MIDNIGHT
DEVOTION

Enjoy!

-Lo≥ XX

MIDNIGHT DEVOTION

By Loz Cadman

Paperback ISBN- 978-1-3999-6251-3

Cover design by: Loz Cadman via CANVA.
Broken Heart Logo by Holly Cadman

Proof read by Philip Mantom, Lisa Conn, Jeff
Stevens

Grammar checks by Edward Jones

Printed in the United Kingdom

Content Warning
The following content contains scenes of
attempted sexual assault, self-harm, gore,
death, and mentions of death, assault, explicit
language, and scenes of sexual nature.
If you are easily triggered by these, this may
not be suitable for you. This novel is intended
for mature audiences.

To Matthew,

Who turned my world upside down, helped me heal, and
showed me how to love again

AUTHOR'S NOTE

On 13th October 2021, I attended a gig in Birmingham with a dear friend of mine. We went to see *Salem*, a small band created by *Creeper's* Will Gould (who we are both fans of) and it was my second band I saw after quarantine lifted; the first band being *Esoterica,* who me and my best friend Philip had waited YEARS to see live! Whilst waiting for one of the support acts to come on stage, my mind began wondering about the possibility of meeting Salem after the gig as there had been many photos on their social medias where people tagged them in selfie photos next to them at their previous tour dates. It also had me think of a scenario where the band were actually vampires (since their music was about eternal love and all things creepy) and were able to perform without breaking a sweat. This caused me to create a story in my mind about a woman who becomes acquainted with the band and is saved by their lead singer, accidentally exposing himself as a vampire. The story then started to grow as more and more ideas began to blossom, which then had me wondering if this was the time to get back into writing.

The next day, after we saw Salem AND met Will Gould, the story still stuck with me. By the time I got home from work, I got the PC up and running and opened a blank document. By this time, the title of the story didn't exist and was simply called *'Untitled Vampire Story'* (a little *Bojack Horseman* joke I thought would be funny to incorporate into my project). The story was coming out of me furiously. The names, locations, plot, lore, it was all there on this word document. I was quite hesitant about whether to attempt to finish it as I had no confidence in writing fiction due to attempting to gain a higher GCSE level back in 2016 and failing miserably. However, this story helped me gain that confidence back as well as give me something I will be forever grateful for.

In four months, the story had finished, and it took me a year and a half to polish and edit it with the help of 4 wonderful people with different views on the structure of this story. It went through 2 different endings before I decided to go with this one. This was also supposed to be a one off story, but it has now ended up becoming a potential series due to the lore expanding that wouldn't work for one book without it being an exposition dump. Originally, this was supposed to take place in 2020/21, but I was given the idea to make it take place in a more nostalgic period, as well as it not working as a modern story because of COVID still being an issue during that time. My brother informed me that society is having nostalgic periods as of lately with the whole 80's and 90's revisits in media, and the *Twilight* comeback appearing all over social media; it gave me the idea to listen to his suggestion and make this story take place in a very nostalgic time for myself: when vampires and alternative music were mainstream! In 2009, I was going through a stage of listening to music constantly, watching *Criss Angel:* MINDFREAK, and reading the Twilight books. Bands like *Green Day, Placebo, Murderdolls, Slipknot, Muse, My Chemical Romance, Avenged Sevenfold, Within Temptaion, Esoterica, Paramore, Kaiser Chiefs, Franz Ferdinand, Crowded House, Rammstein,* and *Korn* were all on my iPod during that time. It was still a nostalgic period for me, so, it made a lot more sense for me to make this story take place during the late 2000s when I was at my most emo.

Music is one of my greatest inspirations, especially when it comes to creating memories and connecting my emotions to something that best suits what I feel. Whether its connecting sadness to a *Low Roar* song, or connecting anger to a *Korn* or *Slipknot* song, music has helped me manage my emotions in the healthiest way imaginable. My Spotify library is filled with hundreds of bands and playlists that I have discovered over the years whose music has comforted me in ways I could not describe.

Being autistic made it more challenging for me to find ways to control my emotions and expressing how I felt. As I grew older, I became more withdrawn and hid how I felt in order to keep my job and my relationships secure. It was a very unhealthy thing for me to do, but because I was so terrified of confrontation, it felt like the right thing to do. For years I isolated myself with music to confront the traumas and emotions that I felt nobody else could help me with. I dealt with self-depreciation and depression since I was eighteen and it took me twelve years to overcome those negative depreciative thoughts and accept myself. A lot of those emotions came from the people and environments I found myself in, whether it be a very unstable relationship; unrequited love; reliving my childhood memories and seeing the way I used to behave and the mistreatments I was given; toxic people and environments, both at work and outside; financial stresses; all on top of not wanting to accept my true self, especially when it came to being autistic.

I will say this though: *Midnight Devotion* has been the creative therapy I so desperately needed. It has helped me overcome so much that was stuck in my mind, whether it was traumas, losses, destroyed ambitions; this novel has helped me overcome them, and for the first time in my life, I feel free from the shackles of those emotions and memories. Just like music, creative writing has helped me maintain my emotions by creating something unique from it and helping me move on to greater things.

This is a story about hope, ambition, and finding love again after being alone for so many years, as well as confronting the past and finding the closure that was so desperately needed in order to move on.

-Loz

.

Prologue

♥

The grand hall sustained collateral damage from the epic battle. Debris, rocks, and ash were scattered all over the hall; the red carpet that trailed down to the large golden throne that belonged to a superior creature had been burnt, and the great chandelier that cradled hundreds of candles had fallen and only a few that remained alight.

Bloodthirsty monstrous red eyes in the shade of hellfire stared down at her prey. They were ready to go in for the kill. Their sharp white teeth extended outwards, their tongue dripping with venomous saliva at the idea of tasting their prey's delicious blood.

The prey showed no remorse or fear, only revenge and resentment were present in her expression. Their hand grasped tightly against the handle of their weapon, the pommel of a sword. The monster and prey glared viciously at each other, waiting for the other to make the first move.

Mortal versus Immortal.

The last few months had been a series of perilous yet exciting events that no mortal could ever dream of; all leading up to this very moment for the renegades to obtain their freedom from control and restriction, to live the rest of their existence the way they had dreamed of doing so. Love, family, vocation, fame, a second chance to live the life that was once stolen from them.

Chapter 1:
♥
Kathryn

In the morning of a late October day in Southampton, England; a young woman woke up to begin the first day of her new life. Like most mortals, she was not aware of what was yet to come, to her it was just like any other mundane day.

Her pale blue eyes reflected at her from the bathroom mirror after a quick shower. Her rounded freckled face with an expression of dread painted on, leered back at her. She sighed heavily before leaving the bathroom with a towel secured around her upper chest. Across the hallway was the bedroom; small and crammed with nooks and crannies, stacked with hair products and accessories, piles of clothes - mostly black or laced.

The curtains were still draped closed, making the bedroom as dark as a crypt, an ideal resting atmosphere for the young woman where no sunlight could disturb her morning's rest. Pulling on her usual daytime outfit of black jeans and her favourite black and white striped half sleeved shirt, she almost felt complete. Once dressed, she pulled the curtains open to reveal the world of the living. The sun had just risen and had left behind its trails of orange and pink to start the cold autumn day.

"Red sky in the morning. . ." she groaned before leaving the bedroom.

Her flat was not exactly the best-looking place to live. Its faded magnolia painted walls had obvious signs of previous tenants living there from the dirty markings on the kitchen cupboards and walls. Unfortunately, it was what she could afford at best with the pub job she had going. She had tried her best to make it look like she owned the place with her posters and spooky art. The most prominent were a trio of classic horror movie posters framed and hung on the walls, signed by cast members of those movies. She could sell them, and they would potentially be worth a year's rent in Southampton but felt as though the sentimental value was too much for her to give up, after the hard work that she had put in to getting them signed at the conventions she had attended.

The large five shelf black bookcase that rested against the wall by the bricked-up fireplace were overflowing with books, both fiction and non-fiction: a lot of them horror themed. The usual Stephen King to H.P Lovecraft. One shelf was dedicated solely to psychology, with a photo of her younger self with long wavy brown hair standing next to two elderly people, whilst she held a framed degree certificate in the subject. Crammed in between the books were small plush toys- one of a fox, with its fur darkened from the years of love it was given; one of a cute little skeleton that held a black heart in between its bony hands, and a brown bear wearing a graduation outfit with the word 'Graduated!' written on its chest. A variety of decorative statues of skeletons and cats were placed in front of some of the books.

The woman had finished her small breakfast of toast coated with strawberry jam before going back into her bedroom to do her daily facial painting. Whilst putting on the palest of foundations onto her already pale skin to ghost herself up, her phone bleeped to notify her that a text had arrived. She had a couple of guesses as to who it would be: one of her parents or Luca-her colleague at the pub she worked at.

She paused when she saw the word 'Mom' on the screen. She slid the phone upwards, revealing the keypad. The little screen showed the following message:

'Hi, Kat! Any idea when you will be nxt visiting?'

Texting was never her mom's strong point. Kat slanted

her mouth to one side before locking her phone off to continue her makeup regimen. Her mind wondered about her shift schedule for the weekend of her potential visit. Paying for train travels was never something she could afford very easily as money was always scarce with her not-so-exciting job at one of the city's music pubs. The only thing she enjoyed at her job was working with Luca, since they were into the same subjects as her. Unfortunately, she knew her shift tonight would not be with them, so she would be stuck working with her manager, who she would call the 'exact opposite of her' due to her tanned skin, long bleach blonde hair, and tight, skimpy outfits that Kat would not dream of wearing! She was not the worst person to be around, but she could not stand to be her around for an extensive amount of time given how obnoxious she was around certain people.

Today's colour theme for her eyeshadow was shades of pinks, with her lipstick being crimson red to give her more of a vampire look. Each day she would choose certain coloured eyeshadow that would best match her outfits, as she would worry that someone would judge her clothes-makeup combination. Mascara was put on last to darken her natural light eyelashes and to extend the curl for people to see.

Tonight, at the Golden Barrel pub where she worked, was live music night; she was eternally thankful that it was not karaoke night at the pub since she was not in the mood to listen to tone deaf oldies singing. Her manager, Sally, had booked in an obscure band that Kat had not heard of before, *Midnight Devotion.* Luca had told her that they were local and new and were looking for places to play locally. They said that Sally was approached by a group of strange looking individuals telling her to have them play at their pub at their next band night. She didn't even question it and had no idea what sort of music they were going to play, which was strange considering how their manager was usually cautious of what was performed.

This band gave their manager a poster promoting the band's gig which had them even more curious about who they were. 'emo' and 'punk rock' were labelled on the poster, which were the sort of genres they never hear played at the Golden Barrell pub, let alone live! If she wasn't doing her shift tonight, she may have been somewhat excited to see this band. But alas, her reality had gotten in the way of fun.

What was more surprising, this band did not have any social media accounts or anything to promote themselves, not even a website could be found!

She had been working at the pub for about a year now and had to suffer many small bands performing with barely any room to move around. It was not permanent, but Kat could not help but feel that her life was at a total standstill with nothing to look forward to.

The clock struck eleven before Kat decided to message her mother back saying that she intended to come and visit. The idea of riding a train back to her hometown of Essex sent a shiver down her spine. She had moved to Southampton solely to escape and start a fresh life of independence. Since she had settled in Southampton for her university degree she felt as though she belonged there rather than Essex and had always struggled with fitting-in at school due to her social withdrawal and not being able to relate to any of her classmates. Being at university was a massive relief for her since she had found people that she could be herself around, which had helped her open up.

After she had texted her mother, saying she would inform her of shift plans and try to get the time off work, Kat pulled out her laptop from the coffee table and sat on her corner sofa, which faced the fireplace. She double clicked on her music library for it to fill the silence of her lonely flat. Her choice of music for the session was an eighties gothic rock band that had hints of new wave and post-punk. The hours went by slowly. An awfully long boring hour of job searching was followed by another. Many of the jobs she saw online were ones at the docks, care work or shop staff.

There were only two jobs she applied for: both reception work; one for a dentist office and one for the local council. It was the best she could do for now but would check every day to see if there was something.

"Looks like I'm still in purgatory for a while longer,"

she groaned and angrily closed the search engine in defeat. She quickly stood up and stormed into the kitchen to make herself some coffee. There was barely enough food for her, which meant a shopping trip was necessary. Kat sighed as she blew into her mug before sipping the coffee.

Kat slipped on her black boots and black coat aggressively before grabbing her set of flat keys to get some food. The cold autumn air hit hard against her face as soon as she had started walking through the city streets. For a Saturday afternoon, it was no surprise to find it filled with people of all walks of life. Gangs of restless teenagers, families of all sizes, couples, and the usual exotic mix of people from the cargo ships meeting up with their crew mates. She envied them for the closeness of human activity whilst she was stuck alone shopping for food rather than treating herself to some new clothes or stuff for the flat. A supermarket was near to her, decorated with Halloween ornaments for the occasion. She could not do a week's worth of shopping but bought herself the necessities such as milk, bread, and shower gel, as well as trying to decide what to have for lunch. A quick shopping trip later and Kat was back at her flat to make some lunch, having seen the last reduced roast chicken hiding at the back of the fridges.

After her lunch, she sat on the sofa and lounged about watching whatever seemed interesting on the internet to watch. She sunk into the comfort of the fabric sofa and could feel the cushions giving way as she fidgeted into her usual cosy corner. It was either going to be a repeat of what she had seen or diving in blindly to whatever channels she followed. She could feel her body slowly attaching itself to the warmth of the sofa as it welcomed her to comfort and solitude.

Her day-to-day living wasn't what she would call exciting. It was rather lonely, mundane, and uneventful, the new clips on the internet weren't diverting her. She craved change and wanted to start doing something about it before going insane from loneliness and repetitiveness, especially since it was becoming close to a new decade.

Chapter 2:

♥

The Band

Kat snoozed the afternoon away before work time, with a playlist on shuffle on her music player's speakers. Her alarm went off at five, a loud buzz awoken her from the slumber. She groaned as she pulled herself off the sofa to top up her make-up before leaving the flat, with a quick trip to a newsagent along the way to grab a snack for her break.

The coldness of autumn had grown bitter as it was close to twilight. Kat's coat kept her warm, along with the brisk walk through the centre of Southampton, egged on by the music she had playing on her MP3. Loud alternative music blared into her eardrums. The loudness of the aggressive drumming and guitar shredding encouraged her to walk faster despite dreading her shift.

The shops were beginning to settle for closing time with their sandwich boards being brought in and the lights turning off before bringing down the shutters. Kat hoped that one day she could return home from a nine to five job and have the evening to spend either by herself or with like-minded friends.

The *Golden Barrel* wasn't exactly the nicest looking pub in the city. Its exterior paint had chipped away, and the sign was never going to be illuminated, and the manager was too busy drinking the profits. Only three out of the four exterior lights were working, and the once shiny lettering was rusting and peeling. "It's character," she'd say to any staff that complained.

The poster for tonight's gig was framed on the wooden door entrance. A large broken heart looking like it had been hand drawn was centralised in a purple background with a pale pink light hiding behind the logo. The band's name was written in white and had a glowing effect like moonlight, and its gothic font printed above the logo. Below the logo it read:

Saturday 24th October 2009
8:30pm start
11:00pm curfew

Kat let out a quick sigh before pushing through the heavy wooden doors of the pub and entering its British ambience. It was what she would call her 'own personal hell'. The place wasn't too packed, but Kat knew it would be soon, as the tide of early drinkers washed in before they flowed out to the clubs. It was a rare sight for Kat to see any teenagers or young adults in this pub, as it was often older people way above her age that she often was nerve wrecking, since she was not the best at socialising with strangers, Kat could just about cope when she had the bar safely between them and her. Maybe tonight could be an exception given how this band performing were labelled as 'emo' and 'punk rock', according to Luca.

The pub felt much larger than the average pub in Southampton. It had been part of a rope warehouse which meant there was room for the bar and the stage- located at the far end of the room on the left-hand side. It was like the pub was still stuck in the nineteenth century with its dark wooden counters, tables, and chairs. The bar area was rough around the edges, with a few broken tiles and yellowing wallpaper. The first thing anyone would see when they walked through the entranceway would be the wooden bar. It was as if the pub was taunting her rather than welcoming her. Even the smell was unwelcoming, creeping into her hair and clothes, a strong scent of beer and smoke, an aroma that followed Kat into her dreams.

Kat would have to stand all night seeing the doors open but unable to go outside until her breaks and when her shift was over.

Her manager Sally would make conversation easily with the older clientele, since she was ten years older than her and easily followed the mainstream news, Kat avoided this like the plague, as she could not relate to any of it or care for anything that was, to her, irrelevant. It was as if Sally had to know all this to strike up conversations with the customers.

"Welcome, Kathryn!" Sally called out from behind the bar, her southern accent sounding sarcastic rather than pleasing. Kat swore that she had gotten herself a tan since the last time she saw her two days prior. It was always strange for Kat to be working alongside someone who was dressed on the other end of the spectrum of fashion and who she had nothing in common with.

"Hey, Sally," Kat muttered as she quickly approached the back room to avoid having a conversation. She could see that Luca was preparing to leave their shift as they hung up their waist apron. Luca was a unique individual with bleach blonde hair combed to the side and the other half shaven. Their rounded face was a riot of blue makeup, from dyed eyebrows, blue mascara, eyeshadow, and lipstick, a look that was not best suited for this sort of place, but they felt comfortable with it regardless. Nobody would comment on their look as diversity was welcomed in this pub, even Sally thought it was captivating!

"Luca!" Kat smiled, happy to see someone that she was comfortable being around. "Are you coming back later for the gig at all?"

"Definitely! It's not every day that we get our kind of music played live at this place!" Luca was ecstatic at the prospect of live music, especially when it came to strangeness. The weirder and more obscure the music was, the more it fascinated them.

Emo and punk rock were one of the few genres within the music world that was beginning to get more attention in the alternative music world. The last few years had been great for alternative music, especially for the rock-loving teenagers who needed nihilistically happy tunes to get through their day!

"When you told me about this band, you had me at punk-rock! Emo was just the icing on the cake!" Kat laughed, taking down her waist apron from the coatrack and tying it through the belt sockets of her jeans. "I'll see you later, then!"

"See you!" Luca left Kat alone with the unrelatable adults as her shift began. Her shifts with Luca were always the most fun. They would spend ages talking about music and recommending each other media to watch or play. It was a friendship that she wished could blossom, but since their work schedules were all over the place, their free time was difficult to arrange.

Two hours into her shift and it was getting busier and busier every few minutes. More people were coming in, ones she would recognise as regulars who would come every Saturday evening. She had developed a small relationship with some of the regulars, who would often compliment her on her makeup work and ask questions about herself, which she was often reluctant to talk much about aside from being a university graduate. She knew that to be a psychiatrist, or work within the field of psychiatry, she would have to start working on her social skills and communication tactics, which wasn't exactly her strongest trait.

Some new people also came in that she had never seen before, and to her surprise, a bunch of them were late teens and young adults dressed in her sort of getup: skinny jeans in a variety of colours, excessive eyeliner, hair that looked as straight as string, teenage girls wearing hoodies a couple of sizes too large.

"Why are so many young people dressed like this for a music gig?" Sally said loudly to Kat.

"Clothing style can show people the sort of music they're into as well as it being an aesthetic for the genre," Kat answered nonchalantly. "Since the band you booked are classed as 'emo', some of the people here will be dressing up to fit the theme of this band. It's like how goths dress gothic when they go and see bands like *Sisters of Mercy* or when the *Sex Pistols* were popular and people dressed up like the band. It's been that way for years. So, you will be seeing a few young people dressed unusual here tonight."

It was precisely seven forty-five on that Saturday evening was when she first saw *them*. She was in the middle of serving someone, looking bored out of her mind as the doors swung open. Since tonight had many people coming in dressed how she liked to dress, her fascination would get the better of her as she would begin to examine people's outfits. This person, however, seemed different to all the rest.

An individual whose looks were as farfetched as hers and Luca's had entered the pub, looking more alien than everyone else here. A lanky man whose hair was as dark as a raven's feather that was slicked upwards and combed over to reveal his widow's peak. The diamond shape of his face twisted and turned to look at his surroundings with an emotionless look.

She was struck with the way he was dressed; black leather jacket, his shirt black buttoned with a silk purple tie wrapped underneath the collar, black skinny jeans that showed his slim physique, and makeup that matched her style with its darker shades of purple and pink on the eyelids. His face, however, was abnormally pale, and not the sort of pale Kat was used to seeing. She wasn't so sure if it was foundation that he was wearing or costume makeup. He seemed old but young at the same time, possibly in his late twenties or early thirties. He made his way over to the far-left hand side of the pub where the performance stage was in the next area. Kat was captivated with the way he looked, and it took her a moment to realise why her hands were wet as she ended up over filling the pint that she was pulling from the tap. She silently cussed as she grabbed a towel nearby to clean her hands before serving the drink to the smirking gentleman across the bar.

"Idiot," she muttered to herself. "Stop gawking at people." The doors opened again, making Kat instinctually turn to see who it was. Her eyes gleamed at another strange looking person. This time, it was a younger man whose chestnut brown hair was combed to the right, covering his forehead, with the rest of his hair shaved to a soft brush. He walked in as though he owned the place, whilst carrying what looked like a guitar case, giving Kat the indication that he was part of the band for sure. His rounded face glared at everyone before turning back to head to the stage. He looked disgusted with the people he saw in that pub. His long dark purple jacket made him look as abnormal as the first person she saw walking in. The ends of the coat flapped along with his stride.

A woman then entered after the surly guitarist. Her light brown hair dangled above her breasts and seemed to float behind her like seaweed. She marched over towards the stage with a guitar case also at hand. Her outfit wasn't purple or black like the other two, since she was wearing a white T-shirt with a crimson leather jacket, black skinny jeans and make up as pallid as the bandmates. Kat stared in awe, trying to think of a way to strike up conversations with this woman.

"We need to help Oliver with the drum kit." Kat heard the woman tell the men on the stage loud and clear.

The raven-haired man nodded and marched his way towards the doors. The emo girls in the crowd were all looking at him with bright eyes that Kat imagined to be filled with giant pink hearts. The usual 'hots for the lead singer of a band' kind of excitement.

The broody-looking band member returned with another man whose short, dark sandy blonde hair was held aloft with gel, which crowned his long oval face. He was lean-looking, carrying the kick drum lightly like it was a bag of feathers. In a quiet moment at the bar Kat tried hard not to watch them set up their instruments and equipment as they walked in and out. Her eyes searched frantically to find the raven-haired member. Every time she saw him, her heart would do a huge jump before shifting into mini jumps.

"You seem distracted, love," Sally's voice caught her by surprised.

"Oh, am I?" Kat chuckled nervously as she turned to face her. "I must be daydreaming! Sorry!"

"You've been gawking at the weirdos over there."

Kat gritted her teeth at the word 'weirdos' and resisted the retort that formed in her head.

"I'm just fascinated with the way they look," she shrugged. "They look how I would dress if I had more time and money." Sally shrugged as she turned to serve another customer.

Before Kat could speak to the person in front of the counter, the handsome dark blonde band member approached, making Kat feel an intense sense of nervousness, like they had the superpower of making the most socially anxious of people even more anxious.

"Excuse me," his deep northern voice echoed at Sally. "We're the band you've booked to play this evening. When is the curfew?"

"Eleven, love!" Sally responded, smiling greatly at him. "Sound curfew is at eleven It does say on the poster you gave me."

"Oh! Yes, you're right!" His teeth shone as he laughed without blushing from embarrassment. "Thank you, Ma'am," the gentleman nodded. He caught Kat watching him and gave her a friendly smile before walking away. His friendly expression gave Kat more heartbeat jumps as she quickly found some imaginary beer to wipe up from the bar.

"Jesus Christ," Kat sighed deeply. "What was that all about?"

"Such manners he has," Sally laughed. "I wonder if he's single."

Kat silently scoffed at her comment, knowing full well that she would fall for any guy that was polite to her. She marched to the back room to sort out the glasses that were in the washer. After bringing in some clean glasses and storing them on the shelves underneath the counter, Sally dismissed her for her break, much to her relief. She raced out the pub to escape the stiff stench. The air outside was much cooler than when she had arrived, giving her some comfort from the heat of the pub's cramping and alcoholic smells.

Kat leaned up against the crumbling wall of the building, lifting her head up to see the star-filled sky. Condensation escaped from her mouth as she sighed heavily. She dug into the large pocket of her apron and pulled out the chocolate bar she had stored for her break. She unwrapped the packet and quickly took a large bite, enjoying every sensation in her mouth as the gooey caramel coated her teeth. Her eyes wondered around the street to help distract herself from what she had going on in her mind. Immediately to her right was a Ford Transit van that was painted purple - a colour you wouldn't often see on vehicles, let alone beat up old vans-parked up on the road near the pavement. On the side of the van was a decal of a broken heart, looking like it had been hand drawn, with a scribbled line underneath the tip of the heart, just like the one on the poster plastered on the door. A very eye-catching look for a vehicle with an abnormal colour.

      The pub door creaked open. Kat jumped as she was too distracted to remember where she was. She had expected one of the pub regulars to leave the building to smoke a cigarette, or some of the teenagers or young adults to gather outside in preparation for the moshing, but to her surprise, when she turned her head around, she saw someone her eyes had been darting at for the last hour. His raven hair glowed under the building's lights, showing small hints of blue shade within the black dye. His lanky figure posed straight as he turned to see the young bartender standing against the wall, gazing further at his marvellous looks. This person was the perfect picture of whom she had often envisioned herself dating; it was like he had stepped out of her imagination and had appeared right in front of her.

      His long jawline was sharp and strong, both his chin and nose were pointing downwards when his face turned to the side. Kat never usually noticed these small features in people, but his stood out from everyone else. This man was what she would define as handsome. It was rare for Kat to be so absorbed in the image of someone, and there was something about this person that seemed more than meets the eye, but Kat couldn't quite figure out what it was that made him so…eye catching.

      The individual walked straight past Kat, getting into the driver's seat of the van. Her head turned to follow his movement. She couldn't figure out why she was watching him with such fascination. There was a strong sensation of lust that had built up within her, which she was not used to feeling. She tried to shrug it off by turning to face away from him, ignoring him completely. Unfortunately, she couldn't turn off the anxiety that easily.

"Aren't you cold?" a sudden voice came from her right where the van was. Her heart stabbed against her ribcage when she saw the leather-jacketed man looking at her with a crooked smile, one that caught her off guard. Kat took a deep breath in to get herself together before responding confidently to his question.

"Not really," she answered nonchalantly. "When you're working in a packed pub, cold air is a bit of a relief!" The gentleman approached Kat further, making her feel the need to step back, but her feet stayed in place to prevent her from potentially running away.

"It seems awfully busy tonight. Is it always this busy on a Saturday?" He continued asking. Kat noticed that his accent sounded more Midland than Southern Southampton.

"Oh yeah! It's music Saturday so there is always shit going on here, better than being bored at home." Kat allowed her words to flow out confidently to show no fear in speaking to him, despite feeling apprehensive. She checked herself and added, "We don't usually have young people attending these gigs since my manager usually books more folksy bands and hires DJs for karaoke." He chuckled at her statement, which made her blush. She could see his teeth were perfectly white but wasn't sure if it was from the pale face, unless he had had them whitened.

"The poster said you were local, but I've not seen you around before," said Kat, trying to get the conversation flowing.

"I've been here with my bandmates for a couple of months. This is our first gig in a long time. We recently moved from Glasgow."

"Why move to Southampton?" Kat raised her eyebrow, seeming suspicious with the change of scenery.

"We wanted to experience life down south. Hence, SOUTHampton!" He and Kat both giggled at the emphasis. His smile looked innocent; the eyes played a major part as they partially closed when his high cheekbones raised. Kat gazed at his eyes when he widened them and had noticed that they were darker, an abnormal crimson shade.

"Why are your eyes red?" She squinted her eyes whilst examining his.

"Contact lenses. For the aesthetic of the band." He casually responded without hesitation. "We like to be a little abnormal, it gives us more of an image."

Kat nodded. "I wish I was brave enough to wear contact lenses. I don't like things going near my eyes."

The man smiled graciously. "It's not as bad as you imagine. It's just a small discomfort that lasts a second and a few blinks later it's all over. Taking them out, however, is more of a pain."

Kat shuddered at the idea of placing her finger and thumb on her eyeball which made him chuckle at her discomfort.

"I'm William, or Will, whichever. I'm the singer of the band."

Kat had spent some time tonight guessing what his name would be and did not expect it to be a name that common.

"Kathryn. But you can call me Kat, which I much prefer." Kat noticed she was still blushing slightly, causing her to turn away and look at the ground out of shyness. She heard Will chuckle under his breath, which made her blush even more. It was strange for her to show this sort of weakness, since she was not used to being bashful around people. But Will's charm seemed to have her behave in a way she had never around people; before it was like he had the superpower of charming people with his voice, much like the blonde gentleman who spoke to Sally earlier.

"Kat," Will smiled. "Well, I hope our performance tonight distracts you a little from the madness of work!"

"I hope so too! How long are you playing for?"

"We start in ten minutes and will be playing for an hour and fifteen." Kat checked her watch and saw that it was close to the end of her break which meant she was due to go back in to continue her dreaded shift. "Shit! I need to go back inside! It was lovely talking with you, Will!" Kat ran past, pressing her hand into his upper arm as a "thank you" gesture which she instinctively did without a thought. Will smiled awkwardly and pulled back as he turned around and watched her run back inside the pub.

Kat dipped past the customers, still blushing, and distracted, and almost bumped into Sally. "Where's the fire, Ms Rhodes?" Sally cried, laughing at her afterwards. She stumbled back behind the bar; feelings of embarrassment clouded over her and caused her to turn red. She tensed up her body as she tried to focus on the queue and shouting, "Who's next?!". But all she could think about was Will's charming behaviours towards her.

'Such a fucking cliché,' Kat thought. *'Why the fuck is he so perfect? There's got to be something wrong with him. Maybe he has a fetish that's frowned upon? Or he's secretly a killer? That tends to be the case with perfect strangers. I need to stop drooling over him. I doubt he would date someone like me. He must be with the woman in the group, or something.'*

The woman member of the band approached the door calling out to Will. "Are you coming in any time soon? We have a show to perform!" Before Will could respond to her, she turned around and took a quick glance at Kat, giving her a stare that could pierce through steel. Kat was caught off guard, making her glance away quickly from her and going back to organising the glasses. The woman marched back to the stage to finish setting up the equipment and instruments.

'I hope she doesn't hate me for talking to Will.'

Kat could see the guitarists placing foot pedals of various shapes and sizes on the floor that were each connected to short and long wires, either to each other or to one of the guitars. The amplifiers resting on the corners of the platform were oversized for a small pub and awfully heavy-looking. More cables were trailing through the platform to reach the amplifiers, to present a louder tone and a variety of treble for both guitars and three microphones. All taped to a stand that looked more like a snake than a piece of the PA system. The drum kit had been set up at the back of the platform, a set up that Kat had never seen before. The barrels of the drums were shiny purple with the skins being pure black, except for the bass drum, the largest one of the entire kit that had a purple background with the same broken heart decal as the van.

Their equipment seemed so expensive despite them being a 'new in town' band. Kat was curious to know how well this band played, and what makes them special enough to play at this pub.

Chapter 3:
♥
The Gig

The pub was beginning to get a little too crowded for Kat's liking. For such a small pub it was surprising that a band could perform there. The younger generations crowding around the place didn't help the situation. She had never seen it so packed before.

Luca had arrived and managed to sneak in behind the bar. Kat was relieved to see Luca right next to her, thinking how clever they were to have dodged the queue.

"Nice outfit!" Kat complimented them. Their outfit for tonight was jean shorts with long red and black striped socks covering their legs, and a black wool jumper that was covered in intentional rips and holes to expose some of their skin, with a black T-shirt hidden underneath.

"Well, this is my usual style, so I am dressed this way for ALL events!" The two of them laughed simultaneously and Luca bumped hips with Kat in their usual greeting for when their hands were full.

Whilst sorting out the microphone stand, Will took notice of Kat's interaction with Luca and remain frozen in place. His curiosity got the better of him as he began wondering what their relationship was. He couldn't tell if they were a couple, or simply good friends. A form of jealously crept in but was automatically pushed away the moment his bandmate with the purple jacket clipped him round the back of the head.

"Don't even bother, William," he whispered. "We're not here to catch prey. We're here to play!"

"Shut up, David," Will muttered angrily as he shrugged him off with aggression to continue his work on the microphone. David chuckled to himself and started to fidget with the guitar pedals.

"I guess you can still watch from behind the counter," Luca informed Kat. "I know you hate music evenings, but this may be the one time that you can enjoy the music that is being presented to us!"

"That's because we've never been presented with punk or rock music, just lame cover bands and mainstream DJs. Karaoke nights are the worst." Kat gave Luca a high five and then got back to work.

The band spent the next ten minutes sound checking everything, making sure that all instruments and microphones were at a suitable volume. The music that was played through the pub's radio was turned off, which notified everyone in the building that the band were due to start playing.

"Good evening, Golden Barrel! We are MIDNIGHT DEVOTION!" Will cried into the microphone with confidence. The crowd welcomed the band with cheers and roars; girls screaming for the attractive band members and wanting to get as close to them as possible.

"Thank you! This first song is called *Twice in a Lifetime!*"

The drummer tapped the sticks together four times before bashing the symbol and the snare drum. The guitarist began strumming the strings with his plectrum on his purple Les Paul guitar, and the woman plucked her black Fender bass.

Nine seconds later, Will began singing. His voice was much higher-toned than Kat had expected. She had expected him to sound grunge or be gruff. Will's voice was a gentle alto, and he really could carry a tune. The song he sung had lyrics about living more than once and using the second life to achieve the impossible. Not a lot of people were focused on the band's performance. The younger crowd were bouncing around and raising their fists in the air, pumping along to the music's beats.

31

Some of the regular pub goers looked confused or were finishing up to leave early. It was not what they were familiar with. This sort of punk music seemed more grunge and alternative.

As the song ended, the crowd cheered loudly. Kat gave it her all to show support and encouragement, which Will managed spot from a distance.

The next song they played was heavier and was about moving on after love and finding it somewhere else. Both guitarists sung into the microphone along with the lead singer during certain parts to add volume and emphasis in the lyrics. One thing that caught Kat's attention about the band that she found quite peculiar was that their performance was quite infallible. Both guitarists never seemed to miss a tab or slip up, the drummer's beats were on point, and the singer's voice was always in tune. This new band didn't seem to break a sweat or stop to drink to stay hydrated. Normally, after every song that other bands would play, the members would quickly drink water or something to keep themselves hydrated; but this band never drank a drop of anything. They continued playing without wearing themselves out throughout the entirety of the set. None of them were even sweaty enough to remove their jackets! The room was filled with people, not only that but the pub had the fireplace on, adding more heat into the already packed room. The sudden acknowledgement of a customer wanting a drink distracted Kat from the realisation of the band's sweatless performance.

An hour and a half of punk rock music later, the band played their final song. It was the heaviest of the bunch, and it encouraged the young audience to start small mosh pits. A few members of the crowd even started crowd surfing, despite it being the worst place to do that sort of thing!

Thankfully, nobody was hurt, and they would immediately go back into the crowd to continue the madness. Kat had never seen the place so packed in the entirety of her employment there! It was quite exciting for her to witness such a scene! Kat found herself laughing at the fact that this punk rock band was causing people to do things the Golden Barrel pub was not used to doing. Sally would need some bouncers to calm the crowd down.

"Thank you!" Will cried to the audience once they had finished playing. The audience cheered and applauded. Will smiled and waved, then walked off the front of the stage to the back of the pub. The band took off their gear and began packing up.

"That was amazing!" Kat could hear some of the audience members saying to each other.

"Their lead singer is so hot!"

"The music sounds unique! *Kerrang!* need to have a listen to them!"

"I'm surprised they don't have social media yet!"

"Where can I download their music?"

"Do they have a website?"

A lot of the crowd made their way outside to get some fresh air or to smoke, which gave the pub more space to walk through. Some made their way to the bar to order some drinks. For about an hour, Kat was working hastily. It was getting close to midnight and the band were still talking to the handful of audience members who took an interest in them. Will couldn't help but glance a peek at Kat every chance he got. She didn't notice his glances as she was always serving someone at the bar. Luca approached the band and gave them a positive reception.

"You need to get an album released! I want more music from you guys!" They said with enthusiasm.

Will chuckled. "We're hoping to next year, but unfortunately, we haven't got any social medias just yet. We're working on it."

"You need to get it going! Grab some new fans! Grow an audience! Maybe someday you can be big enough to be played on the radio!

Luca thanked the band before leaving the pub, then said goodbye to Kat and Sally before leaving.

By half-past eleven, it was last orders. Sally took over the bar shouting to encourage customers to 'Drink Up!'; whilst Kat went to collect any glasses or bottles left behind and wipe down the tables. The pub started to get emptier as closing time approached. As Kat was picking up the glasses from a nearby table, Will came over to say hello. She looked up, surprised to see him still here despite finishing the act over an hour prior. He smiled at her as he picked up the crate and took it to the counter.

"You guys were pretty amazing," Kat told Will as she was wiping down the table. "I should download your music."

Will chuckled. "We're not that famous yet. I will give you a CD on me as soon as we sign with a record label." Kat walked behind the counter, taking the crate to the back of the room, placing the glasses in the dishwasher. Moments later, she came back and saw Will sitting on the stool behind the counter. He handed her a much wider smile than before. It was a smile that would make anyone feel safe. She offered him a drink, but he shook his head with refusal. The other bandmates sat at the far end of the room talking to each other watching, looking like they were watching their lead singer commit a crime.

"So, what's the next venue you guys are going to be playing at?" Kat asked playfully. "You seemed to market your gig awfully well to attract such an audience!"

Will smiled, "We're planning to book more venues later in the week and start touring around the country," he told her. "Next year we want to start promoting ourselves properly, and maybe make the debut album!"

"You know, for a new band, you sounded professional. How long have you guys been going for?"

Will slanted his mouth as he searched for an appropriate answer.

"About a year now? Oliver, the drummer, was in a band before this one. He asked me if I wanted to sing, and I agreed. I write poems, so it was a good idea to turn some into songs."

"Why doesn't it surprise me that you write poems?" Kat laughed nervously. "You look like the sort who writes deep literature.

Will chuckled under his breath with amusement. "Thanks, I guess. The other two, David and Laura, are new to being in a band."

"And what were you guys doing before the band?" She continued her interrogation.

"Before, we were just working in between jobs to save up for the instruments and a place to live."

"And now?"

Will hesitated for a second. "I am out of work now, hoping this band gig will kickstart a new career for us all."

Kat leaned forward on the counter to get closer to Will, showing interest in what he was saying to her.

"Better get yourselves on social media, start spreading the news about your content and upcoming gigs! Social medias are blowing up by the day! If you want this to be a full-time thing, you best start getting serious about it." She smiled and leaned back to finish her work. Will chuckled and dropped his head.

"Oh, but I am serious about it," Will chuckled. "What about you?" Will lifted his head back up and began interrogating her. "How long have you been working here?"

Kat began calculating the time in her head to answer the question. She rolled her eyes and tilted her head to the side whilst thinking and calculating.

"I think it's been a year now," she answered. "This isn't something I'm going to be doing forever, only until I can get myself a job as a psychiatrist."

"Really?" Will widened his eyes and smiled. "That's so cool! So, what were you doing before the pub work?"

"I finished Uni and got a temp job at a clothes store while looking for proper work." Kat laughed; she wasn't so sure why, as it wasn't funny or amusing.

Will and Kat exchanged laughs before David, the lead guitarist, approached the bar. "We're ready to leave. Now." His voice didn't seem pleasant, which caught Kat off guard.

Will dropped his smile and sighed with disappointment. "Duty calls." He smiled as he jumped off the stool. "I'll see you in a bit." Kat giggled whilst watching him walk away. She hoped that he would still be there when she left the pub, but there was a piece of her inside that doubted it.

By midnight, Kat finished her shift. She quickly grabbed her coat and left the pub. She thought how stupid she was thinking the band were still going to be there when she left. Once she was outside, the air was much colder than before. To her surprise, she saw the band next to their van, but there seemed to be a bit of bickering going on between them which Kat caught wind of.

"You need to tone it down, Will," Laura was commanding him. "We can't risk having someone close to us."

"I wasn't going too far; I was just being polite. She probably won't see us again, anyway," Will argued back.

"Can we please talk about this back at the flat?" Oliver intervened.

"With pleasure!" David leaped into the back of the van, leaving the door open. "Come on! I want to get back and sort out the guitar!"

Will turned and immediately jolted as he saw that it was Kat who had left the building.

"Hi!" Kat gently waved, nervously approaching the band. Will's smile made her feel uncomfortable, but in a good way, because not many people made her chest feel heavy and finding it hard to talk to them due to nervousness.

"Do you want a lift back to yours?" he asked politely without hesitation. Kat's heart skipped a beat. She wanted to say "yes" but wasn't sure if that was a good idea.

The rest of the band stared blankly at Will.

"We don't bite!" David jokingly called from inside the van. Will closed his eyes with annoyance.

"Oh! That's okay! I enjoy my evening walks!"

"Are you sure you don't need someone to walk you home?"

"I'm all right, really! Thank you for an awesome evening. Watching you made this shift easier for me."

"That's great!" Will smiled.

"Do you have a boyfriend?" David randomly called from the van. "You can be honest with him!"

"Shut up, David!" Laura hissed at him.

"I don't, no. Though, I would like to be your friend if that's alright?"

Will's face didn't show remorse or resentment towards her rejection. He was somehow relieved but also worried.

He nodded his head and faked a smile. "Of course. Have a safe journey home."

"Thanks. I'll see you soon!" Kat walked swiftly away, her feet picking up the pace with each step. She quickly took one last look at Will before turning around and walked down the street, heading her way home. Will watched before she disappearing around the corner. A sigh escaped his mouth as he gazed at the empty street.

Chapter 4:

♥

Exposure

Kat made her way through Southampton alone. Unlike daytime, the streets were empty, though some of the other pubs were still going despite the midnight curfew. The dimmed streetlights were the guiding light for Kat, as she made her way back to the flats. She enjoyed her evening walks in the city as something was therapeutic about a deserted street; it made her feel like she was the only person left in the world. The music playing through her earphones would add volume to the silence, unhealthily loud depending on what she was playing.

Her handbag contained a spray of deodorant that she could easily use as an alternative for pepper spray, and her flat keys would be a useful weapon if she were threatened in any way.

When she turned towards the main city centre, she noticed someone coming out of a side alleyway. The unexpected approach caused her to suddenly feel uneasy and threatened; her peaceful walk partially disrupted. She avoided giving them eye contact, continued down the avenue, and slightly quickened her pace before walking past the Working Men's Club to avoid looking at the gaggle of men outside smoking.

"Alright, sexy?!" they hallooed her, making Kat feel uncomfortable. Her instincts caused her to begin rummaging for her deodorant spray to use as a potential weapon, only as a last resort. Panic struck as she failed to find it, *"Keys, phone, mirror, purse, tissues. . . where is it?!"* She reached the corner of the street and began walking towards the city centre. A large, open area that was regularly filled with people completely deserted. The streetlights were more frequent here, making her feel safer, more seen.

Kat's arm was caught by a stranger who pulled her off-balance. The sudden pull caused her to gasp loudly, her bag fell off and landed on the ground, the contents scattered all over the floor, including the missing deodorant spray. Her earphones fell off and dangled onto the ground. The faint sound of heavy music was heard from the earbuds.

She began pulling away to see who her attacker was about to throw a punch at them.

"I'm talking to you!" He shouted aggressively. The person who had grabbed her with his thick fingers was a short, bald man with a stubble beard, wearing a tracksuit. His beer belly poked from his tracksuit jacket, showing obesity in his body structure. Dark circles under his eyes were proof of excessive drinking for a long period of time. He licked his dry lips, examining Kat's features. "Well, aren't you a feisty one? Quite the look you've got going! Just in time for Halloween!" His breath smelt strongly of alcohol and cigarettes - an obvious sign of a bender or a pub crawl. The smell of his breath made Kat's stomach turn.

A million thoughts ran through her head, trying to think how she should defend herself. Her bag was too far to reach to use as a weapon. She began throwing punches, but the drunk man reflected on her attack with his other hand and started waving his lit cigarette towards her face. The stench of the smoke made her feel queasier. He pushed her down and used his body weight to push her slim body against the cold damp floor. Kat screamed for help whilst he held her down, trailing his hand up her coat. She kept squirming and screaming, hoping someone nearby would help. The coldness of the air faded as the adrenaline took over, warming her up during that dreadful moment. She squirmed harder until her hand found her bag again. She grabbed it and swung it at her attacker. He flinched and pulled it out of her hand, leaving her defenceless once again. Despite her pleas, the man continued trying to rip her clothes open. His hands made their way to her jeans, and Kat became too terrified as the intention of the attack unfolded.

There was a moment of blackness, and she finally felt the pressure on her body disappear. All that could be heard was muffled struggling and panicked whimpers, followed by a scream, a scream that was so light that Kat wasn't sure if her hearing had deafened.

Kat pulled herself onto all fours ready to run, but her curiosity had gotten the better of her as she turned to see what had happened. The drunk man was held up in the air with a hand penetrating right through his chest and out of his back. Blood gushed out and dripped onto the floor, in between the cracks of the stone pavement. What penetrated him though was someone she recognised; someone she had just said goodbye to. What was different though was there were large silky wings with sharp tips at the ends extended from his back, very much like bat wings. There was a certain grace and beauty as they shimmered in the streetlight enfolding her attacker.

What happened was about to change her life forever, turning her reality into something horrific.

"Will?"

Her eyes widened in shock. She swore she must have been dreaming. The gentleman that was talking to her at the pub earlier tonight, having a wonderful conversation with, and seemed genuine, was lifting someone twice his weight above the ground with one hand through his chest.

Will dropped his arm to release the corpse, causing his bloodied forearm and hand to be free. His entire forearm had been painted crimson red. He licked the blood off his fingers, and slowly licked up his forearm. His wings receded into his back, snapping, and popping like sails in the wind.

"What the fuck?" Kat whispered under her breath. She stayed static from the shock of what she had witnessed. Many thoughts were running through her mind, each one questioned the possible reasoning of what her eyes were witnessing. She figured she was just dreaming and was about to wake up any moment now, but she couldn't recall being in bed before any of this had happened. Maybe she was dying and was having fantasies of being saved? Then the wind blew, and she felt the sea air against her skin, proving that it was indeed real.

Will slowly turned to face Kat; his face filled with rage. The grey eyes were now blood red; his teeth were longer and sharper. Blood dripped from the tips of the fangs, and pooled black and heavy on the pavement. Once Will realised what he had just done, guilt withered him, changing his expression. Kat looked like an injured animal in his eyes, a wounded deer that had been massacred by a savage carnivore.

"I'm so sorry you had to see that," he said with no empathy in his tone. He stared down at her with a look of concern. "Are you alright?"

Kat's heart pounded in her chest, and not just because of what she had, but to have Will be the person doing it; the handsome lad who wooed her, who she thought was amiable, and for him to be something more than human, maybe not even human at all!

"What the fuck are you?" She came close to screaming but didn't want to draw attention to anyone for Will's sake. Even if she wanted to, her throat was throbbing and too dry to be capable of emitting anything close to a scream.

"I'm not going to hurt you," Will crouched down, raising his bloody palms for reassurance, "it's okay." Kat retreated in fear. Will pulled his hand away and watched her panic. Bile suddenly escaped from Kat's mouth from shock, the sight and smell of the blood, and the stench of cigarettes and alcohol caused her stomach to give up. Will backed away slightly to give her some room. Vomit, followed by panic, she began hyperventilating and shivering. She recoiled into a ball and her breathing became hasty as she tried to calm herself. It all became too much for her. Everything then faded to black, like she was falling asleep. Her body went into shutdown, and she went limp. Will grabbed her head before it reached the floor.

41

"Will!" Oliver's voice called out at a distance. Will turned and saw the other band members running towards him, reaching him within seconds. They stopped once they reached him, each of them staring at the body and at Will, putting two and two together.

"What have you done?" David asked him.

"It's bloody obvious what he's done!" Laura cried with a strident tone. "He's gone and fucking killed someone in public AND in front of a human!"

"Guys! Keep your voices down!" Oliver told them in a whisper. "We can't draw any attention!"

"He was going to hurt her," Will explained, showing no signs of guilt to his action.

Laura marched her way forward, feeling compelled to beat the shit out of him. "You have exposed us!"

Oliver ran in between the angry Laura and a bloodied Will. "Guys! We can't do this here! David, get the van here now! Laura, you and I will take the body away. Will," Oliver looked at Will who was cradling Kat in his arms and stroking her hair away from her face. "Will!"

"What?"

"We're taking her with us back to the flat."

"Fuck that!" Will raised his voice, objecting to Oliver's suggestion.

"You can't take her back to her place without permission, Will! And you can't wake her up and explain what just happened! We can't stay here!"

"I am not taking her back to the flat! It's too dangerous!"

"Will. We have no choice. Either you leave her here, to wake up alone and question what had happened, and even call the police and have them track us down. Or you take her back with us, and we sort it out from there." Will could feel the frustration, but mostly the frustration on what his actions had caused. They had to be surreptitious; having any human knowing the existence of their kind would be a transgression. They'd be found out and that could mean death.

The van arrived, pulling up next to the others. Laura picked up the dead man, with no effort, fast enough for no cameras to pick up on the CCTV and carried him to the van. His body thumped onto the flooring of the van's storage.

"What are we going to do about the blood?" David asked the others. "It's all over the place! And I'm fairly sure someone will notice it!"

"I'll sort it out." Laura opened the boot of the van and pulled out a jet washer. She activated it and began spraying the blood and the vomit away from the footpath and into the nearest drain. Both coalesce with the high powered water and was pushed in between the stone pavement. The pungent smell of the blood and vomit began to disappear.

Will removed his bloodied jacket, passed it to Oliver, then picked up Kat and carried her into the front of the van. He stared at her throughout the entire drive, watching her breathe slowly. Nobody in the van said a word throughout the journey.

Will placed Kat in the recovery position, covering her with a blanket. He stared at her for a moment, watching her sleep soundly. He took off his bloodied shirt, changed into a black T-shirt, and swapped his skinny jeans with an identical pair. After changing, he shuffled his way out, still watching Kat sleep, not yet ready to face the temper of the rest of the band.

He walked down the hallway, past the four bedrooms and a bathroom, approaching the living room. The flat they lived in was designed for university students, using it as their hiding space and for band practice. The living room was modernised with laminate flooring, a long kitchen counter that was never used, as well as no utensils or other useful kitchen supplies, only wine glasses.

The rest of the living room had a long grey corner sofa that was the midway point of the room, with a television attached to the green-blue painted walls. A games console and DVD player was found below the television on a TV unit made of glass.

There were two large windows covered by blackout curtains to prevent sunlight. Next to the window sat a large black mat where the drumkit would rest with black foam attached to the wall. Many amplifiers and music equipment surrounded the mat. A couple of guitars were attached, ones that were expensive yet flashy enough to display.

Laura was first to start the conversation and was always very ardent when it came to the laws of their kind. "Right, you need to sort this out. You know what'll happen if we are uncovered."

"I know, I fucked up," Will agreed without looking.

"That's an understatement," Laura said, rolling her eyes in frustration.

"But you need to understand that I went on my instincts and my immediate instinct was to kill him, to save her."

"You only just met her tonight!" Laura raised her voice, showing frustration within her tone. "When you interact with a human, you don't start conversations with them and begin an acquaintanceship with them! You either lure them and kill them, or you hypnotise them into forgetting about us when it becomes too serious."

"Laura," Oliver placed his hand on her shoulder, which she shoved off in an aggressive manner.

"Why couldn't you have just pulled him off her and fought him like a human? Throw a few punches or something? Now we have a dead body in our van and a woman that's witnessed a killing!"

David laughed, showing levity towards the situation. "You do know if we punched a human, they would go skyrocketing across the street and probably smash through a building?"

"David," Oliver muttered.

"I didn't want her to get hurt! That prick was going to violate and possibly kill her! I didn't want to take my chances!"

Laura gave Will an aggressive look. Oliver and David straggled back, thinking that a fight was about to break out.

"I'm going to give you a choice, Will, for the sake of us all. Either you change her, have her join us, or you hypnotise her once she wakes up and have her forget about this whole ideal. We cannot have any witnesses, otherwise, we'll be exposed to the world, and we will be executed for transgression!" Will felt bitterness inside of himself. He didn't like either of those choices. None would have a positive outcome. He felt a strong disapproval towards the ultimatum, which meant he was now butting heads with Laura.

"She's not going to tell anyone," He murmured, waiting a moment for Laura's words to expose her true emotions.

"You don't know her well enough to be so sure of that!" David stated as he walked towards Laura. "Laura's right, we can't take our chances. If you don't do either of these choices, I'll do it myself. Or I could kill her, and we drink her blood?"

"No! I won't let you touch her!" Will growled at David. His voice beginning to transmute with fury, anxiety, and protection.

"Everyone, calm down," Oliver told his bandmates, with the tendency to be the voice of reason and the less argumentative one of the group. "You're lucky we installed soundproofing. Now, this situation is getting us nowhere. I propose we hypnotise this girl into forgetting all about this and get her back to her flat."

"But we cannot go into her building without permission," Laura informed him angrily.

"Why don't we hypnotise her once we get her back then?" David suggested to them. "Will takes her back to the flat, hypnotises her into forgetting any of this, and tell her to go to sleep. He leaves and we move on from it all?" The creatures had special abilities they would use on humans to hypnotise them into submission, some use hypnotism to lure their prey and then feed off their blood. It would be used on humans in case one had witnessed something they shouldn't have, or if they needed to persuade someone to do something against their instinct.

Will thought about the idea. He approved of the given choice that would spare her life from immortality or death. The only thing he disliked about the option was hypnotising her into forgetting all about him. He had found a human connection with someone for the first time in an exceptionally long time, and for it to be taken from him due to his stupid mistakes made him feel worse about it all, and even more so, he felt even more resentful towards what he was. The restrictions of his kind gave him revulsion against it. This was not what he had intended to happen. He had hypnotised humans in the past to get out of situations, but this was the exception where he had to compel himself into doing so.

"I guess that's the best alternative," Will, he raised and dropped his arms with frustration and defeat. "I'll take her back to the flat once she awakens. But what do we tell her when she wakes up and starts asking questions?"

"We just tell her she passed out on the floor; we were nearby and saw that she needed help," David suggested, shrugging his shoulders. "We'll say we didn't know where she lived and couldn't seek help and thought we would take her back to ours to rest?"

"That sounds crazy," Oliver told him with scepticism. "Surely, she would ask why we didn't phone an ambulance? We've kidnapped her by this point."

"AND murdered someone," Laura added grudgingly. "What are we going to do about the body?"

"We need to quickly drain the blood before it gets stale and then we hide the body somewhere," Oliver answered. "Doubt anyone is going to miss him if he's a potential assaulter."

"What if this girl was his first?" Laura wondered.

"Then we may have just saved many lives from violation or potential murder."

Will ignored them. He was fixated about what he had done tonight. He thought about Kat's reaction to his attack, the blood on his clothes, the body hanging through his forearm, the reaction from his bandmates; the regret was eating him alive. He had put his bandmates, and Kat, in potential danger. Laura was right: he could have just pushed the bloke away from her and dealt with it like a regular person. Instead, he had to go through the bloodlust route and full-on murder someone to save a woman's life. There was no turning back now.

He turned around and saw his bandmates in the centre of the spacious living room. In a daze Will wandered back into his bedroom as the others were in discussion. He quietly entered the bedroom and slowly closed the door behind him. He saw that Kat was still asleep. She was breathing slowly, looking peaceful as she slept. Will leaned back against the door and continued watching whilst thinking about the plan. It was a plan that needed to happen before the sun rose, otherwise Kat was going to be going home knowing what she had witnessed, and possibly tell people, although if she did, they may think that she was crazy.

Will didn't want to wake her up, but he had to at some point. She could be asleep for hours. He approached the bed and sat next to her sleeping body.

"Kat?" He hemmed. She slowly began to move, but then fell back asleep. "Kat?" Will placed his cold hand onto her face which caused her to wake up instantly from the sudden shock of his abnormally cold skin. When she saw who had touched her face, she gasped loudly and quickly sat up on the bed. Will stood up and moved away from the hysterical Kat to give her some space.

"It's okay!" He assured her, placing his hands out in front of her.

"Where am I?" Kat asked him, hysterically. "How did I get here?" Will slowly approached the bed with his hands still in front of him to show her reassurance. "Stay away from me!"

"Kat. I'm not going to hurt you!"

"Bullshit! I saw what you did to that person who attacked me! What the hell are you?" Kat leaped from the bed, recoiling to the far corner of the room, as far away from Will as she possibly could get.

"Calm down, and I will explain everything." Will stopped moving and allowed Kat to approach him once she was imperturbable. She was breathing hastily. The adrenaline kicked in again. "I promise you I am not going to harm you. None of us will."

"Us?"

"My bandmates."

47

"Are they monsters too?" Kat asked loud enough for the band to hear in the next room. The word monster made Will flinch as if a sharp pain had suddenly arisen within.

"Oi! I resent that!" David cried from the living room. Will rolled his eyes. They both stared at each other, Kat looking frightened as the monster that saved her leered back; his lips withdrawn. Kat's chest became heavy waiting for her saviour to speak the truth, or to kill her on the spot.

"We're *vampires*," Will finally confessed. He felt dirty telling her the truth, but he couldn't hide it anymore. The word *vampire* made Kat freeze in place. It suddenly made sense to her now: the pale faces, not breaking a sweat during their performance; not drinking anything to stay hydrated; how Will rejected Kat's offers on food and drink.

Kat begun to breathe slowly, calming herself, addressing the situation of what she was just told despite her heart racing immensely. It was very much difficult for her to believe. The more she thought about it, she suddenly realised something.

"Did you follow me?" Kat asked indignantly.

"I did. But I'm glad I did because I managed to save you."

Kat rolled her eyes at his statement. "I walk home at that hour most evenings anyway. And you just happened to be at the right place at the right time to save me from a possible rapist, by stalking me? Were you also curious to know where I lived so you could watch me sleep at night like a creep? It may seem romantic in movies, but it's actually not!" Kat began to feel agitated by what was going on.

"Absolutely not!" Will cried, trying to reason with her and say the right thing. "I know, it does sounds creepy, and I do apologise. But I.. ." Will struggled to finish his sentence. He wanted to say something without it sounding possessive or odious. He bit his tongue and dropped his head.

Kat started to lose her patience with Will.

"Well?" Kat demanded he finish, her eyes wide with fury, which made Will feel underappreciated at the fact he did save her life.

Before Will could answer, Kat's impatience made her leave and head into the living room.

"Wait!" Will cried, but Kat ignored him. She marched down the hallway and saw the rest of the band standing in the middle of the living room, waiting for them to come out. Kat stood still as Will followed to stand behind her.

"So, you're a band of vampires?" She asked, churlishly.

"Shiiiiiit, he told her; of course, he did," David whispered to Laura, still trying to bring levity to the situation. She remained silent.

"Yes," Oliver answered, calmly. "We are a band, who happen to be vampires. We do apologise for taking you back here, but we couldn't leave you there or have the police involved. It would have caused some distress for our kind's community."

Kat felt highly sceptical, but after thinking about the attack, the scepticism became irrelevant.

"I have so many questions to ask," Kat told them. "Like, how long have you all been vampires for? You all don't look like you're hundreds of years old."

The band looked at one another before answering.

"Should we be telling her?" David wondered. "I mean, it's too late now, right?"

Laura heavily sighed. "We've been around for many years: David has been a vampire for thirty-two years, I've been a vampire for sixteen years, Oliver has been a vampire for six years, and Will has been a vampire for-"

"Eighty-eight years," Will completed her sentence, his voice filled with shame.

Kat turned to face Will with shock plastered on her face.

"You're over a hundred years old then?"

"Technically, yes. I'm actually a hundred and twenty years old." Will didn't like telling her this. He didn't have to, but if she was going to forget about it, he may as well state the fact. He wasn't particularly happy about his age, let alone being a vampire.

"Are you day walking vampires?" Kat asked. "You know? Go out during the day?"

"Nope!" David quickly responded. "If it's sunny as fuck we don't! If it's cloudy or overcast then yeah, we technically can! Any hit of sun rays would burn us to a crisp! Sorry to disappoint you, sweetheart, but we don't sparkle in the sun. And to answer your next question, yes, we can sleep in the day, but only so that we can skip the day and go straight to night! Kind of what you humans do to get to the next morning. Tiredness isn't a thing for us either. Sleep is just an optional thing."

Kat nodded to show that she understood their expositions.

"I think that's enough with the twenty questions," Will told everyone. "It's time to get you home, it's getting pretty late." Kat turned to face Will, her face showed disapproval.

"You can't tell me what to do," she informed him scathingly. "I might want to stay here."

"Well, you can't," David told her, his eyebrows raised and eyes widened, a slanted smile grew. "A flat full of vampires is not exactly something you'll be able to sleep with."

"Will is going to take you home," Laura initiated. "And you will not see us again after tonight."

"You do realise I cannot go home with my life being the same as it was yesterday? I live in a world that has vampires, which is so cool!"

"No, it's not cool," Will murmured angrily.

"Anyway, you need to get going," Laura demanded. "Now."

"Okay, fine! But I'm not going to forget what happened tonight!" Kat finally gave in and pointed at the vampire group.

"You'll probably think this was all a dream once you wake up in the morning!" David laughed.

Will gave him a look of disapproval. "Let's get going," Will escorted Kat out. She glanced at the band before she left the room as if she was never going to see them again.

"If you tell anyone, we'll have to kill you!" David jokingly called out from the living room.

Chapter 5:
♥
William

William and Kat left the building without a word. They marched through the quiet city streets, both lost in their own thoughts: Kat, due to what she had witnessed tonight, was still trying to get her head around the situation she was in; and Will, due to not wanting to discuss what she saw, to avoid any more questions about his vampirism, especially with possible witnesses nearby. He spent the entire walk listening to Kat's beating heart pumping at a fast rate.

Twenty minutes of awkward silence later, they arrived at the building where Kat lived. The building itself was four floors high; despite the early hour, many of the flats still had their lights on.

"Kat," Will finally said, his voice soft and calm this time. She stopped to look at Will, highly keen to know what he wanted. He stared at her, his grey eyes connecting with her blue eyes. "Would I be alright to come inside for a minute?"

"Why?" she seemed suspicious with what Will's intentions were.

"I feel like we need to talk more about tonight, just us two, no interruptions." Kat raised her eyebrows, unsure with what Will had planned. Was he going to kill her? Suck her blood dry from the neck and then dispose her body in the ocean nearby?

"Why didn't you ask whilst we were walking through town?"

"I didn't want any citizens nearby hearing us. I had my eyes looking out for people in case you started asking questions." Kat remained still, continuing to stare at Will, thinking about whether it was a good idea to accept his request. There were many questions she had about Will and the band: who they were, what they were, and many more.

"I suppose you HAVE to ask for permission because of what you are?" Kat questioned. All Will had to offer in response was raised eyebrows and shrugged shoulders.

"Okay," she sighed in defeat. "You can come in. But you're not spending the night here! I want you gone once we've finished talking. Understood?"

Will was relieved that his plan had worked.

"Understood," he nodded.

She pulled out her keys from her coat pocket, holding the heavy front door for Will and they made their way up the stairs to the second floor where she lived. Kat again made sure that Will was in front of her and ushered him inside. He made his way through the hallway and into the small living room as Kat turned on the lights. A variety of smells entered his nostrils with each step. One minute he could smell the toiletries from the bathroom – coconut in particular – then the next he could smell hair products: hair sprays, heat protection and hair serums; and deodorants. There was a distinct smell of coffee coming from the kitchen when he walked passed. Once he reached the living room, the smells came in variations: lavender, varnish, paper, and black cherry scented candles.

He slowly examined the contents of her flat, admiring the horror décor. He drew a small smile when his eyes caught the framed retro horror movie posters on the wall. Of course, the woman he saved was a fan of horror. How ironic.

Kat nonchalantly threw her jacket into her bedroom and made her way to the living room. She slowly approached her black sofa to begin her vampire interview or her ultimate demise with the uneasy feeling still present.

"So," she began, "what did you want to talk to me about?" The tone of annoyance made Will uncomfortable. He

52

faced her and saw that her arms were crossed, waiting for his response.

"I wanted to. . ." Hesitation crept up on Will as he paused. This was the moment he was supposed to hypnotise her into a trance, making her forget about him and everything that had happened. It was now or never. There was a war going on in his mind between what was right and what was wrong. How could something that felt so right also be wrong, and something that felt so wrong be right? It didn't make any sense to Will. He was never this hesitant when talking to a human and attempting to hypnotise them. Frustration continued to blaze inside his ice-cold body.

"Wanted to what?" Kat demanded grudgingly. Will hesitated. Both of them stared at each other; Will looking dejected and Kat looking chagrin.

"I wanted to say I'm sorry about tonight," he finally confessed. "I didn't mean for this to happen."

"For what to happen? The murder? Were you speaking to me so generously because you had the intention of eating me?"

The latter made Will flinch, feeling offended with her assumption, despite it being true. That was his initial intention from the beginning, but it slowly started to feel wrong the more he spoke to her, to charm his way into her life so that he could taste her blood. He didn't want to kill an innocent person, but there was something about her scent that made him feel hunger so strong it almost made him think the unimaginable.

"Don't assume that," he told her, almost breaking into an argumentative state. "I had no intention of ever harming you. If I wanted to, I would have done it by now. I only regret the danger I've put you through and the murder I committed. You should be thanking me for saving your life!"

"Yeah, let's not focus on the elephant in the room, Will!" Kat yelled stridently, causing Will to flinch. "Yes, I am grateful that you saved me from that vile, disgusting human being, but I'm not going to avoid what you are! I want to know why you were following me to begin with, did you want to find out where I live so that you could eat me!?"

"I did not want to do that at all," Will finally answered, his tone much quieter than expected, remaining calm to try and control his emotions. "I just wanted to tell you that meeting you tonight has changed how I see things." Kat's eye widened. She felt something strong hit against her chest as the words went through her ears. "If I didn't care about you, I wouldn't have followed you home. I would have just gotten in the van with my bandmates and drove off, then possibly hear on the news the next day about your potential death. I didn't want to take my chances. If I didn't care about you, I would have killed you myself. The smell of you is excruciatingly delicious; I smelt it the moment I entered the pub. It was difficult for me to be there, so when you were outside, I went to the van to have a quick drink of blood that we carry around, but it still wasn't enough. Seeing you outside, that dangerously close to me, almost set me off."

All of this talk of wanting to kill Kat, how delicious her scent was, made her feel queasy and slightly frightened of Will. All she could do was stare at him; she knew he was being sincere.

"Do you want to feast on my blood now?" Kat questioned without hesitation. Will stood silently, not knowing if answering honestly was going to help the situation.

"I don't want to," he chose to answer. "I would much rather drink lava."

Kat nodded, withdrawing her painted lips so that they became invisible.

"What are your vampiric instincts telling you to do now?" She moved closer to Will, which had him instinctively step back, trying not to be too close. The smell of her scent was still tempting. Will could feel his fangs tingling in his gums, getting ready to erupt. He had to control his urge to feed on her since the earlier attack had fed his hunger. But due to the disgusting taste of his victim's blood, it hadn't satisfied his hunger.

"My instinct is to not do what I was told to do," he confessed. "I'm supposed to make you forget about tonight, have you continue your life as it were before you met me. I could either kill you or turn you into a vampire. But the safest option for you is to hypnotise you into forgetting about us."

The words that Will spoke made Kat reflect on it all. It felt as though her life would have turned in a completely different direction if the latter wasn't available.

"I don't want you to forget me. There's something about you. . . I haven't felt for a long time."

"If you feel that way, then why don't you turn me into a vampire?" Kat suggested, shrugging her shoulders. "That way, you can have all of me. And I can be just like you, and nobody gets hurt."

Will's expression shifted into concern.

"You're really willing to sacrifice your humanity to become what I am? A parasitic monster? When you're a vampire, you're not truly living; you're just existing. I would much rather you have a long and happy human life than a long and miserable existence."

Kat scoffed. "I've got news for you! My short human life is more like a long and miserable one. I haven't got much going on that's as exciting as being a vampire! It sounds more exciting than what I have going for me right now!"

Will growled under his breath. "No. Being a vampire gives you restrictions: you can't go out in the day or go anywhere sunny and warm; you can't eat your favourite foods or drink your favourite drinks; you can't see your loved ones anymore; Kat, being a vampire isn't fun. I would rather be human again and experience everything in life than existing for eternity with minimal opportunities."

"But don't you have like cool superpowers and shit? And not eating food saves you so much money! What I would give to not eat anything and save so much money!"

Will turned and stared out of the window, trying to block out the sound of Kat's heart beating rapidly.

"Yes, we do have powers. We can run faster, have super strength and super hearing, and we can hypnotise humans, but I still want to be human again. I want to eat human food, bathe in the sun, be close to someone, get married and have children, I can't do any of those things as a vampire. And you might think you are poor, but you have so much more than I do."

Kat let out a long breath out, glaring down at the floor. It was all so surreal to hear about the life of a vampire in modern time; it was not often people addressed the restrictions of the lifestyle beside the daylight situation. She lowered herself on to the sofa, insisting that Will do the same. He hesitated for a moment before deciding to sit at the far end of the sofa. Kat placed her legs up on the cushions and crossed them, her hands resting under her feet. She decided she could use her psychology degree to her advantage at this very moment. Her first client: a vampire. The feelings of anxieties and confusion were pushed away for her to focus solely on the vampire.

"Tell me, Will," Kat leaned forward with confidence, still in psychologist mode. "What do you want to do to me?" Will hesitated for a second. He moved away from Kat, despite his instincts insisting he be closer. "Do you want to hypnotise me into forgetting about you?" Will sat silently as he wasn't sure how to answer her question and was worried that he may say the wrong thing.

"I don't want to," he finally answered, his voice seeming guilty, "but I HAVE to."

"So why can't you lie to the others? You don't have to do this. If you want me in your life without turning or killing me, you're going to have to compromise on something." Will didn't move or respond. He was still in a dilemma with what was right and wrong. Many thoughts raced through his mind; anxieties, possibilities, the danger he could put her through, but also the chance of being happy for the first time in eighty-eight years.

"I would be putting you in serious danger, you know," Will told her. "We're not the only vampires out there. If you know about us, there will be others coming after you."

"I could just pretend I don't know," Kat shrugged.

"That wouldn't be possible. The others would easily find out, and I don't want to take my chances."

"I don't want to forget you though! You don't get to decide what is best for me! This is the blue pill red pill situation; either I go back to reality, wake up, not remember anything about tonight and never see you again; or I stay in wonderland, see how deep this rabbit hole goes and see the world for what it truly is. I want to take the red pill and be part of the vampire world."

Will placed the palm of his hand over his face in frustration. "I'm not going to let you ruin your life over someone you just met!" Will was beginning to get impatient with her. He came remarkably close to hypnotising her without hesitation. "I'm not worth that kind of sacrifice."

"You're. . . I don't believe that." Kat shook her head, disapprovingly. "Will, you saved my life tonight, and while I didn't react appropriately, because, you know, I witnessed a supernatural being kill someone, I am still grateful that you saved me. I owe you my life."

Will turned to face Kat, "You don't owe me anything. I'm going to have to do the right thing, even if it hurts me to, but this is for your own protection." Kat felt the urge to protest, but they were just going in circles with the argument. She could see where he was coming from with the whole idea, but also wanted to experience this new and exciting life she'd stumbled into. In the past, she had always been told to fight for what she wanted in life, and this was her moment to stand up for what she wanted for herself, even though it was extremely dangerous for a human.

"Is there any way at all we can compromise?" Kat asked him, wanting to get the best of both worlds.

"How?" Will was sceptical but allowed her to explain.

"Well, let's reverse this for a second. Is there any way, at all, that could help us turn you back into a human rather than turn me into a vampire?"

Will thought about it for a moment. It wasn't something that came to mind often; he'd just accepted that he was doomed to be a vampire for the rest of his existence. There were rumours, hints, whispered between blood-drunk vampires shortly before dawn. Stories no human ear had ever heard; there was a potential way, and it was not only extremely difficult, but also suicidal.

"Vampires are hidden. You humans have your stories and a few crumbs of knowledge. In the same way we have our own legends and myths. Fairy stories for vampires. There is a Head Vampire here in the UK, part of the global Vampire Council known as the *Vamperium,* vampires who are more powerful than all of our kind whose job is to keep us vampires hidden." Will dropped his head. "It's a theory- so it may not work- but if you want me to be human again, we have to do the impossible; *Kill the Head Vampire , Mistress Claudette.* Supposedly that breaks the bonds, and any vampire less than a hundred years old will revert to human form. Claudette is well over three hundred years old and is the strongest vampire in the country, ruling the UK and Northern Ireland. We'd certainly have to get through her hoard and then. . . well, no one has done this but I guess the Vamperium won't turn up and hand out rosettes and prizes."

This Mistress Vampire sounded like a daunting individual from her status alone.

"The other Head Vampires, how many are there?"

"There's one in every country," Will explained. "All over the world controlling continents and certain parts of those countries. I'm not sure myself how many there are, but it's a lot."

A large quantity of Head Vampires, and she only needed to kill one to make the potential change. Kat needed a moment to think and excused herself. She put the kettle on, thinking of what she had just been informed.

Head Vampire , human, hypnotism, a hundred years.

Her head spun from the extensive knowledge.

Kat picked up the conversation while she made herself a cup of tea, "Was she the one who turned you?"

Will shook his head and said, "She wasn't, but the person who did was a total stranger."

"And how did that happen? If you don't mind me asking?" Kat's curiosity was entering territory that Will wasn't so sure he wanted to revisit. He stayed silent for a brief moment before reaching his decision to let her in.

Will waited until Kat had finished making herself a drink.

"I was working as a blacksmith in Birmingham," Will began. "I was married, about to be a father to a beautiful boy. My wife, Elizabeth, was eight months pregnant when I turned. I was walking home from a late night at work when I was suddenly attacked down an alleyway. At first, I thought I was being mugged, but I felt the sharp penetration of teeth in my neck. I didn't know the person that attacked me, and I didn't get a look at their face. All I know is it was a man with thick brown hair that curved under his ears. If I hadn't pushed him off, I would have probably bled to death. Or, I would have been drained completely of blood." Kat felt intense sadness within her. The thought of losing a husband whilst carrying his child, and not having the father be there from birth onwards seemed terrifying and upsetting.

"I had managed to escape as people were chasing the creature that attacked me, not realising what he truly was. They didn't see me, thankfully, because I hid behind a wall of pallets as I began changing into the monster I am today. Once I realised what I had become, I knew it meant I could never see my family again. I had my entire life taken from me within the hour. My wife and son are now dead, and all I have now is the band and that's it." Will's voice dropped. The sadness swelled up inside of him.

"I left the city as soon as I realised what I had become and moved from city to city. When I reached Manchester, a vampire found me and took me to Mistress Claudette's castle in the north. The castle is hidden from public view, hidden inside the mountains of Scotland. Only vampires could enter from the summit."

The thought of a snowy mountain made Kat shiver from the imagery of cold weather. She hated being cold and could feel the frosty wind at the thought of it.

"You said that your wife was pregnant before you turned into a vampire. Did you ever see your child at all?"

Will dropped his head as he thought about that fateful day. "I watched my wife give birth to our son; it was snowing that night. I hid by the window, and I'll never forget that night, which I'm thankful happened during that time of day. It was a very sunny day before nightfall. The screaming, the crying, she was saying my name a lot, which hurt even more. I saw my son covered in blood and crying. If I wasn't a vampire, I would have cried tears of joy to see my son being brought into the world. I couldn't hear what Elizabeth called him. She said she wanted to name him Henry, after her grandfather. But shortly after she handed him to the midwife, saying something to her that I couldn't make out, she laid there motionless. I desperately wanted to bash the window to grab their attention, but I couldn't. I watched my wife die right before my eyes. It was the worst thing I had ever witnessed. The best AND worst day of my life.

"My son was put up for adoption. I stayed near the hospice and waited. He was adopted a couple of weeks after his birth. The new parents were well off, they even had their own car! I left Birmingham and have never returned. I never saw him again."

Kat envisioned the story in her mind as if she was watching a clip from a movie and tried to imagine when owning a car was notable. The sadness in Will's tone made her feel pure empathy towards him, but she did her best to stay in professional psychology mode. "Do you still think about your wife?" Kat was expecting Will to reject the question, but his response was full of grief, and he was too deep into the story as it was.

"Every day."

Kat was eager to learn more about his past life. "How did you meet her?"

Will glared aimlessly for a moment as he searched for the words to describe his first encounter. It happened so long ago that the memories seemed blurry to him.

"When I started my job, the Smith was in one of the suburbs, and we did a lot of work for the bakery next door. At the end of my first week, I wanted to treat myself to an iced bun. I walked into the shop and immediately saw her standing by the cakes. I remember staring in awe as she stared at the delicious cakes, looking indecisive on what to choose. I awkwardly approached her, and she immediately turned to face me, making me fluster and blush like mad. She had the most elegant smile; one that would cure sadness in a blink of an eye. Pale skin and long auburn hair tied up in a bun. I saw her hand ring-free, meaning, to my surprise, she was not someone's wife" Will smiled at the thought of her. "I just said that I loved cakes, in such a dumb manner. She giggled, then told me that lemon cake was her favourite, and that was how we began our conversation. Throughout the weekend I couldn't stop thinking about her. So, the following Monday after work I went back, hoping to find her. Luck had it in for me that day, as she was there! I plucked up the courage and asked her out, and she said yes. We took the tram out to the edge of the city for a picnic on the hills with all the other Saturday couples." Kat noticed Will smiling as he told her the story.

"I knew I wanted to spend the rest of my life with her. I took her to the Southeast Coast and proposed to her on the beach. She, of course, said yes. We got married shortly after, and she fell pregnant a few months later. It was the happiest I had ever been." The smile slowly started to fade as Will began entering the tragic part of the story. "I had always wanted children, so being a father was exciting for me. But it seemed as though it was never going to happen, and it may never happen again unless I am broken free from this eternal curse."

Kat understood how difficult it must have been for him, reliving those lovely moments before it was all taken away from him. His family, his humanity, his identity, everything. "Thank you for telling me. I know it was hard for you to relive those memories, but you don't have to ever again."

Will continued to stare on ahead, looking at the window, despite it being draped closed. "I shouldn't be telling you any of this," Will growled in frustration, standing up, still facing the window. "I'm awfully conflicted with this. Why is this so difficult for me to do?" He walked over to the curtain, pushing the fabric away to reveal the window. His reflection was non-existent as the ceiling lights beamed onto the window. According to the myth, vampires cannot be seen in reflective objects as it is believed that do not have a soul, and mirrors usually reflect the souls of those that stare ahead.

"I have to make you forget me, even if I don't want you to." Will averted his face from the window, looking down at the laminate flooring.

"But why haven't you already, though?" Kat got up from the sofa and slowly approached Will. "You have been given so many opportunities to hypnotise me all night. Why do you not want to? If hypnotising me is the right thing to do, why haven't you already?"

Will didn't turn around to face her; he continued to look out the window, contemplating his existence. He thought about how he had gotten there, the journey he had to go through, which had led him to this very moment. Night-time Southampton was dimly lit with the streetlights on, creating a calming yet eery atmosphere, one that Will was used to seeing every night since his transformation. So many years of minimal social experiences, minimal opportunities, forever at the margins and frozen in time.

"To tell you the truth," Will sighed, "meeting you tonight was not what I had expected. I hadn't had this sort of connection with a human in an awfully long time. For a moment, I felt. . . human myself. Whilst we were talking, I forgot for a moment that I was a blood-sucking parasite. My hunger ceased when I drank blood in the van." He finally turned around to face Kat and continued. "I know we have only just met, and it hasn't gone as well as I had hoped, but I feel as though it went in the opposite direction to what I had intended. My bloodlust was itching for your blood, but as I was talking to you, I began to forget what I really was, and that's something I don't want to lose. You make me feel human. I've spoken to so many humans in the years I have been...this, and none of them made me feel this way before. I find you fascinating."

Kat's mouth slowly drew a smile, which gave Will a strong sense of relief that she did not resent him in any way. Both of them slowly walked closer until they were a few inches apart. Kat began to breathe heavily from her strong repetitive heartbeats. Will's hand slowly lifted, then stopped once it was closer to her cheek. He hesitated.

"It's okay," Kat whispered, cupping her hands onto his. "I'm not afraid." Will's smile slowly grew as he pressed his cold vampire finger and thumb under her chin, pushing her chin upwards to face him further. His slow movement towards her face made her feel apprehensive. However, she trusted him.

"I have to go," he whispered softly into her ear, his cold breath sending a sinister chill through her auditory canal. "You did say you wanted me gone once we've finished talking. I will see you soon. I promise." The words gave Kat a strong sense of disappointment as his finger and thumb withdrew from her chin. He was gone before Kat could turn and open her eyes. She saw the door close, and exhaustion swept over her.

"Holy shit," Kat whispered.

Chapter 6:

♥

Decisions

"YOU FUCKING IMBECILE!" Laura roared at Will after he'd told the bandmates what he'd done. He had expected this level of anger coming from her more than Oliver and David.

"Laura, keep your voice down." Oliver placed his hand on her shoulder; she pulled back sharply and glared.

"Fuck off, Oliver! You should be just as angry at this moron! He had ONE job! And he decided to do the EXACT opposite of what he was supposed to do! I knew you taking her back to her flat was a big mistake! One of us should have taken her back instead!"

Will remained still in front of Laura, allowing her to verbally attack him for his supposed 'mistake'. He knew she was going to be this vicious towards him. Given her background, she was the one that took vampire rules more seriously.

"I told you we should have killed her," David muttered. He sat on the sofa watching the fight with amusement like a live soap opera. Laura suddenly turned to face him, which caused him to hesitate from the unexpected acknowledgement of his presence.

"Don't you have anything to say about this?" She demanded. "This involves you as well!"

David shrugged, uncaring about the situation.

"I say we change her into a vampire, since he doesn't want to kill her and refuses to hypnotise her," he answered.

"You don't get a say in this!" Will yelled.

"Guys! Calm down!" Oliver tried to get in between Will and David, but Laura pulled him away.

"Oh, but I do, William." David launched himself off the sofa, standing inches away from him. "Because, what Laura just told me, this involves all of us, not just you, and I say we kill her, or change her, either will do."

Will's anger began to get out of hand. He no longer had control over his negative emotions and allowed himself to succumb to his rage. His fangs extended; his wings started poking out under his shirt. "We are NOT going to take her life away!" Will roared.

"Then why didn't you do it?" Laura demanded. "You've had no trouble doing this before! What makes this one so special?"

"What's it to you!?" Will became agitated and aggressive, something he was not often capable of feeling, especially when it came to the life of a human.

David pulled a face of realisation. He then chuckled under his breath. Laura and Oliver both looked at him with confusion wondering why he was acting so humorously.

"Oh, I see how it is! William Crowell is in love." David asked teasingly.

"Don't," Will whispered aggressively, clenching his teeth together to withhold his anger.

"You are! Oh wow, you are so fucked!" David walked away, placing his hand over his face, letting out a mixture of groaning and laughing. "You must definitely be over your wife then if you've fallen for someone for the first time in decades!"

"David," Oliver muttered.

"You have got to be kidding," Laura shook her head. "You just met this girl tonight and already you want to Romeo your way into her life? You don't just fall in love with someone after one night, Will!"

"I didn't ask for this to happen," Will informed them. "She and I were talking when we got to hers and she seemed interested in our kind and who I was. I then opened up to her about my past and- "

65

"Wait! You told her your history?" asked David, shocked by the revelation. "You didn't need to, Will! Fuck me! You couldn't even keep your mouth shut about this!"

"I'm sorry," Will shrugged, slowly beginning to care less about how the others felt. "But at the same time, I'm not sorry. It felt like the right thing to do. She's a really good listener! She did psychology at university, so she's very empathetic."

"Will, you're missing the bigger picture here!" Laura told him with exasperation. "You have REALLY screwed us over! If Claudette finds out about this, we may all be executed, INCLUDING the girl! Or she will force us to turn her and let us off with a warning! One of the two! There's no escape for her." Laura pointed a finger a Will, exaggerating her words. "I want you to get rid of her! Or else we will leave without you! You can live your existence with her, not us!"

"Laura, don't be like that," said Oliver. "We can work this out, just don't say thing you are going to regret."

Was Will willing to lose his bandmates, his coven-his only family- over a human he'd just met who he may have fallen in love with?

"He's not going to do it, you know!" David announced. "He's already had a chance to do so! We may as well do it ourselves! He's too much of a wuss to do anything with this girl other than to keep her as a pet. Literally, playing with his food!"

In a blink of an eye, Will launched himself at David, grabbing him by the shirt.

"You will NOT lay a finger on her!" He roared to his face. "Touch her, and I will end you!"

"Come on, William," David smirked. "We all know you're not capable of that. You're too much of a softie."

"ENOUGH!" Oliver intervened. "We don't have to fight over this! Will, let go of him." Will stared down at David for a moment before doing as Oliver asked him to, never taking his eyes away from him. "What I suggest we do is sort this out without any uproar or violence. Okay?"

Nobody in the room spoke a word for about half a minute; they just glared at one another intensely.

"Right," Oliver finally broke the silence. "We have a witness- a human witness- who knows what we are, and we need to sort it out."

"I don't want to turn her," Will informed everyone. "And I most certainly don't want to kill her, nor do I want to have her forget me. But I believe there may be an alternative solution. You all know I want to be human again, that I would give anything to live a normal life, and I believe we can make that happen." The eyes of the other bandmates widened; they all knew where he was going with this, and it clicked instantly what he was on about.

"Will," Laura shook her head. "You can't be serious."

"That's fucking suicide, man!" said David. "It's also a fucking theory! It probably isn't even true! Do you really want to risk our lives for something that may not even be true?"

"But it could be possible, especially if we have Kat by our side," Will suggested.

"To use her as bait?" Oliver seemed confused. Why would Will throw a human at the Head Vampire that he was potentially interested in?

"Not necessarily bait. A weapon. She has knowledge on vampire lore and as a human can do things we can't."

"That doesn't mean shit, though," said Laura. "They're dumb books; fictional! Does she even know this plan of yours?"

"No. But I did tell her we would have to kill the Head Vampire to turn human again." The band continued to stare at Will baffled by his suggestion.

"So, you kind of lied to her? Because, again, it's a theory!" David talked in a slow wryly monotone. "No human has ever killed a Head Vampire before. Why do you think we keep our kind a secret? It's funny because, before tonight, you had no intention of thinking such a thing; you just accepted your fate, pushing away the possibility of becoming human again. And now you meet one girl, then suddenly you want to go on this suicide mission to regain your humanity?"

Will seemed unsure of himself. He had always hated being a vampire since it was what destroyed his life. He had a future, and it was taken from him. But now, he had been given a second opportunity, but it was a high risk that he was willing to take.

He lifted his head and looked at his fellow bandmates.

"Don't any of you want to be human again?" Will asked them, ignoring David's question. "Don't you miss eating your favourite foods, sitting in the sun, going out in the day, normal human things?"

"Not really," David shrugged, giving him a careless look. "We have superpowers, and we are superior to humans. We could rule the world if we wanted to! And being a vampire means we never have to eat food and can just spend money on the band! How do you think we've been able to afford the instruments and music equipment?"

"True. But those are just things." Will told him.

"I think being a vampire is WAY better than being a weak, puny human who spends every second closer to death," David argued.

"I disagree," said Laura, taking David by surprise.

"What?" asked David.

"I-" Laura sighed and shook her head. "While I enjoy being young forever, I miss the possibilities and the opportunities. I have spent weeks on end thinking about what could have been. Before I became. . . this, I wanted to get married someday and have a career. So, if there's a slight possibility that I can get that, then I'm on board, regardless. I miss my job as a police officer. I wanted to be promoted and help people stay safe."

Will smiled at Laura, she looked up and smiled back. "I don't like the idea of breaking the rules, but I will have a think about this."

"What?" David cried in disbelief.

"Same here," Oliver immediately told him.

"Why?" David began to freak.

"Because if we become human, we can play festivals and be a normal band! I want us to be big enough to do interviews and attend events!" Oliver walked over to Will and wrapped his arm around his shoulder to show support. "If we're human, we can go anywhere we want in the world without the fear of sunlight! Plus, I want to drink whisky from a silver flask and not blood from a plastic one!"

David groaned and leaned his head back. "You guys are seriously going to consider this? You'll be giving up eternal youth and impressive superpowers!"

"When have we EVER used our vampiric powers, David?" Laura questioned. "We don't get to use them that much! Only when we're getting out of trouble using hypnotism, and that's it!"

"And carrying the equipment to and from the van," Oliver added with a chuckle.

"But it's awesome to be able to lift heavy items without effort or pain and run superfast, jump really high! Or getting to hypnotise people into doing whatever we want! Humans would LOVE to be able to do that! It would fuck up the economy, sure, but my argument still stands."

"At the expense of living a life," Will pointed out. "We're not really living; we're just walking around as lifeless creatures that suck blood. We're parasites! Come to think of it, vampires are pointless. We don't give anything back to the community or anything."

Laura shrugged at his comment, not finding any fault in his logic.

"Well, we do kill humans which decreases the population rate?" David stated. "Which means more resources for them? We don't eat food so that means even more resources for others. If you think about it, the economy would be better balanced if the vampire-human ratio were a little more equal."

Nobody said a word to him. They knew what he meant, but it didn't matter to them anymore.

"My idea is that Kat could kill the Head Vampire as, you know, we can't do that ourselves without one of us becoming the new one. We arm her with stakes, silver, and holy water, and figure out how to get her close enough to kill Claudette. If she kills her by either decapitation or stabbing her in the heart, we *may* become human again."

"Will, your idea is pretty fucking stupid," David judgingly commented. "First of all, I thought you were all about protecting this girl. Now you want to put her at serious risk by throwing her at the most dangerous vampire in the country. And for what? Mortality?"

"She's our only hope, David,"

"YOUR only hope. I have nothing to go back to if I become mortal, so why should I be involved?"

"Because you're one of us," Oliver told him. "Midnight Devotion would be nothing without you. If you become mortal, you can gain recognition as one of the best punk bands around? We've come this far, David. Please don't throw that away for eternal existence with limited activity."

David stared at Oliver, raising an eyebrow at him, wondering if he was just buttering him up and rubbing his ego, but Oliver was always sincere, and he rarely told jokes or was sarcastic. "Ok, whatever," he muttered. "I'll join your stupid vampire killing cult if you do say yes. So long as I don't lose my immortality. If I'm given the option to stay this way, let me be."

Oliver smiled at him without a comment.

"So, how would we go about doing this then?" Laura asked.

"We tour around the country and head up to Scotland; head up to the hideout," Will responded.

"Whereabouts in Scotland is the hideout?" asked Oliver. "I don't remember when I went all those years ago. I remember it being inside a mountain?"

"Ben Nevis: the highest mountain in Scotland," Laura replied. "Her hideout is inside the mountain; the entranceway is hidden at the summit."

Oliver nodded. "So, I think what we could do, and this is just an idea, is we do a tour around the country and make our way up north. Let's take advantage of this! Let's be a vampire band one last time!"

Will and Laura chuckled along with Oliver.

"Our first ever tour, and it's going to end with killing a vampire," Will smiled. David did not contribute to the excitement. He stood there, as ever, feeling the odd one out.

Chapter 7:
♥
Questions

Kat awoke the next morning after a very restless night's sleep. She expected to have little sleep after the previous evening's events.

Before she went to bed, at a time she could not remember, she'd made some strong coffee then spent roughly an hour going through her books. She was looking up information about vampires and how relevant they were to the ones she had met. To her dismay, extraordinarily little information on fictional or mythological vampires seemed to match the ones that were indeed real. She had theorised that maybe vampires had evolved over the centuries of their existence and that the little that human society had learnt was centuries out of date. It could be possible, but she didn't heavily rely on her hypothesis, considering how everything was not what it seemed. Maybe, if she saw Will again, she could show him and the band her books to see what they thought on the subject.

There was so much she had to learn about the world around her. The thought of going through a boring day and then suddenly into the next with a completely different view of the world, was a strange sensation to her, almost like a fever dream.

Kat stared at her horror movie posters in the living room in confusion, her eyes scrolling past each one, and staring solely at the supernatural creature in the framed image. "*How many of you lot are real?*"

Her thoughts were very fixated on Will and what he had done, what he had said to her, and what he wanted to do. A part of her had hoped to see him again that day, but another part had told her to forget about him and move on to save herself from the perilous band of vampires. She felt as though it was too late and that the mundane world that she lived through was no longer normal. Her life now revolved around a group of unnerving beings that were more than meets the eye. Picturesque individuals with supernatural powers, and quite possibly the strongest people in the world. *People;* not *Monsters.*

The large clock on her living room wall read seven-forty in the morning. She sighed with frustration at the lack of sleep she'd had. When she approached the window to draw open her curtains, it was still dark outside. The streetlamps were beginning to dim down ready for the sun to rise. It was her day off work, so she had the day to herself to do whatever she wanted, despite it being awfully limited due to her lack of funds and entertainment. What her mind debated about was whether it was a good idea to go to Will's place, see if he was still alive, and if the band hadn't killed him already after last night's mishap. Guilt withered inside herself as she thought about it, feeling somewhat responsible if it had happened.

After doing her hair and makeup, wanting to look as beautiful as possible in case she saw Will, Kat decided to go out and treat herself to some breakfast at the local café, which she did once a month with the little money she had, since she didn't have anything in the flat that appealed to her and didn't feel like shopping on an empty stomach. She needed strong and expensive coffee to wake her up and think logically about her situation.

Once she left, the dark sky had turned into a grey blanket, low and stifling. From the distance she could hear the waves crashing against the docks and the seagulls calling out whilst gliding around the city.

Kat made her way through Southampton to the café about five minutes from her flat. When she arrived there, it was too packed and noisy for her, so she decided to find somewhere else. She needed to go somewhere that wasn't so crowded and loud so that she could concentrate on what she was going to do. Kat found herself walking back up the hill towards the city centre, close to the same spot where the attack happened. The streets were quiet, for a Sunday morning it was expected.

She stared at the very spot where the life changing moment occurred, replaying the scene again, like it was a dream she had. She then began to wonder whether or not she had actually dreamt it. Unless her mind was gaslighting her into believing such absurdity. Then again, she was so caught up on the fact that vampires were indeed real that it pulled her away from the reality that someone had been murdered and she witnessed it.

She realised something quite peculiar about the very spot where it happened. Her eyes leered to where Will murdered her attacker and saw that there were no traces of blood at all, no sign of police tape, or any indication as to the murder taking place. Surely, if someone had found the body last night, there would be police tape surrounding the area and reporters speaking in front of cameras to describe the incident. The citizens of Southampton were just walking over the emptied crime scene like it never happened.

The thought of Will being all bloodied and cloaked in his silken wings made her gasp under her breath. She pushed away the thoughts as far away as she could. Will staring at her, red eyes crept up in her mind. A gasp escaped silently from her breath. It was enough for her to resume walking and quickly move away from the area. Her feet suddenly decided to race into the nearest café that Kat could find, regardless of the quantity of people inside.

Kat remembered there was a café in the row of shops across the main road, so she scurried away to get some warmth, a seat, and more coffee. Breathing heavily as she entered, the people inside - of which Kat quickly counted seven, all adults - looked at her with concern. She felt embarrassed but ignored them and immediately went to sit at the nearest table by the window. It had a modern make over with sea green and navy grey walls along with fancy ship-shaped menus. The café was thankfully noticeably quiet enough for her. She realised that she looked decidedly out of place, but the few regulars had gone back to tending their own drinks, chatting amongst themselves. Her heart stayed racing, causing pain and discomfort in her chest. The thoughts weren't escaping her mind no matter how hard she tried to push them far away. The visions came back, uninvited, and her thoughts continued to fixate on the images of Will. His charming looks and slim body then morphed into the bloodied, silken winged Will who had killed her attacker, but had obviously been thrilled to kill them in the process of saving her.

Kat sighed and tried to focus on the menu. Part of her just wanted one of everything in the hope the calories would settle her mind despite knowing her stomach not being strong enough to sustain a large amount of food.

The server hovered and Kat made up her mind. "A large, full-fat latte, and a bacon and egg ciabatta, please. I've had a rough night."

Kat looked out the window and watched the world go by. She could see teenagers walking through the streets laughing together and checking their phones. Many of the kids were in groups of three or in pairs, a few of them with intensely straightened hair, showing obvious signs of damages from excessive use of hair-straighteners and lack of conditioner. Their layered fringes covered their entire forehead by sweeping to the side, a popular look for teenagers, or the vampire members of a punk rock band. Their choice of clothing was skinny jeans with oversized hoodies that either had artwork based on a famous band, or an abstract drawing of something cute, modified to look terrifying. Their accessories being studded belts around their wrists, colourful striped fingerless gloves, and quirky necklaces.

Seeing them made Kat realise it had been a while since she'd seen her friends from university. Maybe now it was time to set up a social media other than MySpace, and try to reconnect, and see how they were getting on. Usually, she would receive texts and calls from them, every once in a while, but due to commitments and work schedules, it was incredibly difficult for her to arrange a visit with them, especially if she wanted to have a group of friends together.

Her food arrived, for which she thanked the server. Her stomached roared and Kat obeyed. She lifted her head from the food, turned to face the window again to continue people watching, and almost fell off her chair screaming. Her heart thumped against her chest from who her eyes caught coming towards the cafe, someone she wasn't expecting to see, especially at this time of day! A pale faced figure that she easily recognised, only this time, he was no longer wearing the pink and purple eyeshadow and dark lipstick from last night. His skin, however, remained abnormally pale. His lips, too, were just as pale, almost as if he had painted both his face and lips with the palest foundation. Despite this, he remained picturesque in Kat's view.

He took a quick glance at the café where he spotted Kat. It was the same handsome smile she saw the previous night. He spotted her and slowly waved at her with a look of concern. It looked like the band HADN'T killed him yet.

"*Jesus fucking Christ*," she whispered, watching him approach. Will stepped inside quietly and, without waiting or asking permission, sat down opposite Kat.

"Hello again," he said in a welcoming tone. Kat didn't respond, she stared at him in disbelief. "Aren't you please to see me?" Will smiled.

"I have several questions," she responded with scepticism. "How did you know where I was? Did you follow me *again*?" Kat's tone held more than slight annoyance towards the possibility.

"A little bit," Will shrugged, creating a gap with his thumb and index to exaggerate the size.

"What do you mean 'a little bit'?"

Will shrugged his shoulder and raised his brows. "Well, I was about to walk to your flat to talk to you, finish what we discussed last night. Then, I saw you standing at the spot where. . .you know. You quickly walked away before I could approach you and I got concerned. I stood about for a moment wondering if I should talk to you or not. I went on my instinct, again, and decided to do the right thing, come and talk to you."

Kat grimaced. "You can't stalk me like that," she told him after sipping her cup of coffee. "It may have worked last night and saved my life, but that doesn't mean you get the privilege to do it all the time. It's not romantic at all. If anything, it's problematic and creepy."

Will couldn't help but chuckle. She was partially right about that. "TECHINCALLY, I wasn't stalking you. But I promise not to do it again," he assured her, not bothering to argue with her.

"Good," Kat smiled. "Glad I got that across to you so very easily. I was worried you were going to be difficult with me considering you're…never mind." Kat continued diving into her breakfast.

Will was happy to see Kat smiling rather than grudgingly interrogate him again. "You look like you haven't slept at all," Will pointed out.

"Good to know my make up failed to cover my sleep deprivation," Kat slanted her mouth. "But yeah, I didn't sleep great. When you discover that *you-know-what* are in fact real, it can make your mind race a million miles an hour, make you want to read up everything about them." Kat gave Will a look so he knew she was still wary, but Will responded with half a smile. "So, what did you want to talk about?"

The server interrupted "Can I get you anything?" she asked Will. Will didn't take his eyes off Kat.

"I'm alright, thank you," he told her. "Just here to keep warm, are you?" The server turned her back and strode off leaving Will and Kat alone.

"I wanted to tell you what I had discussed with the others last night," Will informed her. He smiled greatly at her. He was not used to smiling this much.

"I'm glad they didn't tear your head off!" Kat laughed. "So, what did you guys discuss?" She took another big bite of her breakfast and listened to Will's story.

"I told them I didn't do what was intended, which was to hypnotise you into forgetting about us and what had happened, which, of course, meant all hell broke loose when they found out."

Hearing that made Kat feel on edge. Supernatural beings were fighting over her. Drama wasn't something she had to deal with on a regular basis, so this was somewhat new.

"You must have balls of steel to tell your bandmates what you did, rather than lie," said Kat.

"I also told them that there could be a way for us to be human again and we all conformed- well, me, Laura and Oliver did, David didn't want to, but democracy won in the end. Laura is having a think about it since she's not one to break the rules. She's quite. . . law-abiding due to her past."

"What did she use to do?" Kat queried.

"She worked for the Metropolitan Police in London back in the nineties. Even when she turned, she abided by whatever laws our kind have to keep us alive. But since she misses being part of the police force and a normal human life, she's starting to consider it herself despite it being what David called *'suicidal'."*

"Well, he's not wrong," Kat tipped her head sidewards, giving Will a sly smile before biting down on her food.

"So, we have a plan, and we're going to need you to come with us." Kat ceased chewing and stared at Will, frozen in disbelief. She took in the information he had just given to her before she could respond.

"You want me to travel with you? Why? And where?"

"We're going to be touring the UK and make our way up north. Claudette's hideout is inside Ben Nevis Mountain up in Scotland. We'll need you as the only way to kill the Head Vampire would be to stab her in the heart with something either silver or in the shape of a stake, or you decapitate her, whichever you can do."

It all remained surreal for Kat to be talking to someone supernatural about killing a supernatural queen. It was a goth's dream come true!

"And you need a powerless human being to do the job for you?" Kat wondered, looking sceptical at him.

"Vampires can't exactly hold silver items. Nor can we be near holy symbols or items. Our kind are not strong, not in the same way as the fictional vampires your kind are used to reading about or watching on media."

Kat quickly took a bite and swallowed, and then drank some of her coffee, which had cooled down by now. "Can one vampire kill another?" she continued questioning.

"Yes. But it's not as simple as you think. It requires a lot of strength and agility. If a vampire kills a Head Vampire , they become the new Head Vampire . It is theorised that a human killing the Head would reverse vampirism, and all vampires that reside in the country would revert to being human. Which is why your kind are forbidden to have knowledge on our existence, otherwise our kind would be in danger from hunters, and cause a widespread panic."

"But if all the vampires in the country reverted back to human, wouldn't that cause people to start exposing your kind?" Kat queried.

"I don't think anyone would believe them," Will chuckled.

"What about those who went missing for a short period of time because of what they became?"

"The Head Vampire s from around the world would sort them out. Let's just focus on us for now, okay? And worry about the outcome later," Will assured her.

Kat nodded, talking about this helped her focus and think less about the incident.

"So, in other words, you want me to be a vampire hunter?" Kat asked, intrigued.

"Technically, yes?" Will bobbed his head side to side.

"What do I get out of this? Because I would have to go on leave at work, and I don't want to do a job and get nothing out of it," Kat waved the remains of her sandwich around to inform him that she was serious. "Especially if I'm travelling across the country."

"Well, you're definitely not going to be doing this for free," Will assured her with a smile. "I will pay you well. I won't give you a figure as I would need to work it out. It will be more than what you earn each month."

"Will I get a bonus if I kill the vampire lady?" Kat chuckled, which made him smile.

"I'll think of something," Will gave her a suggestive wink.

Kat thought about it for a bit, she'd be sacrificing for this: her job, her flat, her mundane life. Even though she wasn't entirely satisfied with how things were going and how some days felt as though she was in a dead-end position and the temptation for excitement outweighed the danger.

Her moral compass pointed towards the latter.

"I'll do it," Kat concluded as she took another sip of coffee. Will's grey eyes widened, surprised by her response, let alone an agreement.

"Seriously?" He leaned forward, which made Kat nod.

"Fuck yeah! I want to travel the country and help out a band! It beats working shifts in a pub!" Kat became excited with the idea of touring the country and becoming a vampire hunter. "Question though, why can't you go straight to the Head Vampire 's hideout and kill her there? Why do you need to travel the country first?"

"Because we need time to prepare you, as well as continue to be less conspicuous." Kat nodded and finished her bacon sandwich. "I assume you have a long list of questions?"

"A list? I have a novel full of questions!"

Will chuckled at her comment.

Kat sat back and closed her eyes, for the first time in twelve hours she didn't see images of the thing sat across from her covered in someone else's blood.

"What are you doing today?" In his mind, he hoped for Kat to say that she had no plans to go anywhere or have any shifts, so that he could spend the day with her.

"Nothing really," Kat shrugged. "Was just going to chill at mine, think more about what happened last night."

Will half smiled, concealing his excitement. "Okay. Well, I wanted to ask if I could join you on that and come back with you? Maybe you could continue interrogating me?" A handsome vampire asked her to come back to her flat and hang out. She somehow found that extremely exciting despite it being perilous. To her surprise, it did not phase her in the slightest, as if this was all normal for her.

"I think most sane people would reject that idea," Kat smiled. "But I'm not 'most sane people'."

Will and Kat giggled together at her comment about herself.

"So, is that a *'yes'*?" Will continued smiling.

"It is indeed a *'yes'*." Kat exchanged a smile. "Yes, to interrogating you as well as to coming back to mine."

The server came to gather Kat's finished plate and asked if she wanted anything else, which she rejected. Kat also rejected the idea of Will paying for her breakfast, but he had insisted, saying that money didn't mean anything to him.

"You're going to need money when you become human again," Kat muttered as soon as the server left. Will shook his head and laughed as they both left the table to leave the café.

It was still overcast outside which was a safe scene for Will to travel. He explained to Kat that so long as the sun was not directly visible, they were able to walk around in public. Vampires can choose to rest in the day to wait for night-time, but they couldn't dream or properly sleep.   "That's a human thing we lose, it's like when you are tired but can't sleep properly. It is as bad as it sounds."

"That doesn't sound like fun," Kat grumbled. "But then, why do you have a bed?"

"It's a furnished flat for university students. Also, when I rescue humans, they have somewhere to sleep." Kat glanced sideways and checked if Will was making fun of her. He bounced his eyebrows. "I laid you down on it. Was it comfortable for you?"

"I couldn't address the comfort of it because I was too busy losing my shit at the fact that I witnessed a murder by a vampire, supposedly fictitious and mythological creature." Kat lowered her voice and leaned closer to Will's ear, to avoid people hearing her. Will didn't respond.

Since Will had already been in her flat the previous night and was welcomed in, he wasn't restricted from entering again. They happily made their way up the stairs until they reached Kat's door.

The blackout curtains in the living room remained open, but Will informed Kat that due to the overcast, she could leave them open and give the room some natural light. They casually marched over to the sofa and continued the 'twenty questions' despite it being something Kat shouldn't be learning about.

"Whatever is asked in this flat, stays in this flat," she confidently told Will.

"Okay," he smiled, feeling grateful for her hospitality.

"So, let's start with the one I've been itching to ask all night and day that may be difficult, but you don't have to tell me it is too difficult."

"It's okay," Will assured her, placing his hand on top of hers, causing a tingling sensation. It felt as though an icepack had been placed on her skin. "You can ask me anything."

Kat took a deep breath in and prepared herself for the subjective question she was eager to ask.

"How many people have you killed?"

Will didn't flinch. Instead, he stared at her, thinking about all the people in the past he had to kill in order to survive.

"Ten," he concluded.

"In eighty-eight years?" Kat seemed surprised by the figure he gave her. It was much smaller than she had anticipated.

"That includes the man from last night as well."

"So, like, how have you survived for that long and have only killed ten people? That doesn't make ANY sense!"

Will sighed, guilty of the lives he had taken for the sake of his thirst. Every kill he had done-even those too villainous to live- guilt would wither inside with each kill. It felt like a person who was trying to quit smoking continue smoking, and that each cigarette they inhaled was a puff of shame, even if it was pleasurable for them.

"Because we can drink blood from anything with a beating heart, including animals. But sometimes, we kill humans for the extra energy, the extra taste, to wipe away those who are potential harm to others." The way he told Kat this was full of confidence, like he had wanted to tell her, hoping that she would ask about his lifestyle. "Nine people I have killed were all villainous people. The first victim I killed was out of sheer hunger, which was the only kill I regret." Kat had envisioned Will in the early twentieth century wearing fancy clothing roaming the dark industrial streets of Birmingham, stalking his prey from a distance.

"Speaking of," said Kat, "What did you do to the body from last night? There didn't seem to be a crime scene when I walked past that area this morning. Did you do something to him?"

Will slanted his lips and said, "We took the body to the back of the van and cleared up the blood with a power washer we store in the van."

"Why do you keep a power washer at the back of the van? Won't that drench your instruments if it leaks?"

Will chuckled. "No. It's because we don't want to store it in the flat. We use it to clean the van."

"Okay?" Kat slowly nodded. "And, what are you going to do with the body you have stored at the back of your van?"

"We've drained it before the blood went stale."

Kat gazed in confusion, wondering how that was possible. "With equipment that's ten times more expensive than any of your equipment?

"No. We poke holes into the body and put small tubes in, suckle on the tubes and let the blood drip into a large water bottle." Hearing Will say this made Kat feel nauseous, her stomach turning with the idea of a body shrivelling up like a raisin.

"Sorry," Will dropped his head in shame.

Which led to her asking another question to move on.

"Besides your teeth and the hypnotising, the bat wings, super strength, speed, and hearing, do vampires have any other unique abilities?" She knew fictional vampires always had different abilities and weaknesses, but she was eager to know if any of them were close to Will's type.

"We have retractable fangs," Will showed Kat his snow-white teeth and revealed his retractable fangs, which made Kat highly fascinated to see teeth that sharp. She approached her left index finger towards the edge of the tooth before Will recoiled away, making sure that his razor-sharp fangs didn't cause a disastrous consequence.

"We can turn into monstrous creatures on command. I've never turned into the full monster, just the wings and claws.

"We can jump really high; have retractable wings to fly through the sky, which I keep to a minimum because you never know who could see you." Kat nodded whilst listening to the absurd powers of the vampire telling her all his secrets with no hesitation. Will was in too deep, and it was too late for him to turn back, he was unburdening himself, a confession he'd longed to tell.

"There is another reason why I've only killed ten people," he continued. "We usually like to keep a plastic flask filled with blood on ourselves to keep us from getting thirsty. Silver flasks would seriously damage us! Otherwise, we would drain the blood from the bodies before we dispose of them and keep the blood in our fridge and freezer. We would drink some of the blood before we interact with humans, usually before we leave the flat, but we carry the flasks around with us just in case. When our flasks go empty, we fill them back up."

A flask made of plastic was pulled from inside Will's jacket. He unscrewed the small plastic cap and tipped it upside down to reveal the crimson red content on his fingertip. The little red liquid shone from the light; Kat gazed in fascination as she watched Will place his index finger into his mouth and suckled to absorb the content.

"Is that human blood?" she asked curiously without fear or disgust.

"It's pig blood," Will answered in a heartbeat. "Not as tasty as human blood, but it keeps us going for a while."

"How long can you go without drinking blood?"

Will's mouth slanted to one side. "I haven't the faintest idea," he shrugged. "I have survived an entire month without it before giving in. When I became a vampire, I tried to eat regular human food, but it was like eating cardboard, very bland and difficult to digest. The nutrients in food became an anathema." Will shivered at the memory of learning to adopt his new diet.

Kat shuddered at the thought of eating cardboard.

"I'm sorry!" Kat giggled. "I once ate cardboard like the weird child I was out of sheer curiosity!"

"Children do all sorts of weird things out of curiosity!" Will shrugged with a smile. "Any other questions?"

"Oh, loads!" she blurted. "Have the other band members killed people?"

"We all have. David more than any of us. Oliver has the lowest kill count because he has always been empathetic, even as a vampire he cares about people. Laura, well, she struggles with what we are the most. She's killed a few people in her vampire life, but she has always resented herself for it. Which is why I reject the idea of you becoming one of us. I don't want you to start resenting yourself for murdering people due to what you become."

Kat understood this statement and started to realise why a vampire might want to be human again. Being a vampire meant a lot of sacrifices to gain superpowers and unlimited youth. She wasn't that close to her parents, but not being able to see her family or friends ever again was a thought she dreaded. It was the only exception to not wanting to transgress into vampirism.

"My turn to ask a question," Will chuckled.

"Oh?" Kat's eyes widened.

"How old are you?" Will asked her, which caught her off guard completely.

"Oh! I'm twenty-four," she quickly responded. "I always get told I look younger though! What about you? What age were you when you turned?"

"I was thirty-two when I became a vampire, and became a father," his voice saddened as he thought about the son he never got to father. The memories of Will's human years came back to him. The dark evening of when he became a vampire flashed into his thoughts as the image of the creature with red eyes, pale white skin, and sharp teeth came close to him. His final evening as a human. He pushed the memory away and immediately answered her question, trying not to dwell too hard on the worst day of his existence, the day where his life was stolen from him.

"Have you ever tried to track your son down during those eighty years?"

"I couldn't. It was too painful for me to consider doing so. I would rather have forgotten about it and kept him safe from what I was. He deserved a life without any danger or threats."

Kat really wanted to ask him more about his son but decided that it was best to not mention anything about it from now on.

"Let's move on," she shook her head. "My next question was going to be about vampire reproduction."

Will looked at Kat with shock, but in a humorous way. "You want to know if vampires have sex?" he laughed.

"That's what I meant by *reproduction*!" Kat blushed. "What did you think I meant?"

Will let out a small chuckle, which made Kat blush. "I mean, we can, but I haven't had sex as a vampire, nor do I want to, especially with a human."

"And why is that?" Kat anticipated for answers, curious as to why Will vetoed the idea of vampire-human intimacy.

"Because who knows what I might end up doing to a human! I could end up breaking their body!"

"I wasn't trying to suggest that we have sex!" Kat cried with embarrassment. "I was simply curious! Next question!" Will chuckled at Kat's embarrassment but admired her fascination. "Actually, I just thought of something: don't any of your instruments contain silver?"

"Funny you should ask," Will pointed. "None of the instruments we have actually have silver on them. The guitars and the drumkit contain nickel silver, which isn't really silver. It's copper, nickel, and zinc."

"Oh really? I did not know that!" Kat was surprised to learn about this. "Does that include the strings on the guitars?"

"They're made with steel cores and nickel-plated steel wrap wire, no silver at all, so we're perfectly safe."

Kat felt as though she had learnt so much within a single hour, things no human knew about.

"One last question," Kat raised her index finger indicating the single figure.

"One?" Will looked at her with confusion. "I'm surprised you have one more and not half a dozen left!"

"For the meantime, just the one: do werewolves exist as well?"

Will's eyebrows rose. It was not a question he had expected her to ask. "Not as far as I know! We haven't come across any!"

"Good. Less mythical shit to deal with!" Kat and Will laughed together; their hands entwined, connected like fire and ice.

Chapter 8:

♥

Plans

Back at the band's flat, David, Laura and Oliver sat around the kitchen table discussing their current situation; that of the dead body in their van and how they now had a human interfering with their existence thanks to Will's emotions towards her.

Red liquid- too thick to be wine- were drank from wine glasses by each of them.

"Whilst Will is off playing with his food, we're the ones dealing with his mess like a parent of a problem child," David rolled his eyes. "Did he say when he'll be back?"

"God fucking knows," Laura shrugged. "I just hope he hasn't done the Devil's Tango on that poor girl."

"Gross," Oliver shuddered in disgust. "Sex is not something Will thinks about, and you know that, Laura Bates! He's incredibly old fashioned!" Laura gave Oliver an expressionless look. "Can we discuss our current situation? What are we going to do about the body? We haven't killed anyone in a long time. Getting rid of a body is much more difficult now than it has ever been with modern technology and expert forensic scientists. Laura, you should know this!"

Laura and David sat in silence as they thought about it. Oliver drank some of the blood from his glass, gasping as soon as he'd finished.

"I did some research, and apparently this guy has done a lot of dodgy shit." Laura opened her laptop and read out what she had on the victim. Researching into local criminals and their records was something she was good at, having previously worked in the police force back in her human years.

"Declan Shaw. Forty-eight years old, unemployed, and over the past thirty years, charged with sexual assault, possession of drugs, speeding three times, had his license revoked and three counts of physical assault. Short sentences and the sort of usual suspect when something goes missing in his neighbourhood." Laura turned the laptop around for the table to see. The mugshot image of the same person that assaulted Kat the previous night and his criminal record were on the screen.

"How is he NOT in jail?" David seemed surprised.

"He is classed as 'mentally unwell' and went to a psychiatric unit for some time," Laura informed them.

"I suppose Will is going to be happy knowing he killed a criminal, considering he doesn't like killing people like the goody vampire boy that he is," David said sardonically. "So, we bury dear Declan here in the woods, and he becomes worm food."

"Hang on," Oliver objected. "Does he not have any relatives or friends who may start asking questions about his disappearance?"

"A few" Laura answered with little care in her tone. "He didn't have any siblings growing up, his mother died twenty years ago, and his father has dementia and is living in care. He only has the social circle of the pub life."

"Seems as though Will caught himself a vicious wolf," David commented. "As well as a delicate deer."

Laura scowled at David and turned the laptop back to face her. She closed the records on the screen and moved to the next item on their agenda: *the tour.*

"We need to start asking around for venues and such who may let us play," Laura informed the boys. "We should aim for London, Cardiff, Birmingham, Manchester, and Glasgow. We don't want to do small places as it makes us easier for our peers to find us."

David and Oliver looked at one another, their eyes raised and mouths frowning. "What?" Laura raised her eyebrows.

"Birmingham?" Oliver questioned, concerned about her choice. "You do know that Will doesn't want to step foot in that city, right?"

"He needs to fucking get over it," Laura replied bitterly. "It's been over eighty years, and the city has become a different place!" David and Oliver didn't respond to her comment, but they knew Will was not going to like the idea of going back to the city where it all began; the city where his child lived; the city he never wanted to step foot in ever again.

"He's going to rip your head off, you know?" David warned her.

"He can fucking try!" Laura focused on her laptop as she began searching for venues around the country.

"Also," David pointed out, "I thought you weren't supposed to be in London until you've been a vampire for a hundred years? That's like a general rule to vampirism when you sign up to the lifestyle to avoid being seen. What if someone you once knew spotted you? They'd probably get a heart attack seeing you the exact sage you were when you 'disappeared'."

"David," Laura explained, "London is a breeding ground for spotting new talent, especially bands. If we want to get recognition, we need to go to cities that are highly populated, and London is the capital of England. So, it is essential that we play at the capital cities of the United Kingdom. Let me worry about that, and in the meantime, why don't you start practising for our potential shows while I start making some phone calls and emails?"

"And I take it you've made your choice and are going along with Will's suicide mission?" Oliver wondered. "I mean, I'm on board with it as well, but we seriously need to start thinking about ways we are going to do this aside from the gigs."

"I thought long and hard about it all night, and while it is a fucking stupid idea and I am purely against the idea of breaking the rules, I reminded myself on what I said the moment I turned: if the opportunity of becoming human were to present itself, I would take that chance no matter what, even if it meant breaking some rules to get what I wanted."

David and Oliver both nodded before leaving their chairs, taking their blood-filled wine glasses, and separately making their way into their bedrooms. Laura sighed thinking about how difficult this was going to be for Will, but she knew it was something he needed closure on.

Kat and Will spent the day together watching horror movies and listening to their favourite songs. There had been many new tunes that Will discovered through Kat, ones he didn't know existed, ones that he hadn't listened to in a long time, and some that gave him a sense of nostalgia. He was amazed at how music had evolved over the decades that he had been alive, and he gave Kat a potted history of rock'n'roll.

Will found Kat to be an interesting human; she didn't like being part of the mainstream crowd, she was fascinated in classic horror movies, enjoyed haunted houses and goth aesthetics.

"What draws you to classic horror movies then?" Will asked with fascination, pointing at Kat's collection of posters.

"The practical effects are what make them great, as well as how they changed cinema. Oh, how I wish I had been there when they first came out to see the audience's reaction to the gore and silly acting!" Kat smiled. "Let me guess: you saw these movies when they first came out, didn't you?"

"Guilty," Will laughed. "I went to see some of them with David on the big screen. It was an experience, that's for sure!"

"Ah, so jealous!" Kat sighed ruefully.

Will had found himself a friend-a mortal friend- who he felt comfortable being himself around. He also found it ironic that vampires were coming back into popularity through fiction novels and media depictions appearing on the big screen. Kat explained to Will that not all vampire fictions were the same, and how some changed how vampires function. Some more questionable than others.

Will hadn't had this level of innocent fun with anyone for a while and was starting to be thankful about his decision.

He hadn't laughed nor smiled, nor been this happy in an exceptionally long time. Every second with Kat made him feel more human than ever before. Whilst she went to make herself some food, Will had pulled out one of her books from her bookcase. He began reading through the book that Kat had read the night before.

Kat came back into the living room with a bowlful of penne pasta mixed with pasta sauce, a couple of slices of garlic bread in the bowl with it, and a glass of cranberry juice. Will noticed the cranberry juice and laughed a little.

"What?" Kat smiled as she noticed Will looking at her drink. She sat with her legs crossed on the sofa.

"Nothing," Will giggled. "I'm curious: since meeting me, had it encouraged you to read this?" Will raised the book with his hand to reveal the content he was reading.

"Oh, that." Kat crossed her legs to make herself comfortable. "I got curious after last night's incident and wanted to see if your vampires are in anyway the same as the ones in my books."

Will skimmed through the pages. He chuckled quietly at the description of vampires in the section of a book about various mythological creatures.

"There are apparently half vampires in that book," Kat pointed out. "Or *Dhampirs;* do they exist as well?"

"They don't exist as far as we know," Will explained in a formal tone. "But I doubt they exist at all since we cannot procreate with humans. Besides, if half vampires existed, I think they would be exterminated by the Vamperium because they could pose a potential threat of exposure if they were to interact with humans without close supervision."

Kat casually ate some pasta as Will explained the lore of vampires to her. It became so strange how vampire lore was becoming normal for her all of a sudden.

"So, there's only one type of vampire? No hybrids or anything?"

"Vampires are the only mythical creatures to walk this planet. No hybrids, no other folklore; just us. Sorry if that disappoints you."

"It…doesn't, actually. I'm quite surprised really. I mean, if there were other creatures out there then it would be next to impossible to hide from humanity for everyone!"

"It would be difficult, yes." Will and Kat stared at one another for a moment. He then killed the silence with disappointing news. "I should probably get going soon to see what the gang have decided about the plan." Knowing that Will was leaving made Kat feel anxious. She was used to being alone, but the idea of being alone again made her object to the idea. She didn't want to seem possessive, but was still worried for him, especially since he had broken the one essential rule of vampires.

"Okay," she sighed with disappointment. "When will I next see you?"

"As soon as the plan has been discussed with the others, and the sun isn't beaming down," Will assured her. "I just need to make sure that everyone else is onboard."

"Do your bandmates hate me?" Kat queried, speaking her mind. "They didn't sound particularly pleased with me being there."

"No, they were just pissed off at me for what I did; it didn't have anything to do with you, apart from David, but he hates everyone." Will assured her. "If you're that anxious about it, I can take you with me and you can see for yourself that they don't hate you. They're more concerned for you."

"How can you be so sure that they don't want to eat me? You said so yourself that my scent is mouth-watering."

"I've already threatened David that I would tear him apart if he ever harmed you in any way, so that's given them the message of how serious I am."

Kat froze with her eyes wide open. It surprised her greatly at how protective Will was towards her. She knew he would kill for her- she had seen it with her own human eyes- but to threaten a vampire withing his own clan was strange to her, especially since they had only known each other for a little over twelve hours.

"Jeez," she whispered. "You'd kill your own vampire bandmate who you've probably been with for a long time just to protect a weak human being such as myself?"

Will denied her self-depreciation. "I see you as a beautiful human being that's now living around dangerous powerful creatures, and I want to make sure that you don't get taken down by any of them." Will gave Kat a smile despite talking about dangerous creatures and potentially killing someone close to him to protect her.

"So, you would kill your bandmates if they tried to kill me?" Kat waved her fork about as she asked.

"Without hesitation," Will answered immediately. Kat gave him a look of concern. "What?"

"You haven't known me for more than twenty-four hours, and you're already dedicating your existence, and potentially giving up your eternal youth and superpowers to be with me?"

"That's not necessarily the case," said Will. "I did explain that I've been wanting to turn to a human way before I even met you. The reason I want you to come with me is because I think you would be an advantage against vampires. We just need to gear you up with crosses, holy water, silver, and whatever vampires are weak against- whilst also protecting ourselves- and you can use those to stall the Head Vampire and kill her."

Kat imagined herself covered in straps and carriers filled with bottles of holy water, stakes, a necklace covered in garlic and crosses dangling from her wrists as she stabs a vampire in the chest, watching it turn into dust and vaporising into the sky. It reminded her of the action-packed vampires movies. "That does sound pretty fucking epic," she agreed. "I'll come with you to the flat then, on the condition that I spend the night there."

"Deal." Will didn't hesitate and gave her a sly smile. "I won't be sleeping unless the sun is out so I can protect you from the others, potentially."

"Just, please don't watch me sleep like some weirdo," Kat pointed. "I don't find that attractive in the slightest.

Will giggled and said, "I won't."

By mid-afternoon, Will and Kat returned to his flat and entered the living room to find Laura, Oliver and David sitting on the sofa together. Each vampire head turned and gave a surprised expression after seeing Will bring Kat with him to a flat full of vampires. Will examined the room and saw that they had been drinking glasses of blood, which was a positive sight, meaning that they wouldn't be craving Kat's internal essence. A laptop sat on Laura's lap, Will hoped this was a positive sign of progress with the plans.

"We weren't expecting to see you for a while, Kat," Laura politely told her. "I would offer you a drink, but we only have blood, I'm afraid."

Will gave Laura a stern look, which she responded with a shrug.

"It's okay," Kat smiled with sincerity.

"I've told Kat what we'll be doing. She is onboard with the whole idea," Will smiled at them all enthusiastically. "How have you gotten on with venue locations?" David and Oliver looked at each other with looks of worry, like they were expecting an uproar to commence at any second.

"I have found a couple of venues in London. I will give them a call and continue looking in Cardiff, Birmingham, Manchester, and Glasgow." Laura knew that saying *Birmingham* was going to trigger Will, but she said it, nonetheless.

David and Oliver looked at Will as she said the forbidden name, waiting to see his response. Will's expression didn't change.

"Brilliant," Will continued smiling. "We will need to book some shows as soon as possible. I want us to be at Ben Nevis before the beginning of February." The others were surprised to see Will taking this so well.

"What has Kat done to him?" David thought. *"He is never this generous to a human."*

Will wrapped his arm around Kat and pulled her closer, making sure she was feeling calm and secure.

It was all so strange for Kat to be learning about the world of vampires, she was almost led to believe that she was just becoming friends with a group of goths who portrayed themselves as vampires, but after witnessing Will killing someone the way he did right before her human eyes, that thought seemed more absurd.

"How does killing the Head Vampire turn everyone back to human then?" she asked, theoretically.

"The Head vampire being killed by a human could potentially counteract vampirism," Laura educated her. "If a vampire were to kill them, then they would become the Head Vampire and gain all of their powers and abilities. One of the main rules of vampirism is that if a human discovers the existence of vampires, they must either be killed, hypnotised into forgetting, or become a vampire. Will, of course, chose neither of those things because he seems eager to be human again, and so am I." Laura gave Kat a smile, which made Kat relax a little knowing that she didn't hate her. She wanted to have a good relationship with Will's bandmates.

"You'll also be happy to know that the person that attacked Kat last night has quite a criminal record," David informed them so casually. "So, no need to feel so guilty about that now. Will, you did the country a favour."

Will didn't respond to that information. He still felt somewhat guilty that he murdered someone but thankful that he managed to stop them from harming Kat.

"We've drained the blood from the body and plan to bury it in Bramshaw Commons later tonight," Oliver added. "We'll wait until midnight and then leave. It'll be easier to do this when most of the city is asleep."

Will smiled at them all, feeling thankful that his bandmates were doing this. The situation was going in the direction he didn't think was possible; he now has Kat knowing who he is and being surprisingly okay with it as well as being comfortable around her. The thirst for her blood was still something he struggled with, but not to the extent he had expected. He was thankful to have the flask of blood he kept in his coat. Every sip made it easier for him to be around her.

"Kat's going to be staying here tonight, I hope that's okay?" Will told them all, pressing his fingers against her shoulder, pulling her closer to his cold body.

"I suppose?" David shrugged. "But she's not coming

95

with us tonight, you know that, right?" His venomous tone had Kat feel on edge.

"Oh! I didn't think I would be!" Kat interjected, anxiously. "I'd probably be asleep here whilst you're off burying the body."

"You're going to have to get your own food, I'm afraid," Laura directly told her. "We don't have anything in for you to eat."

"I'll order her something," Will assured them.

"What are you going to do about your job at the pub when you come with us?" Oliver asked her.

"I plan to continue working there for a couple of months until you have the venues booked," she answered. "I may also need to start saving up some money for the journey and inform my landlord that I'll be gone for a few weeks, depending on how this works."

"I can pay for your rent for those weeks if they get too difficult with you," Will offered, which made David raise his eyebrow, seeming concerned for Will's sincerity towards a human he had just met.

"Will? Can I talk to you for a second?" David gestured for Will to join him in his bedroom. Will unhooked Kat and followed David down the hallway.

Once they entered the bedroom and closed the door, David folded his arms.

"What are you doing?" he asked him sternly.

"What do you mean?"

"You're going to pay for her rent? Buy her food? You just met this girl last night, and you're already throwing money around and offering her things? Why?"

Will looked at him with confusion.

"I have the money to do so?" Will shrugged. "What's the problem with that?"

"Money that we need to pay for the shows! The van, the equipment, the people who can forge our documents. Especially for the aftermath of killing Claudette!"

"Why are you making such a big deal about this, David?" Will argued. "I have enough money to cover the costs for all sorts! Enough for when my human life potentially happens!"

"IF it does happen!" David shrugged. "You're betting so much on this hypothesis!"

"Quit being so cynical about everything! Just let me do my thing and you do your own thing! Kat is MY responsibility, and I want to take care of her, protect her, and I gave her the choice about this!"

"Are you sure you did? Or did you force her into it because it's what YOU wanted?" Will grabbed David by the throat without hesitation and pushed him onto the door, which he was surprised stayed intact despite the strong force. Will's face came close to David's as he growled loudly at him, his fangs pointing outwards; his inner monster came close to coming out, causing potential destruction.

"What's going on in there?" Oliver shouted from the living room like a parent. Will huffed trying to calm himself down. David didn't react to Will's actions and allowed him to let his frustration out.

"You going to let me go, or what?" David asked. Will released him and then shoved him out of the way before he opened the door, angrily. He saw Laura and Oliver standing next to Kat, which made Will anxious, but also relieved that they may be trying to protect her from a possible fight.

"What the fuck was that all about?" Laura asked him.

"Forget it," Will shook his head as he made his way over towards Kat. "Keep looking for venues for us to play, will you?" He grabbed Kat's hand and dragged her across the living room, through the hallway, and into his bedroom, slamming the door in the process like an angry teenager.

Will pulled Kat towards him and embraced her without hesitation. She didn't respond to it right away, but she suddenly raised her hands slowly, and had her warm arms wrapped around his cold back, holding tightly onto his jacket.

"It's okay," she whispered. "I know how difficult this has been for you, but I'm here, and I trust you." Will stayed silent, still holding onto her, not wanting to let go. A repetitive thumping was heard coming from inside her living body.

"Your heart is beating so fast," Will finally said. He let

go of her, allowing her to move back until she could see his face.

"It's the adrenaline. Being held closely by a handsome vampire wasn't something I thought I'd be doing, in all honesty." Will laughed quietly and held on to Kat. His laughter was very comforting as she rested her head against his hardened chest.

Chapter 9:
♥
Crime

Will ordered Kat an Indian takeaway later that evening. The strong scent of curry herbs permeated the band's flat, but only Kat could appreciate it. The others hid in their rooms so that Will and Kat had the living room to themselves.

"I have never had curry, what's it like?" Will suddenly asked Kat the moment she swallowed her food so as to not let her talk with her mouth full. "I know the smell, but I have no association with it as food."

"Did you ever have spicy food? Or anything that made your mouth tingle? It's like a warming blanket and leaves a happy taste in your mouth. I'm not sure I can describe it. It's a thick cream that has certain spices to add intensity and flavour."

Rather than show envy, Will smiled at Kat's attempt to describe Indian food.

When Kat finished her large meal, Will had her wrapped around his arm and her head resting on his shoulder. He'd brought a blanket from his bedroom to keep her warm as his body was much colder. He smiled at the fact that he finally had someone to hold after years of only holding himself. They were watching movies on the sofa until Kat slowly began drifting off to sleep.

Will could hear the others stirring in their rooms getting ready to leave and bury the body in the woods. By midnight, Kat was fast asleep on Will. He carried her into the bedroom and placed her into his unused bedsheets. Kat was in such a deep sleep that his cold lips didn't even wake her when they pressed against her forehead. He left his bedroom to meet the others downstairs by the van.

Oliver was in the driver's seat, as usual, whilst Laura and David were in the back seats, all waiting patiently for Will.

"Will is lucky we don't lose patience," David muttered sarcastically.

Before Laura could respond to his comment, Oliver turned the ignition, and the van roared into life. Will hopped into the passenger seat, slamming the door behind him.

"Ready?" Will turned at Oliver. He nodded as he drove away from the building.

They made their way through Southampton. The streets were almost deserted; very few cars were driving through the city. There were a few people out and about, and it looked like many of the pubs and clubs were still open. Will looked out the window, thinking about Kat and his first meeting with her at the pub. He also began thinking about his wife, Elizabeth. The idea of being in a relationship had always scared him because of the death of his wife. He didn't want to relive the pain again. What he was doing to Kat was perilous, but with what strength he had left, he knew he had to take the opportunity that presented itself, so that he could once again live a normal life. He had to believe it, or else all hope was lost.

Nobody said a word throughout the journey through Southampton. As soon as they had left the city, David finally spoke up.

"After tonight, let's try and keep the human killing at a non-existent level, shall we?" Will began to get frustrated with David's sarcastic remarks. He knew David was always sarcastic about everything and liked to be the joker of the group, but it was getting too much for him now, especially with the current plan.

Oliver told the others: "We need to bury the body in a secluded area. It shouldn't take us too long if we run deep into the New Forest."

"If we weren't vampires, this would take us all evening," said David with a smile, feeling pure pride with his unlimited strengths and abilities. "Are you sure you want to leave this all behind, not being able to use your strength to bury bodies?"

Will cringed at David's question. He decided to focus his thoughts on Kat and their day together. He thought about what he might do next, which made him chuckle under his breath. He thought about maybe taking her for a midnight stroll in the woods or going to see a movie. He wanted to do so much with her before and after his vampire life.

They drove along the M27 in silence before they reached Bramshaw Commons. They drove through lanes until they reached a dead end, where people would park their cars to go hiking, or walk their dogs. Thankfully, their van was the only vehicle there. David and Will opened the back and saw the body wrapped in large black bin bags and taped up tightly like a plastic mummy. It was so dark that it would be impossible to see where they were going through the woods if they were human; their vampire eyes guided them through the darkness of night-time. It was as if someone had turned the brightness and saturation to maximum.

Laura and David leaned into the van to pick up the body, while Will kept a lookout for anyone or anything that could be watching. Oliver kept the engine running in case they needed a quick getaway, even though they could just outrun whatever spots them committing a crime they couldn't abandon the van under any circumstances, not with a giant broken heart printed on its side, and its unusual paint colour. David effortlessly carried the body over his shoulder whilst Laura grabbed a shovel. Rather than confirming they were ready, they just disappeared deep into the woods without saying a word to one another.

The breeze from their high-speed running caused the branches to rustle, the sound of their footsteps echoed through the trees. Laura and David reached the centre of the woods and found a secluded area full of bracken and gorse.

They glanced at each other and nodded. This was the perfect place.

"I doubt any human would walk through here," David

shrugged.

Laura approached the bushes and begun shovelling into the dirt. She was going at such a fast pace that she reached twelve feet deep within two minutes. Dirt was flung into a pile behind her as she disappeared into the earth.

As soon as she'd finished, she leapt up from the deep grave and landed back on top next to where David stood.

"The grave is done," said Laura.

David could smell the corpse on his shoulders, sour from its last night out, full of beer and the rot starting to eat away at its insides. David dropped the body into the grave in disgust, where it landed with a gentle thud. Declan Shaw disappeared into the soft earth never to be seen again. David then fastidiously brushed his hands together.

"That's the hardest part done," he commented. Laura began collecting all the dirt from its pile with the shovel and quickly filled up the double deep grave. A minute later and it was filled in, and they made sure the bushes and leaves were replanted to disguise their digging.

"That takes care of that!" David rubbed his hands together, again.

"Rest in peace, Declan Shaw," Laura muttered, with no emotion to her tone.

They both gave a quick glance at one another before David finally spoke. "Race you back to the van?" He challenged Laura.

"You're on, Barrett!" Laura smirked wickedly.

In an instant, they raced away from the grave and flew through the darkness. Their vampiric vision helped guide them. The two vampires glided through the forest, flashing amongst the trees so fast that the leaves and branches rustled in their wake. Laura wielding the spade like a demented samurai. Both were laughing as they would outrun each other every second. David had always liked challenging the others, letting the vampire part of him run wild at every opportunity. He would often lose against them at whatever challenges he had to offer, like the tortoise and the hare, he underestimated his bandmates' abilities.

Back at the car park, Will could hear David and

Laura's laughter echoing through the woods, causing him to be slightly concerned with what they were doing. Oliver picked up on his unease.

"Don't fret Will," Oliver laughed lightly. "I have a feeling David challenged Laura to a race. My money is on Laura."

"I was going to say the exact same thing," Will laughed back.

Laura was the first back and used the spade to vault over the van. David was one millisecond later.

"For fuck's sake!" David moaned.

Laura smiled victoriously.

"It was a close one!" she cried triumphantly. "You won't be able to find Mr Deadman anywhere!"

David collected himself and sat down in the rear seats. "Let's get out of here, shall we?"

Laura clambered in, throwing the shovel carefully into the emptiness of the back. Will sighed and got into the passenger seat. He was excited to go back to be with Kat, just the thought of being next to her.

It was two-thirty in the morning when the band got back to the flat. Laura, David, and Oliver all went to do their own thing. When Will entered his bedroom, Kat was in a deep sleep. He carefully closed the door behind him and went over to check on her. Her breathing was slow and even. She was peaceful which assurance him. Will grabbed a book from his small bookshelf, deciding to read whilst lying next to Kat. He figured he may as well kill time whilst waiting for morning. The book he had chosen to read was a novel about a demon and an angel being friends and saving the world from the apocalypse. It was one of his favourites.

By seven-thirty Will was finishing the book. He gently nudged Kat awake. She turned to look at him, and he saw her large blue eyes staring at him, making him smile with delight.

"Morning, sunshine," he whispered, then chuckled to himself when he realised what he said.

Kat stretched her arms and responded in kind, "Hello

Mr. Moonlight."

Will laughed and closed his book, placing it onto one side to kiss her forehead.

"Did you sleep alright?" he asked her. His elegant smile made her feel comfortable despite being inches away from a blood sucking creature.

"I slept surprisingly well. Your bed is cosier than I thought it would be." Will didn't know how to respond to that comment. He never had the luxury of feeling the comfort of his own bed.

"Do you want me to go grab you some breakfast? It's still pretty dark outside?" Dawn was still half an hour away, which gave Will plenty of time to pop to the shops.

"Yes, please if that's not too much trouble? I'm starving!"

"What do you eat, I mean I haven't been food shopping in quite a while," Will wrinkled his brow in thought.

"I'm open to anything. So long as it can keep me full for a few hours," Kat informed him.

Ten minutes later, he arrived back with bags of shopping, enough for a family of four for a week. "I may have got carried away, but there is milk and cereal in there somewhere, and bread..." Will gave Kat the plastic bag filled with potential breakfast.

"And croissants and jam! You did rather get a bit enthusiastic!" Kat sat up on the bed emptying out the bags. "I haven't seen his much shopping in one go since before I went to university!" Will collected the breakfast and made his way out of the bedroom to start.

Kat had stolen one of Will's shirts from his washing basket to place over her body. It was baggy enough and long enough to cover her underwear. She shouted from the doorway, "Were you guys able to do it?"

"It's done, he's gone. Let's not talk about it," Will requested. "I want to talk more about you." Will came back with her breakfast. She leaned on the bed and waited for Will. He handed a plateful of Danish pastry plastered in strawberry jam and a glass of orange juice.

"Thank you," she smiled. "So, what do you want to

know?" she asked as she took a bite out of a sticky Danish pastry.

"I want to know about your parents. Talk to me about them."

Kat nodded as she swallowed her food.

"My mom, Margarette, and my dad, George, have been married for forty years. They live in Essex in the same house I was raised in. My mom is a social worker, and my dad works on building sites doing something with the plans that I never understood."

"No siblings?"

"Nope. I had to rely on other kids to keep me entertained. It was rather lonely growing up. I didn't have many friends in school and often kept to myself." That surprised Will, given how extraordinary she was to him.

"And you get on with your parents?"

"The majority of the time. We have had disagreements from time to time, but I love them no matter what. I was planning to stay with them soon for my dad's birthday, then I'm staying for Christmas and New Year's, so you won't see me for Christmas I'm afraid."

Will smiled despite her disappointing news. "I didn't expect you to sacrifice time with your family to be with me, and Vampire Christmas isn't really a thing," he assured her. "Go and have fun with your family. I'll be all right."

"Because of religious reasons?" Kat giggled.

"Some vampires keep their faith, but it seems odd to me when I could live forever. That and we don't need anything materialistic."

"Except you don't want to live forever."

Will chuckled as she drank some of her orange juice.

"I'm going to need to go back to my flat to freshen up," she informed him. "Did you want to come back with me?"

"Actually, the band and I were going to do some practice. But I can come on by later tonight after your shift and take you on a date?"

The word *date* made Kat choke on her juice. She started coughing as the contents went down the wrong pipe.

"I'm okay," she waved her hand to assure him. "You want to take me out on a date? At midnight?"

"Did I stutter?" Will teased. "Of course, I do!"

"Where are you going to take me?"

"Wrap up warm, I'm going to take you out for a stroll in the park." Kat was very curious about this. If he wasn't a vampire, he would have more options such as dinner and a movie.

"I do have to work tonight, so I'll be done by about eleven thirty, hopefully." she reminded him.

"I can pick you up from the pub. I promise I won't kill anyone tonight."

"Pinkie Promise?" Kat teased back.

When Kat had finished her breakfast, and changed into her own clothes, she said her goodbyes to Will and the band before making her way home. Will wanted to kiss her lips but decided to keep his distance; he wasn't sure if she was ready for that in their unusual relationship. And he wasn't sure that his band mates were ready either.

Later that afternoon, Kat had changed clothes into something to keep her warm. Black wool leggings underneath her black skinny jeans, a thick grey wool turtleneck jumper, with a t-shirt underneath for the extra layer. She wrapped herself up more with her thick black winter coat and fastened her large boots with skull and roses modelled all over the faux Leather. She grabbed some of the leftovers from her fridge and left for work.

Monday shifts were always quiet, and Luca and Kat used the time to give the bar a proper clean after the mayhem of the weekend. Luca suddenly approached Kat once they finished serving a group of women who often came in for a drink after their Pilates.

"So," they said with a flirtatious tone. "The lead singer of that band the other night."

Kat found herself blushing as she thought about him. She avoided eye contact with Luca and continued pulling the lever that pour the beer.

"Yes?" Kat smiled. "What of him?"

"He seemed extremely interested in you. Did you two

exchange phone numbers?"

"Not exactly. We just talked. We met up earlier today, and he's taking me out later, just for a night stroll."

"That sounds. . . pretty Victorian," Luca raised their eyebrows with suspicion. "Are you sure a night walk in the park alone with a man is such a good idea, lass?"

"I don't think he's planning on doing anything to me," Kat assured them. "I know what I'm doing."

"...but does he?" Luca laughed, seeming to trust Kat's words despite their initial worries. "Well, IF he does anything to you, I will bite his head off before the police do."

"Well, you know what to tell the police if I show up missing or dead," Kat turned her head to face Sally. "But I don't think Will is like that."

"If you show up to work tomorrow smiling then I will know to trust him." Kat couldn't help but smile, which was unusual for her to do during her time at work.

At eleven o'clock the bar was dead, so Sally let Kat nip off early. Kat said goodbye to Luca before heading out the door. They waved their goodbye whilst putting away clean glasses. "Enjoy your date!" They yelled as she left the building.

There was a frigid wind in the street and no sign of Will, "*I'm early. Perhaps he hasn't been stalking me today*". There was a sudden rush of air on her face, a black streak in front, and a loud bang as Will landed, smiling like an idiot. Kat jolted from the sudden appearance of her vampire prince.

"'Evening, Ms Rhodes," he smiled, taking her hand, and kissing it gently in an old-fashioned manner, making Kat blush.

"'Evening, Mr Crowell." Kat cupped Will's hand and the pair made their way down the street.

Kat felt safe being with Will. She instinctively knew he wouldn't harm her, despite being a vampire potentially thirsty for her blood at any given moment. He was mature enough to control himself, a strategy to maintain his thirst. And having a vampire who could easily tear anyone apart was strangely reassuring after the Sunday morning attack.

"How was work?" Will began the conversation.

"It went well. It wasn't busy like it was on Saturday," Kat answered. Will pulled her closer to him and kissed the top of her head. The pair made their way down the street and headed towards the city centre, looking for a snack van, and hot coffee to keep Kat warm and awake. Once Kat got her hands on the warm cup, they headed back up the hill towards the park to begin their night-time stroll.

Chapter 10:

♥

Flight

Large puffy clouds hovered in the night sky, underlit by the city's lights, cloaking the stars and the moon, preventing them from being seen by human eyes. The cold air penetrated Kat's body, despite the many layers she wore. It bit into her face and ears. The coffee warmed her up with every sip.

The park they walked through was empty; not a single human - or vampire - in sight. The occasional lights on both sides of the footpath illuminated their way.

"You know that argument about vampires, and how the light of the moon is a reflection from the sun? Does that affect vampires?" Kat wondered aloud, the moment she looked up at the cloudy sky.

"No. The moon isn't warm enough to burn us alive," Will responded casually. "The reason we burn up in sunlight is the UV lighting, and the sun's natural heat. It boils the venom that pulses through our bodies, a corrosive chemical that should never be exposed to fire and sunlight. You know how humans need sunlight to gain vitamin D?"

"Yes? Are you telling me that the reason vampires look so pale is because they cannot go out into the sunlight?" Kat couldn't help but find it ironic how vampires could not gain a single trace of vitamin D without burning up.

"Correct."

"So, vitamin D and UV lighting kills vampires."

Will burst out laughing. "Quite pathetic really, isn't it?"

"No. I think it makes sense. So, if I pushed a vampire into a tanning bed, it would kill it?"

Will shrugged his shoulders. "I haven't thought about that. But yes, it's basically a vampire oven."

"What about the UV lighting in clubs?" Kat looked up at Will, waiting for his answer.

"That UV light wouldn't kill us, it's not strong enough, but it would show the corrosive venom that's inside us, as well as revealing our eyes being abnormal, which is why we cover up and wear sunglasses sometimes, even indoors. People would assume it's part of our 'look'."

"But couldn't you just hypnotise them into ignoring your abnormal skin colour? What about hypnotising your relatives and friends into pretending that you're not a vampire? Or when you have relatives visiting?"

Will remained silent for a moment before responding, staring ahead of them.

"When we become a vampire, we do not know what we are capable of doing until it is too late. Once you are taken to see Mistress Claudette, you are informed of what powers you have as a vampire, but also the limits you are expected to live within."

Kat kept trying to find loopholes in the lore of vampires.

"But what happens when someone discovers that ability when they turn?"

"If they do, they will still need to go see Claudette. Sometimes, her vampires would travel to the families of those vampires, and hypnotise them into forgetting about them, just to make things easier."

The idea of someone's family having their memories erased just so they would not know of vampires made Kat feel grief for those dealing with exile for the sake of their existence. Those that become vampires probably didn't even want it in the first place, which made her wonder more.

"What if someone turns into a vampire, and wants to be killed on the spot because they don't want that particular life?" Kat continued.

"She would give them what they want," Will responded without hesitation. "Execute them right there and then. She once said, *'The fewer vampires, the easier my job'*."

"And how many vampires are there in the UK?" Kat's eyes widened with curiosity as she waited for a high figure.

"A fair few in each county, a few more in the big cities," Will answered, looking down at the pavement lights. With vampire eyes, the streetlights would illuminate brighter, and be visually more stunning through their vision. "We don't know for sure. The Mistress has her secrets, so that it is easier to control us."

"Are there other vampires in Southampton besides yourself and the band?" asked Kat.

"Not that we know of," Will answered with a chuckle. "We haven't come across any."

"That's. . . good, right?"

"It is good. We could possibly be the only vampires in this city."

Kat took another sip of her coffee, which was starting to cool down. "Have you gone to other countries to find more vampires?"

"I've never left the country," Will began. "I have roughly met twenty vampires in the eighty-eight years I have been one. I stayed with my bandmates, accepting my fate that I will forever be in this state. I have been craving change for so exceedingly long. The world may be changing around us, but my life remains the same."

The thought of his fate upset him, knowing he would never have the life he desired. He had hoped that would all change soon but didn't want to get his hopes up too high; he wanted to enjoy his time with Kat before the tour in January. He felt Kat's hand sink into grip around his bicep and pulled herself closer to him, her head leaned against his shoulder. Will was thankful to have drunk some blood so that he could not feel the urge to kill when she leaned in closer to him. Her elegant

111

lavender scent remained to his liking.

"What will you do if you become human again, hypothetically?" Kat queried.

The question made Will wonder about it. It was obvious to him what he would do, but he didn't want to freak Kat out, thinking it may be too soon to think about. So, he thought of the next best thing.

"Like I told you at the pub: I would like to get Midnight Devotion more publicised and get an album out," he told her instantly. "You know that Oliver is incredibly determined to get the band going. Laura and David are on the same page but aren't as determined as Oliver. I know he's been dreaming of being in a band that played festivals and being popular enough to play on the radio. I want that as much as he does."

Kat smiled whilst listening to Will's idea, which led to her next question.

"How did the band start?" She became very curious to know about the origin of Midnight Devotion.

"It was when me and the others came across Oliver back in 2003," Will began the story with a smile. "We were in a club in York; Oliver was playing the drums for a different band, who also happened to be vampires."

"So, you're not the first ever band of vampires?" Kat chuckled.

"Sorry to disappoint you," said Will. "David talked to him after the act, saying how impressive his drumming skills were, and the pair of them spent the evening chatting about music. Then Oliver mentioned that he wanted to start a new band, as he wasn't going to be staying in York for much longer. He wanted to get the band on the move, but the other vampires said they weren't confident enough to be nationally recognised, because of Claudette. The other band members moved back to London, which is sort of vampire central, and Oliver decided to come with us back to Glasgow. We spent the next few years learning instruments and perfecting our skills to the point where we wanted to start a band. Neither Laura nor I knew how to play instruments but were very much on board with the idea. David played guitar back in his human years, but never got proper lessons. I played piano back in my day, but my skills were rusty, so learning piano again on a keyboard helped. We each learned guitar, bass, piano, and drums. We are all multi-instrumentalists, since being a vampire meant that we could spend days on end practising. I learnt how to sing as I was itching to sing about how I felt. Plus, Oliver said I had the best singing voice out of all of us."

Kat looked at Will with her eyebrows raised. "Let me guess, from your poems?"

"My poems are somewhat involved."

"Of course," Kat giggled. She could tell she was giggling constantly due to nervousness, but positive nervousness. She was having a wonderful time having a romantic stroll with a vampire.

"I know," Will acknowledged. "At one point, at around 2005, we each did a degree on Music Technology to get the best knowledge on music theory and history. We bought a lot of books and spent a lot of our spare time - which was as much spare time as you could count - studying and practicing."

Will and Kat entered a park containing a set of swings, both for toddlers and older children; a pirate ship, with a slide and climbable rope; a zip line, and wooden benches. Kat let go of Will and made her way towards the bin to drop her empty coffee cup, then proceeded towards the swing set. She sat on the left swing whilst Will sat on the right.

"So, have you always been a fan of music?" She asked, as she began swinging slightly backwards and forwards, holding onto the chains that supported the seat.

"I've always been a fan of music since I started playing piano at the age of eight. A lot of stuff after the war was sugary pop, but that's what people wanted then. I eventually became a fan of punk rock music in the seventies, *Sex Pistols* and all. I was there in Manchester for their famous gig; I saw *Joy division* when they started up. Each decade I became a fan of a new genre. As soon as we all mastered music, we wanted to start a punk rock band."

"And who came up with the name and logo for the band?" Kat wondered. The image of the van's broken heart decal showing up in her head.

"Me," he answered in a heartbeat, handing her a prideful smile. Both of them laughed. "I drew the broken heart logo; it represents the fact our hearts no longer work. Broken, essentially."

Kat raised her head and widened her eyes.

"Makes sense, I suppose. But why the name *Midnight Devotion*?"

Will shrugged his shoulders. "Vampires hang about at midnight. And devotion means *love* or *loyalty*? So, midnight love? It sounded cliché, so we went for something that was the same but different." Kat dropped her head and snickered. "What?" Will laughed with a hint of a smile.

"That's so cliché," she lifted her head up to look at him, smiling. Will couldn't help but smile at Kat's adorable giggling. "But a perfect fit for vampires, I suppose!"

"That's the purpose of it!"

They sat in silence for a few minutes, each lost in thought. Will was starting to have hopes for a future with Kat.

"And, in the last eighty odd years, what did you do in terms of hobbies?"

Will thought about it for a moment, retracing his history, remembering all the jobs he had.

"Aside from learning how to play instruments, I would sneak my way into music venues and orchestral halls - ironic really, considering I am now in a band, but we would still want to earn some money for future fixtures on the instruments, the van: maybe upgrading ourselves a much bigger van? We have enough money to keep going for a while, but we would like to keep it at a suitable level." Will looked at Kat and offered her a smirk.

"And what else were you doing?" She continued asking.

"I did a lot of studying in terms of keeping up with modern technology and politics, just so that I knew what was going on and not to be an old-fashioned vampire. In the eighties me and David also did night work at factories to get some income, so that we could buy clothes and pay rent for a flat, although we could have hypnotised the property owner into thinking we had paid! But I am a man of honesty."

Kat laughed at the idea of hypnotising people into giving them free stuff. Even though she was against thievery, hypnotising her property owner for a month's free rent had her imagination run wild on what she would buy.

"We always had a guitar or two. Over the years we have bought instruments and the pedals needed," Will continued. "Every time that we moved to a new city, we would find work that helped us for a short period, and when we had earned enough, we would go and spend it on new clothes and equipment, as well as doing music courses."

Kat figured it would be common for people who were eternally living to go back into education to get as many degrees as possible, surely. "If I were a vampire, I would totally go back to university, and use up my eternal time and abilities to learn as much as possible, be the smartest bitch on campus!"

Will's chuckle turned into a laugh. "I haven't attended any other education in seven years."

"Did you have to pretend you were twenty? Because you don't look twenty."

Will looked at Kat with a face that showed how offended he was; his mouth dropped, and his eyes widen. Kat knew he was just teasing her.

"Thanks!" Will wryly cried, causing Kat to laugh loudly. "Hypnotism can get you anywhere. But we were 'mature' students."

"No IDs at all?"

"None. Times have changed, it used to be easy: turn up somewhere and tell people we were from an agency. However, we will need IDs for when we become human and lose our hypnotic abilities, of course."

Kat had that small ray of hope within her that Will would turn human someday.

"This is an odd date Will, but possibly the best one I have had, you are doing well so far!"

Kat smiled, and then reached out her hand to pull on Will's swing till they were moving in unison. Will felt incredibly comfortable just talking to her about his life. It was a transgression within the Vampire Society, but this very moment made him realised that he couldn't care less about the Vampire Rules. Feeling this human made it all worth it.

"How did you meet David and Laura?"

Will looked up as he thought how to start the story. It was always fascinating to him how his little coven came to be.

"I met David first in 1977," he began. "I had just left Scotland and came across him in Sheffield. We were fighting over draining the blood of a local criminal. We compromised and shared, whilst talking about how we became vampires and our interest in music. We went to find the new wave of rock bands that became punk. For many years we moved around, following the music scenes from Liverpool to Manchester, to Leeds, until we found Laura in London, 1994. She had just turned into a vampire, and she needed help. Mistress Claudette's right-hand man took us three to Scotland, telling Laura the rules of vampirism. We left her to it and didn't see her for two weeks. We met up in Glasgow and have stayed together ever since."

The penultimate part of the story suddenly made Kat curious about something.

"And what are the rules to vampirism?"

"That we keep our kind secret, which is the essential rule. Don't use our powers to overcome local governments, or try to take over the country; we don't draw any attention from humans; when we kill people, we must hide the bodies, basically, we need to keep ourselves hidden from humanity and try to blend in."

"Sounds rather challenging," said Kat. "Vampirism doesn't sound as fun as media makes out."

"You get used to it. But I hate living with restrictions. I want to live my life my way. I don't. . . I don't want to be a monster anymore. I want to be just like everyone else. You obviously know that."

Kat grabbed Will's cold hand and grasped it tight, causing a strong sense of cold to shiver through her. She ignored the uncomfortable temperature and allowed herself to shiver. It was worth it, to feel his skin touch hers.

"I'm thankful that you have enough confidence in me

to kill a strong vampire," said Kat.

"I'm kind of gambling my luck as well as your life on this. No pressure, but you're our only hope, Kathryn." Kat understood the risks, but she knew why she was doing this. Will saved her life, and she felt that this could be her way of showing her gratitude. However, there was another reason she wanted to go on this highly dangerous journey. The idea of Will being human again, and the possibility of being closer to him, made her hopeful, even though their chances were as slim as a sewing needle. The pair of them looked up at the partially cloudy night sky. There were barely any stars to see, as they were still covered but the moon glowed from behind a cloud. "For vampires, that's a lucky sign, it means that hunting will be quick". Will looked at Kat and thought it best to change the subject, "What made you stay in Southampton after university?" Will asked.

She turned to look at him and gave an honest reply. "I really like the city," she explained with a smile on her face. "Essex is similar, but it felt cleaner here, I feel free here. I wanted a fresh start and independence. Originally, I was living with two other people, but then they left after six months due to finding work outside the city, and I ended up having to find somewhere else. I wanted to try and find a job in psychiatry here. So far, of course, I'm not having any luck. It might be time to look elsewhere, otherwise I would have to return home to save up more money."

"Never lose hope," Will reminded her. "You seem passionate about it."

"I want to be able to help people mentally. I've had to support my mother during her depressive episodes when I was a teenager. It was challenging but was also rewarding. I basically helped her overcome a battle with her mind."

Will didn't react for a moment. He then nodded and asked "Maybe you could start somewhere different? Maybe counselling first and climb up the ladder to psychiatry?"

Kat nodded, agreeing to his idea.

"That is a possibility. We must all start somewhere, right? I mean I'm currently a bartender that barely gets paid enough to cover the rent and bills. Finding work isn't exactly a walk in the park right now. The world economy has gone to hell in a handcart."

The night air started to get colder. Kat shivered slightly from the late-night chill.

"Not a fan of the cold?" Will asked her.

"Nope! I prefer late Summer and early September weather," Kat informed him, rubbing her hands vigorously together. "I need to get some new winter wear, especially when we go to Scotland! I dread to think how cold it gets up there!" She came remarkably close to joking about being a vampire and not having to suffer from the cold but kept it to herself. "I'm still surprised the band agreed to this risk," said Kat, blowing her warm breath into her cupped hands.

"David doesn't want to be human; he seems to enjoy being a super-strong monster. Laura and Oliver have passions and dreams that cannot be fulfilled as vampires. At the moment, we're focusing on needing to rent a recording studio for a couple of months and getting an album on the go before the tour." The idea made Kat wonder why they hadn't already done so. It would make sense for them to start recording an album, they had the money to do so, they had songs written and performed some gigs, so why wouldn't they use that to their advantage?

"I think you guys should record in the flat to start with, then get the studio album to sell at the tour," Kat suggested. "I guess you can make an album within two months, with the content you've already written. And the internet could help! Bands are promoting themselves on social media these days, so you will need to set one up at some point!"

"We could make an EP, not sure about an entire album?" Will seemed sceptical about his own work. "I could ask the others what they think. We may as well take advantage of our vampire skills and spend hours upon hours recording music without tiredness, we could do it both at the studio and at home."

"That was exactly what I was thinking! Spend your waking hours recording music in a building with little to no windows."

Will and Kat laughed simultaneously. She was enthusiastic about the idea of helping a band kickstart their career and encouraging them to proceed with their dreams.

"You're amazing," Will said to her.

"Not as amazing as you," Kat smiled. "Seriously, first thing tomorrow evening you should get started on the EP. Maybe get someone to make T-shirts to sell on the tour?"

It was amazing for Will to see Kat being encouraging and even managing him into making content to sell on the tour.

"Purple shirts with a broken black heart on?"

Kat laughed. "Emos and goths will LOVE them! It's very fashionable right now."

The pair of them laughed along and continued staring into each other's eyes. Blue and red eyes gleaming at one another with the strong and intense emotions of devotion. Both pairs of eyes that saw the world differently; one saw it more vibrant, but disturbing, the other duller and more uneventful.

Will leapt off the swing and slowly marched to the centre of the park. Kat got off hers to make her way over to Will. He looked up at the sky for a moment before turning around to face Kat, who stood inches away from him. His face gave her a flirtatious smirk, which made Kat's heart melt with desire.

"I have two final questions for you," Will told her with an anticipated smile, whilst lifting two fingers up. "Firstly," he bent the middle finger, "are you afraid of heights?"

Kat gave Will a look of confusion, slowly walking closer to him. "No?"

"Secondly," He lifted the middle finger, "do you like roller coasters? Or fast movement?"

"I'm alright with them?" She shrugged, unsure with where Will was going with his question.

"Good," Will chuckled. He turned Kat around quickly, causing her to gasp in surprise. He wrapped his arms around her stomach softly Kat wasn't sure what was going on, but she trusted him.

"Hold on tight, and try not to scream," he warned her. Before Kat could say anything, her feet were no longer touching the ground. She gasped at the realisation of what was happening. The speed of them rocketing up into the sky caused her stomach to feel like it was no longer in place, her brain felt like it was being pushed down against her skull, and her heart raced along with the speed. The cold air had entered her lungs, making her insides temporarily freeze up.

Will stopped as soon as they were above the clouds. The sound of Will's wings coming out from his back, and ripping through his black winter coat, echoed into the stunning night sky. Kat grasped onto Will's arms as tightly as she could to prevent falling, even though he'd catch her before she could scream. She was speechless. The air was much colder than it was on the ground. They were high enough to not be seen by anyone down below, the midnight sky made sure of that.

"Holy shit," she gasped, her eyes widened.

"I won't let you fall," he informed her. "I've got you." He felt Kat's head nod with agreement.

"I trust you," she whispered. The view was magnificent. The city's lights from the streetlamps and buildings were like fairy lights on a black painted wall. They made her jaw drop with amazement at how beautiful and impossible it all was.

"Here we go!" Will cried enthusiastically.

Will began to flap his wings to start flying across the night sky. Kat looked up and saw more stars in the black painted sky than she could count. She laughed as they flew above the city. She could see cars driving through the streets, people walking on the pavements and people standing by their apartment windows.

She extended her arms out and felt the cold breeze through her fingertips. The wind began to chill her exposed skin, her face in particular.

Will smiled, watching Kat having the time of her Life.

"THIS IS AMAZING!" Kat laughed loudly. "I feel like a bat!"

"Not like a bird?" Will asked, confused but still chuckling along.

"Bats are more like night-time birds!" Kat continued to laugh.

Will flew them over the seaport, where the boats were, away from the city. They hovered high in the sky above the ocean.

Will stopped mid-air. Both were upright and Will carefully turned Kat around so that she was facing him, still holding onto her. His wings kept them hovering in the air.

The adrenaline kicked in and Kat felt the panic rise, she held herself tight around his waist. The pair of them slowly and simultaneously connected their lips, turning it into a passionate kiss. Will's lips were as cold as snow. Kat felt her body shiver from the tip of her toes to the crown of her head. She felt his tongue as she parted her lips and collide with hers, connecting like Fire and Ice.

The kiss went on for a minute before the pair disconnected and leaned their foreheads together, still in mid-air in the mid-autumn night. Will's hands held onto her waist securely, whilst her arms wrapped around his neck, her fingers grasping onto his raven hair, as they kissed the night away.

Chapter 11:

♥

Journey

It was now January; a new decade had arrived for the world to celebrate.

Declan Shaw was reported missing by his pub mates shortly after Halloween. There were no leads to indicate what had happened, and the Police asked around before concluding he'd done a possible runner and was on a 'missing persons' report. Suffice to say, the band were off the hook and hoped it was the last time they'd ever have to take a human life and hide a body.

Kat had spent the last few months working at the pub until handing in her two-weeks' notice. She had also spent time with Will, who had offered to pay for her rent and pay her a great amount once the tour was over – if they came out of it alive. They spent their time doing whatever they could to sustain their relationship, despite Will's vampiric status, and went on several dates, late evening meals and talking into the early hours on Kat's sofa. Kat had continued to ask Will questions about his past life, his hobbies and interests besides music, and he told her that he enjoyed pre-Raphaelite art; history; literature; and wildlife. Will and Kat's new relationship seemed to be going smoothly. They saw each other most evenings in the week, and any available days where the sun wasn't exposed, or whenever Will wasn't busy recording music. On the days that were gloomy or overcast, Will would spend whatever spare time Kat had to offer with her. They were

Kirkland Signature

currently in their 'honeymoon phase'.

Will had spent a lot of his free time with the band recording their debut EP for the tour. The band did exactly what Kat had suggested and spent several weeks renting out a studio and recorded their music. Their EP contained six new songs, all of them being their own. They chose not to record a couple of the song they had played in the pub as they believed they weren't good enough to be on the EP, but maybe suitable to be remastered for their debut album in the future. They rented out a nearby studio in the basement of an old factory for them to record for hours straight without stopping to rest. They couldn't stay in the evening since the studios would be closed past eight o'clock, so they would spend the evening rehearsing in their flat preparing for the following day, designing T-shirts, getting them printed and taking them to sell throughout the tour.

A large box of dark purple T-shirts arrived in the post before Christmas, various sizes with the broken black heart logo and their band name above. The band played at another pub the week before Christmas, which contained a larger and more enthusiastic audience, and even sold a few of the new T-shirts. Their debut self-titled EP was finished and ready to be released for the country to hear. The venues were now booked, and they were due to start touring early in January.

Kat had spent Christmas and New Year's with her parents in Essex on a quiet neighbourhood in the outskirts of the city centre. Initially, she felt restless, and squashed into the comfortable semi-detached life of her parents. During her time there, she had a quick catch up with some of her old school friends she hadn't seen for quite some time. They had a drink at the local pub. Her old friends all informed each other about their exciting news, whether it was getting a promotion at work, starting a new relationship, or getting their dream job at a game-studio. Kat kept her details to a minimum, and said that she had met someone, but it was at its early stages and that he was in a band. "He's a little bit older and very sweet," was all she could say. She wanted to see how things went after the tour, and whether she would make it out alive, and whether Will would become human before making it a more serious conversation.

Christmas was a quiet one with her parents. They had their Christmas meal and watched some Christmas movies. Kat helped her father set up his new tablet and had spent an hour teaching him how to use it. It required a lot of patience for Kat to explain it all to him. It was scary for Kat to think that it may be the last time that she would see her parents and old friends since she was going on a suicidal vampire hunting mission. Kat hid her tears trying not to think about it.

A week later, Kat gave her parents a huge goodbye hug before getting on the train. She didn't want to let go of them since this could be her last hug, ever.

"I'll message you when I get back," she told her mother. "Look after each other, okay?"

"Oh, Kathryn," her mother sighed. "Please come and see us again soon."

"I promise," she whispered, biting her lips to try not to cry. She withdrew the embrace and got on her train, waving goodbye at the window as her parents walked away. The tears began to fall from her eyes and splashed onto her new winter coat. She tried to distract herself with music which didn't work as all of the songs made her even more emotional.

When Kat arrived back in Southampton, it was about six o'clock in the evening. A familiar figure was seen through the window of the train as it came to a halt. Kat saw that Will was waiting for her at the station as they had planned, looking uncomfortable but trying his best to blend in. The excitement eliminated her sadness. Her new sense of comfort was moments away from her. She even went as far as running towards him and launching herself at him with a hug, which he immediately went for, the usual cliché that was seen in movies. He squeezed her so tight that the pressure would inevitably leave bruises on Kat's body. He held her for a moment until they leaned back to kiss each other passionately.

"Happy New Decade," Kat giggled.

"Hopefully, I can start the decade as a human," Will chuckled back, "Are you ready for the adventure of a lifetime?" he teased her.

"I'm still really nervous about it, and what if we fail? What about my parents?" Kat informed him as she and Will made their way out of the station hand in hand.

"I understand, but we have that under control. We can do this," Will assured her.

Will had brought the band's tour van with him to take them back to Kat's place. Their first gig was three days away and Kat wanted to make sure that she had everything packed and ready as well as getting her clothes washed and dried. Will and Kat had both planned to spend the night at her flat. She dreaded thinking how cold it was going to be after the heating had been turned off for a week. As soon as she opened the flat door a wave of cold air spilled out like the opening of a fridge door. Will knew Kat's preference and sped through to turn the heating control on to full blast. Kat made herself a cup of tea whilst waiting for the heating to warm up the flat. He smiled as soon as he saw her approaching with her cup of tea and they snuggled down into the sofa blankets.

She showed off her new winter coat to Will. It draped halfway down her calves with black felt being the main material, and fuzzy black material around the wrists, the bottom stem of the coat and around the hood.

"It looks good!" Will told her. "It suits you!"

Kat smiled, leaning her head on his shoulder.

"I've missed you," said Kat. His arm wrapped around her, pulling her closer

"I missed you too," he whispered. Will and Kat stayed silent for a moment as the heating began to warm up the flat. Kat sipped her tea to warm up her insides. Ten minutes later, the flat had warmed up enough for Kat to relax and take her coat off.

"I bought you a Christmas present," Will whispered suddenly in her ear.

Kat sat up with a mixture of confusion and excitement.

"You did?" she seemed surprised.

"I figured you may need it for the journey." He handed her a small black box with a black ribbon wrapped around.

"You didn't have to," she smiled.

"I wanted to," Will chuckled. "Besides, when you see what it is, it'll make sense."

Kat became highly curious. She took the box from him and opened it up. When she lifted the lid open, her look of surprise was replaced with confusion.

"I'm not going to wear this often you know?"

"I don't expect you to wear it around me. Only use it when you face other vampires, which I guarantee you will come across on this journey besides Claudette." Kat nodded, looking at the present inside the box. It was a necklace, silver, with a cross pendant, which shone in the reflected light of the room.

"How did you obtain this without freaking out, or whatever vampires do when they see one of these?" Kat closed the box, surprised that Will wasn't agitated or anxious about it.

"I ordered it online, knowing exactly what it was as soon as it arrived," Will winked.

"I really want to wear it."

"You can. But you'll just have to wear a turtleneck or a scarf, something to cover it up, and make sure it's not on show near myself or the others." Will thought about what would happen if the band saw the cross. The image of Laura screaming and hissing in terror made him chuckle. Kat closed the lid and placed it on the coffee table.

"Thank you," she hugged him in gratitude. Will embraced her, placing his head on her shoulder. He could hear the pulse of her blood through her jugular, causing his mouth to drench with hunger. His fangs begun to sharpen, making him to react in fear. He had drunk some blood beforehand, but this seemed amiss all of a sudden, to be this close to her. This wasn't the sort of excitement he wanted right now.

"Bear with me," he pulled away and got up from the sofa, making his way into the bathroom. Kat watched him walk away, befuddled by his reaction. Will locked himself in the bathroom and immediately dropped onto the floor in frustration. He dug his head in between his legs and wrapped his arms around his knees. A sigh escaped his mouth.

"What the fuck was that?" he whispered to himself. *"I*

need to get my thirst under control during this tour. I thought I had it under control. Is this because she was gone for too long, and I now have to get used to her scent again?" Will began debating with himself as to why this was happening.

"Will?" A knock on the door caused Will to lift his head. "Are you alright?" Her sweet voice made him relax. Oh, how he missed her elegant voice.

"Get it together, Crowell," Will thought to himself. He quickly took his flask of blood from his coat pocket and took a few sips of the contents. This motivated him to get up from the floor and open the door. A worried-looking Kat stood in the doorway.

"I'm sorry," he said to her in a tone withered with guilt. "I needed a quick drink."

Kat raised her eyebrow, realising what he had meant by that statement.

"Were you thirsty?" Kat queried worryingly.

"I should head back to the flat." The comment made Kat flinch. She didn't want to seem desperate for him to stay, but at the same time, she needed to be honest with him.

"What? Why?" She questioned him. "You just got here. We agreed you would be staying here tonight. Don't let one small mishap cause you to want to leave." Will walked out of the bathroom and made his way towards the front door of the flat. Kat followed him, chasing him to try and grab his hand and pull him away.

"Please," she begged. "I don't want you to go. Really. It's okay."

"I- "Will hesitated. "I was awfully close to doing the unthinkable. And I think it's because I haven't seen you in a while, and I have forgotten how elegant your scent was. Being that close to your neck made me want to dig my fangs into you and drain your blood. Now, I'm anxious that the others may want to do the same to you whilst on tour."

Kat understood where he was coming from and why he was so worried, but she had to convince him that it wasn't going to end that way.

"Will. It'll be alright. Wearing that cross is probably

going to prevent them from doing that. And I do trust you, and the others." Her hand rested on his cheekbone; her sky-blue eyes leered into his bloodied red eyes. She leaned in to give him a reassuring kiss. It made Will want to hold her tightly and lean in more. He allowed her to take control.

Kat leaned back and yawned unexpectedly.

"You should get some sleep," Will recommended.

"I don't want to, I want to spend more time with you," Kat argued. "Please stay until I fall asleep?"

Will rolled his eyes and smiled. "Fine."

Kat kissed him on his cheek before she made her way back into the living room, dragging Will behind her. They chose their movie, but Kat started falling asleep as soon as the titles were over. She kept fighting the tiredness, but lost the battle as her eyelids gave in. Will put her into bed before leaving to make his way back to the flat.

Laura had managed to book the band at a venue in each city they had listed. Their first gig was going to be in London in three days at the Kasbah punk venue. She able to use her vampire persuasion on a couple of people over the phone to hand them a convenient time slot. She was sat on the sofa writing down the itinerary for their journey across the country, making sure that they had time to prepare for the big fight, and that Kat would be ready.

"Once I'm human again, I will need to forgive myself for the crimes I have committed as a vampire," she said as she bounced the pen up and down with her fingers. "The guilt can get too much for me."

"It'll be a fresh start for all of us when we turn human again," Oliver assured her, twirling and playing with his drumsticks whilst walking around the living room. "We can forget our vampiric pasts and live our new lives the way we wanted to. Fresh new human memories. A second life."

Will had walked into the living room, making Laura and Oliver stop what they were doing. Both were surprised with Will's sudden and unexpected return.

"I thought you were staying at Kat's tonight?" Laura seemed concerned.

"I need to talk to you all," he informed her. "Now."

"David!" Oliver cried. A millisecond later, David was in the living room with the others, sitting next to Laura.

"What has Will done now?" David asked in a condescending tone.

"Something happened earlier," Will ignored him and started telling them, his tone showing guilt. "I came close to biting Kat's neck when I leaned in for a hug and . . . I'm worried you'll all try to do the same to her if you get close." None of the other band members said a word to each other for a brief moment. Laura sighed, understanding what Will was worried about. David, being his usual childish self, started acting funny about it.

"Told you! Maybe that's a sign you should turn her into a vampire?" he shrugged.

"I get why you're anxious all of a sudden," Oliver assured him. "But we've got our thirst under control. We have plenty of blood to take with us for the trip, and we can always get more if need be. We've been doing this for years, Will. What difference does one person make compared to the hundreds of people we've come across over the years?"

"Simple," David added, "this one is physical with one of us! Our own ACTUAL groupie!" He laughed at his own joke, but nobody was laughing along with him. Will growled under his breath, grinding his teeth in anger. He hated how David saw Kat as a disposable human thing for him to play with. Laura and Oliver had been respectful towards her, and treating her fairly, helping Will with his emotions towards her, despite how they felt about the situation. But David had been snarky and cynical-as always- about her.

"We promise you that no worst-case scenarios are going to happen during the tour," Oliver promised. "I do have a question though. What are we going to do once we confront Mistress Claudette?" Will knew they were going to ask about that, but thankfully he knew how to respond.

"Kat has it under control," he informed them. "She'll be getting some items along the way that she can use as weapons against vampires. She knows what she's doing."

"And are you positive that she won't use any of these against us?" David questioned, still not willing to trust Kat.

"With all my existence, I am positive she won't use them against any of us," Will replied.

Kat got up the following morning rather early due to her having a restful sleep. She spent the day packing up for the journey and had shopped for essentials such as toiletries. She threw away any food that was due to go out of date while she was away and ate the rest of it for dinner. Thankfully, she hadn't bought any milk since she had returned from Essex.
That evening, Will came over to see Kat to make sure she was ready for the tour. She admitted to feeling nervous, but in a good way.

"Make sure you bring plenty of warm clothing," Will warned her. "It's going to be VERY cold!"

"Lucky for you, I have come prepared!" Kat rolled out her black suitcase, placed it onto the floor and unzipped the case, exposing the contents inside. Will could see that she had indeed come prepared. Plenty of jumpers and shirts, jeans, along with underwear and toiletries.

"You definitely seem ready for this trip," he smiled. "But are you sure this is going to keep you warm when we arrive at Ben Nevis?"

"Probably?" Kat shrugged, unsure of herself.

"I'll take you shopping for some hiking gear soon. You're going to need it for the final day. I can't have you fighting vampires when you're freezing cold!"

Kat did not go hiking much and didn't think it was necessary to purchase expensive hiking clothes when she had her usual sorts to keep her warm and dry. But she hadn't hiked in snow before, let alone on mountains covered in snow, so this meant it was now a necessity for her to purchase the appropriate attire. Oh, how she had wished it was September instead of January.

"We will be staying in hotels each night, I promise."

"I was hoping that was the case, because I cannot sleep in a moving vehicle!" Kat informed him as she zipped up her suitcase. "Will you be with me in the hotel?"

"Why wouldn't I be?" Will wrapped his arm around her shoulder.

"Because you don't need to sleep? I don't want you to get bored or anything," Kat shrugged.

"Kat, come on, we're vampires, we don't get bored," Will pulled her closer to him and as he chuckled.

"Do vampires need permission to enter a venue or a hotel?" Kat suddenly thought and blurted out loud.

Will laughed lightly. "No? Because they're not homes to anyone? They're public buildings?"

Kat nodded, looking up to see Will smiling down at her. He leaned in to give her a kiss on the lips, which made her lean upwards to get closer to him. Once Kat had fallen asleep, Will made his way back to the flat and packed his clothes for the journey. The others were pretty much ready. Their equipment and instruments in the front room in their cases, and next to the boxes of T-shirts and CDs.

The next afternoon at five o'clock – where the night had arrived - the band packed the van, made one last check of the flat and their blood stocks, and headed over to pick up Kat. Oliver was driving as usual. David and Laura sat in the back as they waited for Will to finish faffing around with the inventory.

"Hurry up, Crowell! You can count it again later!" shouted David.

"Right," Will said to Oliver. "Let's go pick up Kat and be on our way!"

The streets of Southampton were busy with the afternoon rush hour traffic as they drove to Kat's place, thirteen minutes away. Oliver saw her standing in front of her flats waiting in the cold evening. Kat wore her black, hooded winter coat and held onto the handle of her black suitcase. Oliver parked next to Kat as Will quickly opened the door to greet her.

"Hey, you!" he swung her with a hug. "Are you ready?"

"Totally," Kat kissed him passionately. He put her down and rolled her suitcase to the back of the van. Kat got in the passenger seat, greeting the other band members as they waited for Will.

"I LOVE your outfit," Laura leaned forward from her seat to complimented Kat with sincerity.

"Thank you!" Kat turned and smiled. She was pleased that Laura was beginning to accept her. Will swung in next to her as soon as she said that, causing her to flinch as he pulled the door shut.

"Right!" cried Oliver. "London, here we come!"

Oliver drove away and off they went, the start of their tour, the journey to human life.

A couple of hours later and they reached Richmond, with the traffic slowing down. Forty boring minutes of traffic later and they had finally arrived in Soho where they pulled up in front of the hotel. Kat stared out the window with fascination written on her face. The bright lights coming from the beautiful old buildings and the refurbished ones. The London taxis that were parked outside pubs and boutique shops, the people walking through the city streets wearing fashionable looking clothes. She had always seen London through media, but in real life it was so much more.

Will took Kat out of the van and went to collect their suitcases. He carried a suspiciously large amount of luggage. It was icy cold, and condensation came out from Kat's mouth whenever she breathed, while Will had nothing coming out of his.

"I'll meet up with you in an hour," Will informed the others. "I'm going to check Kat into the hotel to freshen up. We'll see you guys soon."

"She can take care of herself, you know?" David responded sarcastically.

"We'll see you in an hour then!" Oliver ignored David and quickly drove off to find the car park. Will softly grabbed Kat's hand and took her into the posh-looking building.

Will had checked Kat into a five-star hotel, which made her feel like royalty. It was one of the fanciest hotels in Soho. The reception area was like something out of a movie with its steel and glass décor and large staircases. The art that was displayed on the walls looked incredibly expensive, and

Kat and Will went to stare at it despite it mostly being squiggles.

"Are you going to be checking me into fancy hotels in every city we go to?" Kat asked with curiosity as her eyes took in the beauty. Will handed the receptionist cash in hand to pay for the rooms.

"Of course, I am," Will looked at her with a crooked smile. "You deserve to have a wonderful night's sleep. Plus, I bet you haven't stayed in a five-star hotel before?"

"You guessed right," Kat shrugged and giggled. Will took the key to the hotel room and one of the members of staff grabbed Kat's suitcase, which took Kat by surprise. She hadn't had this sort of luxury before. Will thanked the receptionist as they left and followed the staff member, walking up the large ballroom-esque staircase. Their hotel room was on the top floor of the building, so they had to take the elevator up to the fifth floor. They were directed to their hotel room where they opened the door, Kat's jaw dropped as far as she could let it and her eyes sparkled at the scenery. Will tipped the staff member with whatever cash he had pulled out from his jeans pocket before turning to see Kat's reaction.

Their room was much bigger than Kat had expected, bigger than her flat. The bed was king-size, a size Kat had never imagined herself sleeping in, which had black poles on each corner of the bed and thin see-through curtains wrapped around it, making it seem fit for royalty. The window at the end of the room was large enough for them to see the amazing landscapes of Soho and tall enough to see a lot of London's landmarks. Their room had a large bathroom with a tub in the centre that was big enough for two. Kat giggled with delight as she placed her suitcase onto the bed and unzipped it open to unpack her things, still blown away with how huge their bed was.

"Hey Kat?" Will was standing behind her, placing his hands on her shoulders, causing her to turn around. She could see that he had something going on in his head since he had 'that look' that she had managed to decode over the months they had been dating. She waited for him to begin telling her what it was. "I want to say how thankful I am that you're here. We wouldn't be doing this if it wasn't for you. I almost gave up on the idea of becoming human again, until I met you. I'll probably be less agitated and anxious when I become human again, but I'm also worried that I won't be the same person you fell in love with."

Kat shook her head, disagreeing with his self-comment.

"I fell in love with someone who is kind, supportive, understanding, and is such a gentleman," Kat assured him. "I am positive that has nothing to do with you being a vampire. If you were a werewolf or a demon, it wouldn't have made a difference to me. I love Will Crowell, no matter who or what he is." Kat grabbed his hand and pulled it closer to her, pressing it against her thumping chest.

Will gave her a small smile; the sense of relief escaped him.

"Thank you," he whispered. "I needed to hear that."

Kat stood on her tiptoes to tightly embrace Will. His arms wrapped around her to pull her close as close as possible for a moment. The world had stood still when their bodies entwined.

"I'm going to have a bath before bed," Kat informed him. "Care to join me?"

"I want to check in on the others and see how they are feeling. I'll come by and see you off to bed. Enjoy your fancy bath."

Kat giggled as she kissed Will goodbye. She skipped to the bathroom and ran her bath just as Will had left the hotel room.

Will went to check how the band were getting on in their hotel rooms. Laura was having a nice hot bath herself-even though she wouldn't be able to feel the temperature of the water, she still wanted to clean up. Oliver and David were playing a game of chess on the glass table across the room - which was something they enjoyed doing occasionally, plus it often made David feel smart being able to know a complex game.

"Checkmate," Oliver smirked.

David leaned back and groaned. "Am I ever going to win?"

"Just keep practicing. Maybe do some research on the openings and strategies," Oliver encouraged him.

"But it requires studying!" David turned and saw Will approaching them.

"Kat's currently having a bath, so I figured I would come on over and see how you are all getting on," Will informed them.

"I'm surprised you're not in the bath with her." David commented, leaving his chair to make his way over to the bed.

"I'm giving her some privacy," Will told him, grudgingly. "I'm not one to shadow over her twenty-four-seven."

"We'll see about that," David muttered under his breath, lying on the edge of the bed to watch the chess match.

Will ignored him and decided to play a match with Oliver. Oliver was Will's biggest challenger out of the rest of the band.

Roughly twenty minutes later and Will managed to checkmate Oliver with his queen.

"Nicely done!" Oliver smiled and shook Will's hand, accepting his defeat.

"Right! David? Want a match?" Will offered, smiling with pride from his victory.

David launched himself off the bed and immediately replaced Oliver's position.

Ten minutes later and Will became victorious.

"You only won because you're older than us, so you've got more experience!" David moaned defeatedly.

"Sure, that's how it works, David," Oliver smiled, patting him on the shoulder in a patronising manner.

Will stuck around for about an hour before deciding to head back to his and Kat's room. When he returned to his hotel room, he saw that Kat was lying on the bed in a seductive position wearing a piece of black laced nightwear, one that showed off her thighs. Her left leg laid flat on the silk bedsheets with her right leg bent upwards and crossed over her left.

Will stared at her, examining her outfit, feeling rather confused to what she had planned. It was obvious, but he had told her beforehand how he didn't want what she was implying.

"That was a quick bath!" Will noticed. "I was gone for like an hour."

"You coming to bed?" Kat asked him, salaciously. "I could do with a bedtime story." She kicked her legs slowly up and down. Will just stood there, unsure with what to say or do in a flirtatious manner.

"I...er...," Will smiled and sighed. *"What was put in the bath to make her this seductive?"* "I'm not sure if we should do this right now."

"Wiiiiilllll," Kat playfully groaned. "We are in a five-star hotel that I'm fairly sure only the richest of folks go to on holiday. This room looks like it belongs to the royal family, and what better way to use it than to do what most couples do in the bedroom?"

Will's eyebrows lifted. "Sleep?"

Kat giggled. "No, silly! The OTHER activity!" Kat sat up and dangled her legs on the edge of the bed, then gestured Will to come to her with her index finger.

"Miss Rhodes, are you trying to seduce me?" Will chuckled, knowing full well that she was indeed.

"Isn't it obvious, Mr Crowell? Now, come here so I can give you pleasure for the first time in eighty-eight years." Will was surprised to find himself not feeling as libidinous as he wanted, but he had his reasons as to why he was stalling.

"It's blatantly obvious that you are, but I'm not sure if I should fornicate with you, especially in the physical state that I am in. I did specify to you that I wasn't going to have sex as a vampire."

"Aren't vampires supposed to be seductive?" Kat seemed confused. She thought about all of the media that painted vampires as seductive creatures of the night, forcing humans to get physical with them before biting them for food, or to gain an eternal partner.

"Not all of us are. I want to be close to you, I really do, but not when I am like this. I don't want to risk hurting you."

Will whispered. Kat jumped off the bed and slowly walked closer to him. She looked at his face, which was structured in a way that showed he was worried, which made her worry also.

Kat pursed her lips. "I understand where you are coming from, Will, but I highly doubt you can physically harm me. What's the worst you could possibly do? You did say vampires could have sex but not reproduce? So, it's not pregnancy you're worried about. I do have condoms in my toiletry bag if you're that cautious."

"No, no; it's not that," Will shook his head and raised his hands. "It's more like. . . I'm worried about going too far in terms of my physical abilities. Your body is so fragile; it would be like throwing a boulder onto a flower- I could break you so easily if I'm physically close."

"Not unless I take control and you remain submissive." Kat insisted. "That way, I receive the gratification without you doing any physical harm. I'll just ride on top, and you can keep your hands still. I'll just be the dominant one."

Will hesitantly shook his head. "I'm sorry, Kat," he whispered, disappointed with himself about letting his girlfriend down.

"It's okay, really," Kat sighed, then proceeded to look at him with a reassuring smile. "We could try when you turn human?" Will nodded slowly, looking at the floor. Kat wrapped her hand around his, comforting him, assuring him that she was fine with keeping things to a minimum in their relationship.

Chapter 12:
♥
London

Kat had what she could only describe as the best sleep ever; the large bed was part of that reason, as well as being able to sleep next to her vampire boyfriend. Will had woken her up by gently stroking the side of her face. The coldness of his hand made her shiver and wake up quickly.

"Morning, creep," she teasingly whispered. "Are you watching me sleep?"

"No?" Will chuckled. "I'm trying to wake you up as we're going on a city adventure today."

"Oh?" Kat's eye widened, surprised to hear the possibility of a city outing with her vampire friends.

"The sun isn't out today," he informed her. "It's drizzling." Kat rolled over and stretched out her body, revealing her luxurious nightwear.

"Can we get breakfast first?" she yawned whilst stretching her arms as far out as she could humanly do so.

"Get dressed while I order you some room service." Will kissed the top of her forehead before she got up. He watched Kat collect her clothes and walk into the bathroom to freshen up.

When she got out of the bathroom, she waited ten more minutes before a knock on the door had Will march over to answer. A large platter was presented to him on a trolley, surrounded by an empty white cup, a metal teapot, and a variety of cutlery. Looking at it made Kat's stomach rumble. She was presented with a full English breakfast, the biggest breakfast she had ever eaten. Whilst eating, Will walked into the bathroom to drink some blood. He finished his flask, screwed the plastic cap back on top and washed out the blood from his mouth. Kat had finished and was dressed, ready to go out wearing her best jeans, a jumper, and her black winter coat. Will grabbed his coat by the door and beckoned Kat over to him. She leaned in to kiss and get as close to him as possible; she could feel his tongue slithering into her mouth and wrap around hers. He leaned back and smiled as the pair left the hotel room, seeing the band waiting in the corridor for them. Laura and Oliver gave the pair a welcoming smile while David showed no enthusiasm.

"You took your time," David commented with judgement. "What were you up to in there?"

"Something you've haven't been able to do, I'm guessing, for a long time?" Kat confidently teased him, which caused Laura and Oliver to burst out laughing.

"Ouch," Will muttered, his eyes widened by Kat's sudden confidence in teasing a vampire, a dangerous manoeuvre.

"Ha, ha," David rolled his eyes. "That's for me to know and you to kindly fuck off."

Outside the hotel, it was no longer drizzling; instead, the rain had started to pick up, so Kat pulled up her hood to cover her red-dyed hair. The others didn't seem bothered with getting themselves wet from the rain. The five of them made their way down the street into the underground subway and took a tube to Waterloo. The crowded trains made Kat uncomfortable and anxious from the quantity of people inside a tight space. The layers of clothing added more discomfort for her. Will noticed Kat panting slightly and placed his hand on her forehead to keep her cool.

"Thanks," she muttered to him.

"I've always hated the underground," said Laura, scanning around the tram to people watch. She could see that most of them on the train were either on their phones or reading a book. It always was the case for London transportation. A crowded underground train was quite possibly the worst place for a bloodthirsty vampire to be with the number of sweaty humans on board, but thankfully, the band were already full of their blood-filled breakfast at the hotel. Even the crowded corridors of the underground made Kat hesitant and confused; she was thankful to have her vampire crew to keep her safe from any potential harm or separation. Laura helped the band navigate their way through the underground to get to the exit-which Kat was itching to find.

They walked up the stairs to the exit, and they headed to the London Eye. Kat was astonished as it seemed much larger that she had seen on TV and in films. It was a relatively quiet weekend, and they didn't queue long before entering one of the thirty-two capsules with large windows and waited for the wheel to turn. Will had his arms wrapped around Kat as she stood by the far end of the capsule to see as much as London as she possibly could. She had taken many photos with her small digital camera, which made her wonder if vampires could appear on photographs. After snapping a quick photo of her and Will, her camera showed the image of them together, answering her curiosity.

After they had all left the capsule, they walked over across the bridge to get inside the London Dungeon attraction. The grittiness of London's history had her behave erratically like a child on Christmas eve. Laura had never been inside and was curious to see what it had to offer, and it had more to offer than any of them had expected!

"That was AMAZING!" she cried, hopping around the group.

"It really was!" Laura laughed. "It made it even better hearing Oliver screaming!"

David and Will chuckled and took a glance at Oliver, who was looking less than his usual calm self.

"Can we please get going?" Oliver demanded. "I'm not doing that again."

"Alright, don't have to be so whiny about it," said David, still chuckling away.

"We'd best get back to get ready for the soundcheck," said Oliver.

"It's okay to admit you were scared!" David continued teasing him.

When the band returned to their hotel, after a fun filled day, Will ordered Kat a fancy meal from room service, the best lasagne she'd ever had, along with a glass of expensive wine. The pair got themselves dressed up and ready for the show. Kat wanted to go out in style and wore a laced skirt with black laced tights, with her high black boots with skull and roses printed on. Underneath the black coat she got for Christmas, was a black tank top that had laced lining and a black bow on the chest. Her hands were wrapped with more lace as her fingerless gloves matched the outfit perfectly. Her eyeshadow make-up had the tonality of red and pink, her lipstick dark red, the colour of blood, which she found to be ironic.

Will wore a black button shirt, black skinny jeans, and his black and white Vans trainers again. His makeup was identical to the night at the Golden Barrel; purple and pink eye shadow, black lipstick, along with pure pale foundation to whiten his face further. Kat was astonished at how he flawlessly put makeup on without the use of a reflection for guidance.

"Years and years of practice," Will chuckled. "And the help of my bandmates."

"Let me take a photo," Kat wondered. "I don't quite understand how you come up in photos but not in the reflection of mirrors."

Will almost broke down with laughter as he drew his eyeliner on. "Try not to get one of my non-existing reflections!"

She smiled vividly. "Perfect." She turned her phone around to show Will his painted face.

Will shook his head and smiled. Once he had finished getting ready, Will gulped down some blood from his flask, and placed it back inside his jacket pocket. They left the hotel room made their way down to the reception area and left the building, hand in hand. The visitors and staff of the hotel all took a gander at the odd-looking couple like they were famous.

"Are we walking?" Kat asked Will.

"I can't risk getting into a taxi without the driver looking in the rear-view mirror and not seeing me. They would think they were mad!" Will laughed. "I promise it's not too far; the venue is only a fifteen-minute walk."

"Or a fifteen-second run," Kat jokingly whispered into Will's ear, making him chuckle some more. It was dark already and the magnificent lights of Soho made Kat's head spin round in wonder, as she took in the aesthetic of it all. The busy streets of London awed her as it was exactly how she had expected it and more making Southampton look like a small village to her. She took some quick photos whilst they walked through the busy streets. Kat quickly grabbed herself a cup of coffee and a muffin to go from a café to give herself some extra energy for the gig. On their way to the venue, Will informed Kat that there were going to be three bands performing tonight, and that Midnight Devotion were going to be second on stage, "That was Laura's doing," giving her a conspiratorial wink. Kat remembered that Laura also wanted to show her the place she became a vampire. David and Oliver had planned to go to some clubs after the show, to celebrate their first gig of the tour. Time would be tight as they were in Cardiff the following day.

Will spotted the band's van outside the Kasbah. David "helped" Laura with the equipment. Of course, she wouldn't need help due to her super strength, but to avoid suspicion they had to play along with the 'struggle'.

"Hey!" Laura smiled as she noticed them walking towards them. "We just need to set up the guitar pedals and connect to the amps, and we're ready to go!"

"Brilliant! Our first gig in London!" Will cried with excitement. Kat had never seen Will this excited about something; it made her smile; so happy to see him that happy. He didn't let go of Kat's hand as they watched them carry the packed instruments and equipment from the van.

"Where's Oliver?" Kat asked them as she noticed his absence.

"He's inside sorting out the drum set," David pointed

to the venue without looking at them as he picked up the amplifier. "You should get yourself inside and sort out the merchandise stand."

Will nodded and took himself and Kat inside the venue. Inside, the walls were plastered with old posters of band tours and album covers. The aesthetics of the venue gave off punk vibes with layers of peeling posters and cheap red lighting. They walked down the stairs and into the main room. The room they were going to be performing in had no windows, which was perfect for them. The room itself was much bigger than the Golden Barrel: more spacious and much darker. At the end of the room was the performance stage and PA. Stage lighting and strobe effects were also available for their gig.

Oliver was on the stage preparing his drum kit, with the help of one of the venue workers. David was chatting to the bar's PA and lighting engineer about what the lighting options were. The venue was already half full of people of various groups; punks, goths, teens and young adults, couples, middle aged people, all of them there to see some obscure punk bands play. The headline band had done their check and the first support were running a little late. Midnight Devotion tuned up, checked a few levels, got the thumbs up from the engineer, and were shown to a back room.

Kat went out to the front to get the merchandise sorted. She looked hard at the audience thinking about vampires and the people who were at the venue. There were three table stands that had merchandise for each band performing tonight. One of them was for a band called *Sister Punk*, the other was called *My Grievances*. Midnight Devotion were in the middle table, with Laura was setting up the merchandise they had available: T-shirts of all sizes and their debut EP. Kat was going to be sitting there to sell their merchandise as well as promote the band. Will came over with a glass of lemonade for Kat and the pair compared their offer with the other bands.

"The prices of the items are on the table," Will informed her. "Should we try and be cheaper than the others?"

"Go and get ready! I can handle this! I work at a pub,

for crying out loud!"

Will laughed. He and Kat exchanged a quick kiss before Laura came over and dragged him away. Kat sat down at the table, waiting for anyone to come over and purchase their merch. She felt a sense of tension from the uncertainty of doing a good enough job selling the band's merch, as it was important for them to get their name out there. She figured that there may be some sales after their performance, so she took her camera out and started making little film clips of the people in the club. Kat saw Will and Laura disappear back into the band area to get themselves ready for the gig.

The first band, Sister Punk, were ready for their performance. Their music was very retro and simple, but with a hint of 90's indie thrown in. Kat caught herself bobbling along with the music, watching the performance from the merch table. The crowd were bouncing up and down like a group of baby birds wanting to be fed by their mother. The heavy punk music influenced their dancing, and their need to unleash their inner monster. A couple of people suddenly approached Kat, taking her by surprise. Two teenage boys dressed in skinny clothing and had long, dark hair, curious about the merch. They looked at the album cover and read the song list behind it.

"I like the album art," he told his mate. "It's quite emo."

"I'm tempted to get a T-shirt," his mate responded.

"I'm going to get both!" He looked at Kat and pointed to the T-shirt on the table. "Small, please! And this!" He waved the album. Kat picked up the T-shirt and checked the price list. The CD was ten pounds, and the T-shirt was fifteen pounds. His mate asked for the T-shirt in a medium and offered fifteen pounds in coins.

"Thank you!" Kat cried as they both politely nodded and walked away. She smiled with pride at their first sale.

Forty-five minutes later and Sister Punk had finished, meaning Midnight Devotion were next on stage. She was excited to see her vampire boyfriend and his vampire band perform live on stage. It made her think about the first night she met Will at the pub. The memory of it made her smile.

Ten minutes later, at exactly half-past eight, the background music playing from the speakers died down halfway through a song, and the lights began to dim. The lights on the stage changed colours to purple and blue, to match the theme of the band. David had asked for something static and simple. Each member of Midnight Devotion walked onto the stage; Oliver first, then Laura, then David.

Will came over to give Kat a quick kiss of good luck.

"Get on stage, you daft sod!" Kat cried. Will winked at her as he made his way through the crowd. The band were giving him a slow clap waiting for him to get on stage and the crowd took this as a cue and joined in.

As soon as he had reached the microphone, he screamed "Good evening, London!". His voice echoed through the speakers.

The crowd cheered, rushing over towards the front of the stage to get as close as physically possible.

"We are Midnight Devotion!"

Oliver tapped his drumsticks together four times, before David started his guitar intro for four beats, and Oliver began banging his drumkit, then Laura started slapping her bass guitar. The stage lights began dimming in time to the beat of Oliver's drumming. Kat couldn't help but smile; she felt like a mother watching her children performing on stage as she held her camera to record their performance.

Will began singing, and the band cut to a well-rehearsed solo. The lights turned purple whilst Will sang the first four lines. It was a song they hadn't played at Southampton; it was a new song about the first night he met Kat which made her heart skip a beat from the unexpected lyrics:

> *On a cold and dark October night*
> *Was the first night that I saw you*
> *My heart began to fix itself*
> *Every time I heard your heartbeat.*

The drumming and bass came back into the song,

creating a punk rock sound, which got the crowd going again. The stage lights began flickering multiple colours. There were now more people in the crowd as the excitement built and stragglers from tables moved to join the crush.

What is happening? What is this now?
Are you the one that God had sent me?
Maybe this is the feeling
Of my devotion at midnight

The song must have been about his interaction with Kat.

You are my Midnight Devotion
The one who's going to change me
The darkness will fade
The light will enrage
I will be human once again.

Will took a quick look at Kat in the distance, whilst the others were playing, his vampiric vision helped him see through the lights and Kat clearly, she blushed deeply.

When the night comes, I am awake
I walk around the city streets
Nothing in the day makes me happy
As I only live in darkness.
You are the moonlight in the dark
You are the brightest star in the sky
You are the chisel that carves my stone heart

Was Will trying to make it obvious to the crowd that he was singing about being a vampire? Or was he just being this way for the fun of it? Because to Kat, it seemed as though he was being massively self-aware and meta about it. Were the band okay with these lyrics? They seemed to be since it was the first song they were playing. She still smiled at the alluring vampire singer who sang his motionless heart out. The chorus kicked back in; the crowd went wilder than before. Midnight

Devotion was starting to get some attention.

> *Into my arms, you are fearless*
> *Into your arms, I am lighter*
> *Together we are blood and stone*
> *Together we are life and death.*

David then played a riff solo which made the crowd cheer louder. Will began dancing on stage, bobbing his head up and down at a fast rate. Kat couldn't help but laugh at Will's dancing. She found it to be adorable. David was really killing it with his guitar riff, not dropping a note. As soon as David had finished, Will sung the chorus one last time before the instruments began to slow down and die off. The crowd roared and applauded the band's performance, astounded by what they had witnessed.

"Thank you!" Will called out.

The amplifier reverbed from David's guitar, creating a rock and roll ambience in the room. David leaned into the feedback and gave it rhythm. Oliver banged his drumsticks again to David's guitar, ready for the next song. By beat number four, all three instruments began playing simultaneously. This song was much heavier than the last which made the crowd go even wilder. The crowd began bouncing around, and even moshing to the heavy punk rock that Midnight Devotion were offering them.

Between songs Kat managed sell more CDs and T-shirts, hearing people compliment the band on how their music was more goth than retro punk. She wondered what it would be like if they were able to fulfil their dream of becoming more well-known nationwide, or even worldwide!

Once the song ended, the crowd applauded and were hyped for more.

"How are you all doing tonight?" Will asked everybody, which made them respond with cheering. "We are thankful to be playing here tonight! Thank you all for coming to support us! This is our first time performing in London as well as our first-time touring! You could potentially be making history right now!" That comment made the crowd cheer even wilder. Kat saw David, Laura, and Oliver smiling at each other, hyped up and excited for their biggest show so far.

"Let me quickly introduce you to the band! Firstly, on the drums is the charming Mr Oliver Stokes!" The crowd cheered as Oliver began doing a drum solo. "On bass guitar is the beautiful but feisty, Laura Bates!" Laura began playing a couple of strums on the bass guitar whilst the crowd cheered, some even offered her some flirtatious whistles. "And on guitar is the wonderful and mischievous, David Barrett!" David walked towards the edge of the stage and produced a blast of shredding which made the crowd go wild. He went on for some time before Will introduced himself.

"And finally, your lead singer tonight, yours truly, William Crowell!" Will took a bow as the crowd applauded and cheered.

"We're going to be giving you some more songs before My Grievances play tonight! So, this next song is called *Fractured Dreams!* I want you all to clap along with me and make some noise!"

The audience joined in with Will clapping along to the beginning of the song as Oliver began drumming. As soon as Will stopped, David began playing a riff on his guitar for eight beats before Laura joined in for beat number nine, and Oliver began pressing onto the foot pedal of the bass drum. The audience began to cheer as Will started to dance around the stage as soon as Oliver hit the cymbals of his drumkit for the pre verse. This was the big send off at the end of the set and the crowd cried for more, but there was a schedule they had to stick to.

The lyrics to this song were heavily describing the dreams that the band once had and how they were taken by the harshness of reality and the people who shattered them. They also gave out a message within those lyrics for the listeners to not give in to their negativity and to allow those dreams to remain in your hearts and work hard to achieve the dreams and prove those people wrong.

As soon as the band were done playing, they thanked the audience for their enthusiasm and support, and began packing away their instruments and amplifiers so the final band could prepare. Once they had walked off the stage, they were greeted by some of the audience members before they could reach the merch stand. The crowd were informing them on how amazing they were, and a lot of people had marched over to buy their CDs and t-shirts.

"You're going to be the next best thing for punk music!"

"They sounded like a mixture of *My Chemical Romance* and *AFI!*"

"That guitar solo on the first song was sick!"

Lots of positive comments from the audience were given to them. Sister Punk didn't get as much attention as Midnight Devotion did, so it meant they did something different compared to them. Kat continued to sell the merch whilst the band were busy getting compliments. She wondered if every gig would be like this, if so, they'd need more T-shirts. The band went outside to their van to pack away and were all itching for some blood to drink. They all sat in the back, raised their flasks and yelled simultaneously: "To our first successful gig of the tour!"

Chapter 13:
♥
Closure

As soon as My Grievances had finished their gig and cleared their equipment off the stage, it was time for the band to pack up the merchandise stand and leave the building. They managed to get everything back in the van by eleven o'clock. Kat had both her arms wrapped around Will's left arm and pulled herself closer to him, whilst the others discussed their next plan of action.

"I think we should celebrate our first gig of the tour by going to a club!" David shouted vigorously. "You guys in?"

Oliver nodded. "Absolutely! We have plenty of time before heading to Cardiff. It's only a two-and-a-half-hour journey!"

"Will? Laura?" David looked at them and waited for a response. Will and Laura looked at each other, then back at David.

"I think we're going to pass," Laura responded with a smile. "I want to take Kat to the stadium where I turned into a vampire. It's not far from here."

"How dramatic," David groaned dejectedly with a roll from his eyes. "You need to let that shit go. It was so long ago! Didn't you say Will needed to do the same with Birmingham? Come and have some fun with us!"

Will gazed at Laura with a look of reproachfulness.

"Don't tell me to get over the worst thing that ever happened to me! You cannot let something as traumatic as that go, it stays with you forever! So, keep that attitude in your pocket and stop being a sarcastic prick!"

David stared blankly, unable to respond to her outburst. Will and Oliver looked at each other with faces full of worry.

"You boys go and have fun in the club. And try not to suck on the necks of females that give you attention." Laura turned around and walked aggressively down the street, leaving Will and Kat to walk behind her.

"Is she okay?" Kat whispered to Will.

"Yeah, she's just getting fed up with David and his big gob," Will laughed and pulled her closer. "We're going to find somewhere where we can get up on the roof."

"Why?" Kat looked up at Will in confusion.

"We're going to fly to Tottenham Stadium," Will told her. "Are you going to be okay with that?"

"I've already flown with you once. I trust you enough not to drop me," Kat assured him.

"Hey, Laura?" Will queried from afar. "What did David mean by 'Will needs to get over Birmingham?"

Laura was caught off-guard but didn't contradict him. She was never one to keep secrets or tell lies. "He was unsure about us playing in Birmingham, I just said to him that you needed to get over it because it had been so many years and it has changed drastically since then. We need to tour major cities and Birmingham is one of them. I'm sorry. It makes me sound like a total hypocrite."

Will didn't seem upset with Laura. Instead, he was thankful that he had someone to push him into doing something he had avoided for exceptionally long. It was going to be challenging, but he needed to confront his past at some point to move forward, even if it was going to hurt.

A couple of crossings and turnings later and they found an alleyway that no one would dare to walk through due to the large industrial bins that stank up the place. It was the back way to an independent fast-food restaurant. There were no windows for anyone to see them do inhuman activities. Laura leapt off the ground and reached the roof in a single jump. Kat was mesmerised by how high she could jump. Her body trembled at the idea of leaping that high and at a fast rate.

"Your turn!" Will instantly grabbed Kat and before she could say anything, she was off the ground and ascending towards the sky. She grabbed onto Will, closing her eyes tightly, and felt her stomach press down against her intestines. About a second later she was on the roof with Laura.

"For fuck sake, Will!" she smacked his bicep once he released her. "Don't do things without informing me in advance! I needed to mentally prepare myself!"

"Sorry, I thought you were ready," Will chuckled. Laura giggled under her breath. They all walked over to the ledge of the roof to have a look at the city. Kat was amazed at the skyline view of London. The tall buildings, the city lights, the sounds of people and cars, the smells were so much more than Southampton or her native Essex.

"Let's go for a flight tour, shall we?" Will said to Kat as he held her hand tightly. "You wanted to see London, right?"

"Right," Kat smiled. "I didn't think I would be having a special vampire tour."

Laura took off her leather jacket and tied it around her waist before bending down. She leapt up into the sky, ascending at a speed so fast that no one with human eyes would be able to follow. Kat heard Laura's wing rip out from her back and looked up to see them expanding. Her wings were long, silky, and black, much like a bat's.

"Are you ready to fly?" Will immediately asked Kat's permission this time, which gave her reassurance.

Kat fastened Will's arms around her waist like a seatbelt.

"Let's fly!" Kat cried enthusiastically. Will bent down and launched them up into the sky at the same height as Laura.

Kat was laughing as they ascended into the sky. She felt like she was on a rollercoaster. The chilly air rushed through her body as they flew higher and higher above the city's buildings. When Will was level with Laura, his wings came out and the pair began to glide over the city streets above the clouds. Kat held on tightly to Will's arms, still wrapped around her waist. She could feel the cold air breezing through her face. Down below, the city was still awake with loads of taxis on the move, driving through the lit streets. London was filled with many tall and fancy buildings; some of them were brand new skyscrapers, ones that Kat had never seen in person before, only photographs and videos. She began shivering from the freezing January winter evening; she was surprised that it hadn't snowed in the country yet.

The vampires made sure that there was no one around the stadium before they landed, the surrounding streets were surprisingly empty. They landed on the pavement, right next to a set of stairs, which led to the entrance way of Tottenham Hotspur Stadium. Their wings retracted back into their bodies before Laura began her tour of the events from her past.

"I lived in London all my life before becoming a vampire," Laura began her story." I used to work in the police force, and I haven't been back in this city in nearly sixteen years."

"What year did you turn?" Kat asked her.

"Nineteen ninety-three. I was, or still am, twenty-seven years old," Laura answered. "I was working one night on patrol around the football stadium, since it was common for drunkards and hooligans to lollygag around, when I was suddenly lured away by this bloke who looked like he was playing dress up as a monk. It was there where it happened," Laura pointed to the set of stairs leading up to the stadium. The memory came flooding back to her. "I was lured to the top by a vampire. They walked straight up to me, looked at me dead in the eyes and told me to follow them. My body went into autopilot, and I found myself walking up the stairs without any self-control. The next thing I knew, I felt the sharp pain of their teeth digging into my neck. At first, I thought he was trying to give me a hickey or something, but the sharp pain made it obvious what was going on. I couldn't even scream, as much as I wanted to. He left me there to change into the monster he created." Laura looked down at her pale white hands. "I was slowly turning into one of them and felt my life fading with every heartbeat. My whole life flashed before me. I saw my family, my childhood, my friends and colleagues, my boyfriend Gavin, all of it."

Kat envisioned Laura wearing a police uniform, crying in pain as she slowly had her life taken away. This caused her to hold out her hand, offering her support. Laura gave Kat a smile and accepted her support, not grasping too hard as to break her hand. Kat's winter glove kept the coldness of Laura's skin away.

"It was like I had been stabbed with two thick needles. I felt the venom going inside me, spreading like fire through my veins fire. I collapsed onto the floor, writhing in pain. Nobody was around to help me. I was in so much pain, but I couldn't scream for some strange reason. It was like my body had gone stiff and I had lost all control of myself."

Laura released Kat's hand and began walking up the same steps where it all began. Will and Kat held hands as they watched Laura reliving the memory of her transformation.

"I don't know how long I was in that state for, but once I could finally move again, my senses increased immensely. I could hear more, see more, smell more. I felt stronger but was no longer myself. It was like I went through a metamorphosis, a weevil into am ugly yet powerful moth. As soon as I had stood up, I began craving blood. I saw someone nearby and all I wanted to do was drain them dry and satisfy my thirst. Thankfully, I resisted and ran away, but I'll never forget what he looked like. He wore a red polo shirt and tracksuit bottoms, sports gear, and had a clean-shaven head. He could have been my first victim, but my victims were always criminals, I made sure of it. He may now have a family, and I could have easily changed that timeline. When I realised what I had become, I fled and hid away. It was incredibly difficult as my thirst for blood was insane. I had to hunt criminals at night and feed off them, I had always felt guilty doing it, but had always found ways to cover up my tracks."

Kat let go of Will to walk up of the stairs to comfort Laura. She envisaged what Laura had described like a scene from a movie, or that she had shared that memory through Laura's mind.

"What happened to the vampire that changed you?" Kat asked her.

"He left me to fend for myself. I was on my own until

Will and David found me a week later walking around the streets. They could see that I was a vampire thirsting for blood, and they helped me seek some from a criminal. Claudette's coven came for me about a week later and took me to Scotland to see Mistress Claudette. I stayed there for a while as they wanted to recruit me, but I refused. I was then told I was forbidden from entering London for the rest of my existence, even after the one-hundred-year rule. After I left, me and the boys went to Manchester and made it our home for some time, hiding in abandoned terraces in Rusholme. Illegally squatting, as it were. They gave me the vampire life I never thought possible. I'll always be grateful for this band and what they've done." Laura and Will exchanged smiles, both feeling the same. They had both been through a lot during their transformation, but they were thankful to have found each other.

"Laura Bates?" a wry voice suddenly surprised them. They all turned to see who had called out Laura's full name. Will made sure that Kat was stood right behind him to avoid the vampire from seeing or sensing her. They saw an abnormally tall male wearing a red velvet cloak and Victorian-style clothing, the stereotypical outfit of an old vampire. His hair was pure black and combed back, dropping down to his collarbone. The eyes that stared widely at them were pure red, recently-fed-from-blood kind of red. Both Will and Laura knew who it was just by looking at him, neither of them were not too happy to see him.

"Sven," Laura muttered angrily. "Why are you here?"

Sven slowly approached the trio, giving them a sinister grin. His sharp fangs were exposed with the pasty white smile.

"We thought we told you not to come back to London," he reminded her.

"It's only for one night," she aggressively told him. "We're leaving soon. So, you can tell the Mistress that we're not stopping for long. You can also tell her to stop monitoring our every move!"

Sven couldn't help but laugh at Laura as her anger amused him.

"Funnily enough, she didn't know you were here. I, on

the other hand, was just passing by, when I suddenly heard your voice from a distance. I couldn't believe it was you, especially as you were no longer allowed to be here. Remember?" Sven was beginning to intimidate her.

Laura growled under her breath. She could feel her inner demon sprawling out. She tried her hardest to keep it under control.

"You're lying," she gritted her teeth.

"Am I?"

"You always lie. Why should I trust anything that you say?"

Sven chuckled under his breath.

"You're just so naïve, for an ex-police officer. Mind you, you were just as naïve the night I turned you."

Kat's eyes widened. Will could feel Kat's hand tighten his.

"I don't need you or any vampire arsehole to tell me where I can and can't go," Laura growled. "It's been sixteen years since you robbed me of my life!"

Sven tilted his head with an arched smile painted across his face.

"You were given the ultimatum when you became one of us; join Claudette's coven, or we let you go but you were no longer allowed to come back to London. We wanted you to join our coven because of your dedication to the law, and we figured you would be the perfect candidate as a vampire, tracking down those who broke the vampire law. Of course, you chose to break it instead."

"I clearly made the right decision you piece of shit!" Laura screamed. Sven chortled, which made Laura cringe.

Sven then noticed something peculiar behind Will, who was shielding Kat from view.

"Is that what I think it is?" He smirked as he walked closer towards them. Laura arbitrated and stood between him and Will.

"This is our fight," she retorted. "Leave Will out of this. Will, get out of here."

Will quickly turned whilst holding Kat's hand and they took off with Will making sure that he had the view of Kat completely blocked from Sven's. He gasped in delight when he realised they had a human in their grasp, but Laura had quickly grabbed Sven by the neck and kicked him down the steps.

Laura raced over to finish the job. Whist gliding towards him, her hand had turned into a giant grey claw with razor sharp nails. Sven got up and caught Laura's claw with his own vampire claw. He then twirled his body, still holding onto Laura, and threw her above the stadium. Her body spun into the sky at a speed that no human would be able to see. Sven then broke out his wings and glided through the air to grab Laura, pinning her by the throat, and pushed her into the centre of the football stadium; his cloak fluttered with the speed of the wind as he quickly descended. Laura landed with a hard thump that left a deep impression in the turf as Sven triumphantly stood over her. The lights of the stadium were off, so no camera could pick up the tremendously abnormal activities taking place.

"Not so tough now, are you, dear?" he tormented her, his voice demonic from the transformation he had gone through. His upper body began to grow, muscular, and his face was transforming into something fiendish, "I would suggest you leave London right now, but I think killing you would be the wiser option, given that you have broken many rules. Pretty ironic for someone who used to work in the police force."

By then, Sven had fully turned into a monstrous vampiric beast. His upper body was larger, his legs were longer, his skin darker, and both his hands had become claws. The human-looking features ceased to exist.

Laura was still in her human-like form. She groaned as she got up from the ground and jumped up high enough to land onto the first terrace.

"I wouldn't have broken the rules if you hadn't stolen my life, you tosser!" Laura growled fiercely; her voice echoed through the empty stadium. She began thinking about everything that she had to walk away from to protect the existence of vampires as well as herself. Her mother, her father, her sister, boyfriend, colleagues, friends, everyone that she had loved. Her dreams and her future: destroyed. Thinking further about it made her more furious. She had been thinking about this closure for so long. She knew who had turned her and had always hoped to find them one day and kill them herself without any reinforcements.

The memory of when she was kidnapped and taken to Claudette's hideout crawled back to her. Claudette kept a squad of twenty vampires scattered across the country who would watch any suspicious activities. All newly bitten vampires were taken to Claudette to swear allegiance or be monitored. Laura knew of vampires who had been executed for exposing their existence to humans even if they didn't know the rules.

"You should have joined us, Ms Bates," Sven patronised her.

"Why would I join you and your cult after what you took from me?" Laura screamed furiously. She could feel her body changing from the anger dwelling inside. The transformation was something she experienced only once before; she knew what was happening.

"Yes," Sven begged, his eyes widened, his sinister teeth shining through a patronising grin. "Become the monster you truly are!" Laura wanted to reject the transformation and not give him the satisfaction, but also wanted to be evenly matched in order to destroy him. She welcomed the transformation into the same demonic form as Sven. She screamed at the top of her lungs. Her wings came out from her back, her torso enlarged, her face pointing outwards, her teeth sharpened, and her skin thickened.

Once she finished the transformation, she charged towards Sven and the pair began to clash claws together, causing a loud metallic echo. Each of them tried to get their teeth onto the other's necks; neither of them could succeed due to their equal flexibility. They continued bashing and clashing each other, one flying in the air and the other on the pitch below. Laura leapt up from the ground and flew towards Sven, crashing straight into him at high speed. The sound of their claws clashing echoed through the stadium. Their bodies continued to wrestle in the air. They were like prehistoric pterodactyls fighting over a piece of food.

Sven parried her attacks and grabbed Laura by her

wrists, attempting to dislocate her shoulders. She spun around, using the momentum to land a kick on the back of Sven's head. Sven disappeared beneath her, and Laura panicked thinking he was coming back up for more, but she saw someone pulling him away by his feet. She examined the sudden situation, shocked to see that Will had come back for her. He and Sven crashed across the football pitch. Laura dived back towards the fight at rapid speed. She knew that Will didn't stand a chance against Sven in his human form alone and knew how Mistress Claudette's vampires worked. The two band members fought aggressively with Sven in the centre of the football pitch.

Kat ran over towards the fight, feeling like she should help somehow, but also frightened at a level she was not used to managing. So much adrenaline was flowing through her whilst witnessing an epic fight between three supernatural beings. She stopped and waited for the fight to remain in place before charging towards them. She grabbed something from her bag that she knew would work against Sven: *her silver cross.*

Will and Laura were grappling Sven to the ground and Kat was running as fast as she could across the pitch. She was anxious about hurting Laura and Will, but Will caught her eye and saw her approaching and nodded in understanding.

Both Laura and Will had Sven struggling on the ground, both pinning down his wings and claws. He thrashed his monstrous body around to try and free himself. Kat began to point the silver cross at Sven as she got closer, causing him to go frantic. Laura and Will closed their eyes and looked away from her. Sven began hissing intensely at Kat whilst closing his eyes to avoid contact with the cursed symbol. Before he could do anything, Kat pulled out one of her stakes from her bag to stab him with. The idea of being up close to a monstrous vampire caused her to shudder and hesitate slightly. Her consciousness fought off the anxieties of being close to something so perilous that could potentially rip her apart within a second, even if two friendly vampires were grasping hold of them. Kat stared at the monster, breathing heavily the deeper she looked into the darkened eyes.

"HURRY, KAT!" Will screamed, which encouraged

her to act. She pushed herself out of her comfort zone and went in for the kill. The stake pierced through his tough chest, causing him to scream in agony and his body began twitching. Laura and Will both let go, walking slowly away from him to watch him wither. Kat joined in, letting go of the stake and leaving it inside him. They all watched Sven slowly turn to dust. Black smoke was coming out from his body, was disintegrating into black ash.

"She will end you all..." his voice giving way and fading into the night as he became nothing but ash and smoke.

Kat retched violently at the stench; her first ever vampire kill.

Laura began to turn back into her human form. The excessive muscles shrank, her hair became soft and silky, just like the Laura Bates that they knew and loved. Kat watched her becoming the person she recognised. Once she was back to her old self, Kat ran over to hug and comfort her, offering her coat for modesty. Laura embraced her back and held her lightly. "Thank you," she whispered. "And I'm so sorry."

"Don't be," Kat told her. "I'm just glad you're safe." Laura and Kat both looked at one another and laughed.

"Where did you get a stake from?" Laura questioned her.

"When Will and I left, I begged him to take me back. I've had this in my bag since we started the journey. I had them made back at home before I left to go to my parents for Christmas. I could do with more though, but I'm glad I took one with me tonight! It did freak Will out when I told him." Laura and Kat both looked at Will, who was smiling at the sight of his girlfriend and bandmate getting along.

"I bet it did," she laughed.

They all looked around the football stadium and realised what a mess they had made. The aftermath of the fight was too obvious, and the damage would probably make the local news.

"We ought to get out of here Laura," Will said calmly. "We need to leave London as soon as possible."

In the distance Kat could hear sirens, was that for them or just a normal night in London.

Chapter 14:
Abscond

Will held on tightly to kat as the three flew back to the same rooftop where they launched themselves previously. They leapt back into the alleyway, blending into the crowd, making their way back to the hotel. Will paused outside, telling Kat to quickly pack her things and be ready within the hour.

"Why can't you stay with me?" Kat asked him, concerned about what was going on.

"I need to help Laura find the others. Please, Kat. I'll talk about this later."

Laura was impatiently pacing the pavement, "I've tried calling both of them and neither will are answering their bloody phones!"

"They went clubbing, we'll have to track their scents," Will suggested.

"But isn't London full of scents? How are you going to find David and Oliver?" Kat asked them sceptically.

"Vampires have a distinct smell that no human can pick up," Laura answered. "We know exactly what to look out for."

"But what if you come across another vampire that

wants to kill you?" Kat created more excuses, reasons to have him stay with her.

"It's unlikely, but should it occur, then we will fight." Will cupped his hands around Kat's face before kissing her. "Now, go and get your things. we'll be back as soon as possible." Kat nodded and quickly turned to walk up the flight of stairs that led her to the hotel entrance. Will and Laura ducked into an alleyway to make another unseen flight, heading back to the venue to track David and Oliver. Their scent went the opposite direction that Laura and Will took earlier. They continued down the street, picking up the scent, doing their best to ignore the odours from the bars they passed: alcohol, cigarettes, and the sweat of humans.

For ten minutes, they trailed the scent through Soho, until it led them to a nightclub where a line of humans wearing the newest styles were queuing to get inside. Many of them had similar hair colour and haircuts: trendy and mainstream which made it difficult to tell them apart. They each wore stilettoes that looked too tight and uncomfortable, all for the sake of youth and beauty. An intense amount of tanned foundation painted on their skin, and long thick eyelashes glued over their normal lengths to make them look more involved with the mainstream culture, which made the vampires appear even paler than normal.

There was a bouncer outside the venue which was trouble as they would request IDs. Laura had an idea; she whispered into Will's ear to follow her lead.

They approached the bouncer with confidence. He was the type of person nobody would want to fight, almost filling the doorway to the club, but Laura and Will both knew that they would take him out so very easily if the situation required it. The people in the queue were giving the pair a grimace look, Laura heard one of them loudly say *"she looks like a freak, what is she doing here?"* which made her laugh; she knew she was more unique than the mundane females who built their personality on alcohol and reality television shows. The bouncer gave Will and Laura a look of curiosity as soon as they approached.

"Halloween was three months ago," he huffed. Laura

ignored his snarky comment to immediately stare into the bouncer's eyes, widening hers in the process. He didn't respond to her staring but focused deeply on her mesmerising eyes.

"You will let us in without question or identification," she whispered to his face before backing away towards Will, who watched her hypnotic manoeuvre.

"You may enter," the bouncer nodded. Laura smiled and made her way inside, with Will following behind her. People in the queue were whining about the bouncer letting the "freaks" into the club. The music inside was very loud, much louder than Midnight Devotion's gig as it was shrouded with club music that they couldn't recognise or understand. Laura and Will continued to sniff around for David and Oliver. Most of the scents they picked up were sweet cocktails and perfume, cologne, and sweat, which made it difficult to focus with all the bodies and noise. They kept going, knowing that this was an urgent matter. The club itself was garish; the walls painted burgundy, its tiled flooring being black and red with a glitter effect that picked up the strobing lights to create a more expensive look. Not long later, they found them both on the dancefloor together with a couple of women by their sides, both with long straight hair with blonde highlights that draped down their backs. They looked like they were having the time of their lives. David then saw Laura and Will at the edge of the dance floor, staring at him with visible confusion.

"WILL! LAURA!" David screamed with excitement, regardless of how unresponsive Laura and Will were. Will pushed his way over to the group, staring at the women that stumbled over to him in a salacious manner, and told them, "You need to find someone else to dance with," to which both women acknowledged and walked away.

He turned to David and shouted, "We have to get going!"

"Party Pooper! Why? We've only been here for an hour!"

"We've got a situation at hand!" He made a gesture to indicate vampire trouble, which David picked up right away. He was disconsolate, but reached over to Oliver and tapped his shoulder, causing him to turn and see that it wasn't just David.

"Will! You made it!" Oliver cried enthusiastically.

"We need to leave, now! Out of London, immediately!" The pair of them remained still looking at Will, both concerned. The room was booming with club music as they all looked at one another like statues in the middle of a dancefloor.

"Let's talk outside and make our way back to the hotel!" Laura marched over and started moving the group towards the exit. They walked back across Soho to the hotel, making sure no one was nearby to hear them.

"What the fuck has happened?" David urged for a response.

"We came across one of Mistress Claudette's servants," Laura informed them. "Sven. The one who turned me. We had some conflict, but he's taken care of."

"What do you mean 'taken care of'?" Oliver wondered.

"Kat killed him," Will said without hesitation, choosing not to deny how it had happened.

"She fucking what?!" David launched himself ahead of them until he was right in front of Will, walking backwards and deftly sidestepping the street furniture. "How?"

"Stake in the heart," Laura answered nonchalantly. They continued walking fast to the hotel, with David agog and troubled.

"She had a fucking stake with her this entire time?" David was surprised to learn this, "Even when we were at the venue?"

"Hey! I was just as surprised as you are!" Will cried. "She demanded to go back and help Laura and told me she could take him."

"You mean, he and Laura were battling it out? In public?" Oliver asked erratically.

"Not very public, inside the football stadium, in our Behemoth form," Laura responded. "We tried to tidy up the stadium as much as we could once it was over."

David was still baffled by what had happened.

"We were busy dancing with babes whilst you guys

were battling with a vampire servant. Son of a bitch," he huffed under his breath.

"You wanted to party!" she reminded him.

"Perhaps if you had come with us, you would avoided all of this!" David retorted.

"I'll go and grab the van," Oliver told them, and before anyone could respond, he disappeared.

"Go and fetch Kat, Will. We can wait here for Oliver," Laura instructed Will once they had arrived at the hotel.

"Thanks," Will went inside, got to the floor where Kat's room was, and knocked on the door, "It's safe, it's me". Kat answered it, seeing Will looking concerned.

"Have you packed your things?" Will asked her, walking into the room and closing the door behind him.

"I have, but why do we need to leave now, how soon will they find out?"

"They'll know. When Sven doesn't check back in at daybreak, they will know. We killed a member of Claudette's coven, she'll come for us. We can't be here, we need to get to Cardiff as soon as possible.

"How do you know she'll find us?"

Will raced over to her in a flash and placed both of his hands on her shoulders, causing her to shiver in shock.

"She will know one of her servants is absent. Since we've killed one, she'll come for us as we have just committed a major transgression. She won't know it's us, yet. But she'll start with the unaligned vampires like us. So, let's get going. You can sleep in the van or wait until we get to Cardiff." Will continued incessantly as he didn't need to stop to breathe any air. His tone, however, was full of anxiety. Kat was very tired but decided not to argue, but to trust Will. She nodded her head and got herself packed, ready for the unexpected journey through the night to their next destination.

The band waited for them outside in the van. Kat and Will entered the passenger seats. Oliver revved up the van and left the city. It was the time of night when even London was relatively quiet, so they were able to easily escape by half-past two. Kat had a blanket wrapped around her and the blower on full heat to warm herself up.

"I need a hot water bottle," She leaned against Will and fell asleep on his shoulder. Whilst she was asleep, the band began discussing what had happened.

"First gig of the tour and we're already on the run," David laughed nervously. "How the fuck did this happen?"

Laura felt heavily guilty about it all; she looked down to her feet and confessed. "I wasn't supposed to be in London. Sven found us at Tottenham Hotspur Stadium, and he forcefully reminded me of the agreement I had with the coven."

David exploded, barely containing his emotions, "And you were put in charge of booking venues! Why did you decide to go back to London and why were you in that stadium? Did you not think the risks that would put us in?! I told you this was a bad idea!

"David, keep your voice down, we have someone sleeping here," Oliver told him.

"Fuck off! She knew what she was doing and decided to go against us, the exact thing she shouldn't have been doing in the first place!"

"The city is a breeding ground for music recognition; I wanted us to gain some attention, some fans, and if we can turn human again, we can carry on playing at London venues and maybe, one day, we could get recognised and sign a label deal."

"We did get many compliments tonight, you got to admit that," Will added nonchalantly.

"Could she not have waited until AFTER we kill the Head Vampire ?!" David asked, expressing his frustration with his hands. "Or at least kept her head down after the gig?"

"London has a lot of rock venues. Besides, I knew the risk I was taking but didn't think that we would be spotted by someone familiar! I mean, it was purely a coincidence!"

"It's fucking London, Laura! You flew into a football stadium. You practically announced our arrival. Of course, there was going to be surveillance all over the city!"

"David," Will butted in. "Laura knows what she's done. But she was trying to tell Kat what happened to her, and probably tried to convince her to carry on with the mission and convincing her NOT to take the route of becoming a vampire.

Killing Sven was better than not killing him, think of the band and the gigs we have booked, they still don't know about that."

"Again! Could it not have waited until AFTER we had killed the Head Vampire ?!" David was exasperated. Upset with Laura, with Will, with everything, "All I wanted to do was play gigs and tour the country! Now our lives are on the line because the human killed one of the Mistress' vampire minions!

Laura's guilt was building up. She tried to keep her emotions intact and not explode. She gripped tightly on her jeans to calm herself. She could hear the fabric of the jeans rip lightly from the sharpness of her fingernails.

Will saw that Kat was still fast asleep despite the van roaring with angry voices.

"Can we argue about this later?" Oliver demanded. "I am the driver, and I need to concentrate. Pipe down, or I will turn this car around and there will be no touring!" Everyone in the van remained silent. Throughout the entirety of the journey to Cardiff, nobody said a word to each other. Oliver made good time, they arrived by five o'clock and found their hotel in the city centre. Winter was the perfect time for vampires as it meant more time in darkness and they never felt the cold.

Will had to carry Kat out of the van whilst the band went to collect their belongings. Will carried her into the hotel and had to inform the receptionist that she was very tired. The receptionist was not so sure whether to believe him but gave him the benefit of the doubt.

"There will be four other people coming in who can confirm: two males and a female. They're with me."

She handed him a key card to a room without any further questions. Will nodded a thank you and left with Kat still fast asleep in his arms. The group quietly left the deserted reception and took the lift to their floor.

When they were in their room, Will carefully laid Kat on the bed and pulled the floral quilt over her sleeping body. Will wasn't surprised that she was this exhausted and had slept through the arguing. He kissed her forehead before making his way out of the room to find the others. He was still processing the incident that had happened tonight. When Will got to the end of the corridor, he saw David and Laura bickering at one another, with Oliver placing his direct their chests, preventing them from getting into a physical fight. He stepped in to try and resolve the issue.

"I thought we had resolved this?" Will asked them with confusion.

"Clearly not," Oliver responded, looking like a father trying to stop his kids from fighting. "Not here, not now, okay?"

"I just don't understand why she had to go and do that," David explained to them.

"I've explained myself already!" Laura whispered. "You usually don't give a shit! Why the change of heart?"

"I care about the band, not the vampire situation! I don't want to be executed over your stupidity!" he,was right; she shouldn't have done what she did, but at the same time, she was relieved to have finally gotten her closure, but it meant now that the vampiric council could be tracking them down and arresting them.

"I'm sorry, okay?" Laura finally gave in. "I know what I did wasn't right, but I wanted to cut corners and get us recognised quicker. London is the hotspot for bands to do a tour in."

"If we are arrested for this, and for Will's fuck up, I'm not going to stick around to defend your arses," before Laura could respond David raced off down the corridor and into the lift.

"Let him sulk for a bit," Oliver shrugged defeatedly. "He'll get over it before the gig tonight."

"But what if he doesn't?" Laura asked with worry.

High above the Bristol Channel, David let out a wild scream of frustration, with no care who saw him, because nobody was going to believe them. He performed a perfect high dive with somersaults from five hundred meters into the freezing waters and let himself come to rest in the silt and sand. The cold waters did nothing to him. The watery solitude allowed him to meditate his malicious thoughts.

Chapter 15:
♥
Cardiff

Kat woke up at nine o'clock in the morning, noticing that she was in a bed she could not recall ever getting into. Her first thought was to sit up and investigate her surroundings. The lights of the room were turned off, creating a dark scenery to help her sleep. The small spartan room hinted that she was in a hotel, one that was less classy than the one they stayed at in London. This room was in a nationwide chain hotel instead.

She turned her head and saw Will lying with his eyes closed and his hands cupped together, resting on his lower chest. Her movement made him open one of his eyes to see her looking at him.

"Morning, beautiful," he smiled, leaning to his side and resting his head onto his hand. "How did you sleep?"

Kat smiled back. "I slept okay. Not perfect, but I'm surprised I didn't wake up when you carried me here. I must have been exhausted."

"I'm not surprised considering you fought and killed a vampire! That sounds like an exhausting activity!" Will chuckled whilst sitting up against the headboard. Kat leaned her head against his hardened chest and yawned.

"Are the band okay?" she asked with concern in her tone.

"Er, didn't you hear us in the van at all? They were arguing about what happened last night. David wanted to know why she booked a venue in a city she was not allowed to go into."

"And why did she?"

Will sighed.

"She cares so much about the band, we all do. We want to get it off the ground and gain recognition, but as vampires, it's not possible. Since we have hopes of becoming human again, we wanted to get a head start and get people to know our content. London is one of the best places for people get recognition for talent, which was why she chose it."

Kat nodded, understanding why Laura did what she did.

"It's highly common for bands to do a UK tour and go to London on one of their dates," Kat pointed out.

"Precisely!"

Kat pulled away from Will's chest, stretched her arms upwards and did a big yawn. After a few minutes of snuggling in bed later, Kat suddenly thought about something and asked him, "What's the weather like outside?" .

"I haven't checked. You should go and take a look. I'll hide under the sheets in case it's sunny." Will hid himself completely under the sheets. Kat leapt off the bed to open the curtains. She noticed that the hotel room was very warm from the radiator being on. Will must had turned in on in the night to keep her toasty warm.

When she pulled the curtains apart, she gasped. Snow lay thickly across the buildings, streets and bushes, and tiny white circles were falling from the grey sky above, creating an elegant, picturesque winter image she rarely saw in person.

"It's snowing!" Kat cried out intently. Will lifted the bed covers to have a peek, relieved to hear that it wasn't sunny.

"Okay, I can wrap up and we can go and take a look around the city if you'd like?" His cold arm wrapped around her shoulders and they both gazed at the white wonderland that Cardiff had become.

"I would love to!" Kat held onto Will's arm and squeezed herself closer to him. "Let me have a shower first and sort myself out."

"Okay," Will nodded before giving her a quick peck on the lips.

Once Kat had showered and had gotten dressed - layering herself up in preparation for the cold weather - she and Will left the hotel and made their way into the city to grab some breakfast. They found a café not too far from the hotel where Kat had a full English breakfast and a cup of coffee to start her long adventurous day. Midnight Devotion had a gig later, so it was going to be a long day for everyone.

"I was thinking that we could go and do some sightseeing today, if you would like to?" Will had suggested to her. "There's a museum that I like to go to if that's okay? I haven't been here for about ten years."

Kat had her mouth full of toast and had to quickly chew and swallow before answering.

"I would love to!" Kat responded enthusiastically. "I love museums. I take it you avoid ones with religious symbols or items in?"

"You'd be surprised how very few museums have those sorts of things!"

"And I assume you only go to museums when it's not sunny?"

"Mostly in the winter I go to museums. I've been to all the major city museums in the country in the past eighty-eight years, some of them I've been to multiple times. The thing about having eternal existence is you can learn about anything and everything."

Kat smiled at Will, excited at the idea of going out into the city with him like they were on a date.

"Have you been to this one?"

"Of course, I have," Will winked at her. "I can be your tour guide if that's of any interest?"

Kat giggled. "Professor Crowell."

Will chuckled at the given nickname.

When Kat had finished her breakfast, the vampire and his human girlfriend made their way to the *National Museum of Cardiff*. The huge historic building blew Kat away. The ten columns at the top of the wide stairs added the aesthetic of eighteenth-century America. Kat was surprisingly excited to be walking around the museum with a vampire who had lived almost ninety years of history. When they walked inside, she felt as though they were the most out of place people in the crowd due to their gothic look. Kat was used to the stares now, especially with her deathly pale boyfriend in tow.

The museum contained a gallery full of art, smaller works by twentieth century artists, as well as monumental canvases from the Victorian era. Another gallery of cultural artefacts reflecting Cardiff's trade links with the world and the triangle trade with Africa and America. Then Will took Kat to the Natural History wing of the museum, he smiled to see Kat gawking at the dinosaur fossils and stuffed replicas. It was like a father watching their dinosaur-obsessed child. This train of thought led Will to think about what his child would have been like. He imagined his son would be fascinated by history and arts, making museum visits more frequent. He pushed the pain of that image away and focused back on his lively girlfriend.

After their tour, they went to the St. David shopping centre, where Kat found a homeware shop to buy some garden stakes and a pocketknife to create more vampire stakes. Will felt a little uneasy about it, but knew she needed to do it. A couple of stakes wasn't going to be enough for her, so she needed to increase her inventory.

Kat grabbed a coffee and a sausage roll from a café in the shopping centre, and they ended the day with a walk out past the Senedd and round the Bay. The snow had covered the paths and roads around the harbour, and their footsteps created crackles with each step on the snow, leaving footprints behind with each step they took. The bay was glassily calm under the overcast sky. Kat hoped that one day they could return when they were both human and do this day again in the summer.

They turned back to the city, reluctantly retracing their steps, enjoying every second they had together, both knowing the clock was ticking down before the gig and before their eventual confrontation with Mistress Claudette.

By six o'clock in the evening Kat had eaten at the hotel bar and was back in her room with Will. Both were getting ready for the gig, with the news that David had returned after his day of intense brooding. He was soaking wet but got himself clean for tonight's gig. The band got in the van and made their way to the venue in the centre of the city called *The Five Crows*, and it was much like the Kasbah venue in London: small, smelly, loud, and plastered with retro music décor. Kat congratulated Laura on finding venues that really fitted the band's image.

After their arrival, Oliver and David began unpacking the instruments and equipment, and bringing them inside. They were due to start playing at seven-thirty, so it meant that they needed to set everything up right away. They were the first out of two bands to perform; they were the support act. The band they were going to support tonight were called *Renegade*, a local punk rock band that were well known in the city of Cardiff. They were niche outside of Cardiff but had released three albums in the past five years and performed at smaller punk festivals across Europe. By seven, the venue was getting busy. There was an influx of people that were dressed in ripped jeans, wearing leather jackets with patches on that had band logos embroidered on them, entering the building. Even by punk standards some of the hair styles made Kat blink twice.

Inside, the lights were dim with a variety of shades of purple and pink, the perfect lighting for Midnight Devotion since it was the colour scheme of the band. Whilst David and Laura were setting up the drumkit on stage, looking like they weren't overly strong undead beings, Oliver and Kat shuffled their way through the crowd to set up the merch table with Will walking behind them surveying the gig and trying to get a sense of the crowd. Oliver helped Kat bring in the box of merchandise to a table at the far end of the bar next to the Renegade stand. Kat was, of course, going to be sitting at the stall again, selling to strangers, something that she was still nervous about.

"I feel a little overdressed," Kat told Will anxiously. She was wearing a black lace dress with witchcraft symbols embodied on black leggings and her black boots. "Everyone here is dressed all punk and old classic rock and I look like I'm supposed to be at a *Cradle of Filth* gig."

"You are beautiful. And the best-dressed woman here," Will assured her, holding onto her hand, and spinning her around.

"You're only saying that because you're dating me. So biased of you, Will."

"I'm sure the others would agree with me. I mean, Laura adores your choice in clothing!"

Kat blushed at his comment. He handed her a quick kiss on the lips before leaving her with Oliver. They both set up the T-shirts and CDs on the table, along with the price list whilst Will went to the stage to set up his microphone. Once the stage was set up, the band made their way back to the van to have their quick drink of blood from their plastic flasks. Each of their eyes began to turn red from the digestion of blood. In half an hour the red eyes would quickly turn to grey. The taste of the human blood had them calm and collected, their energy getting stronger and more resilient.

The band returned, fortified, and Will went to get Kat a drink of lemonade before going on stage. He gave her a quick kiss on the cheek after handing her a drink and made his way to the stage. The lights dimmed down until the stage lights were the brightest lights in the room.

"Good evening, Cardiff!" Will screamed into the microphone. "We are Midnight Devotion!" The crowd cheered warmly at their introduction. The setlist and performance was identical to London's, and all the songs went smoothly. Kat wondered if this was going to be the same every night for the next three nights. She figured bands were used to performing the same setlists repeatedly for days. The room wasn't as packed as London was. Some of the people were chilling outside the room in the bar area, and a large group of people stood around the room watching them perform. By the third track, they had a small dense group of keen listeners, though more than half the room were just standing there showing no interest or saving their energy for Renegade.

Kat watched Will dancing around on stage having the time of his afterlife. He seemed happy, excited, lively. All four members of the band seemed relaxed and happy to be there, even David and Laura were exchanging smiles and riffs. Kat couldn't help but admire the look of their enjoyment. It was not every day that vampires could enjoy a moment with the human race. They could if they were able to keep control of their thirst for blood and keep their species disguised. *"None of that will matter once they turn back to human and can re-join them,"* she thought.

Will did the introduction of the band again like he did the other night, bowing to the crowd after introducing himself. He also did his dedication speech for the next song, which he dedicated to Kat. Some members of the crowd were looking for her, causing her to blush slightly and wanting to hide away from the sudden attention. When the band had finished their performance, a few people approached Kat and purchased some CDs and T-shirts. Up close the audience was more diverse than London, quite a few people that approached them were middle-aged men, with their wives or girlfriends and even some family groups with teenage kids. There were also young adults who were at university or college age.

"Their guitarist is well lush!" she heard one of the girls saying aloud.

"Their bass player is even cuter!" the girl's mate told her. "Do you think she's single?"

Whilst she was dealing with the sales of merchandise, Midnight Devotion ended their setlist and thanked the crowd. The band were busy getting their equipment and instruments packed away. They carried them through the performance room, through the bar room to get outside so that they could put them into their van as quickly as they could before another long drive.

They made their way back inside to watch the main act of the evening. The band they supported were all males; their lead singer very, very punk: red and black striped jeans, a ripped white tank top with a hand drawn dragon on the back, and spiky blonde hair that looked painful to touch. The two guitar players were both wearing leather jackets: one of the jackets was red, worn by the slim bodied guitarist with curly black hair that landed on his collar bones. The other guitarist, who had thick brown hair and more muscle than the other one wore a lot of green. Both played their guitars like they were the greatest guitarists in the world, showing off their expensive-looking guitars and swinging them around with the strap going around their torso. The drummer was much older, pale and bald, dressed all in black combat gear and managed to look like he was hardly moving, despite the noise he made.

Will sat next to Kat to watch the main band perform, holding onto her by wrapping his arm around her shoulder. Oliver was at the back of the room with David and Laura watching the band from a distance; all three of them seemed to be enjoying their act. The crowd had gained more people, making the room more packed and having enough people to start moshing. The band were thankful to have control of their thirst as the sweat of the packed room wafted into their nostrils, which would make most vampires either race outside or act out of bloodlust and murder every human in the room, just for the taste of blood, all in a sudden flash, quick enough to escape.

Renegade were a nostalgic seventies-style punk rock band, the type of music that stayed retro and attracted an older audience. The lead singer had an authentic edge despite their young age. The crowd was going wild; jumping up and down and pushing and shoving each other around with laughter showing in their faces, all whilst being friendly to one another. Renegade's performance, and the crowds pushing and shoving, went on till curfew at eleven thirty. When it was over, Kat sold a few more CDs. Will began packing away the merchandise table while the rest of the band waited outside for them to finish. Will approached Renegade to say thanks and gave them a free copy of their CD. Kat hadn't seen him quite this excited before tonight.

Outside, the snow continued falling, adding thicker layers to the snow that already stuck to the ground. Kat shivered as she quickly got into the van to warm herself up. Oliver kindly put the heating on for Kat to get herself warmed up. The blanket Will brought with him was placed around Kat, which she cocooned herself in to embrace her warmth, making sure none of it escaped whilst she snoozed on her cold-skinned lover's hardened chest, all the way to Will's hometown.

Chapter 16:
♥
Revelation

Two o'clock in the morning, after driving up the M50, the M5, and getting lost on the ring road, they arrived in Birmingham city Centre. David was doing his best to shout directions to Oliver from the small map book they had, but many of the roads were closed for building works. Many arguments occurred, making Kat drop in and out of sleep. Will couldn't contribute to the directions as the city had advanced so much since he was last there that it became surreal to him. He looked out the window, amazed at how different his home city had changed since he had last been there in almost ninety years ago. The memories flew back into his thoughts, matching the new buildings to the ones he was familiar with from his time as a human. There were lots houses that had been replaced with shops or cafes. The entire city had been modernised and reconstructed, making it all seem alien to Will. After nearly ninety years his memory had become so out of step as to be useless. The old city that he once knew ceased to exist, and he knew little about these streets and places. Seeing the occasional building he recognised only made him feel more out of time and uneasy.

Kat could tiredly see Will gazing and held onto his hand as they drove through the city, she could feel it tightening, giving her a sense of his apprehension.

"Home Sweet Home, eh, Will?" David teased. "Looks totally different than it did back in the twenties, huh?"

"Now is not the time for your teasing remarks, David," she silently groaned at him.

Will completely ignored him since he was too fixated on the memories of his human life in Birmingham. Images of his wife were coming back to him now more than ever. Each street corner they drove past made him think what used to be there, and what activities took place when he was there all those years ago.

Her beautiful smile that drove his heart wild reappeared. If his heart were beating, he knew it would drop to the pit of his stomach and cause him severe grievance.

"Are you okay, Will?" Kat whispered with concern. He took a second before turning to face her, full of wonder for what he was feeling as well as thinking.

"Yeah," he faked smiled, trying to give her assurance. She wasn't sure if he was lying or not. Could vampires lie without even trying? Could they mask their emotions so easily? "It's just weird to be back here."

Ten minutes later and they arrived at the hotel car park. Will immediately left Kat in the van and strode off to the edge of the car park to get a better view of the city centre. Kat remained seated in the van, watching him from a distance, concerned about his wellbeing.

"He'll be alright," Laura approached her as soon as she got out of the van. "Just let him brood for a bit." Both women watched Will stare at the cold dark sky. Snow was still falling on an icy breeze, landing onto his hair, face, and clothing. Kat couldn't help but see Will standing in the snow staring ahead the city horizon as a work of art. He was beautiful no matter what he did.

"Oi, broody!" David cried as he threw a snowball at him. It was thrown with the strength of a vampire, so it was faster than a bullet. Without looking, or even moving his neck, Will sidestepped it and threw one back at David, who moved his hand so quickly to stop it that the ball appeared to vaporise on collision. Will's face was blank; he then averted his eyes towards the powdered ground, continuing to brood at the winter night sky.

"Laura, please take Kat to the hotel. I need to go for a walk," Will informed her as he walked away without continuing the conversation. This made Kat even more concerned for Will, knowing full well that he was reliving his human years. Laura held Kat's hand, and the pair made their way, by foot, to the hotel around the corner from the car park. Oliver picked up Kat's suitcase and followed them, whilst David was busy getting snow off of his jacket.

"Don't be upset about Will," Laura continued reassuring her.

"Are you guys sure that coming here was the best idea?" Kat asked them lightly.

"You were the one who said he needed to get over it," Oliver reminded Laura.

"He needs closure, Ollie. If he wants to be human again, he needs to face his past and move on from it. If I'm able to do it back in London, then so can he." Oliver didn't argue about it, he knew full well that Will was a sentimental vampire.

Will strode around the quiet Birmingham streets deep in thought, trying and succeeding to get lost in the alleys and back streets of the city that was once his home. At three in the morning, it was much quieter than London was at night. He walked in the middle of the road as the snow continued to fall around him. Despite the emotions, and useless memories, this still felt like a homecoming. His hair became damp, and his shoulders were drenched from the snow. He was still picturing the city streets from what it used to look like and how different it had all become.

The wind changed direction and Will turned to face it, then jumped wildly all the way back to Victoria Square, a place he was remarkably familiar with. He turned his head around to examine the new and old features of the place he once knew. The Town Hall was still there but now looking more of a shiny office block, and there were restaurants and clothing stores which had replaced the red brick buildings he once knew. He could still see down Hill Street to the back of the station, and the road to the markets he and Elizabeth would frequently visit.

Will looked around for a bit before noticing something peculiar standing on top of the roof of the Bullring. Standing above the rooftop, looking down at Will, was the silhouette of a person who stood as if he owned it, but undoubtedly someone who shouldn't be there. Will froze, and with close examination from his vampire eyes, he saw the person more clearly. Will could see that he was a short, slim male who had short wavy brown hair, wearing black trousers, a soft navy-blue trench coat long enough to flutter against the cold breeze. The smell of vampire was in the air, along with something oddly familiar that Will couldn't place. The pair of them stared at one another, wondering what the other was thinking. Will could see that his eyes were red, which immediately labelled him as a vampire that had recently been feeding on blood. The mysterious man saw that Will's eyes were grey, which meant he hadn't drank blood for some time. Seeing this caused the stranger to immediately turn away. Will instinctively jumped high enough to reach the Bullring roof and began chasing after him.

"Hey! Wait!" he pleaded.

The stranger was way ahead of Will, but it didn't stop him from continuing the chase. He saw the stranger jump onto the building ahead, and then run alongside the building at a high speed, fast enough for no human to see or hear. Will followed the exact same path, parkouring his way over the roofs of shops, flats, and business buildings. Neither of them set foot on the streets below.

"Please, stop!" Will cried, but the stranger ignored him. They raced through the city until they reached the Digbeth part of Birmingham. The stranger launched himself off the roof and landed on the side of the building across the way and began running upwards until he reached an open window, where he immediately disappeared into the darkness within. Will copied his moves and followed him until he reached the open window where the stranger had gone through. The room he went into was part of an old building that was due for refurbishment. There were pieces of tarpaulin, timber wood and paint cans on the floor. The walls of the room were grey like concrete blocks;

180

the paint work was yet to begin. Will couldn't see the stranger anywhere; even his vampire vision couldn't find him. His scent was masked due to the recent snow. All he could pick up was the smell of paint and asbestos from the decrepit building.

"My name is Will," Will shouted out, his voice echoed around the room. "I am one of you: a vampire. I just want to talk. I'm not one of Mistress Claudette's servants, if that's what you're worried about. And I know you're not one of her companions, either! I just want to talk." There was nothing but silence that filled the dark room; all that could be heard was the cold wind outside. Will concentrated, shutting down awareness of further noise and light to focus on the building around him, trying to hear vampire activity or movement within his surroundings.

Nothing.

Something kicked Will at the back of the leg causing him to fold double, and then Will felt a blow to his face, and he was down on the hard floor. He cried out from the sudden attack; his voice echoed through the large empty room. They were too fast for Will to see who it was. He sprang up quickly but two people were able to grab him from behind. He was in the air now, rushing towards the nearest wall, causing him to create a crack from the force of the creatures that pushed him up against it. He saw two people pinning him up against the wall, whilst a third person walked slowly towards them. He tried to free himself from their grasp, but their strength was an even match with his. He wondered if they were much older vampires than he was due to their strength, or that they were young vampires that had a joint strength that one vampire wouldn't be able to fight against.

"We thought we were the only vampires in this city," the person approaching him was the person Will chased after. The other two were a young boy and a young girl. The young slim male was dark skinned, wearing black tracksuit bottoms and a green and yellow hoodie. His hair was buzzcut short but had very small curls to them. He seemed just as young as Kat.

The stocky female had dark blonde hair with bleach dipped dye at the ends that fell lankly to her collar bone. She wore dark purple Doc Martin boots, light blue bootcut jeans and a thin army-style khaki coat. Her eyes were much bigger than the male's, mousey even. Will examined her features and concluded that she must have been in her early twenties when she turned. Both of their eyes were as red as the stranger's, which gave Will the impression that they were a small coven of vampires that had been on a hunt around the city, and he feared that if they were hunters then what might they do with him.

"I'm not from around here," Will snarled. "I mean, technically, I was originally from here, but I haven't been here in eighty-eight years. I just arrived here tonight."

The young woman pushed Will further against the wall and yelled "How many of you are there, old man?" in a threatening tone.

"Me and three others," Will told them in a calm tone, purposefully leaving Kat out of the equation.

"He's bluffing," the young man told the stranger. "I bet there's more than three of them!"

"No," the stranger objected. "I believe him. Let him go. Aaron, Tabitha."

"How can you tell?" Aaron sceptically asked him.

"The tone of his voice. No vampire would lie in a tone like that."

The pair of them did what they were commanded, their nostrils flaring, red eyes staring, and Aaron keeping his fist raised, aiming at Will. Will did not try to run or attack; he stood against the dented concrete wall and allowed them to speak but was readying himself in case a fight were to break.

"What brings you to Birmingham, then?" Tabitha aggressively asked him.

"My band I are performing at the Asylum venue tomorrow," Will answered hesitantly. "We're currently doing a tour around the UK, and we're heading up north to pay Mistress Claudette a visit," Will explained himself. He didn't move an inch as he waited for the mysterious vampires to continue interrogating him and throw more questions at him.

"Who is Mistress Claudette?" Aaron questioned, tilting his head to the side.

That was a question he did not expect to hear from the vampires. His eyes widened. "You. . . don't know who she is?"

"Did I fucking stutter?" Aaron spat.

"Aaron," said the stranger calmly.

"Sorry, Henry."

"Tell us more about this Mistress, old man." Tabitha demanded. "What makes her she so special?"

Will was awfully confused with what was going on. These vampires were off the radar from Mistress Claudette, or maybe they were from a different country, or maybe new-borns who hadn't been found by her coven yet.

"She's the Head Vampire of the United Kingdom," Will informed them. "When you become a vampire, one of her servants would take you to her where she would inform you on the vampire rules. If you break her rules, then she will execute you. Which leads me to some questions I would like to ask you."

"I'll allow it," said Henry. "You have one question for each of us." Henry raised his fingers to count the questions.

"It's a question for all three of you, actually."

"Go on?" Aaron raised his eyebrow.

"When did each of you become a vampire? It's important for me to know this."

"Why does that matter?" Tabitha asked him grudgingly.

"Because when you turn into a vampire after two weeks, one of her servants would come and collect you."

"Why two weeks? Why not immediately?"

"It's a trial run that the vampires go through to see how they would instinctively react to their change. The strongest vampires would restrict their urge to kill, which means they are mentally strong. Claudette kills the ones that are not strong enough to resist." The vampire trio stared at Will with looks of further confusion.

"How do they even know when someone becomes a vampire? Does this Claudette get a sensation whenever someone turns?" Tabitha asked with scepticism.

"She has vampires all over the country on the lookout for new-born vampires. They track them down by sniffing out new vampire scent."

"New-born vampires have a distinct smell?" Aaron asked, also with scepticism. All of this seemed surreal for them to believe.

"Yes. The fresh venom within our veins would still be mixed with our human blood, creating a certain smell that only vampires can track."

The room turned silent. Aaron and Tabitha looked at one another, seeming confused with what Will had explained to them.

"We're way older than two weeks, old man," Tabitha informed him. "I turned into a vampire three years ago!"

"Eight years ago, for me," Aaron added.

Henry took a moment to respond.

"Sixty-four years," he finally told him. Will remained silent, shocked at how high a number he had been given. He expected below twenty years at least, the same as the others.

"How. . . how have you survived all these years without detection?"

"That's your question limit!" Tabitha loudly pointed out and punched the wall next to Will's head which failed to make him flinch.

"No. I want to tell him." Henry rejected Tabitha's comment and proceeded to give Will the information. "I was in Germany at the time that I turned, fighting in the war." Henry started to march around the room whilst giving Will his vampire origin story. "I was in my second year in the army. We were in the middle of the battlefield when the Germans attacked our base. It was so unexpected that I was not prepared. A group of Germans were fast approaching me and my comrades. We were given the order to retreat but the captain chose two of my friends to stay and man the guns. I refused to listen, wanting to help them. The thought of losing my two closest friends encouraged me to stay and fight. The next thing I knew a shadow appeared over the trench, and they were both bitten in the neck by one of the Germans whilst they were arguing with me about it.

"The creature then leaped at me, and before I could comprehend what had happened, it took a bite on my neck before being shot by my dying comrade. While it did next to no damage, his shot gave me the chance to escape. I limped back to base over two agonising days, but the doctors pronounced me dead of blood loss the next day. They dumped my body into a pit along with the others. What they didn't know, of course, was that I was very much alive."

Will stared at Henry with fascination. He was intrigued to learn more.

"How did you get out of the country without getting recognised?" Will wondered. "Or even burnt from the sun?"

"It was nightfall when I awoke in the pit," he replied. "I managed to climb out without being noticed. However, I felt the strong urge to consume blood. When they dumped one of the fresh bodies into the pit, I managed to salvage the blood before it became old and gross. After feeding myself, I ran away from the base and just kept running, never stopping. I was so confused. I hadn't noticed that I'd been running for over fifty miles in a short period of time. I reached the coast of France and started swimming; never stopping. The fast swimming and never slowing down or losing my breath was immaculate for my escape. I was back in England before the sun rose. As it burned my flesh, I knew exactly what I had become, and was amazed with how real it all was. I hid in a nearby derelict building, waiting for night-time before setting off to get back to Birmingham.

"I hid from society during the day in the attic of farms and outbuildings and would come out at night to hunt for blood. I was back in Birmingham by the following week. I had to hide in the day and move by night. I was running but didn't know my way back to Birmingham so that was why it took me so long. I was just running blind. Once I got there, I soon realised I couldn't stay without hurting anyone. My thirst was at a high rate, and I needed to remain hidden. For all I knew, everyone I knew and loved thought I had been killed in the battlefield. I would only come back every now and again. I have watched the city I grew up in change with each visit, getting more and more modernised."

His story reminded Will of what he had to do. Leave the city he grew up in to keep his friends and family safe from his new lifestyle. A painful sacrifice, but one that was necessary.

"One night I found Aaron, who had been attacked by a gang of racist scumbags who had stabbed him in an alleyway. I killed all three of them, and because he saw what was happening to him and his undeserved death, I had to make a choice. I chose to save him, turning him into the same creature I was. For the first time in a while, I no longer felt alone."

Henry looked at Aaron and smiled. Aaron grinned back with gratitude. "He decided to join alongside me, and I told him that we had to keep a low profile and that he couldn't go home."

Aaron nodded and began to walk around the room; his eyes focused on his surroundings as the memories played out as he described his story.

"It was incredibly difficult. I had to fake my death for my family to move on," Aaron added to the story. "My parents are from Jamaica, and I was born in West Brom'. I was in Birmingham visiting some friends, and I was on my way to the last bus until I was jumped by this gang. They demanded my money and then proceeded to beat the shit out of me, anyway, stabbing me multiple times. Despite my skills in martial arts, they were able to gang up on me and had me on the ground before I could defend myself. The next thing I knew, the gang has disappeared, then I remember a pain in my neck. . . and, of course, I was saved by becoming a vampire. I was kept hidden for two days before I woke up as a vampire."

Will envisioned the incident in his mind as he told him what had happened. He believed that Henry did the right thing, but at the same time, was death a better option than restricted permanence?

"Then, five years later, we found Tabitha," Aaron concluded.

She shook her head and sighed with grief. "I was a university student, studying film media. I was in my third and final year, and I was at a club with my mates. My drink got spiked and I was kidnapped by these two wankers. I had no idea where they took me, and they proceeded to do serious harm to me.

"They slapped me, punched me, stripped me, tied me up, did...horrendous things to me. I remember their laughter, their encouragements towards each other, the suggestions they offered to each other. I was on the brink of death; I was even begging for death. Then it went dark. I couldn't see what was going on; the laughing and the banters suddenly became screams and blood-filled splatter.

"There was more pain and an odd cold feeling. The boys had decided to *save* me and turn me into a vampire. I woke up in a different derelict building and thought "*here we go again*", but they told me what had happened and all three of us have stayed together ever since. I'm grateful that they saved me, but at the same time, I never got to finish university or say goodbye to my family. I was labelled as missing, and the police had no lead, by now I am officially dead in-absentia. I don't know if my family ever gave up, but it pains me knowing they could never see me again, especially like this. I chose to change my name and my entire identity to remain hidden.

"I've stolen phones from the people we kill to keep up to date with society's news, and also because I would be super bored without internet entertainment!" Tabitha pulled out a sleek black metal block with a glassy looking front from her the back pocket of her jeans. It was not like the buttoned phones that Will was used to; this one was one large screen with a single button underneath, the sort of phones rich people owned. "I have three of these phones on the go! If one dies, I use another one! Then I go to charge them at a nearby café or hotel. I also buy gift cards so that I can buy data to watch stuff on these things or get free Wi-Fi wherever there is any available."

Will gazed at them, amazed at how they each became vampires: one through the war and two that were close to death and were given a second chance, in exchange for their aging and never seeing their friends or family again.

"These two: they're essentially like the two friends I lost during the war," said Henry. "I would do anything to protect them both."

Will felt that way towards the band. He wasn't able to save them from death, but he felt the strong bond he formed with them, but it wasn't as strong as the trio in front of him.

"So, you guys have been travelling around the country and have never come across other vampires?" Will asked curiously.

"We have. But we would slaughter any that approached us with threats," Henry told him. "They would always say the same thing each time. '*By orders of the high council of vampires, the Vamperium, you are ordered to come with us and be given the mark of vampirism. Failure to cooperate will result in your execution.*' We didn't do as we were told. We wanted to be free. So, we killed them."

Will was stunned. It explained a little about how they were able to stay off the Mistress' radar for so long.

"What the fuck? You've killed Claudette's servants? How many?"

"Four," Aaron answered proudly, using his fingers to emphasis the death count. "Two within the last decade. I think they have forgotten us, and now we're Vampire Outlaws! Rogue vampires!"

"How were you able to? They're enormously powerful vampires!"

"Aaron here has some techniques in the field of martial arts, as he stated previously. Not only that, but he trains constantly. His vampire skills, added to that, make him virtually an unstoppable fighter."

"High ranked fighter in my human years. I was a champion at martial arts and won national tournaments. Of course, now, I can't achieve that with being a vampire, unless there's a vampire martial arts tournament. I still get upset about being jumped and beaten to death." Aaron chuckled to himself.

Will figured that the servants they had killed were ones that were below a hundred years old. There was no way Aaron could kill a vampire over that age, because when a vampire turns one hundred, they are given permanent vampirism but with the added bonus of stronger abilities and the abilities to transform into monstrous creatures.

"Now, your turn to answer questions," said Henry as he turned back to Will. "Why are you visiting Mistress Claudette since you claimed she's the ruler of this country? And why haven't you done this already? She's clearly not in Birmingham, as surely, we would know about her given how local we are."

Will hesitated, feeling like he had been cornered. He could lie and not tell them about Kat, but at the same time, if he wanted to ask the three of them to join their group to increase their chances, they would have to know about her. He wanted more vampires to join their coven so that they had more of an advantage if a fight were to break, especially as they had a vampire who knew martial art techniques and could potentially teach them a few fighting techniques.

"Personal reasons," he told them. "We want to tour the country first and be a real band whilst we have the chance. We've already released an EP and played two venues so far."

"What's your band called?" Aaron asked him curiously, crossing his arms with fascination.

"*Midnight Devotion*. We're a punk rock band."

"I LOVE punk music! Maybe we should go and see their gig!" Tabitha suggested, smiling with excitement. "I haven't been to a gig in a long time! I can even send out a signal for some peeps to attend the gig through my anonymous social medias!"

"*Anonymous?*"

"Well, I can't show my real identity when I'm a vampire, can I? I've got a lot of fake accounts, so that I can keep up with the latest trends and news updates! I use fake photos as using my real face would draw attention, even though I've changed my hair and have red eyes." Tabitha flexed her stylish mobile phone at Will. "I'm basically an internet guru! So, I can send out all sorts of announcements to my followers on MySpace and Facebook and Twitter! Like tonight's gig! I'm quite sure a few people who follow me are from Birmingham!"

Will nodded politely, struggling to keep up with what Tabitha suggested but knew Laura would be pleased. So, he had found someone to help the band with fighting techniques, and someone who could do promotional work. Wondering around the streets of Birmingham had indeed done him a favour. Will knew that if they did attend the gig tonight, they would still find out about Kat. The thought of rogue vampires wanting to kill her for her elegant blood made him feel uneasy.

"If you're going to the gig, there's something you should know first." All three of them looked at Will with curiosity. Will sighed and ripped the band aid off. "I kind of lied earlier, there isn't three others with me; there's four."

"Four vampires?" Tabitha inquired.

"No. Three vampires and . . . a human." The word tasted sour in his mouth, as he felt like he was betraying Kat's safety. All three vampires stared at Will: their expressions ceasing any change. "She's my girlfriend, and she's our ticket to turning back human."

Tabitha's eyebrows raised as he told them this. She moved an inch closer to him, eagerly determined for answers to the dilemma.

"You can turn back into a human?" Her voice loudened from the news she was given, her eyes widened with shock but also excitement.

"It's rumoured that killing the Head Vampire would turn young vampires back to their human selves, but only if a human kills them." Will explained to them.

"Why can't a vampire do it?" Aaron asked with a shrug of doubt.

"Because they would then become the new Head Vampire. They would gain their abilities and become the strongest vampire in the country. But yes, Kat is hopefully going to be our saving grace to ending our eternal living."

"So, you and the band are travelling to the hideout of Mistress Claudette's, have this girl kill the Head Vampire, and turn yourselves back to human?" Henry recited their plan, seeming confused by his motive. "But why do you want to be human again? Do you not enjoy having these extraordinary powers and immortality, ageless abilities? Be a superior creature against the snarky and disrespectful humans?"

Will felt like he was having the same conversation as he did with Kat on their first night. He figured it seemed fair given how they had told him their stories. "I want to be human again so that I can have the life that I lost. I was married and expecting a child, until I was attacked and turned into a vampire. My wife thought I had run off, and I never got to tell her what had happened. She died giving birth to our child and I left the city to start my vampiric life. But the band want to be human again so that they can be a band and gain recognition, as well as achieving their own personal dreams. They want to tour the country and do festivals, live normal lives, and live life with no restrictions."

"I understand," Tabitha empathised. "I want to be human again. I miss my family, and I miss going to university and going shopping in the day with friends."

"I miss those too." Aaron added. "Maybe there is hope for us to becoming human again after all! We were all accepting that we were never going to change back and stay this age for the rest of our lives. But if we do turn human, what are we going to do about jobs and such? We don't have money or anything."

"We have someone who can sort out fake identifications and documents to help you out with that," Will assured them. "We don't need identification right now, but as humans, we will need to since we will lose out hypnotic abilities."

Henry stared heavily at Will; he hadn't changed this look since Will finished his earlier story. He had realisation about the consistency of Will's story. He moved passed Aaron and Tabitha and got closer to Will. Will was surprised to see him approaching him this confidently.

"You said you turned into a vampire eighty-eight years ago, didn't you?" he queried.

"I did, yeah."

191

Henry's eyes widened as he looked down at the ground. He stood frozen in place. "And, you said you're from Birmingham, right?"

"Yes?"

"Where in Birmingham?

"Right here, in Digbeth; I was the blacksmith for the dairy depot."

Henry's fist clenched. "It can't be," he whispered under his breath.

"Henry?" Tabitha approached him with concern.

"Henry," Will whispered, realising the impossibility of the situation. "*That's the name Elizabeth wanted to name our son.*"

"How old were you when you became a vampire?" Will asked him, determined to know the answer.

"I was twenty-four years old. I was born in nineteen twenty-one. I was adopted a week after my birth when my mother died, and my father... *disappeared,* that's what I was told." Both Henry and Will looked at each other in the eyes. The pair of them examined each other's looks, drank in each other's scent. Will saw Elizabeth's and his own curls and Elizabeth's brown in his hair and the roundness of her facial structure on his. Henry also had Will's nose.

Will's legs collapsed, making him stumble back against the cracked concrete. He continued to stare at his vampiric offspring; the son he never got to meet, the last part of Elizabeth that was now in his life. Unfortunately, that last part of her had become the very thing he too had become: a vampire. A soulless, pointless creature that leached off the blood of anything with a heartbeat.

"What's going on?" Tabitha questioned, staring at the pair.

Aaron's eyes widened and his mouth dropped. Not a single word escaped from his mouth.

"Guys," Henry didn't move his head to face them, he continued to look at Will. "I may need some time with Will.

Chapter 17:
♥
Birmingham

"Aaron," Tabitha placed her hand onto his shoulder. "We should give them a moment." Aaron nodded, still gobsmacked at the revelation. They both left Will and Henry alone for their unexpected family reunion. Neither of them could say a word to each other; they continued to stare at one another in bewilderment, confusion, and a variety of mixed emotions, both positive and negative, dwelled within them. Will was in complete awe at finally seeing the son that he had envisioned for an exceptionally long, and his expectations had gone above and beyond.

"It's really *you*," Will sniffed with a nervous smile on his lips.

Henry remained frozen in place, still trying to process what was going on, even though he knew for damn sure what was happening.

"Were you adopted into a loving home?"

"I was adopted into a rich family called the Halstead family. I had a sister and two brothers: all of them older than me." Henry didn't blink.

Will slowly smiled, standing silently. He continued looking at the features of the son who he had lost. "I knew you had been adopted into a family, but I couldn't stay around to see you. I just remember watching them leave the adoption building with you in their arms. They both looked ever so happy holding onto you. The mother was cradling you like you

were her son. Seeing that made me know that you were going
to be alright."

"You saw me leave the adoption house?" Henry's
question remained a whisper, but Will heard him perfectly like
he had spoken at a normal volume.

"I did," Will acknowledged. "And were they okay?
Did they treat you well?"

Henry nodded, thinking about his family, especially
his mother. "My adoptive parents were thankfully considerate
people. My new sister and brothers were kind too. We didn't
fight often, mostly childish squabbles and over exaggerations.
They put me in public school, had me learn piano and I joined
the army when I turned twenty-one. Neville joined the army
before I did, but he was killed in the field. My other brother
James went to Wales to join the Civil Service. My sister Enid
married a train driver and had two kids with him. I haven't seen
them since I turned into a vampire, but I guess I am an uncle to
someone, even if I'm not related by blood."

Will was baffled by the life he had been given. Will
wasn't rich back then, but he would have given Henry
everything he could, even if it left him penniless.

"Your mother gave you the name Henry," Will
informed him, nodding his head whilst looking at the ground. "I
was there when you were born. I was outside, watching through
the window. It was painful to watch your mother in pain and
call out for me. It was painful for me to watch her die, and it
was even more painful knowing I couldn't raise my own child."

Henry placed his hand over his face and shook his
head. If he could cry, this would be the moment. Will thought
the same, but tears had gone along with the heartbeat. He
would be crying for both those reasons; happy that he finally
got to meet his son, but also sad that he had landed the same
fate as himself: like father, like son.

"Vampirism has taken so much from us. It was
immensely painful for me to walk away from Birmingham and
leave you behind, but Henry, I had to in order to protect you."

"I know that now, but I have always wondered what
happened to you, but was scared to question it." He lifted his
head back up to see his father. He noticed that his father was

half a foot taller than him. Neither of them had never registered this until now, "I don't resent you one bit. I'm just so sorry that you became a vampire and had to leave mother and me behind to protect us both. I'm grateful you did that. I might not be the person I am today if things had been different. That's not to say that you wouldn't have taken care of me, but I would have been a different person."

Will slanted his lips. "I agree. But at the same time, would you have suffered the same fate?"

Henry thought about it for a moment. He wasn't so sure what the odds were of him becoming a vampire if Will hadn't turned and became his father full time. The cause and effect of their alternate timelines were only going in various directions.

"When you are in the front line in the war there are so many what-ifs and so many near misses, you stop counting." His anger began to rise. He turned around to pick up a can of paint and threw it across the room, causing the tin to squish flat smash against the wall and scatter red paint everywhere. The thrown tin had left a dent on the wall along with the splatter of its innards.

"Henry, son," Will gently approached him. "It's okay."

"No, it's not okay!" Henry roared; his voice echoed.

"You're in shock, and also angry with what's happened. I'm here now." Henry allowed himself to drop to his knees and cover his face with both his hands in defeat. Will knelt down to comfort him, and for the first time hugged is son "I'm here. I'm not going anywhere. I'm not going to leave you ever again."

Aaron and Tabitha returned to see Will and Henry embracing one another. They both stared at the father embracing his long-lost son for a moment before deciding to leave them to it. They ran out of the glassless window and into sky of the night-time Birmingham.

By late morning, Kat stirred from sleep then sat up quickly when she realised that Will was still absent. Laura, on the other

195

hand, was sitting on the other side of the bed, writing in her notebook. She had stayed with her throughout the night to keep guard, whilst waiting for Will. She had tried phoning him multiple times in the night, but each attempted call would immediately go to voicemail, making it frustrating for Laura.

"Has he not come back yet?" Kat asked despite knowing the answer she was about to be given.

"No. I'm sorry." Laura looked at her with sympathy.

Kat became agitated and worried. "What if something has happened to him?! He should have been back by now!" Kat raced out of bed to get to the curtains so that she could take a peek at what the weather was like. The worst-case scenario was right in front of her. The sun beamed in the blue sky, brightening up the busy city of Birmingham.

"Kat! Close the curtains!" Laura screamed as she leapt away and hid by the side of the bed.

"Sorry! I'm going to go out and find him!" Kat closed the curtains, ran over and flung open her suitcase to grab a change of clothes.

"Where are you going to look? He could be anywhere! Plus, he's not going to be out in the daylight! Kat!" Laura got up and was instantly standing in front of her, holding her shoulders to prevent her from continuing.

"Let me go, Laura!" Kat commanded.

"Listen to me!" Kat obeyed Laura and stopped. She allowed Laura to speak. "I will try and call Will and see where he is. But you need to calm down about Will. He can take care of himself. Now, go and have a shower and get yourself dressed. I will call him, again." Kat took a deep breath to relax herself and nodded calmly. She picked up her clothes and walked into the bathroom, closing the door behind her. Laura picked up her phone from the bedside table and called Will. This time he picked up.

"Hello?"

"Where the fuck are you, Will? Kat is freaking out!" Laura remained calm, making sure that Kat couldn't hear her, but using her Police voice so that Will would know she was being serious.

"I. . . ran into some vampires last night and. . . I will

explain later, but please tell Kat that I am alright and that there's nothing for her to worry about."

Laura ignored his latter statement. "You found some vampires? Are any of them Mistress Claudette's servants?"

"No, they actually don't even know who she is!"

"Are they new-born vampires?"

"No."

"What? I thought all vampires knew who she was! Claudette is like the fucking queen of England of the Vampire world!"

"They have killed four of her servants to stay off the radar."

Laura couldn't believe a word Will was saying to her; her jaw dropped and hung for a moment before she could respond to his revelation.

"Are you for real? How is that even possible?"

"I will explain everything later. But please, make sure Kat knows that I am safe."

"When are you coming back? It's sunny as fuck outside!"

"I'll be back at the hotel by dusk. I promise. I'm not in any trouble." Will hung up the phone. Laura sighed and collapsed onto the bed, staring up at the ceiling in disbelief.

Five minutes later, Kat came out refreshed and fully dressed in her other pair of black skinny jeans and layered with two jumpers, one thick black wool jumper that was slightly baggy on her, over one that was fitted and high necked. Her hair was still wrapped around with a towel.

"Anything?" she asked worryingly.

"He's alright. He said he will be back at dusk."

"What was his excuse for not coming back?" Kat felt like a worried mother from continuously asking for his whereabouts and any updates.

"He came across some vampires that apparently don't know who Mistress Claudette is and were able to stay off her radar."

Kat was surprised to hear this. "Eh? He's found some vampires? Friendly ones I hope."

"He seemed confident that they were friendly, but he said he'll tell us more about it later."

Kat sighed with relief but was still slightly anxious about the state he was in, then saw herself in the mirror and looked at the state she was in too. Kat set to work on her make-up and blow-dried her hair to goth-ify herself, then left the hotel room to grab some brunch. She also did some exploring around the Bullring and went to the Oasis market to find the gothic shops. The Oasis was a Birmingham institution; part market and part hang-out with many floors going down into the underground, each floor had a variety of different stores for different items. It was like a maze in a building. There were shops selling statues, jewellery and accessories, expensive clothes that would make the bank accounts of the goths and emos go below zero, band merchandise such as posters, t-shirts, and CDs. After having some brunch and shopping for a new dress for tonight, Kat made her way back to the hotel. It was now three o'clock in the afternoon. In less than two hours, Will would hopefully be back at the hotel.

Will and Henry had set up a fort made of tarpaulin and timber to keep the sun from reflecting on them. Aaron and Tabitha decided to give Will and Henry some alone time by going up onto the next floor.

The father and son had spent the last thirteen hours talking about their lives. Will had told him the story about how he had met his mother and what he had been doing since he became a vampire; how he got the band together, and how he met Kat.

Henry had told Will about his time at school, his job training as an accountant before joining the army. He showed Will his army tags that he still had around his neck and had never taken off. Two circular stainless-steel tags, the size of a two-pound coin, were dangling from the rope that secured them containing his personal details. A trinket such as this would be destroyed by the Vamperium as it would prove evidence of their long-lasting existence.

He had also told him that he was not married and did not have any children, which surprised Will because he would have thought it was common for men to be married, with children at the age of twenty-four. He did, however, have a woman in his life who he had to leave behind as well.

"Her name was Marian. I had planned to marry her when I returned from the war, but, of course, it never came to be."

"I'm so sorry," Will grieved with him.

"She'd be in her eighties now. It was difficult for me to move on from our relationship, but I was just thankful to have spent our final night in the most wonderful of ways. Leaving her to fight the Germans, but never returning, assuming I was dead. I mean, technically, I am dead, but it's probably for the best to keep her safe."

Will had a theory that Mistress Claudette didn't know about Henry as he was in a foreign country, and whoever was the Head Vampire in Germany didn't find Henry in time. He got back to Birmingham the very same day as it was raining throughout the country. The pair of them had more in common than they could have expected. Both of them had left the love of their lives in order to protect them from what they had become.

"So, you play piano as well?" Henry laughed.

"Indeed, I can. We could do with a keyboard player for the band, if you're interested in joining us when we turn back to human?" Henry was surprised that Will would ask him to join his band after only knowing him for less than twenty-four hours. He felt appreciated, and it was all so strange that Henry had found a vampire that happened to be his father. What were the odds?

"You're going to have to explain this to the band first!" Henry laughed.

"And my girlfriend!" Will laughed along.

"Is she older than me?"

"She's twenty-four."

"Didn't expect her to be the same age as me!" Will and Henry both chuckled.

They were both still processing the revelation, one that the pair of them had wondered for many years. Will had always thought about what his son would have looked like by now, who he figured he would be almost one hundred years old or buried underground. He thought about what he would have done workwise; he wondered if he had been a blacksmith like his father, or was doing something else? He had hoped that his son would stay out of trouble and not be involved with anything illegal. He wondered what his grandchildren would have looked like, and if he ever got to see them in the future. All of that was now thrown into the back of his mind as fantasies.

Henry, too, had also wondered what his father would have looked like. He never knew his name, or even questioned it. He just wanted to continue his life like a normal person and even told his adoptive parents that he wasn't upset about it and understood why it happened. There was no reason for him to know who his parents were. He knew what had happened to them, to say the least, and he had no intention of looking up any photos or documents about him. The father and son felt they had found a part of themselves that had been missing for so awfully long.

"How do you hunt for blood?" Will asked him unexpectedly. "Do you just feed off of anyone you see?"

"No," Henry assured his father. "We hunt for people who are potential criminals. Tabitha would find us people in clubs and bars who spike people's drinks or are planning to harm someone."

"How does she know they would do that?"

Henry grinned quite proudly at his father. "The heartbeats of the criminal would accelerate at an immense rate due to the adrenaline of committing a crime, and I notice this whenever I see someone who is stalking someone or has done something criminal. She has managed to find us a couple of people a week, mostly on Friday evenings and weekends. A human's blood would last us a day, and then we starve ourselves for five days before we hunt again, much like lions." Will was very relieved to know that Henry wasn't a rogue vampire that did random attacks on people and was just as empathetic as he was. He couldn't help but be proud of his son for staying out of trouble, and prouder with being able to outmanoeuvre the Mistress's coven, which he found to be increasingly difficult.

"How do you hunt?" His son asked him back.

Will hesitated. "We do something similar, but we also feed off animal blood, which doesn't quite give us the same amount of nutrients and energy as human blood does, but it still gives us the satisfaction of being fed. We have killed humans before, but we do it at a minimum." Henry was fascinated with what Will was telling him. He hadn't thought of hunting animals or feeding from animal blood as an alternative. If it kept vampirism to a minimum and still gave them the feeding satisfaction, but with less power, it would have been more feasible for Henry and his coven, so he kept that in mind. Will suddenly remembered the person who assaulted Kat back in October, who Will had intuitively murdered right in front of her, which was how the chain of events began, the cornerstone of this butterfly effect.

"We have killed a few people in our lives. We extract their blood and place the blood into plastic flasks, as we cannot touch silver. We then hide the bodies."

"Do you have restrictions on who you kill? Like, do you kill murderers or villains?"

Again, the drunken came to mind.

"Yes. We never attack anyone at random," Will responded.

"The men that attacked Aaron, the people that harmed Tabitha, those were the most satisfying kills."

Will quickly changed the subject, "Did you still want to come to the show tonight?"

Henry grinned. "I wouldn't miss it for the world," he told him. "Me and the others will be there."

"You can come and meet the band. I'll introduce you to them, and, if you want to, and if the band agree to, you could join us on the rest of the tour and help us get our humanity back?"

Henry thought about it. He hadn't left Birmingham for quite some time and was itching to travel about with his new crew. Will grinned, being ever so proud of his vampire son.

An hour later and the sun was beginning to set, meaning the vampires could soon leave the building and Will could make his way back to the hotel. Will phoned Kat to let her know that he was on his way back. Kat was relieved.

"I've been worried you wouldn't come back!" she cried.

"I needed some time alone, I'm sorry," he said. "I'll be back shortly, okay?"

Kat nodded. "Okay."

"See you in a bit."

Henry, Aaron, and Tabitha agreed to meet the band at the Asylum venue later that evening.

"I'll see you all there. Just meet us outside the entrance at six o'clock for the sound check," Will told them. All three of them simultaneously nodded. Will took one last glance at his vampiric son, seeing Elizabeth's face in his features, feeling a strong ache in his body. He turned around and leaped out the window, landing directly down below and walked down the snowy streets of Digbeth. He entered Birmingham with a new girlfriend and would be leaving with a vampire son.

Kat was sorting out today's shopping when Will knocked at her door. Her chest tightened as he called for her to let her in. She ran to the door with anticipation. The other half of her soul was missing for some time and her anticipation to be in his arms had her eager to open the door to let him in as soon as possible. She momentarily opened the door and embraced him, holding onto him tightly and refusing to let go. Will embraced her back and saw Laura standing behind them looking displeased and her arms crossed to add further emphasis to her displeasure.

Will's eye caught Laura, staring impatiently. "What happened on your little broody walk last night, huh?" Laura queried like a mother to a teenager. Will let go of Kat, held her hand and gently dragged her into the hotel room. Laura phoned David and told him and Oliver join her in their room. The men arrived in a flash once Laura placed her phone into the front pocket of her jeans. Will sat on the bed whilst Laura, David, Oliver, and Kat stood above him to listen to what he had to say.

He told them about the encounter he had with another vampire and how he chased him through the city until they reached Digbeth, and he was then ambushed by two other vampires. He proceeded to tell each of their stories and how none of them knew who Mistress Claudette was, and how they were able to remain hidden from the Vamperium.

"One of them, Henry, who I assume is their leader, is someone I never knew I would ever meet." All four of them looked at Will with anticipation. They all thought about the people Will had mentioned from his past life; none of them were named Henry.

David was the first to break the silence, "What?"

Kat could feel her heart racing intensely due to the shocking realisation with who Will had found. "You found your son?"

Will dropped his head and nodded, still processing the revelation himself. It was all so surreal, and not just for him. Laura, David, and Oliver all looked at each other; their mouths slightly open, their eyes widened.

"How is that even possible?" Oliver asked him, being brave enough to ask the question, knowing how Will was going to be in pain explaining the story.

Will answered quietly, trying to keep his emotions in check, "He turned into a vampire in nineteen forty-five, when he was twenty-four years old. He was in the army fighting in Germany when a vampire attacked him."

Kat approached Will and sat on the bed next to him, placing her soft hand around his shoulder for comfort.

"This is pretty intense," said David, erratically. "Your own flesh and blood became the very same thing his father had become."

"Like father like fucking son," Will murmured under his breath, then loudly said, "I told them to come to the show tonight, so I hope you're all ready to meet my son and his two companions."

"Seriously?" Laura asked in shock. "Are you sure you want your vampire son to meet his dad's human girlfriend so soon?" She looked at Kat with concern, wondering what she was thinking about all of this. Kat pursed her lips. The idea of being a potential stepmother to someone the same age as her made her feel strange. Hearing the words 'dad' and 'human girlfriend' was something she didn't think she would ever hear in a single sentence.

"No, I want to meet him," Kat assured her. "Will told me he had never met his son, and now that he finally has met his own flesh and blood, I want to meet him."

"But aren't you worried that your son may try and flirt with your girlfriend? Maybe even sweep her off her feet?" David jokingly asked him. "Or feast on her delicious blood?"

"David," Oliver snapped.

Will ignored them as he continued thinking about Henry, his wife, his previous human life, a million thoughts raced through his mind simultaneously. He struggled to focus on a singular thought as one conquered the other instantly. He gently bit the tip of his thumb as he thought about the situation.

"Are you going to be okay performing tonight, Will?" Laura wondered.

"Oh, I'm not letting this get to me, don't worry! Best show ever, promise!" Will promised her, despite it being partially true. He got up from the bed and sighed. "It's going to be okay. Me and my son had a chat together for hours and had a catch up. We're both alright."

"Are you, or have you asked your son, if he would join us on our journey?" Oliver asked him. "Because I am positively sure that is something you would do."

"I told him I would talk to you guys about it first. I didn't make any immediate decisions. I do want them to. We could do with the extra strength to take on Claudette, especially since one of them is proficient at martial arts."

David nodded with a facial expression of approval; his lips dropped as he nodded. "Smart decision."

"Let's get ourselves fed and get to the Asylum venue! Less drama, more music!" Oliver clapped his hands together, making him and David leave the hotel room with Laura and Kat left behind. Kat looked at Will, concerned with the whole situation. Laura was also on the same boat as her, worried for her friend and his new discovery.

"How did you take the news when you first found out?" Kat didn't hesitate to ask.

"I was . . . shocked. But then I was happy. I had always wondered what my son would look like, and it exceeded my expectations." Will offered her half a smile and knelt down to her level, until his face was levelled with hers. He grabbed both her hands and kissed her on the lips. "I'm okay, I promise. Now, go and get yourself wrapped up and ready. We've got a gig to perform."

The band got into their van for the short drive to the venue and parked in the darkest part of the loading bay at the stage door. Kat was incredibly nervous at the prospect of meeting Will's son. Kat held onto Will's hand and tightened it as they approached the venue. She figured he would be nervous about his son meeting his girlfriend as she was. She wondered if vampires could feel nervous or anxious. She had no idea how she would react to him, or how to speak to him. She wondered what his personality was like, if he was as much of a gentleman as his father was; kind, caring, honest, protective, talented. Did Henry resent being vampire as much as Will did? Tonight, she was hoping to find all that out.

The band left the van, Will left hurriedly with eagerness to search the area in hopes of seeing if he could spot his son and his coven. All he could see were humans approaching the venue to queue up for the show despite being an hour before opening. Kat wandered towards Will who stood ahead of them on the pavement. He ignored the people passing through and continued his search for his son and his coven. The roofs of the buildings around them were empty. He expected to see them standing on the edge of one of them. As the rest of the band got their equipment from the van and headed into the building, with the help of some of the staff, Will and Kat held hands and made their way to the front of the venue to keep looking for Henry.

"Hey, Will!" He suddenly heard a familiar voice cry out from the distance, a young and enthusiastic tone, which made him smile right away and quickly turn around. Ahead of him were three vampires approaching them from the end of the street, waving their arm to indicate their presence. Kat was grasping harder on Will's hand, feeling mildly intimidated in meeting new vampires who may or may not be as loyal to humans as Midnight Devotion were. Her anxieties were mostly regarding their thoughts about Will being in a relationship with a human. She pursed her lips and steadied herself.

"You made it!" Will laughed joyously.

"Of course, we made it! We said we wanted to come to the show!" Tabitha cried with excitement. Kat had gotten more anxious as they got closer to them. She was often fine with meeting new people; she would meet new people most nights when she worked at the Golden Barrel pub, and even at these gigs selling band merchandise, but in this instance, she was nervous at meeting new people now, and she knew exactly why. These people weren't, of course, human. Will was surprised to allow them to approach Kat at such a close proximity without getting to know her scent. Maybe Will trusted them, or he knew being by her side at all times was going to add extra security in case one of them were to break their concentration.

"You must be Kat," Henry smiled cheerfully. Kat's chest tightened the moment her name was spoken. She gazed at the boy's features, seeing parts of her vampire boyfriend on him, even his smile was somewhat similar. "My father here has told me so much about you." Kat stood frozen; this was her first interaction with friendly vampires outside the band. She knew Will wouldn't have allowed this if he knew it wasn't safe for her or the attendees.

"Yes, and you're Will's son, Henry," she smiled as Henry offered to shake her hand. His cold hands shook hers, causing her to tremble slightly from the usual coldness of vampiric skin.

"We're not going to suck your blood or murder you if that's what you're worried about," Tabitha assured her. "I'm Tabitha, by the way! I take it you haven't met many of our kind in your life?" Tabitha spoke so casually and with confidence.

Kat nodded slightly. "I only met the band and that's basically it. I've known for few months." The quietness of her

tone indicated her nervousness as well as her rapid heartbeats.
Will placed his arm across her shoulders and pulled her closer
to him to add security.

"So, you're the vampire hunter," Aaron smirked
nervously. "I'm Aaron. I hope you don't slay us tonight."

Kat chuckled awkwardly. "I promise I won't, just
don't attempt to suck my blood and we're good." Henry,
Aaron, Tabitha, and Will chuckled simultaneously, making Kat
vastly blush, adding further pink into her cheeks which were
already showing through her foundation due to the coldness of
January.

"We need to go and get ourselves ready for the gig so
we shall see you guys inside," Will told them as he softly
grabbed Kat's hand.

"What time are you on?" Aaron asked him.

"We're the second act, so we will be on at half eight.
First band are on at half seven."

"Brilliant! We'll see you in a sec!" Tabitha cried with
enthusiasm. "By the way! I posted the event on my social
medias and many people have responded saying they want to
check it out! You are most welcome, old man!" Will smiled at
Tabitha before he and Kat walked away from the group, with
Kat still trembling from both nervousness and the January cold.

"Are you okay?" Will asked her, worried about her
state of mind.

"I'm. . . alright. Just a little cold," she lied. Will could
sense her nervousness by the way she was breathing heavily;
the pulse of her heartbeat had increased. The cold weather
would cover her shaking from anxiety, but Will could see right
through it. It almost next to impossible for Kat to lie to him.

David, Oliver, and Laura were already inside, waiting
backstage. They kept apart from the other two bands who were
already inside drinking and mingling with each other. One band
consisted of four members who were all male, each of them had
dark hair ranging from brown to black, one of them with a dark
red dye patch on the fringe that covered his right eye. They
were each wearing black skinny jeans and black tops, each with
a different style, from a tank top to a long sleeve. This rock

band were known as *Salem's Lot,* named after the Stephen King novel. They were the main act for tonight's gig.

The other band had three members; one girl who had short bright blue hair that was half shaven at the right-hand side and draped over the left-hand side of her head. Her outfit was more casual than what they have seen from other acts: a baggy white tee and black jean shorts that reached her knees.

The other two members were men; one had short light brown hair and other had thick dark brown hair. They were known as *Overture*, a pop punk band that recently formed through university students who were doing a degree in music. They both welcomed Midnight Devotion as they entered the building with their equipment. The vampire band kept it together and smiled nonchalantly. They were offered handshakes by the other bands, and because of the cold weather outside, it meant they could easily get away with shaking hands with other people and disguising it as cold weather.

All three bands introduced themselves, including Kat, calling herself the 'merch girl'. They had about forty-five minutes to relax in the backstage room before they opened the doors, but Kat had to get the merch store set up fifteen minutes prior to the opening time. She and Laura went to grab the merchandise from the van and made their way upstairs to get into the upper floor. The venue had two stage rooms: one large room that would run weekly alternative and metal raves on a Saturday, and the smaller room which was designed for decade dedicated music that is occasionally used for smaller acts to perform. The bands tonight were due to perform in the small room upstairs right above the large room.

They needed to set up the merch table at the end of the corridor around the corner from the stairs. The walls around them were plastered with stickers and band posters from bands within the subgenres of rock and metal. Some of the posters were advertising countrywide tours of well-known bands. The performance room was at the far end of the corridor. The room was the smallest room the band were going to perform at so far, but regardless of size, they just wanted to perform.

"Did you see Will's son earlier?" Kat casually asked Laura.

Laura ceased the unpacking and looked at Kat. "No? What's he like? And were you okay meeting him?"

Kat thought about their earlier encounter and how nervous she was. She quickly looked around the room to check that nobody was listening in on their weird conversation.

"He's quite a gentleman, much like his dad. But it's all so weird for me, having a potential stepson who is the same age as me, well, not technically, but he's twenty-four, but has been that age for like sixty-four years."

Laura laughed under her breath. "I would be weirded out a little as well, so I don't blame you one bit." Kat gave her a smile as she placed the CDs onto the table in a neat order.

Once it was seven o'clock, Overture got their equipment on stage. People began making their way up the stairs and into the performance room, some stuck around to check out the merch, some immediately went into the bathrooms. There was a bar in the corner of the performance room opposite the stage where people went to buy drinks.

Overture came on stage at seven thirty. The performance room was half packed with people. Kat could hear the music but couldn't see much of the performance. Henry, Tabitha, and Aaron approached Kat, causing her to jump slightly as she hadn't expected to see them this soon.

"Hey," she smiled awkwardly, trying to mask her anxieties. "Did you hypnotise your way in?"

"Wait, we can do that?" Aaron widened his eyes and looked at Tabitha. The pair of them laughed and looked back at Kat. "Just kidding. Of course, we did. We don't have much money so we may as well!" Kat shook her head and laughed.

"You need to support the independent artists, Aaron!" Tabitha laughingly groaned.

"How are you getting on with the merch? Made any sales yet?" Henry asked.

"Not many, but I've made quite a bit when we were in Cardiff and London. We're heading to Manchester after the gig. We usually go to the next city straight after the gig and "book" a hotel to avoid potential sunlight."

Henry picked up one of Midnight Devotion's CDs

from the table to examine it. He read the song list at the back and nodded.

"Can I buy this? I want a piece of my father's work."

"Of course!" Kat smiled. "Do you have a CD player or anything to play it on?"

"We can easily get one," he gave her a wicked wink as he handed her a ten-pound note. The coven made their way into the performance room to wait for Midnight Devotion to come on. The minute Overture were over, and the crowd had given them a standing ovation, they took their equipment and got off the stage. Oliver and David got onto the stage as soon as it was empty with their equipment and got themselves ready for their set. As soon as they had finish setting up, they walked out of the room to get themselves ready for their entrance.

Henry and his crew stood against the wall on the far right close to the stage. Whilst Henry was looking at the CD, Aaron and Tabitha were talking to each other, discussing how they felt about Kat. Tabitha was excited to potentially have new female friends; Aaron could see how nervous Kat was but liked her regardless, and not just because his friend's father was dating her. Aaron had a way of knowing who was kind-spirited and who was troublesome. Even before he became a vampire, he would have his human instincts tell him who to trust.

At half past eight, the lights dropped, and Oliver was the first to enter, followed by David. Laura gave Kat a smile as she passed the merch table and walked down the corridor. Will came from around the corner and gave her a quick kiss on the lips.

"Is Henry here?" he whispered.

"He is. He's pretty excited to see you perform," Kat kissed him back. "Go and show him what you've got!"

Will walked his way into the performance room, which was roaring with cheers from the audience. He quickly searched the room to spot his son, but the nervousness got to him and he pushed himself to get on stage as soon as possible. He casually grabbed the microphone that stood in the centre of the stage.

"GOOD EVENING, BIRMINGHAM!" Will screamed into the microphone the moment he grabbed it. The crowd welcomed them with intense cheering, a louder welcoming than the previous gigs. For starters, Will was distracted by trying to locate his son in the audience. His vampiric vision helped him locate him standing against the wall on his left-hand side. He was smiling, which made Will relax and continue his performance with pride. The crowd were loving the music. There were a lot of people dressed goth or punk tonight, which has been the norm for them during this tour. The performance was identical to the ones over the last two nights; but Will was even more animated. Forty-five minutes later, the band had finished, and Will made his way off the stage after thanking the audience for their support, and immediately approached Henry and his coven. He was happy to have seen his son enjoying his music.

"You were incredible!" Henry complimented. "And I'm not being biased either. I've not heard music like that before."

"Thank you," Will placed his hands in the pockets of his jeans and nodded.

"He bought your CD, by the way!" Aaron pointed at Henry.

Will was surprised to hear that. "You did?"

"I figured why not? You are my father after all and want to support you any way I can," Henry shrugged.

"I'm honoured," Will dropped his head with nervousness and honour. "I need to go grab a drink from the van, do you want to join us? Meet my band?"

"Yes please," said Tabitha. "Your guitarist is hot. Is he single?"

"Aw, Tabs!" Aaron rolled his eyes and laughed.

Chapter 18:
♥
Doubts

Will, Henry, Tabitha, and Aaron stood outside the venue by the band's van and waited for the others to come downstairs with their equipment. Will rushed around and hurried everyone so that they could all share a drink of blood and introduce the band to his son. Nervousness raced through Will. He knew that if his dead heart could beat, it would be immensely racing at the speed of a drummer for a death metal band: fast paced, loud, beating aggressively. Was Henry feeling the same way as he did?

David emerged from the venue with his guitar case at hand.

"Are the others coming down? We could do with a drink soon." Will casually asked.

"Shortly. Oliver is packing away the drum kit." David leaned his guitar case against the side of the van, then proceeded to look at Henry and the coven. He examined each of them carefully. "So, this your son?"

"Indeed, it is," Will grinned greatly, excited to introduce his son to his bandmates. He had thought about this moment throughout the day. Henry did an awkward wave.

"This is Henry Halstead. Henry, this is the guitarist of my band, even though I already told you from the introduction part of the gig, David Barrett."

"Pleasure to meet you," Henry offered to shake his hand, which David accepted.

"Likewise," David nodded.

"Hi! I'm Tabitha! I thought you were amazing!"

Tabitha marched over towards David and smiled, offering him her hand. David noticed her crimson red eyes, her skin immensely pale, her teeth pure white as she flashed a smile at him, her friendliness making him feel uneasy. He didn't think much of her: she seemed too modern and inconspicuous. David just shook her hand slowly and thanked her, his tone showing discomfort, which Tabitha failed to notice or ignore. Kat appeared from the venue and jogged across the loading bay to Will and the others.

"I've got a member of staff to cover for me whilst I went out for some fresh air," Kat gave half a smile before greeting Will with a quick kiss. Oliver and Laura finally left the venue with their equipment, and noticed Will, Kat, and David talking to a group of three. They walked over to them, assuming it was Will's son and his coven.

"Guys! This is my son, Henry Halstead. Henry, this is Oliver Stokes and Laura Bates."

Both Laura and Oliver each gave a welcoming smile and shook his hand.

"It's a pleasure to meet you, Henry," Oliver politely told him. He knew this meant an awful lot to Will, and he wanted Will to feel comfortable about the situation. He did, however, wonder how David would behave around him, that was his biggest concern.

"These are my friends, Aaron and Tabitha," Henry introduced them to Oliver and Laura with pride. They all shook each other's cold hands, which felt equal to each member. Oliver opened the back of the van to pack away the equipment and grab the vampires a drink of blood they had stored in a cooler. Kat felt like the pariah of the group being the only one who wasn't a super powered vampire. She hoped that this wouldn't be permanent if she would be able put an end to their perpetual existence.

"Are you going to be joining us on the journey? I assume Will has told you what we are getting up to, right?" Oliver asked them. Will looked at Oliver with gratitude; he knew that Oliver would respect Will about all of this. He had always been respectful towards people, no matter who they were. Patience was his strongest virtue.

"He has told us what you are all up to," Aaron told the band. "Kill some vampire bitch to become humans again? I am all game for that!"

"Me too," Tabitha added, still looking at David. "I've only been a vampire for three years, but I am already sick of it. I want to drink alcohol again and go to the beach on a hot summer day."

"We all have our reasons for wanting to be human again, and I am sure, with the help of Kat, we will hopefully achieve this." Laura was determined more than ever. Each day they were getting closer and closer to the date of the encounter, which gave them a sense of hope. Kat, on the other hand, was beginning to have second thoughts about it all. She doubted her abilities and she did not feel prepared at all. Yes, she did have some stakes and the cross Will had given her, but she felt as though this wasn't enough. There needed to be more weapons and equipment for her to use against a potential army of vampires. If the Mistress's vampires are over a hundred years old, chances are they were going to be much stronger than her vampire boyfriend and her newly acquired family. One vampire from that army could potentially be stronger than all members of Midnight Devotion combined. A sigh of nervousness left Kat. Will heard the increase of Kat's heartbeat in an instant from his acute hearing. He nudged her slightly to check to see if she was still present.

"Are you okay?" he queried with concern.

"I'm going back inside," she quickly averted herself from the group and traced her steps back into the building and back to the merch table. The warmth of the building comforted her. Her anxiety, on the other hand, was still present. She felt the heaviness within her like her heart was dangling an anchor underneath, dragging it down towards her stomach.

The third and final band for the evening, Salem's Lot, came on the stage and began playing their gig. Kat could see that the performance room was packed to the brim. The crowd bounced around in every possible direction, circling around to form an empty pit before colliding into one another. The band's music was Halloween-based with a mixture of modern rock music.

Will approached the merch stand where Kat was, looking anxious, which made her even more anxious because it meant that he knew something was up.

"Can I talk to you for a second?" Will offered his hand to her. She grabbed the last of the merch and boxed it up, then took Will's hand and left the empty table. He took her to the room backstage in the downstairs part of the building, where nobody was around for them to discuss what was needed to be said. The room felt odd after the crowded rooms above.

"You look worried, why is that?" Will wasn't upset with Kat, but it still made her feel uneasy. She knew that Will wouldn't get angry at her, however her anxieties begged to differ on that. She bit her tongue, but that only made her feel worse.

"I can't say, you'll be angry at me," Kat dropped her head in shame.

"Why would I be angry at you? You can tell me; I'm not going to hurt you. Kat?"

His pale hands cupped her cheeks, raising her head to look into his ruby-red eyes which immediately beamed down at her sapphire-blue eyes. For a fleeting moment, she wondered if Will would hypnotise her into telling him what was wrong, but she trusted him to never do that to her. He wanted the relationship to be as human as possible, as well as equal.

"Talk to me, please," Will begged.

Kat shook her head, letting Will release her from his gentle grasp. She moved herself away from him, and faced the opposite direction, ashamed of her emotions. She could feel the intensity of her emotions building up; the tears flooding around her eyes.

"I'm beginning to have my doubts about this," she finally confessed, her head still facing the grey carpet, her arms folded together as tightly as she could manage. Despite being inside, she was still very cold from having anxiety running through her thoughts. "I'm not sure I am ready to face such a dangerous task. I'm not prepared for this, and I'm not sure why, because I was so determined before, but now I'm going in the opposite direction. This doesn't have anything to do with meeting your son, but I do feel a little left out slightly because I'm not like you guys, and I cannot relate to any of you." Kat still couldn't look at Will; it would break her heart to see him look so disappointed in her. The thought of it brought tears to her eyes. She tried insanely hard not to let a single drop out and soak the carpet and mess up her make up.

Will, however, could sense the salt of her tears developing. He chose not to say anything about it and allowed Kat to spill out her emotions and express what was going on in that beautiful human mind of hers.

Kat sniffed and said, "I'm not usually this doubtful of myself, but this is the most difficult thing I have ever had to prepare for, and I don't even know what to do once it happens. I need training, or at least some form of preparation. I mean, isn't this what the tour was about? Preparing and planning for the encounter once we reach Scotland? We have barely planned this entire trip and we will be in Glasgow in two days." The more words that escaped Kat's mouth, the harder it had gotten for her to stop. She paused for a moment to regain her emotional balance before continuing. Her mouth quivered, her chest became heavier every second as the pain of holding in her tears became uncomfortable.

"I know you finding your son is a massive deal to you, and I couldn't be happier that you got given back what you had lost, but I am currently feeling ever so lonely." The latter word made her tear up even more. She was worried that her makeup was going to smudge all over her face and make her look a mess. A hand was right in front of her that contained a piece of white, soft fabric paper. Kat looked up and saw Will handing her something to wipe away the black tears that had blended with her eyeshadow and eye liner.

"Thanks," she sniffed, taking the tissue, and wiping the tears away before blowing her nose.

"You don't have to hide anything from me," Will assured her, placing both his hands on each of her shoulders to comfort her. "I understand where you are coming from, and I am sorry we haven't prepared you properly. But I promise, after tonight, we will get you prepared and taught."

216

Kat nodded slowly. "You are right, and it's not your fault; we've been side-tracked with touring and site seeing and finding old relatives we didn't know were still alive and fighting a vampire in a football stadium." Will chuckled, making Kat feel calmer knowing that he wasn't upset with her.

"To tell you the truth, I've been so excited with being in an actual band and performing on stages and making music. It's made me feel more human than ever. Not only that, but I also get to share these moments with the woman I love." Kat smiled graciously before looking at the ground, blushing immensely at his comment. "And, whilst we're being honest here, I am also scared."

Kat quickly looked at Will, bewildered at the fact a vampire - a strong, monstrous creature - was scared. "Why are you scared?"

"I'm scared that if I turn human, I will be a totally different person, that you won't recognise me. I'm worried that you've gotten too used to me being. . . this," Will gestured his hands up and down his body to show himself. "What if turning human will change my personality and my way of thinking?"

Kat took a moment to think about what he had said. She knew where he was coming from and understood the whole idea of change. Will wanted to change for his benefit, not hers, she knew that. He had his mind set on turning back human since the day he turned, and that mindset had never changed, despite him losing hope. He would risk anything to be human again, even if it meant changing his personality or way of thinking. However, he was now worried about how his personality will change, and how Kat may not look at him the same way she did when she first met him.

"You can't know that until it happens," she assured him, bringing herself closer to him without hesitation. "And, even if you do change, it'll be for the better, I am sure of it. I fell in love with Will Crowell, not the idea or personality of Will Crowell. I love ALL of you, no matter who or what you are, or what you become."

Hearing Kat tell him that she loved him gave him hope. She felt his cold lips pressed against her exposed forehead, which made her shiver with cold excitement.

"I love you too," Will told her with a reassuring smile. "This may sound scary, but I wanted to experience a normal relationship during this trip. If the worst-case scenario happens when we face Mistress Claudette, then I would die not having any memories to look back on when my life flashes before my eyes if that does actually happen. Should this happen, then I want all those memories to be of us, our times together. If you get killed, I will live with the guilt for the rest of my existence. And I know what we both signed up for, but I am still terrified that you're going to get killed."

Will and Kat stared at one another. Both their souls were frightened of the possible outcome of their mission, but knowing that they will be together until death meant it was inevitable no matter what the outcome were to be.

"I'm thankful we've got to spend this time together and be a couple in various parts of the trip, but I still think we need to focus on the inevitable, especially if we are now on the hit list after London's incident," Kat said in a serious manner.

"I know. We're going to stick around until half eleven and then we will drive to Manchester. Tomorrow, we will start getting you prepared and ready for vampire killing," Kat nodded and went to embrace Will. She still felt anxious about the whole thing but was less anxious knowing that Will was going to help her.

Chapter 19:
♥
Weakness

The band stuck around watching Salem's lot. The crowd went mental for the punk music played, mosh pits were formed and continued until a song ended. The finale song of the set blew up in the small performance room with most of the crowd shouting along and pogoing on the spot in unison.

After Salem's Lot had finished, all three bands had a chat about what they had going on next; the Salem's Lot musicians were going to go on a hiatus after the tour saying they were loving it but were nearly burnt out, whereas Overture were going straight into the studio to make a new album after the tour had ended. Midnight Devotion explained that they weren't a hundred percent sure what they were going to do and had to join in the chat, even though they had a clear plan: they were going to attempt to kill the Head Vampire of the United Kingdom to become humans. Laura explained that they needed to record these songs and they wanted to do some festivals too. All three bands left the building, and a crowd of fans were waiting outside to get photos of themselves with the members and paying them compliments.

Tabitha, Aaron, and Henry were waiting by the van. Kat walked over to them and watched the band being bombarded with newly developed fans who admired their music.

"Looks like your boyfriend is pretty popular," Aaron smirked.

"Can't blame him; he is a good-looking guy," Tabitha commented.

Henry wanted to jokingly remind her that she was saying his father was good-looking, but kept it to himself, focusing on the joy his father was giving to people. Music brought people together, and this moment was one to celebrate and share. It was something that healed people, gave people something to talk about, and it has given people the strength to go on.

After about half an hour of photos, compliments, laughter and joy, the band bid farewell to their newly formed fans, and the other two bands, then got into the van. Henry, Tabitha, and Aaron sat at the back with Laura and David. They would lean forward against the seat and rest their arms on the headrest so they could talk to the others.

Tabitha tried to make conversation with David, trying to impress him by talking about herself. She would occasionally ask about him, and he would respond ambiguously. This went on for about half an hour and Oliver couldn't help but laugh slightly that David had to put up with it as it was he that usually did all of the talking. Kat curled up in her blanket whilst leaning against Will as he wrapped his arm around her. Henry, Tabitha, and Aaron all viewed Birmingham one last time before they left the city; the dark streets that they had grown to know over the years of being vagabond vampires.

Laura spoke to Henry and Aaron, asking them about their first few years as vampires and how they managed to hide from the Vamperium. Henry had informed her that he was in Germany at the time he was turned, and immediately went back to England and hid in Birmingham, making sure that no one he knew was nearby when he went hunting. Henry also told her that he had spent fifteen years in Ireland before returning to England and hibernating in Birmingham again. Every visit he made to the city it would have always been revamped and to fit with the relevant decade; the buildings would be modernised, and the transportation would be more advanced than before.

"Do any of you know how to drive?" Laura asked them.

"Aaron does, I don't," Henry responded.

"Beside Oliver, who else here can drive?" Aaron queried.

"I can," said Laura. "I had to drive as part of my role as a police officer."

"You were in the police force?" ask Aaron, enthusiastically.

"David?" Tabitha nudged him, despite knowing full well that he wasn't part of the conversation. He turned his head away from the window to look at Tabitha, who was still smiling at him.

"Oh, erm, yeah, I can," David said with absolutely effrontery.

The journey was the most pleasant one on the tour so far. Will couldn't help but smile graciously at the hearing of his bandmates getting along with his son and his friends. The Midnight Devotion family was expanding.

After a couple of hours on the M6 motorway, they arrived in Manchester, in the half-light of the streetlamps it looked a lot like the other cities. Will nudged Kat awake to get her ready for the move from sleeping in the van to sleeping in another hotel.

Laura had booked in the fanciest hotel they could afford, thinking that by now they would need some proper undisturbed privacy. Oliver parked in the multistorey car park of the hotel. The band, Kat, and Henry's coven all left the van and made their way down the stairs to get to the bottom floor where the street was.

"We have enough money to get rooms for you guys too. Go ahead with Will and I'll get you sorted out." Laura counted the cash from the gigs so far and made neat piles of twenties.

The hotel was something straight out of a movie with brand new modernist-industrial fittings and colours. Will and Laura approached the night receptionist who was a middle-aged man wearing a fancy uniform with a small pillbox hat and stripes around the lapels. Henry, Tabitha, and Aaron were silent, awed at the possibility of staying in such a place.

Henry and Aaron, David and Oliver had their own

room with two double beds, Laura and Tabitha stayed together also with two double beds, and Will and Kat stayed together in their room with a queen bed. Tabitha was having her first bath in three years, filled to the brim, she slipped under the waters and stayed cocooned most of the night, playing music from her phone and singing along to the lyrics.

"I'm going to go and freshen up before going back to sleep again," Kat smiled at Will. He leaned down to kiss her lips before placing his suitcase on the foot of the bed. Kat went into the bathroom to get changed and wipe off her make up. She unhooked the silver cross she wore underneath her shirt to hide it from the band and placed it in the box that came with it. Once Kat had showered, she pulled on one of the hotel robes from the back of the bathroom door and left to find Will standing by the large window. She walked over and stood next to him, and her clean hand found his, straining at what his eyes could see clearly in the last of the night.

Thousands of lights coming from the windows of buildings and the streetlights down below. The snow began to fall from the skies, making the view more elegant and comforting. Kat tried to imagine what being cold like the snow was like to Will and his friends. Was everything just physically numbing to them?

They both glanced at the magnificent view of the city of Manchester and turned to watch the lights of a low plane flying towards the horizon. Kat pulled Will round to face her, then pushed up onto her tiptoes so that their eyes were levelled, and her lips could find his. He gave in to the temptation and kissed her back with further passion. Her fingers slid through the buttons of his shirt to gain access to his icy cold skin.

"Are you sure you don't want some sleep?" Will asked, with a laugh within his tone. "We just did a long drive." Kat ignored him and proceeded to kiss him vehemently, pushing him onto the large double bed and laid on top of him, asserting her dominance.

"I know you said you didn't want to have sex as a vampire, but I would like to at least try and experience what it's like to be close to you. We don't have to perform anything. . . penetrable."

Will responded with a nod, "I said no before I really knew you, but now I want to know you more," and lent forward to kiss her again. Kat's heart raced from the unexpected answer from Will. She chose not to question it to ruin the moment.

He stroked her gently from her neck and down her spine. They slowly made their way to her hips and slid into the robe and around her naked waist.

"I haven't felt warmth like this in years," Will whispered softly into her ear. "Right now, I feel nothing but joy and hope, and it's all thanks to you."

Kat slowly wriggled her shoulders free of the robe until her breasts were exposed and arched her back upwards to look Will in the eye. Kat pulled Will upwards until they were both sitting upright on the bed. The apprehension of being connected to Will skin to skin overtook her. She unbuttoned his shirt until his bare pale chest was available for her to touch. She stroked his empty chest and then immediately went for the neck, and began kissing his cold hard skin, causing him to groan with pleasure and causing her to shiver from his coldness.

His hands remained around her waist, causing her to shiver again, but the contentment helped warm her body as she was itching to be close to him. She pushed him back down onto the mattress and sheets and continued to give him bliss by kissing his sensitive areas, making him groan and wanting more. She took charge of their communion and made sure that she was indeed the dominant one. Will could just as easily have taken control, but he knew that doing so could cause physical harm; he wanted her to take the lead. Kat was glistening with sweat, and Will could smell her excitement and couldn't stop himself from giving in to her. The closeness he had longed for was finally there. He arched his waist upwards so that he could unbutton his jeans, but Kat beat him to it the moment he moved his waist. She hurriedly grabbed the linings of his underwear and jeans together and pulled them down to his knees. She never took his eyes off him as he wiggled them off his legs and let them land onto the floor. She felt his excitement poking her genitals, making her feel further excitement and urgency for them to come into contact with her inside.

Kat glared down at Will. He slowly opened his eyes to reveal his light grey irises and gazed upon her brilliant blue eyes. Her hands touched both sides of his face, handing her a tiny shock through her fingertips and the palms of her hands.

She slowly pushed herself down and let out a loud gasp as he went inside her.

"Does it hurt?" Will asked with concern.

"No. It's just. . . you feel amazing," Kat whispered, her warm breath breezing onto his lips, which encouraged him to collide them onto hers to gain more of her warmth. The coldness of his skin tingled through her, making the experience more exciting for her. She began to slowly thrust herself repeatedly, with Will raising his waist to go deeper into her warm human body. He lightly grasped her waist with the urge to grasp tighter when they picked up the pace, but he maintained his control and kept himself at a gentle level of pleasure.

This was a blissful and emotional moment for the lovers, and it ended with both of them letting out a strong and powerful sigh, followed by heavy breathing once they were finished.

When their communion ended, Kat fell asleep on Will's bare chest. Will pulled the covers over to keep her warm from his cold skin. He stared at the white painted ceiling, contemplating the events that had occurred since he met Kat amazed at what had happened, not just tonight but in the months since they met, and of the possibilities of what lies ahead for them. He gazed at his sleeping partner who slept peacefully after the eventful twenty-four hours she'd had. He took in the scenery of their first physical connection, and how beautiful and successful it was. He was more pleased that his vampiric instincts didn't overtake him, which could have ended in a bloodbath. He didn't feel anything remotely close to bloodlust or hunger when he was with her.

In one night, he had regained his son, and had become physically close to the woman, a human woman, that he loved with all his dead heart.

For the first time in many years, Will was genuinely

happy and content; he smiled and closed his eyes, but rather than dreaming, he was deep in thought of what was yet to come.

The next morning, Kat was woken up by a knock at the door from room service with breakfast. Will was gone but she was getting used to that. This gave her the opportunity to text her parents and let them know that she was healthy and happy. Her father would often message her questions about the phone and how he could do certain things on there, to which Kat managed to offer guidance like his own personal technical support assistant. She heard the clunk of a card key unlocking the door which caused her to look up from her phone. Will had bought more coffee and the smell of the morning air was fresh on his coat.

"Are you trying to fatten me up or something?" Kat giggled, itching to get a bite of the pancakes, her sweet tooth intensified.

"You're going to need the extra energy for today," he told her. "We're going to have a meeting in this room with the others and start planning our next move for when we reach the hideout. We need to show you the ropes of how vampires function and what they're weak against. It's important for you to remember everything we tell you." Kat nodded, listening whilst devouring the delicious pancakes.

"Last night was amazing," Kat told him. "How do you feel about it?"

Will's smile grew the more he thought about it.

"I'm quite glad I opposed to abstinence and decided to consummate the relationship," he chuckled. "I haven't been that physically closed to anyone in long time. I assume it was good for you too, since you fell asleep immediately after."

"It was the best I've ever had," said Kat, after drinking some of her coffee. "And I'm not just saying that to be biased and stroke your ego; I've been physically connected with a couple of guys in the past, but you were the more memorable experience. Who knew that sex with a vampire could be so. . . exhilarating!" Will shook his head and laughed. "Can we go for round two later tonight?"

Will's eyes widened, but his smile remained present. "I'm up for that." He gave her a quick kiss before leaving her to eat her breakfast.

After eating, Kat showered and got dressed whilst Will got the band and Henry's coven together in the hotel room. David, Oliver, and Laura were sitting on the sofa next to the window, the curtains were draped shut to cover up any potential daylight. Henry, Aaron, and Tabitha stood in front of the curtains. Tension rose as soon as Kat walked out of the bathroom, dressed in her black jeans and laced T-shirt. She walked over to Will who stood in front of the television stand and placed his arm around her shoulder.

"We have roughly less than a week until we reach Ben Nevis," Will informed the vampires in a serious presented tone of voice. "We need to start planning our manoeuvre."

"And by manoeuvre, you mean 'training Kat to become the ultimate vampire killer'?" David asked with his usual sarcastic tone. He expected Laura or Oliver to aggressively nudge him as a warning, but they were nodding expectantly.

"After our gig in Glasgow, we need to spend an extra night or two at the hotel and get Kat geared up and ready. Today, I want us to help Kat understand the anatomy of vampires and how she could use their weaknesses to her advantage." Everyone in the room looked at Kat, causing her heart to skip a beat with the sudden attention from the vampires. Were they waiting for her to add anything to that?

"Yesterday I told Will that I don't feel prepared for the ultimate fight with Mistress C," she spoke aloud without thinking about what the best thing to tell them was. She was anxious about how they would take the news that she had no confidence in the plan since she wasn't properly prepared. "I can't go on a vampire killing spree without an actual plan. Some of you have actually been to the hideout, you know what to expect, and I assume you know or have memorised the layout of the hideout?"

Laura nodded as a response, which didn't surprise Kat one bit.

"I can draw up a floor plan for you. I was there for some time having multiple meetings when Sven took me in. One of the advantages of being a vampire is having a strong recollections of memories. I remember the place like I was there yesterday."

Will was thankful that Laura contributed to this idea. She was right though: vampires did have intense memory recollection and never had trouble with forgetfulness.

Will took up the conversation, "If Laura draws up the floor plan of the hideout, the others and I will discuss weaknesses and what each of us will be responsible for." He never saw himself as a leader, not even when he was a human, he often found himself following orders, but this was his time to shine as the leader of his plan.

"David, could you please stand in front of me for a minute."

David gave Will a perplexed look, like he was being told by a teacher to stand in front of the class for a presentation. He shrugged his shoulders and got up from the sofa. He stood awkwardly in the centre of the area in between the television stand and the sofa for whatever Will had planned.

"A lot of media illustrates vampire weaknesses mostly identical to our type of vampires, however, we have many different aspects that are not depicted in folklore. For example: we can be killed by being stabbed in the heart, which is not beating at all, but is the cornerstone of the human anatomy as well as the vampire anatomy." Will pointed to David's chest where his non-beating heart rested within. "A wooden stake to the heart or something silver with a sharp tip will work for an instant kill. The same can be said for the brain." Will tapped the centre of David's crown. "Stabbing the brain kills the vampire also."

David paid no attention to Will but was focused on Kat who attentively watched Will explain vampire anatomy to her.

"We also have the instant killer known as decapitation since the brain is still active despite not having blood running in our veins. Not only that, but vampires cannot regenerate after decapitation. Using silver to decapitate a vampire is your best bet as it's an instant kill." Will placed the palm of his hand on top of David's head to illustrate decapitation, which caused him to roll his eyes upwards awkwardly, intimidating strangulation, which made Tabitha the only one in the room to giggle a response to his silly humour.

"Can vampires decapitate one another with their bare hands?" Kat raised her hand.

"Oh yeah! It's possible to do!" Henry responded, which took Will by surprise, like he had first-hand experiences of pulling the head off a vampire. He figured it must have been when he fought Claudette's workers.

"So, vampires can reconnect their limbs if they're ripped off?" Kat asked him, surprised to know that this was possible.

"Yes," Will nodded. "None of us ever had to deal with ripped limbs, thankfully. We would take the limb and place it in its original place and our body fixes itself after some time."

"You don't know that for sure," Aaron teased.

"Have you had your limbs ripped off?" Oliver jokingly asked with curiosity.

"Nah. I'm just joking with you," Aaron chortled.

"I haven't, if that helps," Tabitha raised her hand, still looking at David. Everyone looked at Henry, who turned his head left to right when David turned to look at him.

"Oh. Sorry," Henry shook his head. "I have actually had my leg ripped off by another vampire when I got into a fight ten years after I turned. It was excruciatingly painful, but I had the upper hand and got them decapitated with my arms." Will was stunned to hear that his son experienced an amputation. He imagined his son screaming in agony, which then led to sudden flashbacks of his wife screaming as she gave birth to their son. The painful memory was immediately pushed away as Will shook his head and focused on the present.

"As I was saying," Will cleared his throat. "Decapitation and stake to the heart or brain are instant kills. Now, let's talk fire."

David then hesitated when he heard the word *fire*.

"Do NOT do a pyrotechnics demonstration on me!" he

cried. "I may be hot but not flaming hot!" Laura and Oliver chuckled under their breaths, which made David turn to give them a stern look of annoyance. Tabitha laughed along but was much louder than the others.

"So, fire is bad?" asked Kat and everyone else nodded gravely. "Just like the sun."

David spoke up, being serious, "Think about sunlight, think how cold we are. Fire is quick and always fatal. It would be like putting a flame torch onto an ice cube. We would turn into ash rather than water!"

"I have another question," Kat tried to lighten the tone. "Garlic and holy water: I know you said religious symbols and certain words trigger vampires, but does holy water do just as much damage?"

"Excellent question, Kathryn," Will approached her and turned towards the group. "Holy water does indeed deal partial damage. Granted, if you throw holy water at a vampire's face - particularly in the eyes - you'll have the advantage of taking them out much more swiftly as you will have made them partially blind. So, if you do get your hands on holy water, throw it in the eyes or on the skin, and proceed to stab them in the chest. Holy water is like a corrosive liquid!"

"Though Garlic doesn't actually affect us," Laura added. Kat was very surprised to learn that garlic, the most common weakness for vampires in media, wasn't effective towards them.

"One other thing," Oliver stood up and approached David. "I recommend you put holy water on something that'll spray at close proximity, like a water gun or a pump spray people use on plants, or what hairdressers use on people's hair."

"Like in *The Lost Boys!*" Kat laughed, pointing at Oliver.

"Exactly like *The Lost Boys!*" Oliver chuckled along, pointing back at her. "I'm glad you remembered that!"

"Or in that one episode of *Tales From The Crypt* about the vampire security guard," Kat laughed.

"You could use the spray bottles that people use on

cats and dogs when they misbehave," David told her.

"Yes, that too," Oliver pointed at David without turning. "Obviously, it'll have to be something small enough for you to carry and to hide away."

Kat thought back to the summers in Southampton, with the kids and their pump-action water guns; they could be ideal.

"So, we've got the weaknesses established, now we need to devise the plan on how we are going to get Kat into the hideout and defeat the vampires." Will clapped his hands together to grab their attention. "Kat and I are going to go shopping in a bit, weather depending, otherwise Kat will have to go out by herself, worse-case scenario, to grab some supplies and gear."

"I'm going to look so badass, Van Helsing style!" Kat smirked, knowing she was being partially embarrassing.

"Can I come along too?" Tabitha pleaded. "I want to go shopping for some new threads for tonight's gig. Manchester will be full of different shops and styles!"

"If the weather isn't sunny, then sure thing! If anyone else wants to come, they're more than welcome to!" Kat told the vampires. Tabitha had hoped that David would tag along but hadn't gotten her hopes up too high knowing how distant he was. Henry and Aaron wanted to come with them, whilst Laura and Oliver wanted to stay behind to get their equipment ready for tonight, as well as having Laura draw up the floor plan of Mistress Claudette's hideout. David quietly informed them that he wanted to go off on his own, which disappointed Tabitha since she wanted to spend some time with him and get to know him more.

"We'll meet back here at five o'clock on the dot," Will demanded. "Get tonight's gig out of the way and then immediately make our way to Glasgow."

Chapter 20:
♥
Manchester

The weather in Manchester was damp and dreary, perfect for the vampires to go out and enjoy their time in the city. The snow was still thick, but the drizzle was melting through the ice, leaving pavements slippery for Kat, but it wasn't an issue for the vampires since their bodies were heavier and not prone to clumsiness. Kat was itching to go to Affleck's Palace shopping centre, which was quite a walk to get to from the hotel, but it was worth it for the multiple stores they had inside. The building had three floors, each with multiple independent stores and small rooms that had independent sellers who sold chic clothing and nostalgic memorabilia.

There was a music shop where Will and Henry immediately went to have a look through the vinyl collections. The pair of them introduced each other to some of the music they enjoyed and found themselves having similar music taste, especially during the eighties. Whilst the vampire father and son were browsing through music records, Kat and Tabitha were looking at the small shop of goth ornaments and decorations. The pair of them were discussing their favourite horror movies: Kat's favourite was *A Nightmare On Elm Street* and Tabitha's was *The Texas Chainsaw Massacre*. Kat was surprised that she was into horror given her quirkiness, but Tabitha informed her that looks don't defy a person's interest. The most colourful looking person could be into the darkest stuffs.

The girls went into a clothing store on the bottom floor where alternative and gothic clothing were sold. Kat bought herself a new pair of black and purple striped jeans, along with a tight black t-shirt with a creepy white rabbit on the front. She also purchased a pair of black laced fingerless gloves, along with two silver crosses, making sure they were out of site from Tabitha. Kat had the distinctive idea of having her hands containing crosses and easily revealing them to the vampires when she needed them to halt.

Aaron went into the small retro video game store that contained classic games as well as memorabilia that he used to own and play. He missed out on playing modern video games and was looking forward to catching up with what he had missed out on over the years if he were to survive the mission.

Once they had finished shopping, Kat grabbed some lunch from a nearby restaurant. She ate her Katsu chicken and rice whilst the others were laughing away at the table having conversations, which made Will smile at Kat with gratitude. He thought about how she is the reason this is happening, if he hadn't met her, he wouldn't have found his son and found his chance to potentially become mortal again. For the first time in his existence as a vampire, he didn't resent what he was. If he hadn't become a vampire, he wouldn't have found Kat, or have found the band, his *family*.

David had wandered off to get supplies from the music instrument shop as the touring and practising meant new strings and sticks were essential.

"Can I ask: what is David all about?" Tabitha finally asked Will and Kat. "He seems. . . inconsiderate? It's like he doesn't want to be there or talk to anyone? 'Antisocial' might be the best word to describe him?"

Will dropped his head and let out a light chuckled.

"David is a complicated guy," he began telling her. "He doesn't want to become human like we do. He wants to remain a vampire and keep his abilities."

"Does he not have something worth being human for then?" Henry asked.

"He didn't have anything before, and the only thing he has at the moment is the band. He's ambitious with the band, but he doesn't think this mission is worth sacrificing his immortality and abilities. He wants both." Will just shrugged his shoulders. Tabitha was nodding her head, still a little hesitant about David's petulance.

"Do you think he act sarcastic and funny as a cover up to his problems, like, a coping mechanism?" She queried.

"That wouldn't be a surprise," Aaron thought aloud. "The guy seems like he has demons within him that he wants to hide rather than confront."

"It's possible, but we accept him and gloss over most of his backbiting; it comes out in his playing, and we value that." Will laughed.

"Maybe he just needs someone to talk to?" Tabitha suggested. "I mean, someone who can listen to what's going on in his mind?"

"'Are you suggesting that you be his therapist?" Henry asked her with laughter in his tone.

"I mean, Kat does have a psychology degree, so she could undertake being his therapist!" Will lightly nudged Kat's shoulder. She smirked and lightly shook her head.

"I don't think he'd appreciate it," Kat muttered with her mouth full.

"I suppose so. But he does seem distant, judging from what I've seen since we've been travelling with you guys."

"You've only known the guy for less than twenty-four hours and you already think something is up with him and you want to try and decode his thoughts?" Aaron seemed confused with Tabitha's intentions with getting close to David. "I mean, you said last night at the gig that you though he was hot, but I honestly don't think he's healthy for you, Tabs. I sense some strong red flags with that guy."

"I don't. . . want to date him," Tabitha denied, dropping her head down to look at the table and avoid looking at the others, making it more obvious to them that she is in denial. "I just want to understand what his deal is."

"You can do better, Tabs, trust me," Kat pointed her fork at her.

After lunch, the gang made their way out and headed back to the hotel. Will and Kat were holding hands whilst walking, with Henry, Tabitha, and Aaron walking behind.

Laura and Oliver stayed behind to plan the assault on the hideout. They had mapped out a plan of the floors and made lists of places they would need to go through in case they separated or something were to happen. The table was covered in sheets of paper from their notebooks.

The others came back from their shopping trip into the large, warm hotel room.

"We've just finished drawing up the floor plans," Oliver lifted one of the sheets and waved it in the air enthusiastically.

"Brilliant," Will grinned. He, Kat, and Henry went over to the sofa to have a look at the floorplans.

Tabitha launched herself onto the bed, whilst Aaron went into the mini fridge and pulled out a plastic flask of blood. The cold thick liquid slid down his throat, and he could feel his body quicken, which made him shudder delightfully from the elegant taste of blood, releasing a long refreshing gasp once he had finished.

"De-fucking-licious!"

Everyone in the room let out a laugh except for Tabitha. She noticed that David hadn't returned yet. She chose not to say anything, even though she was itching for answers, hoping that he was alright. She continued playing on her phone to distract herself.

"Has David not come back yet?" Kat asked, which made Tabitha flinch slightly.

"Nah, he'll be back before the gig, or before the sun makes an appearance!" Oliver answered as he gathered the sheets together and passed them to Will, who sat on the sofa with Kat sitting on his lap.

Tabitha leaned over to Aaron and grabbed the last of the blood flask from him.

"What?" she asked, sourly.

"Nothing," Aaron shook his head, knowing well what was up with her, but chose to stay quiet.

Kat played with Will's black hair, whilst he was looking attentively at Laura's drawing of the floor plan. It was sketched out professionally; neat, clear, and easy to understand.

"Is the hideout some sort of castle?" Tabitha asked the vampires.

"Kind of," Laura told her.

"Kind of?"

"It is a castle. . . inside the mountain."

"Inside? What? How? That's pretty cliché! Very villainous indeed. So, how do you get into the mountain hideout?"

"You get to the top of the mountain," Laura answered.

"Of course," Aaron jokingly commented whilst rolling his eyes.

"At the top of the mountain, there is a stone cairn. Vampiric blood must be spilt onto it to open the entrance. A set of stairs leads halfway down the mountain to where the castle is." Will pointed his index finger on the paper and followed Laura's instructions, making sure Kat was watching him.

"Vampires can bleed?" asked Tabitha, shocked from the realisation.

"They do," said Laura. "It's difficult for a vampire to have its skin torn open. But the coven has their way of getting vampiric blood and using it to gain entry to the hideout."

Kat thought about the process of gaining entrance to the hideout. It was going to be difficult to get vampiric blood without doing real harm to one of the band members. The idea of her harming one of her vampire friends had left her feeling uneasy.

"What weapons does Kat currently have?" Oliver queried. "Besides wooden stakes?" Everyone in the room turned to look at Kat, who remained seated on Will's lap.

She glanced upwards and quickly answered, "I have some stakes and some silver crosses today. I lack holy water though," Kat informed him. "I will need to get some from a church within the next forty-eight hours."

"Glasgow should have plenty of churches," Will informed her. "It'll just be weird for you to request for some holy water."

"Can't she steal some?" Tabitha wondered.

235

"I mean if they still have holy water available in basins within the church. But it would be weird for her to take lots of bottles and fill them up with holy water." Will looked up at Kat, wondering what she thought about the idea.

"I'll find a way to sneak some out," Kat kissed the top of Will's head before leaping off the sofa to go to the bathroom.

Once she washed her hands, she heard the door to the room open and then close. She hurriedly washed her hands and opened the bathroom door a crack. Kat saw a broody looking David with his back against the front door looking aggravated and fidgety. He turned to face Kat when she opened the bathroom door, making her feel more anxious. His eyes were shining red as the large light of the bedroom beamed onto him. Had he been feeding off human blood whilst he was out? He stepped towards the bathroom door, not acknowledging Kat's presence. She stepped out of the way, and they swapped places. David locked himself in the bathroom, and Kat stood perplexed and fidgety by the door. She breathed deeply and then walked over to Laura and Oliver, who were looking over the plans again. No one seemed to have noticed David returning, or were they just pretending it was all okay? David emerged and sauntered over confidently. He seemed disinterested in what they had to say, which Kat noticed Tabitha looking more concerned and confused.

"This is your friendly time check, we have one hour before we head out," Oliver informed everybody as he and Laura made their way out of the room. David turned around and followed behind them without saying a word.

Once the door closed, Tabitha glanced over at Kat and whispered, "What was that about?" Kat shrugged and stared back towards the closed door.

"Are we okay stay here for a bit?" Henry asked the unusual couple.

"Of course," Will answered with a reassuring smile. "I need to get changed and put my makeup on, so you can chill here for a bit."

Kat skipped over to the bed and giddily asked Tabitha if she wanted to do make up with her, which she happily agreed to do. It had been years since Tabitha had been able to have female companionships. Henry and Aaron took the floor plans of the hideout and examined the details, trying to memorise the route in case they lost the plans, or became separated or lost. Tabitha had Kat put on natural eye shadow colours on her eye lids. Kat hadn't put makeup on another girl since she was a teenager, so it felt nostalgic for her to be doing this with a friend, even if they were a vampire. It all became natural for her to be around vampires to the point where it hadn't crossed her mind that they were indeed that.

"I take it you steal makeup from stores?" Kat asked her with a small giggle in her voice, making sure that she wasn't being serious or judgemental.

"I'm not proud of it, but yes," Tabitha shrugged with guilt in her tone. "It's the same with clothing. But I had no choice, especially as I had no money."

The makeup brush was pressed lightly onto her eyelids and painted her stone skin with beige tones. Tabitha was thankful to have drank blood earlier today, otherwise she would have been thirsty for Kat's blood. Being able to drink blood almost every day had put her mind at ease since she was worried that she and the others, having been on a five-day starvation before drinking blood for the past three years, would immediately rip Kat apart to feast on her essence.

Will finished in the bathroom and was wearing his usual pink, purple, and black eye makeup, along with the same outfit from the previous nights: the long black sleeve shirt that rolled up to his elbows, black skinny jeans that showed off his thin legs, and a purple silk tie that wrapped round his collar. It was a good thing that vampires couldn't sweat, otherwise his clothes would wreak of body odour.

"Do you have enough blood to sustain us for the next two days?" Henry asked Will.

"There are some blood bags and plastic flasks in our cooler case," Will pointed out. "They should last us another four days. We're planning to hunt for more blood tomorrow evening."

Everyone was dressed, packed, and ready, making their way to the van enthusiastically, with David trailing behind them, looking lost in thought. He was the last to enter the van and closed the door behind him after everyone had packed their belongings into the back of the van. The van was filled with joyful singing as they drove to the venue, which was about a ten-minute drive through the city. They were singing a well-known song from the eighties that blared through the radio. David, however, was busy looking out the window and watched the city go by. Tabitha turned to see that he was not enjoying himself but listened to what Kat had told her and just ignored him.

They reached *Dead Town*, a small wild western themed venue that allowed any band of any genre to perform there. The exterior of the building was clad in wood and was painted with cowboy scenes from old movies. A big plastic cactus stood on either side of the shuttered swing-doors.

Oliver drove the van to the back where there was a small loading bay surrounded by high brick walls. The gang saw two groups of humans standing by their own vans: the other acts for the night. Once they parked up and ceased the engine, David and Oliver made their way to the back of the van to open it up and get the equipment ready to be taken inside. Will, Kat, and Laura confidently approached the humans across the lot to introduce themselves. One of the bands was *MindMatter*, an industrial metal band that had travelled from Leeds to be there tonight. They were the main act for the evening. There were two women and three men in the band; one of the females had thick curly hair that was dyed green, while the rest of the band had natural coloured hair, ranging from blondes to brunettes to black.

The other band were called *Parasix* which had two men and two women as band members. They were a pop punk band from Morecambe and were heavily inspired by the bands *Paramore* and *You, Me At Six*. They were going to be the first band on at seven thirty, with Midnight Devotion being on at eight thirty, and MindMatter being on at nine thirty.

A couple of the band members of Parasix went into the building with boxes filled with merchandise while the other members spoke to Midnight Devotion.

"Where have you guys travelled from?" one of the women of Parasix asked them.

"We are from Southampton," Will informed them, flashing a gracious smile. "This is our fourth night into the tour, the penultimate gig. We're going to Glasgow tomorrow to perform our final gig of the tour."

"That's awesome! How's it been going?"

Kat left the bands to chat music while she fetched the merchandise box from the van. There wasn't much left, and she was deciding to split it between today and tomorrow. Despite initial reservations, Kat had settled into the sales role and it was good to share the band's music with new fans. Inside, the venue was laid out like a saloon from the wild west; tables and chairs scattered around the room with the bar being across the long side of the room. The performance room was up the stairs and into the room above the bar. The room itself was as large as the room at the Asylum, enough to hold a capacity of a hundred people. MindMatter had their kit to one side of the stage, so Midnight Devotion set up in the back room ready for the second slot, it would be good to have a bit of quiet before the show and be able to see the crowd from behind the stage before they played.

Kat, Henry, Tabitha, and Aaron were setting up the merchandise table near the stage where the other bands were preparing their merch on their side of the table. Kat had gotten compliments from two members of Parasix regarding her purple and black striped skinny jeans and bunny t-shirt.

One of them, Amy, approached Kat and asked, "Are you dating the lead singer?" The woman with bright orange hair that was cut below her heart-shaped face that contained a sincere smile.

"I am, yeah," Kat nodded as she was placing the CDs onto the table.

"How long has that been going for?"

"Only three months, but so far it's going great," Kat gave Amy a smile. "Will is such a gentleman."

"You're lucky! I can tell some of the girls here are going to be swooning for him tonight!"

"Their guitarist has had some compliments too," Aaron jokingly added, which made Tabitha freeze for a moment. She was moments away from giving Aaron a strong backhand but was worried that the force would send him flying across the room. She knew he was doing that to wind her up and nothing more.

"I've not actually seen the other two members," Amy told him. "Just Will and Laura."

"Well, here comes Oliver now! He's the drummer of the band," Aaron pointed out. Oliver approached the merch stand when he saw Aaron wave him over to the table.

"Oliver, this is Amy, Parasix's guitar player!" Aaron introduced her with enthusiasm.

Oliver gave Amy a welcoming smile that made her blush intensely. "Your hair is. . . colourful," Oliver muttered, trying to compliment her. "Very. . . Hayley Williams."

"That's kind of the point!" Amy giggled, still blushing immensely. "I want to wear her style and look as badass as her!" Oliver looked at her outfit from head to toe. Her body was decorated with a pair of tight red skinny jeans that were faded, and a white tank top that had black paint written on the fabric that said *RIOT!*

"One day, you may discover your own style without looking up to someone famous. Fashion changes quite regularly and before you know it, the emo style will die out and something new will take over. It happens! I've seen it happen with the nu metal scene - the nineties - it's going to happen. But enjoy the emo style while it lasts!"

Amy stared at Oliver with no emotion, but her smile grew, then turn into a snicker.

"I don't think what you're wearing is going to last either! You look like you're stuck in the Matrix period," Amy laughed. Oliver laughed along with her. "So, YOU enjoy it while it lasts, because you're a generation behind some of us!"

"Perhaps you could give me fashion tips over a drink?" Oliver chuckled out of shyness.

Kat, Henry, Aaron, and Tabitha all gawked at the pair with bewilderment. Kat's mouth had dropped. Tabitha couldn't help but laugh.

"Maybe later, we are on soon, here's Lilly and Jake. Kat, if you are staying here, could you keep an eye on the table?"

"We can do that for you," Henry added.

"Hi, we're on soon so make sure everything is ready and get your shit together," Jake informed Amy, puzzled by her distracted face, "Are you ok?"

"Well, I best be off, see you soon Oliver!"

"It was lovely meeting you. Amy." Oliver's smile never ceased.

"Pleasure is all mine."

Amy said her goodbye to Kat and the others and went to get ready for the show.

"Oliver? What the fuck was that? Have you ever spoken to a human woman before that isn't Kat?" Tabitha poked fun at him.

"I. . . need to get going." Oliver's smile was still in place as he turned around to awkwardly walk away to find the others in the back room. Henry and Aaron chuckled as they watch him walk away.

"Bless him," Henry muttered.

"I don't think it's such a good idea for him to try and flirt with humans, period!" Aaron exaggerated.

Kat, Henry, Tabitha, and Aaron stayed on the merch tables waiting for the first act to go on, and a few of the attendees approached the stall to have a look at the merch. There were many compliments for the logo of Midnight Devotion, saying how it reminded them of their emo phase. Some of the attendees just bought the CD and T-shirt without having listened to Midnight Devotion. A few of the attendees were family or friends of the other bands and were offering them their support by buying their merch; some were already wearing their t-shirt.

Whilst Parasix were getting set upon stage, Midnight Devotion were in the backroom getting their instruments and equipment out from the storage boxes. Oliver looked at David, noticing how indifferent he was being. He sat on one of the boxes tuning his guitar.

"You doing okay, David?" Oliver warily asked him.

"Yeah? Why wouldn't I be?" David shrugged his shoulders without looking at him. His attention focused solely on his guitar.

"You've become distant from us more than usual and not showing any dedication to the band," Laura expressed her thoughts. "Where did you go earlier today?"

"Why do you care?" David snapped. "It's not like you give a shit what I want?"

"And what exactly is it that you want, David?" Laura argued back. Oliver went to the door to make sure that no one nearby was listening to their conversation.

David indignantly stood up. "What I want is to not become human again, yet you're all putting my life at risk by killing the Mistress's servants and bringing along rogued vampires with us! Why are you allowing yourselves to do this?" David became agitated. It had all built up to this ever since the night Will saved Kat.

"One of those vampires is MY son and I want him to help us," Will informed him, keeping his voice to a minimum. "And I want to help him."

"But why bring the other two? I get it you want some extra pair of hands, but I'm beginning to feel like this isn't feasible. I am telling you now Will, this will end badly, for you and for us!"

"Why isn't feasible?" Laura asked him. "David, please don't bail out on us just because you feel indifferent about all of this. Remember why we agreed to do this in the first place."

"It was democracy! I didn't want to go on this mission! I just wanted us to tour and then go home! Which is why, after tomorrow's gig in Glasgow, I'm going to leave." Will, Oliver, and Laura were left speechless. They waited to hear what David had to say about it and allowed him to fully express himself.

Will was the first to speak up.

"David, you were the first vampire to join my coven; why are you backing away from what we have built together? Do you not care about us?"

"I do care! Urgh! You just don't get it, do you? I don't want to be human again because I have nothing. You all have your reasons to wanting to be human again, but I don't! No family, no job, no future, or ambitions, all I have are my vampire powers and I want to hold onto that. Before I was a vampire, I had nothing! Nothing! Shitty childhood, shitty life, shitty house, and shitty friends. That's why I've been distancing myself, because I want nothing to do with your plan. It's been painful for me to have to listen to you all talk about how you want to kill the Head Vampire and get rid of our gifts! I embrace my gifts, unlike you, you ungrateful sods! So, I'm leaving after Glasgow, and you can find yourselves a replacement guitarist. Maybe your prodigal son can take my place!" And with that, David antagonistically walked away from the band and left the backroom, making his way over to the exit of the performance room and downstairs.

Will growled through his teeth with David's statement about his son.

"Looks like we're going to have to look for a new guitarist soon," Oliver said defeatedly.

"Well, we better look within the next hour," Laura added. "In case he decides not to come back."

"I have an idea," Will marched out the door, not going at the vampiric speed he was used to and went over to the merch table. He saw his girlfriend, son, and his two coven members sitting at the merch table, whilst Parasix were performing on stage. The crowd were singing along to the songs since they played recognisable pop punk songs.

"I need one of you to follow David and make sure he comes back!" Will requested.

"What's up with him?" Aaron asked. "Throwing a strop?"

"We got into a fight and I'm worried that he won't come back!"

"I'll go!" Tabitha instantly volunteered, and before Will could say anything, she was instantly gone. She hurriedly ran down the stairs and through the bar area to get outside. She saw David walking away at a human pace through the swing-doors.

"David!" Tabitha cried. "Wait!" David ignored her and left the building.

"Stop fucking following me, will you?" David roared. Tabitha froze in shock from David's anger. "Leave me alone! I'm not into you, and I don't want anything to do with you!" David leapt into the night sky and was gone in a flash, leaving Tabitha distraught and upset. She was about to give up but decided that she had to ignore his commands and try and get him to come back to the venue, for the sake of the band.

Suddenly, she heard the screams of two males in the distance. They were faint enough for her vampiric hearing to pick up. It sounded like the noises came from the back of the venue. She leapt up into the air and managed to land a few metres away from David. To her disbelief, she saw a lot of blood on the ground of the car park of where the bands' vans were. In the middle of the car park were two grown men - wearing ski masks to disguise their faces and wore black clothing - lying on the ground covered in blood. Standing triumphantly above them was a bloodied David whose fangs were exposed, and his mouth covered in the same blood as the two men. Both his arms were monstrously long and grey with long red fingernails as claws. Grey veins were showing all over his skin from the digestion of blood.

There were two crowbars that were on the ground next to the purple van that belonged to Midnight Devotion, which made Tabitha realise what had happened; the two men had tried to break into the van, and David, being at the right place and at the right time but in the wrong mindset, caught them in the act and butchered the pair of them in an instant, without showing any mercy.

"I thought I told you to leave me alone," David silently and aggressively told Tabitha, who stood there looking incredulous, staring at David's bloodlust eyes as he swung his arms threateningly.

"I heard screaming," Tabitha whispered, terrified of what David might now do to her. "You're not going to hurt me, are you?"

"It depends; are you going to help me get rid of these bodies?" David marched his way over to her, his bloodied fangs still exposed, his eyes filled with blood and anger.

"I know you're not capable of hurting your friends."

"You don't know anything." David grabbed her by her shirt's collar and lifted her into the air. She grasped onto his hand with both of hers, trying to break free, but David's strength was too much for her to do anything about it. "You're such an ignorant bitch."

In a sudden flash, Tabitha was on the ground and David was sprawled next to her. She gasped loudly, then saw Aaron grabbing David by the collar of his coat with both of his hands and slammed him up against the brick wall, developing a small crack.

"What the fuck do you think you're doing to her!" Aaron growled in his face. "Why are there two bodies on the floor and your hands on Tabitha? And your mouth covered in blood?"

David chuckled menacingly, exposing more blood and teeth.

"The right thing," David glowered. "She should have minded her own fucking business." His response encouraged Aaron to forcefully smash David even further into the wall, causing it to crack upwards.

"Aaron!" Tabitha flashed over and placed her hand on his shoulder.

"Are you okay?" Aaron growled under his breath trying to remain calm.

"I'm fine, but you need to let him go,"

"Why the fuck should I? He had you by the throat; it's so disrespectful!"

"I'd do as she tells you," David wryly suggested, showing bravery and no empathy. "You don't want people to see you in this position." Aaron stared into David's bloodied eyes for a moment before letting him go. He let David drop to the ground whilst the boys continued to lock their focus onto each other, looking aggressively at one another.

"When you guys are done eye fucking each other, we need to clear up this crime scene, like right now," Tabitha informed them both with worry. "And David, you need to clean yourself up and get your shit together. I don't give a fuck what's going on with you and the band, but you have a job to do. Also, after what you just said to me, I don't find you attractive anymore. I find you disrespectful and emotionally repulsive." She marched over and slapped David across the face and instantly leapt away, heading back to the venue to find the others and inform them what had happened. David rubbed his check from the slapping aftermath despite it doing little harm to him. It was obvious what had happened, but Aaron still wanted to hear David's perspective on the situation.

"Why did you do it?" he crossed his arms.

"They were trying to break into our van," David argued.

"No, no! I know why you killed *them,* but why did you have Tabitha held like that? What could she have possibly done to upset you that much that you would hold her up by the collar, huh?" David stared down at Aaron; he was unable to come up with a reasonable answer to his question, other than the fact that he was upset. His vampiric urges had obviously kicked in with the mixture of emotions that led to violence and potential harm to his kind.

"I honestly don't know, Aaron," he finally spoke, crestfallen, seeming guilty suddenly. He wasn't so sure himself what came over him. He wasn't usually this aggressive towards people, just at himself. Laura, Oliver, and Will arrived at the scene. All three examined what was in front of them, and then looked at David and Aaron. Each of them gave David a look of anger mixed with shock.

"David," Laura whispered angrily, grinding her teeth. "Explain yourself."

Oliver and Will quickly picked up the bodies on the car park floor and moved them to the back of the van in a flash. The blood remained on the floor, still fresh and wet like a rain puddle.

"Tabitha told us you murdered two people trying to rob our van, as well as physically assaulting her!" Laura continued bitterly. "The assault is what I'm more concerned about right now!"

"That's an over exaggeration! I did not assault her! I grabbed her by her shirt because she wouldn't leave me alone!" David explained himself poorly.

"We told her to follow you and have you come back to the venue as you have a show to perform tonight! And your response to her helping you was grabbing her?!" Will marched his way towards him, angry with what he had done to Tabitha. Just because she was a vampire, didn't mean she was immune from violence.

"I wanted to be alone, and she wouldn't take no for an answer! She's been pestering me ever since she met me!"

"She hasn't been pestering you, David!" Laura screamed, frustrated with his excuses. "She's interested in you, and you could have just spoken to her like a civil person. Instead, you act all moody and antisocial! She was worried about you, you know! Didn't you ever stop to think that maybe people do care about you despite your shitty attitude towards them?" David stood frozen, taking in Laura's outbursts. A towel was thrown at David's face by Oliver.

"Clean yourself up," Oliver commanded. "Nobody wants to see a guitarist with blood on his face, not unless they're in a death metal band."

"It's not my fault I am how I am!" David began rubbing his face with the towel to wipe away the blood before throwing it back to Oliver who instantly caught it. "Maybe I'm just one of those vampires who, unlike yourselves, have no emotion towards anything or anyone? I mean, right now, all I feel is anger!"

"I think you owe all of us an apology, especially Tabitha," said Will. "We're due on in 15 minutes so get your shit together and get back to the venue. We'll clean up this mess."

"You aren't going to thank me for saving the van?" David shrugged his shoulders.

"By coincidence, yes, thank you, but fucking hell, David," Laura murmured acidly, rolling her eyes as she walked away from the car park and back to the venue, with David trailing behind her. Aaron made his way back to the venue to find Tabitha.

Will brought out the jet washer from the back of the van and began washing away the blood on the floor, having the strong water push the blood to the nearest drain. Oliver loaded the cadavers into the van, using his strength to fold them into the space behind the empty cases. Once the car park had been cleared from blood and bodies, Oliver and Will headed back to the venue to get ready for the performance.

"We'll bury the bodies on the way to Glasgow tonight," Oliver whispered into Will's ear when they left the car park. Will responded with a nod, agreeing to the plan. Tabitha, Kat, and Henry saw Laura storm her way towards the back room, followed by David. Kat got up from the merch stand to see if Will was following behind. She could see him eagerly enter the performance room, which made her jog her way towards him.

"Is everything okay?" she asked with concern, holding onto both of his hands for moral support.

"Not really," Will said sternly. Oliver squeezed past them to get into the backroom.

"David being a prick as always." Will leaned closer to Kat to talk in her ear since the music from Parasix was too loud for them to talk normal. "We now have two dead bodies in the back of the van because of him."

Kat's eyes widened in horror to hear the news.

"What did he do?" she leaned forward to speak into his ear.

"He killed two people trying to break into our van," Will told her.

"Holy shit!" Kat held his cold hands tighter.

"We'll talk more later! I need to get ready for the gig!" Will gave Kat a quick kiss on her forehead and made his way to the backroom. Kat slowly walked through the crowds and back to the merchandise table to continue her job.

Once Parasix were done, Midnight Devotion began getting their instruments and equipment on stage and connecting everything to amplifiers and pedals. David was ready first and standing like a monolith on stage; he surveyed the audience, quietly strumming a few solemn chords.

Five minutes later and the band were ready to perform their penultimate gig.

Chapter 21:

♥

David

Throughout the gig, the band had to put on fake smiles and put aside the situation that had just occurred in the parking lot. It was important for them to remain calm and inconspicuous. The crowd still enjoyed their music; the proof was in the excitement that they offered them in return for their music. Jumping around, bobbing their heads, and fist pumping in the air. When the band had finished their gig, they unplugged their instruments and disassembled the drumkit, then made their way to the backroom to pack up. They wanted to leave immediately, but needed to wait for MindMatter to finish their gig so that there wasn't any suspicions. They silently waited for the evening to end, with all of them feeling uneasy and sharing guilty glances. Kat stayed on the merch table during and after Midnight Devotion's performance. They received a lot of compliments from the people who attended the show.

MindMatter had the crowd going wild. A lot of the people that attended tonight's event were fans of industrial metal, wearing heavy black boots and branded t-shirts from other industrial bands. Will and Oliver stood against the wall watching the crowd bounce around the room to the sounds of heavy drumming, metallic keyboard sounds, strong bass, and deep guitar rhythms. Kat could tell Will wasn't in the right mindset. He seemed normal on stage, but off stage, he had changed. It must had been difficult for Will to put on a fake face to cover up how he was truly feeling, like a mask and for once David had fallen into line and played along. Kat was worried that it was going to be an awkward journey to Glasgow after tonight. She considered staying here and getting the train up tomorrow as the thought of the band arguing in that cramped van made her queasy. Her eyes glanced at Will across the crowd, and she could see his arms folded and his eyes watching the band, but his face seemed as though he was a million miles away, which worried her even more.

When MindMatter had finished, Will and Oliver made their way to the back room to move the kit into the van. Kat, Henry, Tabitha, and Aaron had to stay with the merch for another ten minutes before packing away. They watched the band travel back and forth from the back room to the bar room.

Amy suddenly approached Oliver which caught him by surprise. He hadn't thought about her much that evening due to thinking about how they were going to dispose the bodies they had in the back of their van.

"Hey!" she called out with enthusiasm. "Are you sticking around for drinks?"

Oliver delivered the disappointing news, "I wish we could, but we need to get going. However, I would like to see you again at some point if that's okay?"

Amy's smile never changed. "I would like to. If you're ever near Morecambe, give me a call!"

"If you're ever near Southampton, call me." Oliver and Amy quickly exchanged phone numbers and smiles. Aaron watched from a distance, smiling with pride knowing that he was responsible for this pleasant encounter. Hopefully, the next time they see each other, Oliver would have become mortal, just like her.

Oliver brought the van to the front of the venue so that they could pack away their instruments, making sure the dead bodies were hidden behind the flight-cases. Once the merch had been stored away in the van, everyone got in - with Henry and Aaron sitting on top of the equipment carriers - and they started their journey to Glasgow. It was now midnight, and it was going to take them three and a half hours to get to their next hotel.

For about ten minutes nobody spoke a word as Oliver navigated the van out of the city centre to get onto the motorway.

"We need to bury the bodies somewhere," Will finally said to everyone. "We'll need to find somewhere remote and secluded."

Henry looked behind him and saw the tarpaulin behind the amplifier cases. "I take it this isn't the first time you guys have had to bury dead bodies?"

"Nope," David sighed. "We've done this one too many times. How do you usually dispose of bodies of those you murdered?"

"We rip them apart limb for limb and bury them," Aaron responded, nonchalantly.

Will raised his eyebrows and turned to look at Henry, who shrugged in response.

The last few days had not been what Kat had hoped for - a lot of revelations and conflict were surfacing - and she knew that more were to come.

"Are we going to talk about what happened tonight then?" Oliver suddenly said aloud like he was reprimanding children that had gotten into a fight.

"What's there to talk about?" David shrugged his shoulders as he continued to look out the window like a troubled teenager. "I got upset, I killed two arseholes who were trying to break into our van and possibly exposing what we are due to the amount of blood we carry in here, and you guys won't get off my back about it."

"David," Laura sighed angrily.

"Oh, what? You going to lecture me about how much of a prick I am and should be more empathetic towards people? We've had this discussion already and I do not want to go through with it again. Fucking get over it! It's not going to change who I am nor what I want!"

Will could feel Kat's heart racing abnormally, causing him to instinctively reach out to hug her closely, giving her a sense of comfort.

"You still haven't apologised to Tabitha, have you?"

Laura asked him. He was reluctant to respond and chose to sit in silence. The motorway was nearly empty and very few cars had passed them in the last fifteen minutes. David stared out of the window at the outline of the distant hills and signed deeply. Accepting he was in the wrong, especially with what he did to Tabitha, he knew she meant no harm and was looking out for him, but he still didn't understand why she should care about him? He had nothing to offer her or anything to the band. He felt like the outcast of the group, and his vampirism was the only thing that gave his life purpose. David turned to face Tabitha, who remained seated in the back with Henry and Aaron.

"I'm sorry, Tabitha," David looked at her deep in the eyes with sincerity. She knew he meant it. "I didn't mean to hold you like that. I lost control."

Tabitha couldn't help but smile, thankful for David to acknowledge his actions as well as speaking to her properly.

"Thank you," she replied. David then continue looking out the window, reminiscing his actions and how he had gotten to where he was today, which meant opening doors to dangerous territory.

The van's occupants fell back into silence, but the atmosphere had changed to calmness. Kat snuggled into her blanket and lay her head on Will's shoulder. Oliver drove on past Lancaster, counting off the miles to go to Glasgow. As they approached the South Lakes, Henry spoke up, "Would it be wise to go deep into a nearby forest and bury the bodies? I would suggest we rip the limbs and scatter them all over the place."

"OK but I'd rather we stay in one place and get it over and done with as soon as we can," Laura objected. "Bury them both together in one spot."

"No," Tabitha protested, "I think it would be best if we bury them both separately. Half of us can take one body on one side of a lake, and the other half can go on the other side?"

"That's not actually a bad idea," David casually spoke his thoughts loudly. "Unless we do both and half of us go one side and then each of us take a limb and bury them about?"

253

Tabitha was surprised to hear David supporting her idea. She knew she would be blushing if she had blood running through her.

"Midnight Devotion can take one body and the Birmingham Coven take the other body?" Will suggested.

"I was about to say!" said Aaron. "Let's do it!"

"Great name for us, by the way," Henry chuckled, which made Will smile as his son was laughing.

"I have a better idea..." David spoke quietly and let it hang.

"Go on" said Oliver, curious to know what he had in mind.

"Could we not bury the bodies deep in the lake? Like, dive straight to the bottom, dig a large hole and bury them there? Nobody would think to go in there. They're probably never going to dive down there for hundreds of years!"

The rest of the group thought about it, and while it would mean less people to do the job, it did mean they had a better chance hiding the body in the lake as they were able to stay underwater for unlimited time.

"For once, David, you have a good plan," Laura said with an impressed tone.

"Wow, you guys ACTUALLY listened and agreed with me!" David waved his hands about exaggeratedly, but he was smiling for a change.

An hour later and they were off the M6 motorway and driving through Lowther and Askham, until they arrived at Howstown car park near Ullswater. With it being the early hours of the morning, it was completely deserted. Oliver still parked the van in the darkest corner of the rolled gravel. Will decided to stay in the car with Kat, who was fast asleep on his shoulder wrapped in her blanket to keep warm. He was determined not to see another dead body; killing that creeper in Southampton for Kat was his last. Everyone else got out of the van and pulled the bodies out from the back. The Birmingham Coven took one of the bodies, while Midnight Devotion's Laura and David took the other body.

"I think it's best that we bury both bodies in the lake

but have them be separated from each other," Oliver suggested as he opened the driver's door. "Laura and David can bury one at one part of the lake, Aaron and Henry can go and bury the other at another part of the lake. I'll stay alert for any disturbance."

"I hope this is the last time we will be doing this," said Laura. "I am not going to miss burying bodies and killing people with my own set of teeth."

"Hopefully," Aaron responded. "I much prefer to drink blood from those plastic flasks you carry around."

"Blood is not free, unfortunately," Henry told them, his voice being quite stern. "We have to kill to obtain the resources."

"Damn, Henry," said Tabitha, "So philosophical of you!"

In a flash, the group of vampires disappeared into the night. David and Laura quickly made it down to the shore, although they could see the other side the lake stretched off into the distance on their left and right. It was perfect for them to dive into the water and bury the body deep in the flooring. The two band members stood by the water, seeing the moon reflecting down onto the lake, creating an elegant panorama. Both David and Laura remained still with their feet grounded to the grass whilst staring at the night sky and mountains. There was not a soul in sight, and even their vampire hearing could hardly detect any human noise.

David let the stillness settle again and continued to stare at the countless stars that shone in the night like a fairy tale sky.

Laura suddenly caught David taking off his coat, followed by unbuckling his belt.

"Why are you taking your clothes off?" she groaned and averted her eyes to avoid seeing the nudity.

"I'm not getting this outfit wet again. Besides, we can't get hypothermia or the common cold. So, why not go in barely clothed?"

"Okay, fine! But I still don't want to see you naked!" David rolled his eyes, ignoring her as he neatly folded his trousers and top by his boots.

Laura began taking her clothes off with the intention to strip off to her bra and pants, following David's plan.

David stripped down until he was in his boxer shorts before he picked up the dead body over his shoulder like a mannequin. He then leapt into the sky, high above the centre of the lake, then dove in feet first. The impact of the water caused a loud crashing sound as waves of water rippled down to the shore. Underneath the waters, it was dark, impossible for a human to see. He felt the shock of Laura's dive and saw her as she streaked past him, headfirst towards the bottom of the lake. For the vampires, the moonlight was a guiding light under the waters.

David swam down to the bottom of the lake with the body; his breath was absent, meaning he could stay under the water for as long as he needed to be. It took him about a minute to reach the bottom of the lake, and he found Laura was already kicking a depression into the bottom of the lake. The speed of Laura's digging was not as fast as it was as on land due to the density of the water, and the sand and gravel mixture began to swirl, muddying the water and making it much harder for them to see. The further she dug, the harder it became. David pushed the body as deep as it would go into the hole, holding it down while Laura piled on rocks to keep it weighted to the floor of the lake and into the watery grave until they could no longer see the body.

Once the body was completely buried, David pressed his feet onto the lake floor, crouched down, and then jumped through the water before a human could blink, followed quickly by Laura. He and Laura were up in the air and landed back in to the water like dolphins. They swam side by side racing to the shore as fast as vampirically possible.

David walked out of the water and approached his pile of clothes. He quickly started dressing himself just as Laura left the lake. "Let's get out of here. I want to get to the hotel as soon as possible."

"Before we do that, can I talk to you?" Laura suddenly asked, eagerly. "I think now is the time to do so."

David looked at Laura as he was putting his jeans back

on, surprised with her sudden request. "Really? Now? We need to get back to the van."

"We can run back shortly. What I said before, I mean it."

David folded his arms with a blank expression. "I'm all ears. The floor is yours, Miss Bates."

Laura stared at David and spoke her emotions aloud, knowing that an argument between was about to commence.

"I'm sorry you don't feel valued by us. But please, don't abandon us. We need you, now more than ever." Laura began dressing herself, not caring that her wet marble skin was going to dampen the clothes.

David shook his head, disagreeing with her statement.

"No, you don't. I guarantee you guys would be much happier if I wasn't around to make derisive remarks and expressing how I feel. You don't even care about the fact that I don't want to be human. You want to go off and kill the queen of the vampires and take away the one good thing I have, just so that you could all be a successful band."

Laura couldn't believe what he had said. It made her feel like she meant nothing to him. She stood feeling ambivalent whilst also offended by his accusation.

"Are we not good enough for you? Is that it? Because I thought you wanted this; to be in a band and tour the country!"

"I don't want it if it means I must sacrifice my powers, Laura. You know my history; I hated my life and was willing to end it because I had nothing to live for. But as soon as I became a vampire, I felt like I could take on the world and kill anyone who would get in my way. I felt invincible! Why do you want to take that away from me?" David's voice echoed off the crags and reverberated through the night.

"I do not want to take anything away from you!" Laura assured him. "I understand where you are coming from, David, but I am sure there is some way that we could compromise on this. We just need to discuss this with the others like adults rather than rambling and ranting at each other."

David turned to face the lake and looked up abruptly at

257

the moon again, thinking about the situation.

"I'm sorry Laura, I am just me. It's what I want, and I don't have anything to go back to."

"You've got us. It's not easy for any of us, even Will."

"If I turn back into a human, I want you to find a vampire and have them turn me back," he advised her. "No questions asked. If there's an alternative where killing the queen vampire won't turn us back into humans, keep it that way for my sake. If Claudette threatens me, I'll work for her if I must, whatever spares me from being killed or human."

Laura remained speechless. It was a difficult circumstance for them both as they wanted the opposite thing from the other. They were two different people wanting different things. One was yin and one was yang. One was light, and one was darkness. One was fire, and one was ice.

"I'm sorry, and I hope it won't come to that. We will support you, and we will try and find a way for you, but you are more than your vampirism," she finally said solemnly, refusing to continue the debate they had repeated. "But David, whether or not you do stay as a vampire, please don't leave the band." She slowly approached him, keeping her wet hands in her pockets and stood closer than she ever had been towards him. "It won't be the same without you. You're a really good guitarist and I don't see Midnight Devotion happening without you. We've grown to seeing the band as us four. I don't imagine the band replacing you."

"You're bullshitting me," David seemed sceptical about Laura's comments. He was not used to having compliments off anyone, let alone Laura, who he had always butted head with over the years, but they became comrades.

"No, I'm not. You know me, David, I don't lie. I was a police officer, lying wasn't something I did. Will and Oliver would say the same to you."

David averted his face to hide his sorrows. The idea of people caring about him that much was something he found incredulous and abnormal. Nobody had cared for him before, so he had been expecting the rest of eternity to be like this, believing nobody would ever care about him, especially with the things he had done before.

"I'm still unsure the others are going to want me to stay after what happened with Tabitha, especially Aaron."

"Tabitha got your apology and has moved on from it. She does care about you, you know. She was worried about you when you wondered off."

David arched his eyebrows. "But why, though? What have I got that the other two in her coven don't? Or Oliver? Oliver is a charming, empathetic man, quite frankly he is the opposite of myself! I, on the other hand, am neither of those things. I think she's not mentally right in the head to think that I'm fit for her."

"That's just your shitty low self-esteem talking. If we didn't care about you, we would have kicked you out of the band a long time ago. But we didn't, because we like having you around, despite your snarky insolence and comments. We like you for that. We understand why you are the way you are. So, please, for now. Let it go and enjoy the gigs."

Laura reached out her hand, solemnly offering it to David. He looked at her hand like it was something extraordinary to him. He was not used to this level of emotional or physical connection with anyone else. He had often pushed those possibilities and opportunities out of the way to avoid any close connection. In that moment, he pushed away the idea of rejecting Laura's offering and took her hand, tightly grasping it. The pair of them slowly smiled before Laura came closer to embrace David, which took him by surprise. He almost ran away from it but fought his fears and accepted Laura's compassion. He embraced her back and held her lightly, allowing her to hold him tightly. It was a sensation he had not felt in a long time, a sense of comfort, trust, love. He didn't want to let go of that feeling as it brought on so much positive energy for him. Neither of them had been this close to each other before. It was their first physical connection, one that healed David from his internal wounds the longer she held him.

Laura withdrew her embrace but held onto his forearms. Their eyes locked on each other's; Laura was wondering what the colour of his eyes were before he transformed.

"Let's get back to the van." Laura let go of their embrace and gave David a grin. "Race ya!" And in an instant, she was gone.

"I wasn't ready, for fuck sake!" David moaned as he chased after her.

David and Laura raced back to the van through the lake district; the pair of them acting boisterous as they were gliding their way down the path. They were neck and neck: one second David was in the lead, then the roles were reversed. Back and forth the positions of the pair changed every few seconds.

"I'm not going to let you win this time, Bates!" David laughed. Laura was so focused with getting to the van first that she wasn't aware that he spoke. She was simply happy to hear David laughing. They continued running through the fields, jumping over the dry-stone walls and gliding through the night. David enjoyed racing at high speeds; he adored having the ability to outrun anything and be almost invisible to the human eye, like he would disappear in an instant and people would assume that he had teleported. He let out a wild whoop and jumped high into the sky.

Chapter 22:

♥

Glasgow

Will gently held on to Kat whilst she slept in his arms. Oliver sat in the driver's seat waiting for the other vampires to return from burying the bodies. Tabitha remained seated in the back playing on her phone whilst waiting for her coven to return.

For once there was no noise, no lights, no one to avoid or hide from, and Oliver let himself relax fully into the silence.

David landed with a loud thump next to the van and they heard Laura shouting.

"You got lucky!"

"Next time, Laura, will be the deciding round!" David smirked at her in friendly triumph. She was happy to see him smiling and joking about.

The Birmingham coven returned shortly after.

"All done!" Aaron announced proudly. "It's been a while since I went for a swim!"

"We buried the body at the bottom of the lake and deep underneath the flooring," David bragged. "Did you do that as well?

"Yeah, of course we did!" Aaron laughed. "We don't want no criminal floating around a giant lake for anyone to find!"

"Can we please get going?" Henry asked them whilst opening up the door to the van, waking up Kat in the process. She groaned with tiredness as the rest of the band got in.

"To Glasgow, please!" David enthusiastically told Oliver. David's sudden mood change made Oliver confused; he just shrugged his shoulders and started the engine. Will shushed them to remain quiet as Kat stirred and went back to sleep on Will.

During the journey to Glasgow, David talked to Tabitha, Henry, and Aaron about his history about being a vampire and how he met the other band members. Laura couldn't help but smile at him for being social and seeming happier about himself and joining in conversations with the others. She was proud of herself for getting through to him about how important he was to her and the band. This was the last day of the tour and then they would be on their way to potentially becoming human, and even though David could be sacrificing his immortality and vampiric powers, having him in the band was essential.

Despite the laughing and the talking, Kat remained fast asleep, which amazed Will. This was the deepest he had seen her sleep in the van; he could hear her slow breathing. He had hoped that she was dreaming about something pleasant, such as himself, but given the current circumstances that she was in, it was likely that her subconscious would be just as abnormal as the world she was facing in her waking life. He dreaded the moment he would have to wake her up; he thought about the possibility of carrying her to the hotel room like he did in Cardiff. By the time they had reached the hotel, the shutdown of the van made Kat groan, and she moved closer against Will, using the blanket that swaddled her to rub her eyes. Kat had woken up but was still in a sleepy stupor.

"Come on, sweetheart," Will whispered. "Let me carry you inside. Go back to sleep." Kat did not say a word and allowed Will to carry her. She was looking forward to being in a soft bed and was grateful that vampires were nocturnal creatures which meant she could sleep in for as long as she needed to. David and Henry carried the suitcases whilst Oliver spoke to the receptionist, gently using his persuasive powers to add extra rooms at little extra cost. When they reached the hotel rooms, Will took Kat into theirs and laid her down on the bed, covering her with the floral quilt. He decided to stay with her and write lyric ideas in his purple notebook. He found himself randomly writing his and Kat's name inside a heart doodle. He then glanced at his sleeping girlfriend, still wondering as to what she could be dreaming about. The exhaustion must have knocked her out as soon as she was in the bed.

By morning, Kat was still fast asleep. Will had left the hotel room to go and speak to the others who were all hanging out in their own hotel rooms. Laura and Oliver had the floorplans to the hideout on the table, whilst Henry, Tabitha, Aaron, and (for once) David stood in a circle around the table with Laura and Oliver sitting on the chairs.

"We will, of course, need to run or fly to the top of the mountain. Will needs to make sure Kat is wrapped up and geared up because we are due some harsh snow soon," Laura informed the gang.

"I will take Kat shopping today to make sure she has everything ready. Kat needs time but I want to get to the hideout quite soon," Will had insisted.

"Will she be ready by then?" Henry asked his father. "She's only had two days to prepare and has had no physical training." Everyone looked at Will, waiting for him to answer.

"She isn't entirely confident, I must admit, but I want to spend the next couple of days making sure she's ready," Will answered.

"I want to help," Henry insisted.

"Me too," Aaron intervened. "I can teach her a thing or two about reflexes and how to maintain her stamina." Aaron was rapidly pushing his fists forward to make kung fu moves.

"Stamina?" David looked at Aaron, curious about what he meant.

"So that she's not out of breath when running away, and how to control her adrenaline. One false move and it would be all over for her. I can teach her self-defence."

"Against vampires?" David asked sceptically.

"Yes, but she could use some evasive moves, along with handling the stakes and silver, she will have at hand. I can teach her how to throw them, how to be stealthy, take them by surprise, basically turn her into a greater badass." It was starting to dawn on Will how quickly this could go badly and fatally wrong for Kat. He was essentially putting her life in extreme danger, but it was what was needed to get what they wanted. Kat wanted to be with him, and Will wanted to be with her. The pair of them wanted the same thing, but the curse that was bestowed upon him was the brick wall between their dreams of being together equally.

"You get a badass vampire killing machine of a girlfriend, Will," David chuckled. Will didn't respond, despite it being meant as a compliment.

"Me, Henry, and Aaron will give Kat some training tomorrow, and I will take her shopping for the last few things she needs."

"Which are?" Laura asked him.

"Holy water, silver items, whatever else is on her written list. She has some stakes on her, but she could do with a load more, and maybe a holster belt to store them in."

Laura nodded. "Does she have the relevant winter clothing for when we get to Ben Nevis? Hiking boots, coat, trousers? It will be absolutely freezing up there."

"You've seen her wardrobe," Will chuckled, "I mean she looks cool, but also cold a lot of the time. I don't think layering her up with her current gear will do her any good. She needs practical clothes, even if she outside her usual looks."

"Can I join you guys with shopping for the clothes then?" Tabitha requested.

"I don't see why not," Will shrugged with a smile. "Laura?"

"I would love to, but I need to finish going over these plans and make sure that I've drawn out everything legitimately. I don't want to take any risks in getting any of us lost."

David smiled, watching Laura organise and plan in advanced. He had always quietly admired how organised she was and always preparing for anything that was yet to come.

"Come on, Laura," David encouraged her. "Go and have some fun with the girls, and Will, for a couple of hours doing some shopping! Me, Oliver and the others can sort out the plans."

"Technically, we don't know anything about this place, so we won't be of much use," Henry told him. "Me and Aaron could have a look over what you've drawn out and memorise the paths. This could possibly be your last chance to have a 'fun shopping trip' before you either become human or become dust."

"Very charming," Oliver muttered. "David is right though. You should go out with Will and the girls for a bit. I can stay with Henry, Aaron, and David, and go over the plans." Laura looked at Will who stood patiently as he waited for her response. Henry was correct about it being possibly their final days as vampires. If she were to become human, she and the other women would have all the time afterwards to do shopping trips and nights out together, something she didn't get to do much in her human days in the police force.

"Is it going to be sunny today?" Laura queried.

"It's Glasgow," Will smirked. "Although, I heard it's due to be sunny tomorrow."

Laura defeatedly sighed. "Okay, I'll come with you and help get Kat the gear she needs for the journey. We should have done this days ago, but of course, we had other issues at hand."

Will looked at his son and the pair of them exchanged smiles. "Issues that I'm thankful to have come across."

Will went back to the hotel room and saw that Kat was not in her bed. The covers on the double bed were thrown back, revealing an empty mattress with no body on top. He saw from under the bathroom door that the light was on and he could hear water running in the shower. He quickly made the bed and then sat on the foot of it, waiting for Kat. Moments later, the water stopped running. Kat opened the bathroom door and revealed herself to be in a towel that wrapped around her torso. She jumped slightly at the sight of Will.

"I didn't hear you come in," she giggled. "Stealthy vampire."

"I have no control over being stealthy; it's part of the package." Will gave her an enigmatic smile. Kat walked over to

Will and leaned down to give him a kiss, threw the towel dramatically across the room and sat sown on his lap.

"What's the plan for today then?" she smiled.

"You're going to go shopping with Laura, Tabitha and myself," Will winked, "that means weapons and clothing."

"Laura's actually joining us?" Kat raised an eyebrow, surprised to hear that the planning officer of the hideout raid was coming to shop with them.

"We convinced her to spare a couple of hours to spend some time with you and Tabitha. She needs a day out away from the planning and running the tour."

Kat chuckled. "Why do we need to go clothes shopping?"

Will chuckled as he noticed the irony of the question judging how she was sitting on him.

"You need warmer clothing for when we go to Ben Nevis. The ones you have won't do the job of keeping you warm. You'll need a proper coat over something you can then run and fight in, and some way to store your stakes and weapons. Your boots as well will need an upgrade to handle deep snow."

Kat dropped her eyebrows in disapproval. "Not really a cool gothic look though."

"You'll always be beautiful to me no matter what you wear. Clothed or unclothed, young or old, it won't stop me from loving you."

The comment made Kat cutely twitch her nose upwards. "You're so biased."

"Am I? Because I thought I was being honest!" The pair of them began passionately kissing again. Will allowed Kat to push him onto the bed until his back hit the sheets. His hands caressed her bare thighs as she knelt on top of him, her lips still connected to his.

"We should get you some breakfast before we go shopping," Will suddenly objected, his lips still intact with hers as he spoke.

"Can't I just have *you* for breakfast?" Kat teased Will, pressing her lips onto his cold neck. Will chortled at her.

"You need human food; I don't think I have much nutrition to offer that fragile body of yours. And, judging by what you're trying to do, I don't think you have the energy to undertake that activity with me."

"You're so naïve," Kat told him, biting his lips as she continued kissing him.

"No, I just don't want to do this right now. As much as I want to, I don't think now is the time to." Will's gracious smile had her withdraw from the kissing, making her blush when his snow-white teeth gleamed.

Kat's stomach suddenly growled, proving Will's point. Will covered his mouth to hide his chuckle.

"Okay, fine!" she groaned as she got off him to get changed. "Stupid human anatomy." Her grumbling made Will chuckle; he found her adorable when she was annoyed over petty things.

Kat quickly got dressed, then they left their room and went next door to meet with the others. Despite the overcast skies, the mood in the room was positive, and the argument in Manchester seemed to have been long forgotten. They were both greeted with smiles from every vampire in the room. Tabitha approached Kat eagerly and hugged her, which Kat did not expect but found it pleasant, nonetheless.

"You ready to go weapon and clothes shopping?" Tabitha jokingly asked her.

"You bet!" Kat verified enthusiastically.

"Laura?" Tabitha turned to face Laura, who was still sitting by the table.

"Yes, I'm coming with you," Laura confirmed. She got up from the table and put on her jacket.

"Have fun!" David told them, extravagantly, which made everyone else in the room turn to face him, giving him a look of confusion.

Outside, the weather remained overcast. The group agreed to get Kat some breakfast before going shopping for weapons and winterwear. There was a nearby café where Kat bought herself a cup of coffee and a bacon sandwich to go. Tabitha began asking Laura about her life in the police force and what it was like being in her twenties in the 1990s. Laura explained the intense training and exams she had to undertake for her to get into the Force, and how she had to restrict herself in terms of her diet to stay physically fit. She told Tabitha some stories of the crime scenes she'd been in and the most gruesome ones she had seen. But also, the office drudgery of typing out reports and the older men in the ranks who had prehistoric attitudes to everything. Kat grinned, watching Laura and Tabitha bonding. It was nice to see Laura loosen up and bond with others rather than be demanding.

The vampires and Kat walked to an outdoor activity store to help Kat pick out some hiking wear. She chose a pair of waterproof boots in burgundy, in size 6, which were high enough to cover her ankles. They looked at crampons as weapons but decided it was too risky for the stone floors of the castle in the mountain. A pair of thermal socks were essential as her current socks were too thin to keep her feet warm in the snow. Tabitha picked out a pair of black walking trousers, which managed to fit her perfectly, and a pair of warm thermal leggings so she could strip down to give herself more fighting comfort. Laura had found Kat the perfect hooded waterproof jacket that was black, along with three thin layered tops (again, in black) that Kat could discard as needed once indoors. Will picked out a pair of ice-axe gloves that would help her hands keep warm, as well as help her grip onto anything she would use without slipping.

Kat went to choose a backpack that she felt was the right size, one with not so many pockets but enough storage space. She picked out a purple backpack that had two large pockets and enough storage to put in a first aid kit, bottles of water and plastic bags full of blood for her vampire friends. She shocked the shop assistant by swinging it about and pulling on the straps to see how strong it was. It could also act as a bit of body armour for her back.

After picking out the gear, Kat went into the changing room to try on her outfit and was astounded with the result. Will mouthed a 'wow' as soon as she came out. She spread her arms out to demonstrate her satisfaction with the outfit. "And you said you wouldn't look cool!"

"You look like you're going on an epic adventure!" Laura complimented. "But are you comfortable with what we've chosen?"

"Absolutely!" Kat shimmed about, stretched up and grinned. "Now I just need a holster for the stakes and I'm ready!"

Will produced a big roll of money that made Kat do a double take. He paid for Kat's things, and then the gang left the store. Tabitha wanted to get some new clothes for tonight's show, and Kat wanted to get a belt, some fabric and a glue gun to make holsters for the stakes. Tabitha picked out a pair of faux leather leggings, a long white t-shirt with floral patterns on, and a black leather jacket. Laura was engrossed by her new outfit, raising her eyebrows.

"What?" Tabitha giggled. "Your look inspired me!"

Laura giggled back. "It suits you! I'm honoured to be a. . . fashion inspiration?" The girls laughed as they paid for the clothes and left the store, wandering out whispering conspiratorially. Will and Kat bought a simple leather belt and a couple of cheap shirts they could pull apart, and then found a hobby store for a sewing kit and a glue gun.

Back at the hotel, the other vampires had managed to discuss the floorplans that were currently drawn up by Laura. They had clarified that once they got to the hideout, they would need to take out as many vampires as possible to decrease Claudette's reinforcements. They wanted to keep Will and Kat separate from the main group to ensure the element of surprise. It was going to be a difficult mission for them, as her hideout had about a hundred vampires, sometimes more, roaming inside the mountain hideout.

Henry, however, objected to something. "I would like myself and Aaron to go with Kat for extra support. Claudette probably doesn't know about me and my coven, so having Aaron help us with his martial art skills to fight off any vampires in our way, may give us an advantage."

"I agree," Aaron added. "If I can get a vampire onto the ground, it would give Kat the opportunity to go in for the kill."

"Not a bad suggestion," said David, waving his hand, with his index finger pointed outwards to show his agreement. "Me and the others will go in first and head to Mistress Claudette, then Will and the others will follow behind later and use the map to find their way through the hideout and wipe out any vampires roaming the halls."

"Why can't Laura go with you?" Oliver asked Henry. "Surely, she would benefit your group better?"

"She committed a crime, so it would make sense for her to come clean and confess her crime to Claudette," said David. "Not only that, but Tabitha is also the youngest vampire out of all of us and we could just say we're there to get her known to the vampiric rules and regulations and whatnot."

"So, in other words, a confession and a recruitment?"

"Exactly, Oliver. If you and I turn up with Laura, they may ask about Will, but we could say there was no point in him being there too. I can be Laura's moral support and you can be Tabitha's moral support."

"That doesn't make any sense," Oliver objected. "Surely, Will is on the blacklist for being in a relationship with a human and exposing our kind to her. And do they actually know he was with Laura that night in Tottenham Stadium? Do they even know what happened to Sven? How does the information get back to her?"

"It is likely. I wouldn't be surprised if Claudette is the type to 'sense' the death of her servants." David marched over to the mini fridge to grab two flasks of blood. "It's kind of like a voodoo doll, only instead of putting pin into a doll to give her pain, we kill her servants to give her the indication that someone out there is going against authority."

"Hold on," Henry interrupted. "What happened in Tottenham Stadium?"

"Laura, Will, and Kat had a run in with one of Mistress Claudette's servants and killed him," David told him without hesitation. "Let's just say Laura wasn't supposed to be in London and they found her roaming around the city she was momentarily banned from. She wanted us to perform in a city known to be popular for recognition, as well as wanting to show off to the human the location where she became a vampire."

"Fuck," Aaron muttered. "And they know she's with you guys?"

"Probably," Oliver shrugged as David passed him some blood.

"So, shouldn't Will be with you two as well?" Henry questioned. "They would expect Will to be with Kat."

"Will is Kat's responsibility. He would demand to stay with her at all times," said David after he drank some blood. "I mean, we need to wait for them to come back and discuss this with them first."

"I would agree that my father wouldn't want to abandon Kat, he loves her too much to be apart from her."

Kat and the vampires returned to the hotel room with their newly purchased items. Kat wanted to get started with fixing up her equipment for the vampire battle but said she would need to keep her distance as she wanted to glue some crosses onto the laced gloves she had purchased in Manchester. She listened in to what the band were discussing, as this involved her. Everything was repeated to them, and the plan was agreed on, keeping in mind they were unsure about what Sven's death meant for Laura and Will.

Dusk fell as the band put the plans to one side and focused on immediate concerns.

"Final gig of the tour!" David shrilled.

"Then it's the big day soon!" Tabitha added. "Possible humanity is getting closer to us!"

Oliver stood up and faced David, "Mate, I don't know what happened but it's good to see you in a good mood. And, whatever happens in Ben Nevis, you really are part of this band, always." The whole group cheered and quickly piled out of the room and down to the van, singing loudly as they went.

271

The venue they were to be performing at was called *Pandemonium*, known for psychedelic and cyberpunk décor and theme. Ultraviolet lights on the ceilings, revealed UV and bright coloured graffiti on the walls. The UV light would have caused some discomfort for the vampires, thankfully it wouldn't be strong enough to burn them to a crisp. Since they had puffed themselves in white foundation, they shone in the dark, and they were the band, so people just saw them as being really goth.

Industrial music blasted out. The other punters at the venue were wearing a variety of gothic and cyberpunk clothing with vibrant neon colours, outlandish makeup, and spiked jewellery. Kat gazed in awe at every person that walked past her who were dressed to the extreme, this was a real home for a hardcore of alternative lifestyle. The performance room was the largest out of all the ones they had performed in on the tour. Kat guessed that about three hundred people were crammed into the room, it was going to be a great way to end the tour.

Tabitha and Aaron took the box of merchandise over to the table next to the other bands' tables. The other two bands performing tonight were called *Cyber-Goths* - an industrial punk band - and *Starstruck* - a punk rock band with a hint of Krautrock drone. Midnight Devotion were going to be playing first, followed by Cyber-Goths, and then Starstruck would be the finale performance.

Oliver and David were on stage setting up the usual equipment and drum kit. Kat saw Laura, Will and Henry approaching the table with looks of determination.

"Can I get you a drink?" Laura asked Kat loudly over the grinding beats coming from the speakers.

"Yes please! I'll have a fruit cider, any flavour!" Kat loudly responded back. Laura put her thumbs up as she walked away to the bar. Will approached the stage to do the sound check of the microphones. David connected his purple guitar to the amplifier, strummed a few times to make sure it was in tune, and loud enough to be heard but not too loud for nobody to hear Will singing. He turned the dials up on the amplifier to a suitable volume. Some of the long wires connected to the foot pedals that were placed on the floor to add further distortion and different tuning effects to the guitar.

Laura returned to the table with three bottles of Cider for Kat, whose eyes widened at the look of being given three bottles of cider. *"They were on offer!"* before leaving to go get the stage to prepare her bass guitar. Kat shrugged it off and began drinking from one of the bottles, tasting the fruits mixed with fizzy alcohol.

The music playing in the background was very mechanic and futuristic; the sort of music you would hear in a movie about a futuristic city, where people are made into machines or have mechanical limbs replacing their human body parts.

Ten minutes later and the band were ready to begin their performance for the final evening of the tour. Will gave Kat a kiss before departing to join the band.

"This is it!" said David, fervently. "The last night of the tour!"

"And then it's off to Ben Nevis," Laura smiled. "To regain our humanity."

"Once we've gotten Kat trained and ready!" Will bitterly added. "We can't go until she's ready."

"Relax, Will," David turned towards Will and wrapped his arm around Will's shoulder, pulling Will closer towards him. "It'll all work out! Let's just enjoy tonight and worry about the battle another time! Let's show these Cyberpunks what we're made of!" Will handed David a smile of courtesy and released a chuckle as he was surprised to see David's tendencies being this positive and optimistic.

The music died off, causing the crowd to start cheering. The lights darkened and changed from variegated colours to solely purple, pink, and blue. The band made their way onto the stage one by one. The crowd welcomed them with a loud round of applause.

"Good evening, Glasgow!" Will screamed into the microphone. "We are Midnight Devotion! It's our last night on tour, who wants a party?!" The roars of the crowd cheered for the band to begin.

Oliver smacked his drumsticks together four times before David began playing his guitar, followed by Laura. This encouraged the crowd to start bouncing around to the music. Will began singing the intro to the first song of the playlist. The crowd were bobbing their heads up and down to the beat of the music; a few of the members of the crowd seemed to have wanted to get a mosh pit going. When the chorus hit, more bodies were bouncing up and down along to the music, creating a familiar experience for Kat to witness from afar, feeling an essential part of this amazing soft machine. After half an hour, the band and crowd were reaching a crescendo.

As the final chorus to their song ended, darkness erupted as the room suddenly turned pitch black. The lights ceased; the sounds of punk rock turned to silence. The crowd assumed this was intentional and went wild. Kat grabbed Tabitha's cold hand in fear. At first, Kat thought it was just her vision and hearing acting up and that something was going horribly wrong with her body, but the tumult of the crowd indicated that she wasn't the only one experiencing confusion or a feeling of apprehension. Henry and Aaron quickly stood up as the blackout continued. The shouts of the crowd died out, and a handful of faint lights appeared in the room from the screens of people's phones to try and illuminate their surroundings.

"What the fuck?" someone in the audience cried.

"Is this part of the show?" someone else asked their mates.

"Nah, mate! Must be a power cut!"

A loud metallic crash caused the audience to scream in terror. Nobody could see what was going on. Kat panicked as she couldn't see what was happening to her friends.

Silence descended.

The lights were back on. The audience looked around to see what had happened. Then there was even more confusion, as the stage turned empty. No sign of Will, David, Laura, or Oliver. Their instruments were still on the stage, lying on the floor. Seeing this caused Kat to gaze at the empty stage in terror, her heart frozen and heavy. She looked around the room to see if they were still nearby. To her consternation, there was no sign of Midnight Devotion. Kat immediately pushed her way through the crowd to get out of the room and made her way through the corridor and into the entrance of the building. Once outside, she looked around attentively to see if she could spot any of her vampire friends. The van was still where it was parked, but still no sign of them. There wasn't anything suspicious for her to see.

"Kat!" Tabitha called from behind, jogging out of the venue to find Kat standing in the middle of the footpath. She could see that Kat was beginning to breathe rapidly with anxiety.

The urge to sob built up inside of her. She could feel her chest, like it was about to explode, which had her gasping for air.

Aaron and Henry managed to find the girls outside, Kat seemed to be wandering off in confusion.

"Come back inside. It's not safe to run off like that," Henry told the girls.

"What happened?" Tabitha questioned.

"I saw something happening on stage. Smoke had formed and four figures had grabbed hold of them, and then they instantaneously vanished!"

"What the fuck?" Aaron cried. "I didn't even know vampires could do that!"

"Maybe these vampires are special, or different?" Henry wondered.

Kat collapsed onto her knees and began beathing violently. Tabitha leaned down to comfort her, allowing her to sob onto her new t-shirt. The band were gone, taken from her. Will was gone.

Chapter 23:
♥
Preparation

Members of the crowd inquired about the situation with Henry and Aaron whilst they were packing away the band's instruments, but they were able to hypnotise people to forget the situation, allowing them to continue putting their kit back into the van. Oliver had already started giving the keys to Henry for safety during the shows. Tabitha had packed away the merch stand, similarly, hypnotising anyone that tried to ask questions. All this was at double time, without freaking out the attendees too much. The Birmingham Coven piled into the van and Henry started the engine, taking a moment to work the gear stick and try the brakes. He was comfortable driving the van despite not having driven in a long, long time. Meanwhile Kat sat in the van staring into nothingness. Many emotions built up inside her; confusion, sadness, loss, anger, worry, it was beginning to eat her alive. She desperately held back her tears to remain calm, refusing to give in to despair.

"What the fuck are we going to do?" Kat whimpered as tears finally escaped from her eyes. "They're gone"

Tabitha rubbed her shoulder ruefully.

"I have a feeling I know what's going on," Henry told them, causing all three of them to turn and face him to listen in. "I can only think of one thing that would make sense. They might have been taken by Claudette's coven." Kat withheld her breath as she choked. She dreaded the name being mentioned, it felt like trouble, which it was given their current position.

"But then why didn't they take us?" Tabitha wondered aloud.

"Probably because she doesn't know we exist?" Aaron shrugged.

"Yes, it's because we're off the radar and are not traceable," said Henry.

"So, why was Kat spared? Surely, they would take out the potential threat?" Aaron wondered.

"I don't know, perhaps they are only interested in the vampires that broke the rules? But we need to get back to the hotel and get ourselves prepared," Henry suggested as he drove his way through the city.

They arrived and tried to act normal through reception and into the lift, but something was amiss as soon as they reached their rooms. The door to the vampires' hotel room was open, with no sign of forced entry. They went in and saw that the room had been ransacked. Bedsheets were everywhere, clothes were everywhere, furniture had been turned over, and mirrors had been smashed. All of them anxiously walked in slowly, examining the damage of the hotel room.

"They've been here," Henry angrily muttered. "But what were they looking for?"

Kat noticed something peculiar on the window, which encouraged her to walk slowly over to open the curtains to see what it was. She was hoping that her mind was playing tricks on her due to the excessive anxiety pulsing through her, however, she was seeing clearly. A message written on the window. . . with blood.

See you soon, Ms Rhodes.

"It seems they purposely spared Kat to make this a challenge for her," Henry concluded. "And my theory was right; they've taken the band."

"They're onto me," Kat whimpered. "We need to go to Ben Nevis, right now!"

"No Kat, we can't," Henry told her.

"Why the fuck not?! They've taken them! We need to rescue them!"

"You're not ready! We need to give you more training and get you more weapons!"

"Fuck the training! I have you guys to help me out!" Kat raced out of the room and hurriedly went into her and Will's room next door. After unlocking the door with the hotel key card, she began collecting her belongings and packed them into her suitcase. Tabitha immediately followed behind her.

"Stop, Kat," she grabbed her forearms to prevent her from packing further.

"Let go of me! I need to save them!" Kat screamed at her. "I don't want them to die!" Kat's sobs came back as she knelt to the carpet, feeling desperate. "I can't lose Will! I love him! We're so close to getting the life that we want!" Tabitha embraced her crying friend who allowed her to sob more. She kept silent as Kat's sobbing increased. She tried not to be too loud, but she couldn't help but unleash her internal pain.

Henry and Aaron entered the room with the floor plans at hand.

"We've quickly tidied up the hotel room to the best of our abilities," Aaron informed them. "The blood has been cleaned off the window."

"The maps weren't taken, thankfully," Henry added. "However, our plan has now been compromised and we need a new strategy."

"We're all going in together," Aaron placed his hand on Henry's shoulder. "No splitting up, we stick together."

"Kat should get some sleep, if possible, and we get an early start with getting her set up and ready," Tabitha suggested to the boys.

"I don't want to sleep!" Kat snapped. "How can I sleep at a time like this?"

"You can at least try! Do you want me to hypnotise you into sleeping?" Tabitha crossed her arms.

"No," Kat angrily muttered.

"Okay, but I will stay in case you need me to force you to sleep," said Tabitha.

Kat was unable to sleep. She was still fully clothed and unable to relax due to the anxieties of her missing friends. She wondered what was happening to them at that very moment. Were there ways for vampires to torture other vampires? Their skin being exposed to silver? Holy symbols and images being shown or spoken? Or sunlight exposure? The thought of Will being tortured made Kat's heart thump wildly. Tears began building up in her eyes again at the thought of losing him and the fact that she was in bed without him.

Tabitha stayed in the hotel room to keep her safe, sitting on the edge of the bed. She noticed that Kat was still wide awake, and unable to relax which did not surprise her at all.

"You're going to need to get some sleep at some point," Tabitha told her.

"My body clock is fucked, my mind is racing, my chest hurts, it's impossible to sleep in the state I am in," Kat responded, staring at the ceiling. "I give up. Could you please hypnotise me into sleeping?"

"I will give it a try, but I have no idea if it'll work, so don't get your hopes up." Tabitha leaned over Kat so that her eyes were aimed at hers. She stared down at her for a moment and began her hypnotism.

"You are getting verrrrrrry sleeeeeepy," she began telling Kat and trying not to giggle too much, waving her hand over her eyes. "You will get a good eight hours of sleep and feel refreshed as soon as you awake." And with that, Kat was instantly out of it, to Tabitha's surprise. "Shit. That actually worked! Nice!"

Tabitha proudly leapt off the bed and went next door to see how Aaron and Henry were doing. Both of them were sitting on the bed reading through the floor plans of the hideout.

"What's the last thing Kat needs for her weapons inventory?" Aaron asked Tabitha.

"I think she only needs holy water, vodka, and rags," said Tabitha. "She'll need to go to a church with a bottle of water and get it blessed by a priest or something. Unless churches give out free holy water?"

"I doubt that, but will she need an excuse to get a bottle of water blessed?"

"I think when they see her in her gothic outfit, they'll just conclude that she's into vampires and witchcraft and wants a collection of religious stuff," Tabitha shrugged her shoulders. "As for the vodka and rags: molotovs."

"Damn! She's really going all out!" Aaron cried. "David was right, she'll be a badass vampire killer!"

"If the weather is sun-free, I will take her out to get what she needs and when we get back, you will need to teach her a thing or two about combat and stealth."

By nine o'clock in the morning, Kat was wide awake, just as Tabitha had expected. She walked into the room to find Kat opening the curtains to have a look at the weather. It was snowing heavily across the city and the Trossachs.

"I'm taking you shopping today," Tabitha verified as soon as she saw Kat. "We're getting the last two things on the list." Kat remained silent, staring out of the window and watched the snow fall from the sky.

"Will," she whispered gently.

"Come on now," Tabitha encouraged her. "We're not going to spend today brooding. I'm dragging you out to the nearest church so that you can get some holy water."

Kat's emotions prevented her from returning any positive response. She didn't turn around to respond; she continued staring at the window, feeling useless and weak.

"I can't go and get holy water myself you know? I'm a vampire. You're the only one who can get it."

"Do we really need holy water?" Kat mumbled quietly but was still sound perfect to Tabitha's hearing.

"It would give us more of an advantage?" Tabitha shrugged. "The more weapons we have, the merrier." Kat's head collapsed against the large curtain, and she grasped tightly on to the soft red fabric. "I can go and get you some breakfast?"

"I'm not hungry," Kat continued mumbling.

"I'll make you hungry. I can manipulate you into doing whatever I want."

"Tabs, please leave me alone." Kat still didn't turn around to look at her. Tabitha obeyed and headed back to the other hotel room, granting Kat her wish. Sooner or later, Kat would need to snap out of her broodiness in order to focus on saving her friends.

One hour of staring out of the window later - crying and listening to sad songs through her mind to release the tears further - Kat got herself dressed and ready to go out. She put on a pair of her black skinny jeans, with long knee length socks underneath, her woolly black and white striped jumper with a black t shirt underneath, and her new hiking boots. She didn't bother with her hair and makeup due to the sadness that may erupt at any given moment. She grabbed her new hiking coat and her backpack, then snuck out the hotel room to make her way outside without Tabitha or the others.

It was still snowing when she left the hotel. The cold breeze made her face and ears feel uncomfortable instantly. Her headphones, which connected to her MP3 player, helped her ears keep warm along with some heavy rock tunes to keep her indignant.

Kat wondered alone in the cold snow filled busy streets of Glasgow. She felt determined and eager to get the final parts for her vampire hunting inventory and get the last-minute training out of the way. An hour had flown by and she had successfully bought more garden stakes and toy water guns, along with a two-litre bottle of water that would need to be blessed in order to be converted into holy water.

After grabbing late breakfast from a nearby cafe, she made her way to the nearest newsagents to purchase two small bottles of vodka - for arson use rather than recreational use. The person behind the counter thankfully didn't query about her early hour alcohol purchase. Kat left the newsagents and continued her way through the city, wandering aimlessly, until she reached a nearby church. One final thing was needed for Kat, one she was most anxious about getting: holy water. Her large bottle of water was going to be of great help against the vampires.

When she walked into the Cathedral, she was

astounded with how huge it was on the inside. She did not often go to church as her family were not religious in any way but was taken to churches many times as a child for weddings and school trips as well as Christmas performances. With a more mature mindset, she examined the features of the church. Being there made her feel a little more at ease and relaxed; it was quiet, calm and insulated from the world outside. There were a few investments who strode gently down the aisles, some were sitting on the benches, praying for loved ones, and a couple were talking to what Kat could see was a priest, judging by the familiar black attire that was often depicted in media. She immediately marched her way towards him and faked her smile.

"Hi there," he turned and grinned at Kat.

"Hello," he greeted her with a smile. "How may I help you?"

"This may sound daft, but I need you to help me turn this bottle of water into a bottle of holy water," Kat went straight to the point with no hesitation. It was not the time for her to be stammering about and asking a stranger for holy water. It was now or later.

"It is not daft at all, but may I ask why you want holy water?" The priest seemed curious. Kat pushed away her social anxieties and forced it out of herself.

"To ward off potential evil that lurks in my life," said Kat with a straight face and monotone voice. "Let's just say my life has been taken over by what you would call 'demonic' overtones, and I've been purchasing the items needed to ward off vampires." The priest just started at Kat, dazed at what she had just told him. He had suspicions that she was maybe live-action roleplaying as a fantasy character, who was requesting items for her quest against vampires; or maybe she was just messing with him. Regardless, he ignored his possible hypothesis and nodded.

"Allow me to take the bottled water from you and I will bless the water for your 'vampire hunting'," Kat smiled, handing over the bottle of water to the priest. She watched as he went to place it on the pedestal where the large cross was and knelt to the ground. Kat watched as he was reciting the words of God, blessing the holy water with each word that left his mouth. She was surprised how easy this turned out to be; she thought he would have rejected her, and she would have had to search every church in Glasgow to get her bottled water blessed. It all turned out better than she had predicted.

Moments later, the priest returned to Kat with her holy water, giving her an awkward smile.

"Thank you so much for this," Kat smiled awkwardly. "You have no idea how important this is for me."

"Not a problem. God bless you," the priest bowed his head and walked away. Kat smiled her way out of the church and headed back to the hotel.

When she got to the hotel room, she found Tabitha waiting outside her room, judging by her look of disapproval, she seemed annoyed with her, and Kat knew exactly why, without a doubt.

"Did you go out without us?" Tabitha asked, seemingly offended by her actions.

"Obviously!" Kat shrugged her shoulders. "I bought what I needed. I want to get to Will and the others as soon as possible. Could you please kindly go away and let me be alone."

Tabitha's mouth dropped in shock as Kat opened her hotel room door and walked in. She almost expected Tabitha to follow behind and start a scene but was not given that expectation. Kat locked the door behind her, indicating her need for privacy, wanting to finish her stake holster and get everything ready for the rescue mission. Kat left her headphones in and turned the volume up as loud as her delicate ear would allow her. She filled the water pistols in the bathroom so that none of the holy water would fall onto the carpet and harm her vampire friends. Once her holsters and belts were completed, she placed them on her waist and chest and looked in the mirror to check if it would all stay on. She had never felt so badass in her entire life. She felt like a proper vampire hunter. The final piece of her kit sat in a small black box on the side of the sink. She opened it to reveal its content: the silver cross that Will gave her for Christmas. She wasn't able to wear it during the tour, but she was now at the stage where it was needed.

"I'm coming for you, Will," she repeated to herself like a mantra, holding tightly onto the cross and placing her fist against her chest. By mid-afternoon she felt ready, but her exhaustion had gotten the better of her, so set an alarm and took a short nap.

Kat knocked on the door to the vampires' hotel room. Henry answered the door and was stunned to see Kat in her vampire hunting gear.

"Kat?" Tabitha shouted elatedly from the far end of the room. Henry moved to let Kat into the room. Aaron walked out of the bathroom and suddenly stopped to a halt once he saw her.

"Woah!" he cried. "You look like you've jumped straight out of a Blade film! So, fucking badass!"

Kat grinned softly. The outfit had made her feel ever so confident and determined.

"Time to teach me some physical skills," she told them with determination.

All three of the Birmingham coven continued staring at Kat and her new outfit with astoundment.

The snow began to pick up again. Kat and the vampires made their way to the rooftop of the hotel, making sure that no member of staff had noticed them. Each snowflake that landed on Kat's face made her feel cold, but the tenaciousness of getting her vampire boyfriend and their vampire friends (along with the thermal hiking coat she was wearing) helped keep her upper body warm enough to focus and move about. She also knew that the fighting and constant moving about was also going to help her stay warm. Tabitha leaned against the door to watch Henry and Aaron try to train Kat into becoming a skilled vampire hunter.

"Let's use the other end of the stake as a safe point for this practice," Henry confirmed. "For this part of the training, I need you to use the flat end piece as I will need you to practice stealth attacks." Kat took off her laced gloves that had the crosses glued onto the palms so that they could not come into contact with her vampire friends.

"I like what you've done with the gloves, by the way," Henry commented. "Very smart. Also, for the purpose of this training, we'll pretend you are wearing the gloves as you will need them for a line of defence. It'll be a great way to stop a vampire from getting to close, but it's going to be a last line of defence, OK?"

"I guess so, I think I am ready. Are you going to pretend to react to my hands?" Kat wondered, smiling at him from excitement.

"This training needs to be legitimate, so, of course, Aaron and I will be reacting if you reach out your hands. Also, we won't be throwing you around or trying to bite you but do keep in mind that you will be at risk of being attacked by these vampires, but all three of us will always be with you. We won't separate."

Kat nodded with gratitude, and pulled out one of her stakes from her chest belt and made sure she was holding onto it with the flat end pointing outwards.

"Aaron," said Henry, "would you do the honours of being a potential vampire threat?"

"Gladly," Aaron responded. In an instant, he vanished. Kat began searching around the rooftop trying to find him. There weren't many obstacles or platforms for Aaron or Kat to hide behind.

"This is a test of reflex and the ability to sense danger," Henry informed her. "Listen carefully for any unusual noises. Use your ears as your eyes." Kat rolled her eyes from the cliché. All Kat could hear was the sound of the wind, cars driving from street to street down below, but she couldn't pick up on anything else. Before she could react, Aaron raced behind her and grabbed her from behind.

"Got you," he whispered into her ear.

Kat could feel the chagrin building up.

"Henry!" Kat cried as Aaron let go of her. "How am I supposed to listen to a vampire with all this noise going around? The wind, the cars, it's so difficult to pick up on a vampire. Besides, Vampires are stealthy like ninjas!"

Henry chuckled. "You will have many sounds distracting you from picking up what you need to listen out for. Vampires have a distinct sound when they're running, one that is quite difficult for humans to instantly pick up on. Because you're potentially the only human in existence to know of our kind, you need to listen out for it."

"*BULLSHIT!*" Kat shouted in frustration. Aaron ran off again, which was so unexpected that Kat didn't pick up on what it sounded like, and he was nowhere to be seen.

"Listen carefully," said Henry. "If you can hear a vampire running in the distance, you will be more aware of its presence."

Kat began pacing around the rooftop whilst listening out for the sound of the vampire. The winter breeze made it more challenging for her to pick it up. Her ears suddenly picked up on something abnormal; a whooshing sound that was so faint that it could have easily mixed with the winter breeze. This caused her to turn to the direction she was sure it came from. As soon as she did, Aaron was straight ahead. He gave her a smile of encouragement.

"Well done, a few more goes." he told her. This went on for what felt like hours to Kat.

"Now for the next stage. Aaron will do the same, but he will approach you quickly, and you will need to react."

"But vampires are so fast that a human would probably not have time to react," Kat complained.

"You have protection to use, Kathryn," Henry informed her, holding his arms as he watched her. Aaron was gone in a flash, which made Kat go into listening mode. She kept her hearing focused on the abnormal noise of a vampire running. For about thirty seconds, she could not hear it. Then, her hearing picked up on the whooshing sound, she turned to see where it was coming from, saw Aaron, and immediately placed her palm up away from her face. Aaron ran up to her at a high speed and then came to a halt when he saw her palm, pretending to see a crucifix and freaking out by screeching and backing away.

"Go! Attack!" Henry cried at her. Kat held the stake in

her hand up high, her palm still facing Aaron. She ran to Aaron as fast as she could and pretended to stab him in the chest with the flat end rather than the pointy end.

"Good!" Henry grinned. "Make sure you don't pull your palm away when you are stabbing them in the chest. You can also use it to ward off other vampires that are approaching you. Let's add Tabitha to the training by being a second vampire."

"You have to aim through me, not what you can see as my clothes, but think about where my heart is and how much force you need to stake it," Aaron said with encouragement. Kat nodded with agreement and was determined to progress with the training. She turned to face Tabitha and watched her run over to Aaron and was standing next to him half a second later.

"If you have two vampires coming at once, put your palm up and pick your target. Focus on one for a moment and then the other. When both are freaking out, stab one of them, then quickly stab the other once the target disintegrates. And you've got to be quick about it!"

Aaron and Tabitha vanished in an instant. Kat was more determined to get this right, thinking about what will happen when they reach the hideout, pretending that in the very moment that she was there, looking for Will and the others. She began walking around the rooftop, imagining it to be a dark, cold, wet, rocky corridor that she had envisioned a secret mountain lair would look like. The woosh sound of the running vampires came from opposite directions, which threw her off, causing her to turn around in the wrong direction. She then quickly turned around to her left and saw two vampires approaching her, which caused her to reach her left palm out and watch her vampire friends react. The next step she took was to choose her target to "stab" with her stake, whilst using her palm to have the other vampires react to the holy symbol that was glued onto her laced glove. She chose to "stab" Aaron first whilst having Tabitha paralysed by her crucifix. Aaron overreacted to her pretend stabbing, whilst Tabitha, who was waving her hands around, cried out 'No!' repeatedly, not taking it seriously. When Aaron collapsed onto the ground, Kat quickly pretended to stab Tabitha and waited for her to be on the ground as well.

"You guys need to act serious about this, you know," Kat told the pair of them. "Pretend we are acting for a movie and acting out a scene. None of the actors cry out 'no' and laugh about it." But the two had collapsed into giggles and even Kat broke a smile at the sight of them.

Kat practised the same routine with all three vampires, Aaron kept her going into the evening and Kat was tired and sweaty but could discern the vampire noises clearly. But whenever she messed up or failed, she would get frustrated with herself as she wanted to perfect vampire hunting to save her friends. She knew it wasn't going to happen instantly, which frustrated her even more. Would Will and the others have taught her the same way she was being taught now? She was slightly frustrated at the fact that she wasn't given training before. But then again, she didn't expect the band to be taken away so suddenly, but it still would have been useful to have been given physical training beforehand, especially after what had happened with Sven in Tottenham Stadium. They were lucky that Henry and his coven weren't hostile and were willing to help. She'd wished that she had taken this more seriously and had not messed about roaming around cities and hiding bodies.

"We need to get you something to eat," Tabitha told Kat. "We can continue training afterwards.

"When are we actually going to go up to Ben Nevis?" Kat queried impatiently. "How long do I need to be training for?"

"You seem to be doing better than I expected," Aaron complimented her.

"We'll see how you feel by late afternoon, and if we think you're ready, we'll take you," said Henry. "But, for my father's sake, I'm not going to take you there when you're not ready, only be killed. I would feel like I'm letting him down. He's probably hoping I'm taking care of you."

"At least another day, and maybe tomorrow night we could..."

Kat gritted her teeth. "But what if they've taken them separately and they don't know if they're the only ones who were taken?" Kat wondered. "What if Will was taken by one of the Mistress's vampires, and the others were each taken by one of the other vampires and are in separate prison cells or whatever they put bad vampires into? Either they think they've all been taken, including yourselves, or they each think they were taken solo."

Henry looked at his comrades. "It's possible," he said. "But we still need to have you ready, nonetheless. We have four vampiric lives on the line."

Kat and the vampires headed to the door of the roof and made their way back to the hotel room. They ordered room service for Kat, having her eat whatever she desired, which was beef stir fry and a side of chips, and a glass of Cherry coke. She needed the salt to help her stay hydrated when she was fighting. They had to fill the van but they needed to take of Kat too.

Whilst she waited for the food to arrive, she and the vampires went through the floor plan that Laura and Oliver had worked on, trying to make sense of it whilst envisioning what it would look like. Kat had the same vision in her head as she did during training- the wet rocky corridor that had water drops echoing through. Afterwards, Tabitha and Aaron began making some targets to pretend they were vampires for the next part of the training. They managed to find some wooden poles and used pillows and rope to create a 'body'. Henry suggested to Kat to replace her holy water with regular water inside her water pistols, as she was going to be doing target practice and would need to save the holy water as well to avoid the risk of smouldering her friends.

After Kat ate her dinner, she was determined to get back into training despite her tiredness and the late hour. They all went back outside onto the roof top. By this time the snow had stopped, but the winter breeze was still there. She shivered slightly as she waited for Henry's instructions.

"We can keep going, but you'll need to sleep soon," he began. "You have holy water guns, and you can use them to cause a vampire to react worse than the crucifixes. We will practice by using these makeshift targets we just made." Henry pointed to the three targets they made that were scattered around the roof.

Kat examined each of them.

"I want you to shoot some water at the centre of those targets," said Henry.

"Seems easy enough," Kat thought. She pulled out her dual holy water pistols and approached the nearest one to her. Before she could take aim, the makeshift target had vanished.

"What the?" Kat cried with shock. "Where the fuck did it go?"

"You've got to be quick, Rhodes!" Henry told her, commandingly.

Kat turned to look for the nearest one and immediately started running towards it as fast as she could possibly go. When she got close enough, she started to take aim, making sure it was going to hit the centre of the target. Unfortunately, she could see Tabitha racing towards her from the corner of her eye. This caused Kat to quickly react by dropping one of her water guns to have her crucifix palm available to use against Tabitha, whilst using her gun to shoot the target. Once holy water had hit the pillow, she quickly aimed the gun at Tabitha and pretended to shoot her.

"Bam!" she cried out, pretending she shot holy water at her. Tabitha dropped onto the floor and Kat quickly raced over to her and "stabbed" Tabitha. Kat picked up her gun off the floor, turned around and raced towards the next target whilst hearing out for Aaron, who she knew was coming for her. The next target was close to her, and she shot it from a distance and then quickly turned around to see if Aaron was nearby. There wasn't anyone there to catch her out, but she quickly turned and saw Henry approaching her, which caused her to pull her gun forwards quickly, and pretend to shoot Henry. Henry knelt to the floor and Kat raced to pretend to stab him, her breathing going rapid as she ran.

She could feel the determination racing through her veins as she was excited to see how well she was doing. All she could think about was how proud Will would have be of her if he was there right now.

Chapter 24:

♥

Training

By the end of the day, Kat felt she was ready to head to Ben Nevis Mountain to save the band, despite feeling weary from training.

"I think we should keep training tomorrow and head up there tomorrow evening," Henry suggested to her.

"I disagree," Kat argued. "I am ready to go now! Every second I spend not trying to save them, the closer they are to potential death. We must go now!"

"You're not ready; not just yet. You need to do a trial run tomorrow morning."

"And what if it's sunny tomorrow? Are we just going to have to wait until the sun sets? Wait until it's snowing again? I don't think so!"

Aaron and Tabitha sat awkwardly on the bed as they both watched the vampire and the human argue about the plan.

"Kat, I served in the military, we had to do training before we went into combat, so I know you're in need of more training first." Henry tried to get it into Kat's naïve mind that she needed to continue training. The thought of not being able to start driving up to Ben Nevis to save the band frustrated Kat. She tried awfully hard to put herself in Henry's shoes but was not successful.

"I promise you; I will get you in that van as soon as I know you are ready."

"And WHEN will I be ready, huh? Tomorrow? Next week? We don't have time! They could be dead by now!"

"I'm not saying you have to wait long. But judging by how well you've done today, we might be able to start heading up tomorrow evening."

"No, we go in the afternoon! Because it will take us a couple of hours to get there!"

Tabitha groaned in frustration before approaching Kat. She immediately stood in between her and Henry.

"Kat," she said to her. "Time to go to sleep." Tabitha waved her hand in front of Kat's eyes and stared at her. "Sleep for eight hours."

"Okay," Kat said softly, making her way out of the hotel room and going into hers.

"That was mean," Aaron whispered.

"It was necessary," said Tabitha. "I didn't want to do it, but she needs her rest."

"It's only seven o'clock though!"

"Exactly! The sooner she sleeps, the earlier she wakes up and the more time she will have for training!"

Aaron raised his head and nodded. "I see. That makes sense. I reckon all three of us should do some physical training tonight in preparation. I can teach you both more marital arts and self-defence techniques?"

"That is a smart idea. We can train ourselves whilst Kat is asleep. And by morning, she can do her training with us."

"Do you think she will be ready by tomorrow?" Tabitha queried at Henry.

Henry shrugged his shoulders, feeling tentative about it. "I would say by the way things are going, she could very well be. But I'm just worried that the vampires she will be facing will be more powerful than we can expect them to be. The last thing I want to happen is for Kat to be torn to pieces and become a blood bag."

"We all don't want that to happen, but she has us to help her," Tabitha marched over to the table to look at the floor plans of the hideout. "I think, if she didn't have us, she wouldn't be nearly as ready."

Kat woke up feeling groggy, and still in her clothes. Tabitha was sat on the bed next to her reading a celebrity magazine.

"Er did you?"

"Yes, it was late, and you wouldn't let us stop practice, even though you were getting sloppy and frustrated."

Kat frustratingly flopped backwards onto the pillows, motionless for a minute before raising her arm, aiming her finger towards the door, and yelled, "Out! I need to shower and get my shit together."

"Okay, but I'll be sat with my back against the door, we need to work on this together after breakfast."

Kat felt physically and mentally drained; the vampire sleep hadn't helped as she remembered a dream that had seemed to play on repeat all night. Kat found herself running down the corridor of the hideout, calling out for Will. There was no sign of Henry, Tabitha, or Aaron, as it should be. Kat also noticed that she was not wearing her vampire hunting gear and was wearing her normal everyday attire, which would be the worst thing to wear inside a snowy mountain filled with blood thirsty vampires.

The sounds of Will's screams echoed through the damp corridor, followed by Laura's, then David's, and then Oliver's. Kat began running much faster to get to the source of the screams. A few corners later, she saw four bodies lying on the floor, all of them covered in black blood, and their eyes remained open. A tall female figure stood above them, covered in pure human blood and laughed manically. She couldn't see the face, but could see that it was a woman, judging by the figure of the monster that killed her vampire friends. She stood there, looking defenceless at the monster.

The creature began running at high speeds towards Kat, her teeth visibly showing with her vicious smile, causing Kat to wake up screaming. Her hands clenched onto the pillow tightly as her screams muffled into the fabric. When she

realised what was going on, she stopped screaming and quickly
lifted her head up to see that she was in the hotel room . Relief
struck her as she saw she wasn't standing in front of the bodies
of her lover and his band.

Kat was still feeling fuzzy after the shower and her eyes lighted
on Will's purple notebook that rested on their bedside table. Her
curiosity had gotten the best of her as she slid across the bed,
turned on the bedside lamp, and went to pick up the notebook,
knowing full well whose it was. On the front of the book were
doodles drawn with a black ink biro pen. The pages of the book
were graffitied with black lines overlapping one another,
creating a border. Ink had splattered onto various parts of the
cover. In the centre of the book was the band's broken heart
logo hand drawn by Will. Kat rubbed her index and middle
finger against the heart drawing and could feel the pressures of
where the pen had been pressed down hard against the paper.

She opened up the notebook, and the first thing she
found written in the notebook were more drawings of broken
hearts, each of them drawn different to each other like they
were design choices.

Kat scrolled through the notebook and had found
pages upon pages filled with wordings and drawings of the sort
of thing she would expect a high school student to write or
draw during class. Words that had been underlined and
repeatedly written, especially the pages that contained the lyrics
to the songs she had seen Midnight Devotion perform.

One of the pages was written like a poem. At the top of
the page was the title of the poem: *My Thawed Hope,* Kat saw
that some of the words on the poem were written in red biro
and overlapped repeatedly to add emphasis.

> *These rivers once flowed **red***
> *Tho' **winter** conquered my world*
> *The roots of beauty are now **dead***
> *And my heart and soul cry and yearned*
> *For the life that was once mine*
> *Tho' now shackled by a **curse***
> *These **frozen** lands stand lost in time*

*Unknown to when the **frost** will reverse*
*For **eternity** these lands remain **pale***
Until further notice, or never at all
*My home becomes a wasteland and **stale***
*But some day, the warmth of **you** may come*
To thaw

     Kat stared at the poem, rereading it repeatedly until she had memorised the first half of it. She wondered when he had written the poem and what it all meant. It may seem obvious to most people, but due to Kat's restlessness she was unable to decode Will's poem.

     When she turned over to the next page, she saw a doodle of Will and Kat's initials written within drawn hearts. *WC + KR*. There was also a cute drawing attempt of Will and Kat as little cartoons, with Will being given fangs that were dripping blood from the tips. Kat was quite curious as to why Will would draw himself as a vampire if he desired to be human so as to spend the rest of his life with her. Just seeing Will's name next to hers was enough to make her feel emotional again from his absence, and unknown activities that may had taken place whilst she was reading his book.

     Kat could hear voices in the corridor and the door burst open.

     "Have you eaten yet?" Aaron asked her as he entered the room with the other two vampires.

     "No?"

     "Eat first, training after," Henry responded, not taking his eyes off the map. "We're going to fill you up with food before we head to the hideout. Don't want you killing vampires on an empty stomach."

     Kat groaned and collapsed onto the bed next to Tabitha. "Stupid human necessities!"

     "Let's get you some pancakes," she elated.

     "And orange juice?" Kat verified.

     "And orange juice."

     Tabitha placed an order for room service for Kat's breakfast. A stack of pancakes and a glass of orange juice arrived at the vampire's hotel room, where Tabitha collected the breakfast and handed it to Kat, who was itching to eat it.

"Don't scoff it down all at once," Aaron warned her, laughing at how determined she was to eat it. "Slow down, we have plenty of time. The weather is fine, and we can do a session before lunch, and then decide on what to do next over lunch!"

Kat 'took her time' with eating her breakfast as she was determined to start training as soon as she had finished.

"You do know we can't let you do any training until your body has digested the food," Aaron informed her.

"Bollocks! But what about giving me verbal demonstrations. Tell me what I should do, and tell me how to do it, and I'll do some slow moves, a bit like Tai Chi then we can practice as soon as you say so," Kat drank the entire glass of orange juice in one gulp.

"What we're going to be doing is everything you were doing yesterday, but you will be doing it with all three of us tracking you down," Henry told her seriously, "We won't be doing this on the roof top either. You'll have time for your digestion before we start."

"Huh?" Kat looked at Henry, anxious about the sudden change of scenery. "Where are we going?"

"Somewhere you're not familiar with. Bring your backpack as well."

Kat and her vampire associates got into the purple van, with the sky teeming with snow. Kat sat in the front with Henry sitting next to her and Aaron at the wheel, and Tabitha ensconcing at the back with all the leg room she had to herself.

"Will we need to fuel this vehicle before we head up north?" Henry queried to Aaron as he placed the blanket around Kat's shivering shoulders. She handed him a smile filled with gratitude and thanked him.

"I would advise that we do and we can use the merch money as we are done with the tour," Aaron confirmed.

"We're not going too far anyway and it's in the right direction. Just follow the main road and keep going straight."

Kat begun to feel the apprehension hitting her. She had hoped that after they've done the training that they would immediately head up Ben Nevis Mountain to rescue the band. The coven were in traffic for half an hour, which made Kat incredibly impatient, before they were at the outskirts of Glasgow. They then soon reached Bardowie, where Henry intended to have Kat train in the woods near Bardowie Loch. She needed to be in much harsher conditions to help her train in a more realistic and spacious environment. She did well on the roof, but Henry wanted somewhere more pragmatic for her and his coven to train. He was confident about Aaron, but he also wanted to train Tabitha with fighting vampires as well. When they arrived at Bardowie Loch, they got out of the van and Henry guided Kat and the coven to a remote part of the forest where nobody would spot them. His hearing would be able to detect any nearby hikers, or his sense of smell would be able to pick up dogs that the humans would be walking with.

The place Henry chose to train them in was quiet and isolated; it had the space for Kat to walk around, and the space for the vampires to hide and hunt.

"Same as yesterday, but this time all three of us will be hunting you and hiding up above," said Henry. "Use your ears at all times! Don't get distracted."

Before Kat could agree, the vampires were gone. She quickly pulled out one of the stakes from her belt and began walking and turning every few seconds from the anticipation of capturing one of them. The adrenaline that went through her was so immense that her legs began shaking, causing her to lose her footing and slip onto the cold muddy ground. She immediately picked herself back up and stood still for a moment, listening to her surroundings before she moved forward, trying to stay calm. The sounds of the winter winds and shaking branches entered her ears, along with the cold breeze, causing Kat to feel physical and emotional discomfort.

The fall of a branch caused Kat to gasp and immediately look up to investigate the sound. There wasn't anything or anyone up on the tree, but she knew that they were nearby. She got into the mindset that she was in the damp corridor of the hideout, or what she perceived to be the hideout, using her imagination of what the inside of a mountain may look like, back in the dream of last night.

The sound of rustling caused Kat to turn around quickly and see Tabitha racing towards her. Before Kat could react to the attack, she froze, allowing Tabitha to grab her by the shoulders and yelled "TAG!"

Kat stood there, impassively.

"You got me," she defeatedly shrugged. "Let's go for round two." And with that, Tabitha was gone.

Kat shook her head, trying not to lose her focus. She knew she was a novice vampire hunter, but she was quite complacent with upgrading her status in a short period of time. It had always been that way for her ever since she was a child; wanting to prove to people that she was able, normal, fitted in. Unfortunately, she was currently in a position where she would be fighting off omnipotent creatures that no human today knew existed, aside from herself: *"way to go!"* she thought. The sound of the branches swaying from the wind was distracting her slightly, camouflaging the possible sound of light footsteps. She continued to walk, with each footstep crunching down on the untouched snow. This was not going to be an issue when they get inside the mountain hideout, but she figured this was a hearing test, since vampires were incredibly furtive and quick.

There was a sound of crunching snow from a distance, which made Kat turn to see who it was that was coming for her, raising the palm of her hand in the process. This time, Aaron was the one who raced towards her. When Aaron saw the palm raised, he moved away from her, pretending to be staggered from what would be a crucifix glued to her palm. Another sound from the other side caught her attention; the sound of someone landing on the snowy ground. She instinctively dropped her stake from her other hand and placed her palm up to Henry. He dropped to the ground, pretending to be frightened. Once he was on his knees, she quickly took out another stake from her belt and raced over to Aaron to "stab" him in the chest. She suddenly noticed that she had almost stabbed him with the sharp end, causing her to yell out in disgust with herself.

"For fuck's sake!" She furiously cried. "I almost killed you!" Everything came to a halt. Aaron looked up at Kat and noticed the stake. He froze after realising what could have been, if she had not noticed.

"It's all right," Aaron assured her as he got up from the ground.

"No, it isn't! I almost killed you!" Kat marched away from Aaron, her head dropped and threw the stake on the ground out of sheer frustration. Tabitha was immediately in front of her, trying to offer her assurance and stifling her. "I'm so fucking stupid. So fixated with killing vampires to save a group or vampires that I almost killed a friend- who is a vampire."

"Kat!" Tabitha stared down at Kat, making sure she was looking back in her eyes. But Kat just looked down in shame. Tabitha used her index finger to place onto Kat's chin to raise it upwards, much like how Will did. She purposefully refused to look at Tabitha's, knowing what Tabitha's intentions were,, and did not want to give her the satisfaction.

"Look at me," she commanded her with a pleasant tone. Kat still refused. "I'm not going to hypnotise you, I promise." Kat trusted Tabitha this time and looked up to see her grey eyes showing lamentation. "It's okay. Really."

She wistfully nodded her head and suddenly embraced Tabitha.

"I'm sorry," Kat mumbled softly.

"Hey!" cried Aaron, smiling as he raced over to the girls in a flash. "Where's my hug? I'm the one you almost stabbed!" Tabitha and Kat both giggled as all three of them created a group embrace. Once they let go, they went back to the middle of the forest and continued their training.

For two long hours, they had Kat continue spotting vampires at a distance and quickly reacted to potential threats. She was getting better with each wave of training, and the exercise kept her warm, but she also had to catch breath before continuing. Henry had himself and Aaron fight each other to show their vampiric powers to Kat. Tabitha was not the fighting type but needed to be to fight the vampires they would potentially be facing. Henry taught Tabitha basic techniques in both attack and defence. Snow flicked everywhere with every crash that was caused by Aaron pinning Tabitha to the ground. Aaron's martial art techniques were mostly reactive, which gave them more of a chance to succeed. He offered his vampire friends some martial art techniques to use against the older vampires.

Kat continued to watch them race around the trees and clash their elbows and fists; the mid-air fighting reminded Kat of many movies and anime she had previously seen. The sounds of the limb clashing echoed through the trees. Kat was impressively surprised that nobody could hear the commotion happening from afar. Even if someone were to approach them to see a huge fight occurring, they would easily be able to escape the situation via hypnotism.

Tabitha joined in with a couple of the fights and her inexperience showed but she was not able to learn some of the new techniques quickly enough. Aaron had taught her some kung fu moves that he felt would benefit her greatly such as some novice kicking and punching manoeuvres.

"One last fight?" Henry asked Aaron, handing him a smile of determination. "Shall we have some fun?"

"Let's do this!" Aaron crashed his fist against the palm of his other hand. The boys were in immediate combat as they bought their hands together with a sound like thunder and began pirouetting around the forest. Kat could not keep up with the fighting; it was like they were teleporting through the trees, and she could not process where they were going. She decided to just keep her eyes focused on the centre of the area, so that her peripheral vision could pick up on any of the movement. Aaron was able to hit Henry, which caused him to fly through a tree trunk and land on the snow, winded but otherwise unscathed.

"Fucking hell," Kat whispered under her breath, covering her mouth with her hands. Tabitha just laughed at them. Henry quickly got up from the ground and approached the others in a flash. He chuckled as he and Aaron shook hands.

"Good fight!" Aaron laughed.

"Indeed!" Henry laughed along. "I think we're ready," Henry confirmed, smirking as he looked at Kat. "I think we are all ready."

Chapter 25:

♥

Ben Nevis

It was early afternoon when Kat and the vampires got to the hotel to collect their belongings. All Kat could feel was apprehension; her heart was racing more than ever. She calmed herself by closing her eyes and breathing in slow, rhythmic breaths as she packed her belongings.

Will's purple notebook rested on Kat's bedside table. She gazed at it before approaching the table to collect it and placed it into her bag. She knew Will wouldn't appreciate her reading his notebook, but the notebook was the only thing she had of his that gave her a sense of comfort and emotion. Whenever she would read the words written by him on the pieces of paper, she would feel his presence as well as hearing his voice with every word she read in her head.

This was it: the day Kat could change vampire history.

Tabitha came into the room to see if Kat was ready.

"I've never been more ready for anything," she responded, determined to get out of the hotel as soon as possible. She grabbed her suitcase and left the room without doing any last-minute checks. Tabitha shrugged as she followed behind.

Henry and Aaron were already in the van when Tabitha and Kat came out the building's entranceway. They had parked up in front and while Kat jumped into the front seat with Henry, Tabitha took Kat's suitcase and placed it in the back of the van where the music equipment and instruments were.

It was going to be a four-hour journey, meaning they would need to stop somewhere along the motorway to fuel up the van and give Kat the time to eat.

"This is it," said Tabitha indifferently. "By this time tomorrow, we could be human."

"I'm nervous as fuck," said Aaron as he started the ignition. "I'm not even sure what's going to happen to us when we turn human."

"What do you mean?" Henry asked.

"Like, will we all still be friends? Or will we all move on and start new lives? How are we going to start new lives with no money? No job? No legitimate ID?"

"I'm sure Laura has that under control," Kat informed him.

"And, whatever happens," said Henry, "We will always be friends. You two have been my family for the past five years and I would never want to be without you."

"Aww," Tabitha felt Henry's sincere words touch her non-beating heart.

The entire journey was prolonged. Kat was beginning to get more and more apprehensive by the minute. She checked her backpack to make sure she had everything packed and ready. There were a few snacks inside for the journey, but she would need to get more along the way.

She envisaged what may happen inside the hideout: the possible outcomes to certain actions she or the other vampires may take, what she may expect to see, and how she and Will would potentially be reunited. The image of Will being in any danger made her heart sink with heaviness. She hoped that they were not too late.

Aaron pulled up at a service station two and a half hours into the journey for Kat to grab some food whilst he went to fuel the van. Kat bought herself a hamburger and chips special from a fast-food restaurant, and wanted to eat in the van, wanting to waste no time at all. She also grabbed herself a bacon sandwich and a bottle of orange juice for later.

Once Aaron had finished fuelling up the van, the gang got in and drove the remaining two hours to Ben Nevis.

The sky was beginning to show a tonality of pink and orange shades in the sky behind the grey overcast, meaning it was becoming January twilight. It was potentially their last twilight as vampires, or as existing entities, depending on the outcome of tonight.

Kat's adrenaline made her restless. She would check her phone every few minutes to check the time, or to check if she had received any messages. Her parents had messaged her asking how she was doing, and Kat responding dishonestly saying she was okay, when in actuality she was anything but okay.

In the background, the vampires were conferring about what they were expecting to find inside the hideout. She also noticed that Laura had written on the side that the prison cells were small and built with silver materials to prevent breakouts. The vampires must have used some form of protection clothing when touching the silver to construct these prisons.

"So, do you reckon that's where they might be imprisoned?" Aaron asked her.

"Quite possibly" said Tabitha, "But, we can't immediately get in there as it is deep within the hideout."

"What's important is that we stick together, always, no matter what," Henry added. "We are Kat's extra pairs of eyes and ears."

"As well as her fists and feet!" Aaron pointed out. "I don't know about you guys, but I am so stoked to be vampire hunting tonight!"

Kat sat in silence, wishing she could contribute to the conversation, but was too busy staring out the window, anxious out of her mind, thinking whether she was truly ready. The motivation within her was driven by the thought of her companion, her lover, her soulmate, being in great danger, and she was doing all of this for their future, for the band's future, for the coven's future.

By six thirty in the evening, the sky was pitch black and shrouded with clouds, not a single star in the sky could be seen. They arrived at the North Face car park, the bottom of the mountain.

When Kat got out of the van, she felt the strong cold air kicking into her, making her shiver intensely despite wearing multiple layers of clothing and proper hiking gear. She stared up at the sight of the mountain with discontent. Four thousand three hundred feet; she feared how cold it was going to be at the summit.

"Don't worry," Henry assured her. "We're not going to be walking up the mountain."

"I know we're not! But we are definitely not going to be running, are we?"

"Nope!" Tabitha grabbed Kat around her waist like Will did, which indicated to Kat that she was about to go into the air. She was thankful for that, because she didn't want to walk in the cold night and trudge her way through heavy snow. If she didn't have the three vampires, she would have failed, which made her wonder:

"Do you think Mistress Claudette wanted to spare you so that you guys could get me into the hideout?"

"Maybe." Tabitha shrugged. "But let's not dally around thinking about it."

Aaron leapt up into the sky, followed by Henry, and then Tabitha - still holding onto Kat. The cold air was much worse as it stroked the skin of her face. It began causing discomfort to her throat every time Kat breathed in through her mouth. She closed her mouth and breathed through her nose.

All three had their wings extended from their backs and were ready to take flight. Kat heard their clothes being ripped to let the wings come out from their skin.

The vampires glided their way through the arctic air, their wings flapped in unison as they made their way through the fields and the trail below.

For ten whole minutes, Kat felt the apprehension growing stronger as they approached the largest mountain in Scotland - the secret hideout of the Head Vampire who ruled all vampires in the United Kingdom - where her lover and his lifelong companions were imprisoned. This was either going to be the start of a new life for her, or the end of her current life. She thought to herself that so long as she was with Will when she died, she would feel at peace knowing she died alongside him.

When they reached the top of the mountain, the vampires descended onto the flat surface of the mountain peak. The air was immensely cold for Kat; the worst cold environment she had ever delt with. The wind howled savagely as it created snow dust.

"The thermal clothing don't do shit to keep me warm!" Kat shivered as she folded her arms as tightly against her chest as possible to try and keep herself warm, even though it was doing nothing to change that. The thickness of the snow came halfway up her legs, making her saunter towards the vampires, who weren't affected by the weather's challenges or aggressively low temperature.

Tabitha scavenged through all her pockets until she found the sheets of paper that Laura had drawn up. She unfolded it, making sure the strong gust of mountain wind didn't blow them away. She scanned through the papers with her vampiric vision to read in the dark.

"She wrote that we need vampire blood to open the entrance and place it in the cairn." Tabitha loudly announced.

"We need to extract blood from ourselves. However, as soon as we develop a wound, it would heal instantly. So, we would need to be quick," Henry clarified.

"How do we cut the flesh of a vampire then?" Kat queried.

"Silver, of course," Henry responded as he marched over to her. "You'll need to cut my skin to get my blood." Kat stared down at Henry's hand when he offered it to her.

"Laura wrote that there should be a concrete cairn. That's where the blood needs to go," Tabitha informed them.

"Why vampire blood?"

"It's a vampire hideout; it makes sense that they would need something vampiric to enter," said Henry.

"Kind of like an entrance fee to get into a club," said Tabitha as she walked over to the trig point where she saw a small hole on top of the stones, which she assumed was where the blood needed to be placed. There didn't seem to be evidence of blood spillage on the rocks since vampire blood evaporates in a minute. "This must be where we need to spill the blood."

Aaron, Henry, and Kat all walked over to the cairn. They analysed the detail of the concrete and concluded that this was the entranceway.

Kat rummaged through her backpack to find her pocketknife. The cold air didn't make her go any faster.

She finally found her knife and quickly pulled it out, extracted the blade from the choice of tools, then proceeded to cut Henry's palm. As the silver tip of the blade came into contact with his vampiric skin, Henry winced as the pain became real, the pain he had not felt in a long time. Black ooze came out from the wound. Henry quickly went to the entranceway to pour his blood into the hole in the stone. He made sure many drops of it were used - he wasn't so sure how much was needed but he had to be sure that there was enough blood to suffice.

The blood began seeping into the concrete as they heard what sounded like a boulder being pushed. They saw that the cairn was moving away from them, revealing a large stairway into the mountain. All that could be seen was complete darkness.

Henry's wound healed instantly as Kat quickly went to grab her backpack and placed it on her shoulders. She took one last look at the sky; the Moon being visible through the parting clouds, since it could be the last time that she saw the sky.

"You ready, Kat?" Henry asked her.

"Let's go," Kat confirmed and quickly turned to make her way down the steps with her vampire friends right beside her. The concrete cairn began to move back into its original position, as soon as all four were inside the mountain. Kat could feel the apprehension dwelling up inside herself again as they were approaching the endgame of the mission. Her fate, and the fate of the vampires, rested upon her.

Chapter 26:
♥
Castle

The rescue coven walked down the wet stony steps of the interior mountain. Inside Ben Nevis was dimly lit, making it impossible for Kat to see, but the vampires had no trouble finding their way down the steps. The walls were quite closed in, giving Kat a sense of claustrophobia. The only sounds that could be heard, besides Kat's heavy footsteps, were the echoes of water dripping onto the ground from the rocky ceiling, creating an ominous atmosphere.

Kat could feel Tabitha's hand cup hers for moral support as well as making sure her human vulnerability didn't let her fall, which Kat appreciated. Her nervousness would have gotten the best of her and caused her to be clumsy in a dire situation.

"How deep into the mountain are we going?" Kat wondered aloud; her voice echoed through the stairwell.

"Two thousand feet, roughly halfway down the mountain," Tabitha responded.

"Then why couldn't they have the entranceway halfway down the mountain?"

Nobody responded to her question, unsure themselves on why that was.

"Do you want me to pick you up and run down the steps?" Tabitha joked.

"No, no, I'll be fine!" Kat shook her head, denying her offer. "I don't want to risk vomiting after the high-speed run. I can't be doing with illness right now. I just hope that we don't have to climb back up!"

"If we all turn human, we will be hoping the same!" Henry chuckled.

After what felt like a long trek down the stairs, the site of the castle was in full view as they reached the threshold entrance to a flat pavement. They entered what looked like a huge cave, above them was complete darkness and the ceiling could not be identified by Kat's eyes. She looked up briefly and wondered if the ceiling top was the peak of the mountain, but her mind then focused on the primary view. At the end of the long pavement was the castle of Mistress Claudette. The strong lighting from the window illuminated the mountain's interior, making it the centre of attention. Kat's heart skipped a beat when her eyes leered at the castle in sheer determination and anger. She stopped to take in the view of the castle's elegance.

The castle itself was the type she had seen before in fantasy books and media: large wooden entranceway; many windows in various shapes and sizes - some with coloured glass; slim towers near the top of the building, and the colour of the building itself was a mixture of greys and reds. This was what she would describe as the biggest castle she had ever seen in person. The idea of potentially being the very first human to set eyes on a vampire hideout this elegant and mysterious made her somewhat fortunate, but she did not have that feeling for awfully long.

Without a word, Kat made her way down the pavement, with Tabitha's hand still grasping onto hers. She felt more and more uneasy with each step she took.

The castle grew larger as they approached closer. Kat pushed her fears away and allowed the adrenaline to conquer and push her to go towards the doors rather than hesitate.

"Are we going to need vampire blood to open this door too?" asked Kat. "Or do a secret vampire knocking technique?"

"No, and no," said Tabitha. "I guess we just push the door open?"

"Allow me," Aaron approached the wooden doors. He grunted as he pushed the doors without any setbacks. A loud creek echoed through the mountain; it was almost comical how it sounded like a creaky door in a horror film.

"I don't think I would have been able to do that if I was by myself," Kat pointed at the door. "It looks very heavy. Though you vampires make everything heavy look light."

In front of them through the doorway was the lobby of the castle. They could see in front of them two stairways, one on each side that curled up to the next floor, and in between those stairs was a corridor that led to a large door.

Everyone in the group walked through the doorway of the castle and were greeted with the scent of burning candles and varnished wood. The chandelier above the centre of the lobby held one hundred candles burning bright. The walls of the castle lobby were coloured with shades of burgundy, creating a royal vintage aesthetic to the room. The flooring had black and white checked tiles that were diagonal like diamonds rather than squares. Placed on top of the tiles were a few pieces of furniture. A long red velvet sofa was next to the wall underneath a painted portrait of Ben Nevis Mountain, painted from a distance on a cold snowy morning, with bright orange, pink, and blue background.

Another red velvet sofa was seen opposite the sofa under the portrait, and a black fabric rug was centralised between the sofas with an incredibly old coffee table placed on top.

"Where to first?" Aaron asked everyone, seeming unsure himself where the best place to start would be.

"The dungeons are going to be down below the castle. If I were to guess that's where the band will be kept imprisoned?" Tabitha informed the gang.

"What's at the end of that corridor?" Kat pointed to where she could see the door. Tabitha took a quick look at the map of the castle to confirm.

"That will be where the throne room is. Where Claudette trials the vampires. I wouldn't go in there just yet though."

Kat turned to look at Tabitha, confused as to why she told her this.

"Why not?"

"Because we can't know for certain if they're in there," said Henry. "Tabitha's right, we need to find the dungeon first and see if they're in there. Otherwise, we will be going in there blindly and not have the potential reinforcement. If we find the band, we may have extra power to fight her off."

"But what if they're not in the dungeon?" Kat argued. "What if they're behind those doors about to get tortured? Or even killed right now?"

"Isn't Claudette expecting you to be here, though?" asked Aaron. "Judging by the blood on the window back at the hotel, it seemed as though she wants you here. Maybe this is all a game to her, and she wants you to go off searching for them."

"I think we should head to the dungeon first," said Henry.

"How long will that take us?" Kat begun to get impatient with the situation and was itching to charge through the doors to the throne room without hesitation, but knew she wouldn't be fast enough to escape the vampires.

"I'm not sure but let me take the lead and we'll be there in no time." Tabitha approached the set of stairs to her left and the gang followed behind, allowing her to take the lead. Kat heavily relied on her to know where she was going, as the lives of her vampire friends rested on her shoulders which added more pressure onto her.

The corridor on the first floor had two doors on each side. Tabitha informed them that according to Laura's drawing they were just cloakrooms for visitors. They moved on to approach the door at the end of the corridor. Tabitha pushed the door open, and the next room revealed to them a corridor with a left turn about twenty feet away.

Around the corner of the corridor was the entrance to a balcony with stairs straight ahead. On their right, after the doorway, was the balcony that led to the next door that would lead them to the next part of the first floor.

Down below the balcony was a grand piano that was centred on a large green floor mat with two red sofas on either sides and a large fireplace against the wall. Above the fireplace was a large painting of a woman with long blonde hair that rested around her waistline, and a black laced dress that covered her legs and feet completely. She stood with an expression of jubilance as her blood red eyes gazed at them. Kat did not expect the Mistress to look like that. She had envisaged someone wearing a large royal robe and a golden crown on the top of her head. Claudette was deadly beautiful. She was the very definition of 'if looks could kill'.

Below the painting was a golden plaque that had engraved *"Mistress Claudette Hemming. 1706".*

"This must be the piano room," said Tabitha. "We need to get a move on and go down the corridor into the next room."

Kat continued to gaze at the woman who had stolen her friends, looks of resentment plastered on her face as her eyes took in every inch of the woman's features on the painted image. She had known the name for months, but never saw the face until now, and already, despite never meeting, she hated her.

"Kat?" Aaron leaned close to her. "We need to get going."

She nodded, taking one last look of the painting, making sure that she had the image imprinted on her mind to give her further motivation. She turned and hurriedly made her way to the end of the corridor where Henry and Tabitha stood waiting for her and Aaron.

When Kat opened the door, she gasped in amazement. In front of her was an enormous golden chandelier, much bigger than the one in the lobby. No candles were lit to illuminate the room, however, a glass dome ceiling above them was what was keeping the room alight. Golden banisters were seen all over the large room, with a giant black and white checked floor below which Kat could describe as a ballroom. There were many seats and tables that surrounded the outside of the dancefloor and a drinks bar at the far-right side of the room underneath one of the balconies.

She felt as though she had stumbled into a fairy-tale or a scene from a period drama. Just looking at its elegance made her feel incredibly underdressed and unprepared, despite there being no one in the room to judge her.

"No balls happening here tonight, then?" said Tabitha. "Shame. A vampire ball sounds like a picturesque experience to witness."

"Reminds me of a theatre I went to in the early forties before I went to war," Henry thought. "Only with less gold and less formal-looking."

Ahead of them were the stairs leading down to the dance floor. On their right would lead them across the balcony and they would then have to go left and down the other balcony where the next door was. The temptation to go downstairs onto the dance floor was overcasting Kat's reasoning. She pushed the temptation away and marched her way forwards across the balcony. Tabitha and Aaron raced down the stairs to examine the dance floor in case anything or anyone was hiding or preparing an ambush, whilst Henry stayed with Kat.

Before Kat could approach the door, a loud crash occurred down below, causing her and Henry to lean over the balcony to see what had happened. Tabitha had been thrown across the room and had disappeared through the wall, however they couldn't see what had done this to her.

"Tabitha!" Aaron cried. They heard him grunting and saw him fly backwards, his feet landing on the ground but causing the dance floor to crumble beneath his soles.

A slim woman with large monster claws and bat wings flew across the room to approach Aaron. Her long black hair waved through the air when she glided towards him. The pointy fangs of the monster poked through her black lips.

Henry quickly leapt off the balcony to help Aaron. Kat, meanwhile, ran across the balcony to get to the stairs as the balcony was much too high for her to jump from. Henry grabbed hold of the vampire and tackle her to the ground. Unfortunately, she immediately threw him off her and was thrown across the room, crashing through one of the golden pillars and onto the upper floor. Dust settled around the damage as debris started falling onto the floor below.

Kat pulled off her winter gloves and revealed her fingerless gloves with the crucifix on. She then pulled out one of her holy water pistols and charged towards the vampire head on with her open hand in front of her. The vampire paid no attention to her as she was focused on Aaron, so she did not expect holy water to come shooting towards her. The holy water caused the vampire's skin to start smoking, making her scream in pain from the burning. When she turned to look where it came from, she screamed in horror to see how close the crucifix was to her. The vampire recoiled and hissed, hovering in mid-air.

Kat continued to shoot holy water at the vampire, but the vampire became too high up for the water gun to take effect. She continued hissing at Kat, waiting for her to let her guard down so she could take the first strike. Unfortunately for the vampire, Kat wasn't gullible enough for that to happen.

Tabitha launched herself at the vampire in mid-air, and the pair collided, beginning their battle above the dance floor.

"I can't get a shot when she's in the air," Kat informed Aaron as soon as she approached him.

"I'll try and get her to come down and we'll pin her for you to stake her heart," Aaron devised the plan aloud. Henry leapt from the balcony and approached Aaron when he saw him gesture a sign to get to him. In a flash Henry was next to Aaron and Kat. They watched Tabitha and the vampire battle above the dance floor, trying to slash each other and grab hold of the other's neck to decapitate them.

Without a word, Aaron left Henry and Kat and ran up the stairs onto the upper floor, immediately leaping off to launch himself at the vampire brawl. He tried to grab onto the vampire that had her hands wrapped around Tabitha's arms making it impossible for her to move. Thankfully, Aaron crashing onto the vampire set Tabitha free from her grasp and start the fight with him, leaving Tabitha to fall onto the floor below, landing swiftly like a cat. Henry and Kat raced over to make sure she wasn't hurt.

"I'm fine," she reassured her. "She almost had me."

Aaron comically yelled 'hiya' as he used all his martial art skills to fend off the vampire woman and roundhouse kicked her across the head, getting her back on the ground, which he was surprised didn't rip her head clean off. The impact of the crash caused the tiling of the dance floor to break, creating a large dent on the flooring.

Henry and Tabitha ran to the vampire and made sure she was unable to move by wrapping their arms around her shoulders and legs. Aaron landed on the ground and added the extra weight to the vampire. She growled and hissed, trying to fight off the weight on her Kat approached her with a wooden stake at hand. Kat instinctively pushed the stake with all her human force right through the vampire's tough grey skin. The force of the sharp stake penetrated through without hesitation. Smoke leaked from the wound as the vampire's screams echo through the ballroom, loud enough to break the glass dome ceiling above. Large shards of glass rained down onto the dance floor where the action took place. Aaron quickly pushed Kat away from the dance floor as the glass came crashing down onto the vampires. Tabitha and Henry were able to escape the falling glass shards, leaving them to penetrate through the vampire. While the glass didn't take effect on the vampire, the stake to the heart began turning her into smoke and ash. Her screams began to die down when most of her body deteriorated. The gang waited for the vampire to completely disintegrate before moving on.

"Second vampire kill," Kat muttered to herself.

"Well done," said Henry.

"Well done to you guys, I don't think I would have succeeded without your help." Kat smiled at Henry before moving it to Tabitha and Aaron.

"By the way, Aaron," said Tabitha. "What the fuck was up with the 'hiya' that you were doing?"

Henry and Kat both let out a quiet laugh.

"Dramatic effect!" Aaron shrugged. "It worked, didn't it? I should do it more often if it works!"

Chapter 27:

♥

Weapons

The next room behind the door from the ballroom was another corridor with four doors, two on each side of the burgundy painted walls. The end of the corridor had two turnings, left and right, so Tabitha had to direct them to get to their destination since she had the map.

"Behind these doors are bedrooms," Tabitha informed them. "Probably for vampires to get freaky, if you know what I mean?"

"Gross," Aaron cringed. "So, they're sex rooms, basically?"

"Nothing wrong with people getting intimate," Tabitha objected. "Or should I say: vampires getting it on."

"I don't want to know what orgy shit vampires do! Or what vampire sex is like!"

"Probably the same as regular human sex?" Tabitha shrugged.

Kat didn't pay any attention to their ribald conversation. Her mind was fixated in making their way through the castle and preparing herself for whatever vampire came their way next. She figured that they would need to fight off a few vampires before getting into the dungeon, though she was surprised how far away the dungeon was from the lobby. She thought that it would have been convenient for them to have an elevator or something to get to the dungeon from the courtroom or the lobby. Even if they did have super speed to get from point A to point B, she still thought it would be a good idea to have an elevator.

They turned right at the end of the corridor and saw more doors, presumably more "bedrooms". On the left was a stairway going up to the third floor, but they weren't going to be going that way just yet.

When they walked past one of the doors, they could hear sexual activities happening, causing them to cringe and increase their walk speed to get to the door at the end of the corridor.

Tabitha quickly opened the door, and everyone raced through the doorway to leave the corridor of sexual fulfilments.

Aaron shuddered as the door closed behind them.

Kat gazed at their surroundings to see where they were. Stacks of books were stacked on immensely tall bookshelves. Every inch of the walls were plastered with shelves of books. In the centre of the room was a platform with a table set and a couple of green leather sofas.

"A reading room," Kat said aloud, her voice echoed through the tall library. "Wouldn't be surprised if they own every book known to man in here."

"Or it's filled with vampire literature and vampire history?" Henry wondered. "I reckon the birth of vampires is written in one of these books!"

"We don't have time to be reading books, unfortunately," Kat told him.

"We're not here to read books in general," Tabitha announced like a schoolteacher. "We're here to grab some weapons."

"Weapons?" Henry asked, seeming surprised to hear the word in a room full of books of all places.

"Behind that door over there is a small collection of ancient weapons throughout the last few centuries." Tabitha pointed to the door that was at the far end of the room that had the shelves arched around the doorway. "We could do with more weaponry. I have a strong suspicious feeling-"

"Hold up!" Aaron interrupted. "Did you just say, 'ancient weapons'?"

". . . yeah?"

"Like, crossbows, swords, and cool shit?"

"Probably, I don't know."

Aaron ran abruptly across the library and approached the door. He could see that there was a doorknob with a keyhole below it. He turned the knob, but the door wouldn't budge.

"It needs a key!" he called out. "But not to worry! I AM the key!" Aaron pressed his fingers together and pushed his hands forward to prepare for what he was about to do. Everyone else wasn't surprised with what he was about to do, and they let him do it anyway. They watched Aaron start punching at the door and breaking it into bits, all while doing the 'hi-yaaa!' call with each punch. The debris started flying around the room with every punch that struck on the door. His punching was at a high speed, making the breaking of the door easier and quicker.

Aaron finally destroyed the door and bowed at his peers with self-approval.

"You are most welcome!"

"Must you make those 'hi-ya' noises every time you do an attack?" Tabitha queried.

"Hey, don't judge my techniques and ways of fighting!" Aaron gave Tabitha a cunning smirk.

They approached the door and could see from afar that there were display cabinets and display stands containing a variety of old-fashioned weapons. The first weapon that caught their eye was an old crossbow that was held by a stand. Henry took immediate fascination by removing it from its display and examined its features. It's body was made of wood with a steel contraption to place the bolt on when connecting it to its large black elastic string, and the trigger below to release it.

"I will be taking this!" Henry announced, smiling at the beauty of the crossbow.

"Where are the bolts?" Kat wondered.

"They must be around this room somewhere."

"OH SHIT!" Aaron screamed enthusiastically. "Guys! I found nunchucks! AHA HA!" Everyone turned to see Aaron grasping a pair of varnished nunchucks that had red painted handles and stainless-steel chains in between the handles. "I'm totally taking these bad boys!"

"Be my guest," Tabitha rolled her eyes and chuckled.

Kat wandered around the room, feeling like she was in a museum, reminding her of the day she spent in Cardiff with Will. There were a variety of swords from all over the world.

"Why does Claudette have all these weapons?" Kat wondered aloud.

"They were probably gifts or peace offerings, maybe trophies," said Tabitha. "Or she has a thing for ancient weapons? Like when someone collects stuff within a certain interest, spend a fuck-ton of money to flex their wealth or ability to own decorative shit? I never really got it." Kat instantly thought about her collection of gothic and witchcraft décor, which made her miss her small flat back in her serene, mundane human life. "Yeah, I suppose you're right."

Her eyes suddenly gazed on a sword as its blade gleamed from the lighting of the wall sconces. She was mesmerised by the elegance of the sword's unique style; its grip was wrapped in red leather, the pommel was pure white gold that was shaped like a butterfly with red rubies on its body, and its guard was red steel that curled like a heart around the grip. Its blood red scabbard was placed below the stand, which Kat took and wrapped its leather straps around her belt. The sword was taken from its stand; it was much heavier than she had expected. After lifting it with all her might, Kat continued gazing at the sword's beauty, moving her hand slightly to the left and then the right to shine the blade before sliding it into the scabbard.

Whilst Aaron was spinning the nunchucks around like a child being given a new toy, Henry had found the quiver holding some steel tipped bolts for the crossbow.

Tabitha looked at a dagger that had roses painted on its long golden grip, and its blade was roughly twelve inches long. She picked up the dagger that was resting inside a white

319

scabbard with roses also painted on it and pulled out the blade
by its grip. The blade shone as it was revealed.

"This will do," Tabitha told herself, wrapping the
string onto her belt.

Kat approached Tabitha, asking her where they will be
heading to next.

"We need to go back to the corridor and go up the
stairs onto the third floor."

The room grew silent as Aaron ceased his nunchuck
playing.

"You mean we have to go back into the sex corridor?"
His horrified tone exclaimed.

"Just cover your ears if it bothers you so much!"
Tabitha told them from across the room. "We need to get to the
third floor, and we will then find the passage into the
dungeons!"

"We have weapons, let's get going then!" Kat
commanded, leaving the weapons room and going back into the
library. The others followed behind her; Tabitha raced ahead to
make sure she was in front of her, which almost threw Kat off
guard, but she kept her balance from the sudden surprise.

When Tabitha walked through the door, they were
suddenly greeted by a tall gentleman wearing nothing but black
leather jeans, who had dishevelled orange hair.

"Going somewhere?" he asked in a cocky tone. He
immediately grabbed Tabitha by the throat and lifted her in the
air. Before the others could react, a woman wearing a red and
black laced tank top who had long red hair that was tied up in a
ponytail which ended halfway down her back, flew past him,
and grabbed Henry. Aaron grabbed onto Kat to pull her out of
the way but then had to leave her a sitting duck to help his
friends. Kat immediately pulled out one of her holy water guns
and took her chance with saving Tabitha whilst Aaron went
after Henry.

Kat quickly revealed the palm of her hand to expose
the vampire to the crucifix. He was too busy staring up at
Tabitha, watching her fight against his grasp. This encouraged
Kat to start shooting, aiming for his bare skin. The vampire
quickly turned Tabitha to use her body as a shield against the

holy water. This made Kat suddenly stop. She felt useless, unable to help her friend. She heard Henry being thrown against a shelf, causing books and broken pieces of wood to fall onto the floor.

Aaron was in the middle of combat with the red-haired vampire, which meant Henry was now available to help Kat. He saw what was happening with Tabitha and immediately acted on the situation by getting up and going into the corridor. Henry pulled Kat away from the doorway to put himself where she had stood.

"Keep your eyes peeled," Henry whispered to her, handing Kat something heavy. "And watch your back too."

Before Kat could say anything, Henry had run ahead towards the vampire and tried tackling him to the ground. Unfortunately, he deflected his attack by standing to the side and used Tabitha as a bodily shield, causing Henry to miss. The vampire instantly grabbed onto Henry by the back of his collar and pulled him away. He then threw him out of the corridor and back onto the bookshelf, causing more books to come raining down onto the ground. When the vampire turned to grab Henry, his body was finally exposed, and he saw that Kat had replaced her holy water guns with a crossbow in her hands. She immediately pulled the trigger, and the bolt flew straight into the vampire's shoulder, piercing through his rough skin, making the vampire screech in rage.

Tabitha kicked the vampire in the chest when he instinctively pulled her closer to his body, releasing her. She quickly pulled out her dagger from its scabbard and immediately approached him. Without letting the vampire react, she began stabbing him through his chest with the dagger, at the same time letting out a revolting scream. His eyes widened with the sudden realisation that his vampire life had now come to an end. The pain of his heart being stabbed made him shrill in agony as smoke started to sprawl from where the blade had entered the skin and black blood spewed out with every stab.

Images began appearing in her mind that she was familiar with, ones that she had forbade herself from remembering, despite it being from the time she turned after her

human life had ended. The images of two older men who had
her tied to a chair and proceeded to beat her senseless for fun.
The pain dwelled within her, causing her to lash out at the
shirtless vampire by repeatedly stabbing him through the chest
and letting out a loud cry filled with anger, grief, sadness, built
up emotions that she had suppressed herself from confronting
for years.

Having a male, no matter what species they were,
physically grab hold of her without her consent was something
that would trigger a hidden emotion that she had locked away
inside in a long time. She almost had this reaction when David
attacked her out of anger, but she put herself in his shoes and
understand why he reacted the way he did, and she forgave him
when he had apologised. But now was a moment she knew, no
matter what, she wasn't going to receive an apology from this.

She stabbed her attacker unrelentingly, refusing to
stop. Kat tried to pull Tabitha away from the vampire, but she
was so fixated on her emotions that she ignored her. The cries
of the vampire were drowned out by Tabitha's intense,
emotional, rage-filled screaming.

"You perverted bastard!" she yelled. "You sick,
perverted, sadist prick!"

"Tabitha!" Kat cried. "Stop!" Tabitha stopped
screaming and left the dagger inside the vampire, watching him
deteriorate into ash. The dagger collapsed on top of the
vampire's ashy remains.

She turned to hug Kat, breathing rapidly with each
breath slowing down.

"I'm sorry," she whispered, seeming guilty to have Kat
witness her outburst.

"I'm just glad you're okay," Kat assured her.

A loud feminine cry was heard from the library,
followed by a loud crash from glass and metallic items. The
girls turned to see what was happening in the library. The other
vampire was on her knees, her face plastered with grief. Aaron
and Henry had been thrown into the weapons room and had
crashed into the display stands. Aaron's groans could be heard.

"My love!" she keened, collapsing herself onto the
floor and wailed with grief. "My Jack! You will PAY!" Her skin

started to turn dark grey, and her figure began to morph into a muscular creature. Large bat wings extracted from her back and her hands became large claws with long red nails. Her face was no longer beautiful as it had become the face of a monster. The teeth inside her monstrous-looking mouth had grown larger and sharper, the type of teeth that children would draw, thin triangular teeth. Her ears were pointing outwards, her hair became frizzy and out of control, and her upper torso grew large muscles with her legs being smaller than her arms.

"I WILL KILL YOU!" she roared venomously as she marched her way towards the girls. Tabitha pulled Kat behind her to become her vampiric shield and prevent any harm. Henry and Aaron left the weapons room and gazed at the female's transformation.

"What the actual fuck?" said Aaron. "Where did she go? Who's this hideous creature?"

Henry tried to strategize a way to reach the girls and get them away from the doorway. An idea finally came to mind.

"Throw it," he whispered to Aaron. He knew immediately what he meant, and, without questioning it, Aaron threw his nunchucks at the vampire monster. They spun in mid-air like a throwing star at a high speed and ripped through one of her wings.

She pirouetted to face the culprit and growled at the boys.

"Oops," Aaron shrugged sarcastically. "My bad!"

The monster's screams caused many of the bookshelves to vibrate viciously and several books to fall to the floor.

She glided awkwardly towards Aaron which gave Henry the opportunity to run to the girls. He quickly grabbed the crossbow from Kat and picked up the bolt that laid in the ashes of the vampire that Tabitha had killed and place it into the crossbow. He prepared the loading of the bolt before he turned quickly to aim at the monster that was trying to grab onto Aaron, but she was unable to, as he was parrying around in constant flashes. He dodged every slash attack the monster attempted and flew from one end of the room to the next, pushing himself from the bookshelves to get more speed when gliding across the room. Henry struggled to get a good aim at the monster as she was continuously gliding around chasing after Aaron. She stopped mid-air in the centre of the room and began spiralling rapidly until her body formed a black tornado. Books began lifting off the ground and flew around the library, some hitting Aaron in the process as the strong gale force winds slowed him down. He too, along with the books, were spiralling around the room and was unable to gain control of his movements.

"Shoot her!" Tabitha commanded Henry.

"I can't! The bolt will just fly away from her!" Tabitha and Kat both tried to come up with a solution to their situation. They had to act fast in case the monster was planning a final blow on Aaron. The apprehension made Tabitha act when she had an idea spring to mind; one she was a little reluctant about.

"I never wanted to do this, but it seems I have no choice," Tabitha closed her eyes. "Let's fight fire with fire." She allowed her inner emotions to get the better of her and had her body morph into the very thing she never wanted to become: a *monster*, just like the one in front of them. She began huffing violently as black smoke began to develop around her outline, creating a dark aura.

Kat stood away from her to allow Tabitha the room for her conversion. Just like the vampire, her muscles expanded and her beautifully pale skin turned a ghastly grey. Henry turned to see his friend becoming the very thing they were fighting against. She was no longer recognisable to him.

When her transformation was complete, she let out a vicious growl before launching herself into the eye of the storm. Her wings were able to deflect the books that were spiralling around the room whilst making her way to tackle the vampire. Tabitha used all her strength to break through the tornado and grab hold of its source, disrupting its spiralling attack and cancelling out the tornado. The women crashed onto the upper bookshelf above the weapons room. The impact was so intense that it caused it to have every book in the room collapse off the shelves and onto the floor, creating a mountain of books. The site of the library was like an earthquake had hit the castle at a remarkably high magnitude.

Aaron and the books all fell onto the ground. Aaron landed like a cat when he reached the floor.

"Woo! That was pretty intense!" he laughed. The nunchucks he had thrown earlier landed right on top of his head, causing him to collapse onto the floor. "Fuck!" he groaned.

Henry and Kat both gazed at what Tabitha had become and watched her fight off the enemy vampire. Aaron got up with his nunchucks at hand and was shocked to see what Tabitha had become.

"Tabitha?!"

"Yup! That's her alright!" Kat confirmed, looking just as shocked as he was.

The Behemoths were grasping onto each other's claws whilst staring down at one another viciously, fighting as if they were the only ones in the room.

"Shouldn't we help her?" Aaron pointed out, seeming worried for his friend. Henry got his bolt ready and aimed it steadily at the enemy vampire. Once he felt confident enough, he pulled the trigger, and the bolt flew across the room at a high speed and successfully penetrated through the vampire's wing and into her upper back.

"Nice shot!" Aaron cried enthusiastically. The vampire growled in pain but refused to acknowledge the culprit who shot her.

Henry pulled out his right arm and said to Kat, "Stake". She handed him one of her stakes and then he immediately ran through the heavily damaged library. He jumped high enough to be above the fight and landed heavily on top of the enemy vampire. The force of his fall caused her to lean back away from Tabitha but still heavily hung onto her claws. Henry continued pulling the vampire away from Tabitha while simultaneously trying to get the stake to penetrate through her chest and into her heart. Unfortunately, her upper muscles were too large for him to get his arm to where the stake needed to go.

Aaron decided to give Henry help by leaping up to the vampire battle and use all of his strength to pull the enemy vampire away from Tabitha. Her claws were still colliding with the Behemoth but decided that enough was enough. Tabitha leaned her head backwards and with full force she shot her head forward fast enough to bash onto her opponent's forehead, headbutting her. It leaned back even further which gave Henry and Aaron the advantage to get the vampire off Tabitha and onto the ground. The impact of the fall caused the books around them to stumble around the library.

Kat ran over to the scene with a stake in hand and was ready to finish her off.

Tabitha had her claws wrapped around the vampire's throat and pinned her down hard enough to prevent escape. Henry and Aaron's weight on her arms and legs kept her restrained.

Kat stabbed the vampire monster heavily through the chest with the wooden stake. Just like the last two vampires, the wound started to sprawl smoke and black blood, oozing out as the monster hollered in pain and began to disintegrate into ash.

Tabitha slowly began turning back into her normal self while the vampire enemy was putrefying. She shook her head and let her hair wave around.

"That was intense," she sighed with a smile.

"That was still pretty fucking cool though, you've got to admit that!" Aaron told her. She just handed him a chuckle and raised her eyebrows.

Kat stared down at the pile of ash and rubble remains of the vampire she and the others had just killed. She could feel parts of herself physically and mentally changing, one vampire kill after another. The adventure she had been on the last week was one she knew was going to change her immensely, one that she would never be able to forget.

Chapter 28:
♥
Dungeon

The gang went up the stairs onto the third floor. The stairway was tighter than the last one. It spiralled its way upwards with torch scones attached to its brick walls. Kat figured that this was one of the side towers that she had spotted outside the castle.

"So many stairs," Kat huffed wearily. "Why?"

"Do you want me to carry you?" Henry politely offered.

"Please." Kat allowed Henry to lift her up with his arms under her legs and her body resting on his back. He walked up the stairs easily with Kat on his back, and it turned out they didn't have far to go, which slightly irritated Kat.

"I'll carry you the next time we find a set of spiral stairs," Henry laughed whilst placing Kat back on the ground once they had reached the threshold. Kat didn't respond as she felt useless; a weak human being who was basically the odd one out of the group for being this powerless. The only thing she was good for in her eyes was stabbing vampires in the chest with a wooden stake and squirting holy water at them. She couldn't physically take on a vampire, nor could she transform herself into a large vampiric monster and gain the ability to fly or have acute senses. The more she thought about how fragile she was, the more it made her feel like a thin piece of glass; easily breakable with a single bend and being dropped from a height.

The third-floor corridor was where they needed to be to get to the dungeon, according to Tabitha, who continued reading Laura's map of the castle.

"At the end of the corridor we need to turn left, and there should be a stairway going down, followed by another corridor with an elevator at the end of that," Tabitha informed her team.

"An elevator?" Aaron seemed surprised to hear this. "In an old castle like this?"

"That's what the map says!" Tabitha gave Aaron the map for him to read to prove she wasn't wrong. He was astounded to see that she wasn't lying about it.

"Then why the hell wasn't there an elevator in the lobby to take us to where we needed to go then?"

"Because this castle is weirdly structured?" Kat frowned. "I swear you better be right about the band being in the dungeon or else I'm going to be PISSED!" She began striding her way down the corridor with her hand grasping tightly on the grip of her new sword. She hoped to use it at some point in the evening and then take it home with her as a prize for their victory, if they won.

There were three doors on each side of the walls that had numbers on each one.

"Bedrooms?" Kat pointed out.

"Correct." Tabitha confirmed.

"Do some vampires actually sleep in coffins?" Aaron inquired, whilst raising his eyebrows and listening in to any activities occurring in the bedrooms. He was thankful to hear nothing but silence as they walked past the doors.

"I mean, it's got its advantages! Blocking out all sunlight exposures, peace and quiet, it's a safe space for them." Henry thought aloud.

"You know, for a vampire castle, there are barely any vampires about!" Kat noticed. "We've come across three vampires so far and I expected us to be fighting an army of vampires. Did Laura ever mention the number of vampires living in this castle at all?"

"Not really. She never spoke about it," Tabitha responded.

"There could be a lot of them hanging about in the courtroom," Henry suggested. "Waiting for the trial of the band to begin? I just hope we haven't jinxed it."

Tabitha turned and gave Henry a stern look of disapproval, her eyes beckoned towards Kat for Henry to be careful of what he was saying about the band. No reaction came from Kat, but she felt her chest ache intensely at the idea of her friends standing trial against the country's vampire ruler who would determine their fate.

The elevator at the end of the corridor was very out of place. Henry approached the rustic-looking elevator and perused its features. He slid the door open, which made a ruckus as it revealed its interior. There was a lever on the left-hand side with no floor indications.

"This is an old coal mining elevator shaft," Henry had concluded.

"I thought this place has been around for hundreds of years?" Kat wondered. "Unless this is an upgrade from the forties, and they haven't upgraded since?"

"It's possible," said Henry. Kat and the vampires approached the inside of the shaft. Once they were all inside, Henry slid the door shut as Kat pushed the lever down to activate the elevator.

The loud metallic contraptions activated as the elevator began to descend slowly to its destination. The apprehension had gotten intense for Kat. She had hoped that Will and the others were going to be where they were heading to. She envisaged herself holding onto Will tightly and allowing her emotions to overtake her to show him how much she loved him, how much she had missed him, allowing their reunion to linger, making up for the time they had lost during their separation. She had always been told that separation would make the heart grow fonder, but to her, the separation made her heart feel sullen and tense.

She knew Will probably felt the same, especially since his love interest was a human who had stumbled into his world filled with parasitic creatures, a place she didn't belong in unless she became one of them herself.

The elevator stopped once it had reached its destination. Henry slid the rustic door open and out everyone went. The corridor was dimly lit with candles that hung on ripped wallpaper. Cobwebs filled the ceiling and corners of the room, showing signs of dilapidation. The derelict and haunting aesthetics of the room would usually make Kat excited, however, she felt no satisfaction at being there.

"Claudette could do with a redo on this floor," Aaron commented on her home furnishing. "It's got spooky haunted house vibes!"

"Unless it's intentional," said Tabitha. "Dungeons aren't supposed to be luxurious or look like a spa, you know."

"Well, duh," Aaron muttered, rolling his eyes. The gang hastened down the corridor and turned right where they had found the large metallic bar door. Without perusing, Kat immediately went to open the door, hoping it was unlocked.

Down they went into the dungeon. Kat's heart was pounding now more than ever. The determination, the psychological state of mind that had her thinking of the worst possible outcomes of tonight's conflicts, the reunion she had hoped to have with Will, the safety of the band, the safety of herself and her friends all raced through her mind.

The final step was just ahead, which made the pain in Kat's chest rise at its highest. The dungeon was the worst of the rooms they had been in; stone walls, soggy flooring that shone, it was like they had walked into the underground of a medieval dungeon-unless the scenery was intentional. The far end of the corridor could not be seen; darkness was all she could see ahead. No torches were on the walls to help her find her way to the dungeon. This, of course, wasn't a problem for the vampires.

"Will?" she instinctively called out, hoping to get a response from him. Her voice reverberated through the stone walls of the dungeon. "Will!" She shouted again.

"Kat," Henry whispered. "Be careful. We will lead the way for you." He grabbed her hand and then flinched when a pang of coldness hit.

"Oh! Sorry!" Kat quickly removed her crucifix glove for Henry to hold her hand softly.

"We're right here," Tabitha assured her. Aaron led the way with Tabitha behind, followed by Henry holding onto Kat's hand. Two minutes of non-stop walking later and they finally found a door that was made of old crumbled wood.

"The door needs a key," Aaron informed them.

"No problem," Tabitha told him "Never stopped any of us! Let me have some fun for a change!" She kicked the door several times, causing the door to crumble piece by piece, until there was enough space for all of them to walk through.

"Nicely done," Aaron complimented.

"Thank you," Tabitha said in a gleeful tone as she skipped her way through the decimated door with pride.

The room through the doors was filled with prison cells. The bars of each cell were made with pure silver, making it impossible for vampires to try and escape.

Kat was eager to scream out for Will again but remained silent. She pulled out one of her water pistols and made her way through the room, quickly glancing at each cell to see if her or any of the vampires could find someone familiar to them. Each prison cells they looked at were empty with the exception of silver chains that connected to the back walls with a silver cuff at the end of the link.

A low groan was heard at the far end of the room which caught everyone's attention.

"Did anyone else hear that?" Tabitha asked, making sure she wasn't the only one hearing things. "Hello?"

"Tabitha?" a faint cry echoed. "Is that you?"

"I definitely heard THAT!" said Aaron. "I can't make out who it is though."

Kat immediately sprinted towards the location of the sound with the vampires following behind. The groans became louder as they approached the cell where the source came from.

Inside the cell was a male with dark brown hair and was wearing a purple coat, and heavy boots which had shackles above the ankles.

"David!" Kat cried, feeling a strong sense of relief to see him alive. She placed her hands on the silver bars to examine the damage done to him. He slowly lifted his head up to see who it was that had approached him. His eyes were black from starvation, his skin was grey with the bones of his face revealed, and his clothes had been ripped and were filthy. He could barely lift his head up to look at Kat. He seemed to be in a stupor state.

"David?" Kat became concerned for his well-being. He looked awfully pallid. "What did they do to you?"

The thought of Will being what had happened to David made her anxieties hit an all-time high.

David silently growled, causing Henry to instinctively pull Kat away from the bars. The beating of Kat's heart sent David in to a bloodlust state, with the idea of tearing her apart to feast on her blood. He revealed his razor sharp teeth with the intention of using them to tear through Kat's skin. The sudden movement caused the shackles on him to burn against his skin, making him shrill in pain. He froze in place, waiting for the burning to stop.

"You need to keep your distance," Henry warned Kat. "His mind isn't in the right place as his starvation seems to be making him think illogically."

"Pass him a blood bag then!" Tabitha informed her. "Let's get him back to normal!" Kat hastily pulled off her backpack and unzipped it to find a bag of blood. She had four bags, one for each of her vampire friends. It was what was left in their storage cooler.

"I'll go and see if the others are here," Aaron told them, and then immediately left.

Kat quickly pulled out one of the bags of blood from her backpack and under passed it to David through the bars. The bag safely landed on his legs. David slowly picked it up and bit through the plastic with his sharp teeth. The blood poured out from the plastic bag and stained his hands. He placed the opening of the blood bag into his mouth and started sucking it dry. The coppery taste warmed his body like fire; a strong sensation that made him want more. The blood drenched his throat; it was the greatest feeling David had ever felt as his thirst quenched.

Aaron came back with the bad news. "The other's aren't in here. There's only David." Kat's heart dropped when she heard the news that the rest were absent. Where could they be then?

Kat and the vampires could see David's skin lightening up to the paleness it used to be. When the bag was empty, David threw it on the ground and let out a loud sigh of relief. His eyes were the darkest of red, the reddest that Kat had ever seen.

"That felt so fucking good!" David screamed with excitement. "I would jump up in a celebratory fashion, but my fucking ankles are chained up in silver and it bloody hurts!"

"Shhhh!" Henry placed his finger on his lips and whispered. "Where are the others?"

"Three of Claudette's vampire slaves took Oliver and Laura downstairs into the interrogation room, which was where they drained me of my strength, putting me in a starvation state."

"Why would they do that?" Aaron wondered.

"Claudette knew you were coming here so she wanted to have us be in a state where the very sight of Kat would cause us to lash out and rip her apart."

"To keep her away from them?" Aaron asked.

"Yes. She wants Kat to face her alone without the help of vampires."

"What about Will?" Kat asked eagerly. "Where is he?"

"They just took him upstairs into the courtroom with Claudette. They're going to be putting him on trial soon and determine his fate. My guess is they'll wait for you to arrive and either have you killed in front of him or have him kill you as they've also put him in a starvation state." Kat felt her body getting cold despite wearing layers of clothing. Bile burnt her throat as she came close to vomiting from the stress and physical struggle, she was currently in.

333

"We've got to get you out of here," Kat shook the sickness off, determined to move on.

"How? The bars are made of pure silver. Touching them would only burn the skin of vampires and Kat won't be able to pull them apart," David pointed out the problem.

"Let me try something. Kat, lend me your snow gloves, please?" Tabitha approached the cell whilst Kat passed over her gloves. She placed them onto her hands and proceeded to place her covered hands onto the silver bars. With all of her vampiric strength, she pulled two of the bars away from each other and created an opening for them to enter David's cell. David watched quizzically as Tabitha managed to find a way to get the silver bars bent without grimacing or have pain inflicted on her.

"You are fucking amazing, Tabitha Davis!" David shook his head, seeming proud of her. Tabitha chortled from the compliment and proceeded to enter the prison cell to get the cuffs off David's ankles.

"Hold still, please," Tabitha smiled proudly as she pulled the chain to disconnect halfway and then approached the shackles on his ankles. David squirmed as the cuff touched his vampiric skin, causing a burning sensation, followed by smoke. Tabitha snapped the cuff open, freeing his ankle from the silver. The other ankle was also free from the silver shortly after.

David jumped up from the floor and waited for Tabitha to get up before embracing her, which took her and everybody else by surprise, as David was never the hugging type.

"Thank you," he mumbled on her shoulder.

"Erm . . . you're welcome," Tabitha shrugged and hugged him back.

"We need to get Oliver and Laura out of here before we go back upstairs to the courtroom." Henry announced. "You said the interrogation room is downstairs?"

"Yes," David confirmed as he and Tabitha left the prison cell. "I'll lead you to it, but we've got to be-"

Something suddenly grabbed onto Kat from above, pulling her upwards towards the ceiling. She screamed in terror as her vampire friends tried to see what it was that pulled her away from them. Henry launched himself from the ground to grab hold of her, but something suddenly pushed him away and he flew across the dungeon. Aaron raced over to help Henry whilst Tabitha leapt up towards the ceiling to rescue Kat.

A monstrous high-pitched scream was heard from above, followed by Kat falling onto Tabitha, who caught her and safely land back on the ground. The screaming continued from above.

"You BITCH!" a woman shrilled angrily. David, Tabitha, and Kat could see a vampire woman descending to the ground with smoke coming from her face. Her brown hair was plaited back showing all her facial skin.

"Holy water," Kat simpered, lifting her water pistol to reveal the source of her pain. "The power of Christ compels you, bitch!" Kat confidently squirted more holy water at the vampire's face. Tabitha then raced over to grab hold of the vampire whilst she shrilled in pain. David had gotten his strength back and proceeded to help Tabitha with the fight.

Henry and Aaron were in battle with another female vampire with short, curly blonde hair that curved under her chin. She was a feisty fighter compared to the previous vampire they had fought as she danced around giving high kicks.

Aaron had his nunchucks to fight with. The wooden handles would collide swiftly with the vampire's arms and claws with every hit. Henry tried to get himself into the fight to give Aaron the advantage, but the vampire sensed when he was about to strike her and would backflip, then kick Henry across the room, and go back to fighting Aaron.

The other vampire woman was eager to get her claws on Kat, but Tabitha and David weren't letting that happen. Every opportunity that was presented to the vampire was stripped away, either by Kat's palms containing the crucifixes, or her holy water gun, which would then give Tabitha and David the chance to grab onto the vampire, but she would then use all her strength to push the pair off her and resume trying to grab Kat.

A crossbow bolt flew above Kat's head and a critical shot pierced the vampire woman's shoulder. Kat knew this was Henry's work, and quickly raced over to Tabitha and David, before the vampire could grab her, without looking back. Henry quickly reloaded the crossbow and took another aim at the vampire, who glided towards him from the other side of the room, fuelled by sheer anger. The trigger was pulled as soon as Henry had a clear shot and the crossbow bolt penetrated through the vampire's cheek. She crashed onto the ground and began wincing in pain before pulling out the bolt from her cheek, leaking black blood before the wound healed. David and Tabitha ran over to grab hold of the vampire's arms and pinned her down.

Kat sprinted as fast as she could with one of the stakes held in her hand to get to the vampire so she could end its eternal damnation.

The other vampire who was fighting Aaron could hear what was happening from behind and flew away from him to save her comrade.

"Hey! We're not done here!" Aaron called out, chasing after the vampire. She quickly turned towards Aaron and immediately slapped him across the face, sending him flying across the room and crashing through one of the prison cells, breaking the bars. He screamed in intense agony as the silver came into contact with his skin, which gave him an intense burning sensation. He quickly got up and tried to get away from the silver.

The vampire foiled the execution of her comrade by crashing herself into the group, causing them to separate from the vampire and scatter across the room. Kat quickly dropped onto the floor to prevent the vampire from hitting her as she flew over her with her large vampire wings.

Tabitha pulled out her dagger and quickly got back up. She ran towards the flying vampire who was gliding her way back to the gang.

Aaron and Henry, in a flash, ran over to the other side of the room where Henry shot a crossbow bolt straight at the vampire that was standing on the ground. The bolt pierced through her shoulder which made the vampire screech at them. Her body began to morph into her Behemoth form as her body crackled and shifted into a muscular, grey skinned beast with sharp claws, which were able to hit at Aaron and Henry directly, causing them to fly backwards until they hit the back wall of the dungeon.

"What the fuck is going on in here?" a male's voice called out from the doorway leading downstairs. A rounded individual with short dirty blonde hair wearing a hooded red cloak that draped down to his ankles came in to investigate the commotion happening in the dungeon. He spotted David, who was halfway down the dungeon and realised what had happened. David gave him a cheeky smile like he recognised him.

"You should be in your prison cell, you prick!" he yelled. "Girls! Get each of them into a cell, now!"

"We're TRYING!" One of the women yelled, whilst fighting Tabitha, who was trying to stab her with her dagger. "But they put up a good fight for a bunch of young ones!" She grabbed hold of Tabitha by her hair and lifted her in the air, ready to pull her head apart from her body.

Something hit the vampire's chest causing her to drop Tabitha to the ground and begin withering in pain. She looked down and noticed that a wooden stake had pierced through her. Looking up to see her attacker, David stood next to Kat who then ran over to help Tabitha get up and made sure she was alright.

The vampire cried out for mercy as her body decomposed into dust. Her screams were ear piercing, echoing through the dungeon and distracting the male vampire and the vampire monster who turned and saw their comrade dying.

The Behemoth vampire glided towards David to avenge her comrade in a rage-filled outburst. Kat quickly gave him one of her stakes and he went in for the attack. The vampire managed to get David by the shoulders and pin him to the ground.

The male vampire raced over to the right to try and get hold of Aaron and Henry. He attempted to launch a punch at Henry but was caught off guard by Aaron who had his nunchucks at the ready, standing in between him and Henry. He smacked him across the face with the nunchucks, causing him to be knocked to the ground. He instantly got back up and gave Aaron a look of wrath.

"You want to catch these fists, newbie?" he asked in an intimidating tone.

Aaron clocked his head to the side and smirked. "You bet I do!" Aaron began the fight using his martial art manoeuvres. His kicks were blocked by the vampire's elbows one by one. He attempted to use his nunchucks but they too were deflected by the vampire's elbows. He parried his way round Aaron and kick him down.

David noticed how much trouble Aaron was in and decided to lend him a helping hand.

"Tag team?" David asked, parrying his way around the vampire.

"Tag Team!" Aaron nodded.

David and Aaron charged at the vampire with everything they had and were immediately in close combat. They managed to push him to the ground and came close to stabbing him in the chest with a stake, however, he deflected the attempt by rolling quickly to the side before leaping back onto his feet and grab David's arm whilst attempting to kick Aaron who parried away from him.

Henry approached Kat and whispered something into her ear. She nodded at his words. Whilst Tabitha, David, and Aaron were busy fighting the vampire, Kat quickly rummaged through her backpack with Henry standing in front to hide her away from the fight. Something was passed to Henry which made him race away from her whilst she ran to the far opposite end of the room where the door was.

Tabitha struggled to get hold of the Behemoth vampire who blocked all her attacks and managed to get a hit on her. She was on the ground trying desperately to get the monster off her. Its teeth were inching closer and closer to her neck with the intention of biting her head off and going in for an instant kill. She knew that she had to keep holding on a little while longer until one of her vampire friends could hopefully find the time to free her.

"Hey!" Kat called out at the top of her lungs from the far end of the room. A knife was dropped from her hand , landing on to the soggy ground, creating a small splash on the puddle. The enemy vampires ceased their attack on the others and paid attention to the red liquid that was dripping in between Kat's fingertips. The scent of her blood caused a frenzy for the vampires, a great distraction for the pair to focus on the crimson drink that was offered to them for free. In an instant, they were away from the others to feast on the live meal that stood in front of them.

When Kat saw them getting closer, both of her palms were swiftly raised to reveal the crucifixes. Both the enemy vampires reacted adversely to the sight of the holy symbols, closing their eyes and hissing in terror. Kat bravely started walking closer to the vampires with her palms still open, making the vampires withdraw out of fear.

A loud crash of glass, followed by an ignition of flames erupted on the ground from the combination of vodka and a flamed rag that was soaked from the alcohol. The flames engulfed the vodka that spread across the floor and lit up the two vampires who were covering their eyes to avoid looking at the crucifixes. Kat walked backwards to watch the vampires wailing in agony, their skin turning to ash from toe to head.

The vampires tried to run to get to Kat, but the pain slowed them down, like a heated ball and chain. Their immortal bodies were becoming ash with the flames. The screams of pain and the burning of the bodies didn't faze Kat in the slightest as she knew these were the people who hurt her friends, and possibly the ones who have hurt Will, so empathy was not present in her emotions or her expression.

The screams died off as the bodies of the vampires crumbled onto the floor. The flames slowly began to disappear.

"Thanks, Henry," Kat nodded, expressionless.

"That was fucking SICK!" Aaron cried out, clapping his hands enthusiastically. Tabitha and Henry chuckled as they watched Aaron bounce around the room. "Henry, you are such an arsonist!"

Henry laughed and shrugged his shoulders before approaching Kat. He could see that she wasn't behaving like her usual, cheery self. "Are you okay?"

"Yeah," Kat sighed as she took her backpack off to grab her first aid kit. She pulled out a cloth to wipe the blood off her skin before dressing her wound with a plaster "David, show us where the interrogation room is, please. I'm hoping we're not too late to save Laura and Oliver." Kat finished aiding her wound and pointed to the end of the dungeon, directing David to lead the way. He nodded and turned away from the group, having the others trail behind him, with Tabitha holding onto Kat's arm as extra support in case of another ceiling ambush.

Chapter 29:
♥
Rescue

David led Kat and the vampires down the stairs onto the
bottom floor and turned left where a metal door was seen at the
far end of the corridor. There were four doors, two on each
wall. All were military-style doors, heavy and metallic.

"The first door on the left is where they held me for
interrogation," David pointed at the door. "They asked me
questions about what had happened to Sven and the whole
transgression of having a human knowing who we were. They
then took me into that room there and-"

The screams of a woman were heard behind the
door, one that was familiar to David, which prompted him to
instinctively charge towards the door.

"Laura!" he cried out, banging on the door eagerly.
The pounding of his hitting on the metallic door loudly echo
down the corridor. He tried smashing the door down with his
fists, but he wasn't having any luck. "Open this door, you
vampiric bastards!"

The door instantly blew out from its hinges and flew
across the other side of the corridor, making David fly back
along with it. He was sandwiched between the doors as it
landed on the other side. The door collapsed onto the ground,
and the others saw that David's body had dented on the other
door. Not a scratch was on him.

"Son of a bitch," David moaned as he walked away
from the door and brushed off the dirt from his purple coat.

341

The gang looked at the doorway to see what it was that caused the destruction of the door. To their dismay, a vampire who was more muscular, more intimidating than the previous vampires they had encountered approached them. Kat felt Tabitha's hand grip slightly tighter on her coat when they saw him entering the room. He ignored them as if they weren't in the room and approached David. He picked him up and immediately threw him down the corridor. He disappeared into the darkness and crashed into something metallic.

"Fuck!" his voice echoed.

The vampire turned to face the others. Kat had her palm open and a water gun in the other, with Henry and Aaron loaded with their crossbow and nunchucks and Tabitha with her dagger at hand. His body began morphing into his Behemoth form, his already huge muscles grew even larger. This was the largest vampire monster Kat had faced so far on her journey.

Once the transformation was complete, Kat instinctively began squirting the last of the holy water that was in the gun before replacing it with the other one. The water caused the vampire to cry out in pain before launching itself onto her. Thankfully, Henry pulled Kat out of the way as the vampire crashed onto the floor, creating a rubble pile from the broken ground.

Henry pulled the trigger of the crossbow, launching the bolt right through the vampire's head. It roared violently from the hit. Henry grabbed Kat and leapt high enough for her to quickly unsheathe her sword and immediately stab the vampire through its back, hitting its heart in the process and causing it to wither in pain before deteriorating into dust and ash.

The group looked at one another, confused as to why that was such an easy fight.

Kat sighed in relief and said, "Thanks, Henry."

"Pleasure," he smiled and nodded.

"Laura?" David's voice called out whilst urgently going into the interrogation room. A metallic table was centred in the room along with four wooden chairs. The sight of Laura tied up to one of the chairs with her wrists and ankles locked in silver to prevent her from escaping appeared before David, which he dreaded seeing. Her face had dropped, her hair curtained her face, making it impossible to see the state they had put her in.

"Laura?" David eagerly approached the chair and knelt to the floor. He moved his head around to try and see underneath her long locks to get a look at her face.

"Can you hear me?" David tried communicating with her, but she was not responsive.

Kat and the others got into the interrogation room and saw David trying to get Laura to respond to his pleas.

"What did they do to you?" he asked her, his voice filled with anguish.

A small groan came from her, followed by a little head lift, which made her wince from the pain.

"Hey," David whispered, half smiling with relief. "It's David. You're safe now."

"D. . . David?" Laura's voice croaked. Her face showed malnutrition from the lack of human blood, the same way David was.

"Kat! I need some blood!" David called out. Within a second, Kat knelt down, rummaging through her backpack to find the bag of blood. She passed it to Henry who then went over to David immediately. After passing the bag to David, he tried persuaded Laura to drink it.

"David," Tabitha pointed out. "Let me get the silver cuffs off her first." David agreed and allowed Tabitha to kneel where he was, placing the gloves back onto her hands before pulling the cuffs off her ankles. Laura cringed at the sudden burning of the silver that touched her skin.

"Sorry, Laura," Tabitha whispered apologetically. When both cuffs were off, she got up from the floor and proceeded to get the shackles off her. As soon as they were off, Laura collapsed into David's arms. Her face was revealed, showing the wrinkles and signs of hunger.

"Drink this," he encouraged her, placing the bag of blood against her lips. "It's blood."

Laura groaned as she slowly opened her dry mouth to allow the blood to enter. David squeezed the plastic bag as hard as he could to allow the blood to gush out, fall into her mouth and slide down her throat. The blood soothed her throat, making her crave for more to shower her throat. Once the bag was empty, she swallowed the remaining drops of blood in her mouth and gasped with relief.

A minute later and Laura's face began glowing back to her usual look that David admired. He smiled when she opened her eyes to reveal its shade of red.

"Hey," he chuckled with relief, smiling down at her.

"What the fuck happened?" Laura quietly asked him. "Where are the others?"

"Right here!" Tabitha called out enthusiastically. Laura's eye widened from seeing her. "Almost all of us are here!"

"Laura," Kat knelt to the floor and held her hand.

"Hey, Kat," Laura smiled, sitting up to hand her an embrace of gratitude. "I was worried you weren't going to get here."

"Without the help of Henry and his coven, I don't think I would have made it," Kat smiled gracefully.

Laura withdrew her embrace when she had realised there were two people missing from the party.

"Where are Oliver and Will?" Laura queried in a worried tone when she saw that they weren't with them.

"Oliver is here somewhere," Henry responded. "Will's up in the courtroom, quite possibly with Claudette."

"Why didn't you go straight to the courtroom?" Laura asked them.

"Because we thought you would all be here in the dungeon," Kat answered. "We also ran into trouble along the way."

"And got some awesome weapons!" Aaron flexed on the nunchucks he took, making Laura chuckle. She got up from the floor with the help of David and they all left the interrogation room.

"Your floor plans were a lot of help," Tabitha encouraged. "You must have explored this castle from head to toe."

"I was here for a while," Laura told her. "A trial run, should I say, as they were persuading me to stay as one of their coven members."

"Thank fuck you didn't stay," said David with a sly smile.

"When did you last see Oliver?" Henry asked Laura.

"The last time I saw him he was taken into the other interrogation room after they finished interrogating me."

"Which room is it?" Kat asked with urgency.

"The one down the hall and on the right."

Tabitha immediately took charge in leading everyone down the hall to the other interrogation room. David stood closely to Laura, making sure she was stable enough to move.

Tabitha began banging furiously on the door, her knuckles bashing against the metal echoed with each knock. The door opened immediately, revealing a woman wearing a salacious outfit consisting of a tight, black-laced corset with the skinniest of jeans and highest of heels. Her black hair weaved down to her breasts like seaweed. Her heavy lipstick shone from the corridor lights, revealing a glossy red colour. Her eyelids were shaded with the darkest of red.

She glared at Tabitha with a look of revulsion, ignoring the rest of the group.

"Can I help you?" she asked aggressively.

"No. I'm just here to collect my friend and be on my way," Tabitha said with a smug look. "Move."

"Or what?" The lady vampire approached Tabitha, revealing her height to be much taller than Tabitha, even without the high heels she would still be taller. She looked up without a change in expression. The pair of them stared heatedly into each other's eyes, full of resentment and hostility.

"You're outnumbered, honey," Tabitha tilted her head to the side as Henry and Aaron stood next to her with their weapons at the ready. "I suggest you move!"

345

"Hmm," the lady vampire smirked. "Is that so?"

With the snap of her fingers, a group of vampires dropped to the ground from the ceiling above her. Everyone counted four vampires that sided with her: two men and two women, all wearing black leather and laced clothing.

"I hope this isn't going to be a vampire orgy," Aaron quietly winced.

"You're still outnumbered?" David raised his eyebrows with scepticism.

"I would say we're even since this little gang has five vampires and a puny human, which I don't believe really counts." The female vampire seductively walked through the door with her companions following behind. Tabitha started backing away from the doorway so the others could space themselves out whilst she pulled out her dagger from its scabbard. Laura made sure she was close to Kat to shield her from the threat in front of them. Kat had her hand gripped tightly on the hilt of her sword, ready to pull it out from its scabbard.

"Let's have some fun, shall we?" The leader waved her head coyly. Her arm extended forward as an indication for her vampire crew to charge forward and attack. All four of her comrades glided through the doorway and chose their target.

One of the vampire males, who had thick wavy brown hair, began attacking Henry, while the other, who had very short light brown hair, went for an attack on Aaron.

The leader launched onto Tabitha and pinned her to the ground. Tabitha grasped her hands tightly around the vampire's throat and pushed her off. When she got free, she immediately leapt back up onto her feet and started waving her dagger about. The girls charged at one another for close combat. Tabitha was alternating her dagger left and right, and her opponent parried backwards to get away from the silver she was holding onto.

Laura grabbed hold of one of the females that wanted to grab hold of Kat. She jumped into the air and twisted the vampire so that they switched places and pushed her onto the ground, pushing her knees onto her stomach to prevent her from getting back up. Kat quickly pulled the trigger of her holy water gun to inflict damage on the woman vampire and weakened her struggle. The water landed on her face which caused her to wince immensely and cry out in agony. This gave Kat the opportunity to quickly pass Laura one of her stakes for her to finish the job. When the vampire woman tried to get back up to attack Laura, Kat pulled the trigger to squirt more holy water at her to cancel her attack. The vampire lost her guard and covered her face to shield herself from the burning. Laura finished her off with the stake. Once she was no longer able to counterattack, Laura got up from the ground and approached Kat who continued to gaze at her vampire friends battling around. It was difficult for her to see what was going on due to the high speeds of all the vampires. It all became a blur to her eyes.

"I need to do something," Kat told Laura, seeming hopeless.

Laura placed the palm of her hand onto Kat's shoulder. "The others need me, what have you got on you that you could use to defend yourself with?"

Kat looked down at her waist and grasped onto the grip of her sword "This sword?"

"Good. Now, do you know how to use it?"

"Not really. I just took it because I wanted to. I figured it might come in handy."

"Well, I think you could do some serious damage with that sword if you improvise with what you have on you," Laura gave her a wink before racing off to help the others. Kat looked confused and wondered about what she had meant by that.

David fought with the other woman vampire who had long thick blonde hair. She easily got the upper hand by blocking and counterattacking every one of David's moves. He fell to the ground with every kick and punch she threw at him.

Henry couldn't use his crossbow during close combat, so he had to try and be tactical with his fists. The person he was fighting seemed very swift and parried his way around him and kicked him in the back.

Aaron, meanwhile, used his nunchucks and martial art manoeuvres to his advantage. The male he was fighting struggled to keep up with him and was astounded with how quick Aaron was.

"You're fighting techniques are extraordinary!" he commented, trying hard not to compliment him.

"Thirteen years of martial arts, baby!" Aaron continued spinning his nunchucks over his shoulders and around his upper torso. "Add a grain of vampirism and I'm basically unstoppable!"

"Until tonight!" The vampire went for his hardest blow and tried his hardest to grab hold of Aaron, but he regretted choosing him as his opponent. His nunchucks were able to smack the vampire across the face multiple times, creating a loud crash with each hit. By the time the vampire was close enough, Aaron roundhouse kicked the vampire hard enough to send him flying across the corridor and crash against the wall.

Laura grabbed the flying vampire by the neck and pushed him against the floor with her left hand around his throat, and the stake she took from Kat in the other. The stake pierced through the vampire's thick leather clothing and into his dead vampiric heart. He gasped at the realisation that he had reached his final moment of eternity. Laura didn't stick around to watch the demise of the vampire, she took off to help the others.

David, Henry, and Tabitha were still struggling against their opponents. Aaron helped David whilst Laura lent Tabitha an extra pair of hands.

Kat couldn't keep up with the fighting, which gave her immense anxiety about what was going to happen when she would have to fight Mistress Claudette. How was she supposed to fight the strongest vampire in the country when she couldn't singlehandedly fight off a vampire alone? The image of her in the courtroom, with a possible influx of vampires and one head vampire made her feel queasy.

Kat thought about what Laura had just told her. The image of her inventory came to mind: the bottles of vodka, rags and a lighter, the bottle of holy water, her first aid kit, her pocketknife, and blood bags.

"What can I combine together to create something better?"

Her hand grasped onto her sword's grip again, and an idea suddenly arose in her mind. This immediately made her rummage through her backpack. When she unzipped the bag, the vampire that was fighting David ceased her fight after kicking him across the corridor and leered at Kat. She immediately went after Kat and flew across the corridor to grab hold of her. The sight of a venomously terrifying vampire woman flying at a high speed towards her caused Kat to react immediately by screaming at the top of her lungs, and she raised her hands forward. The female vampire was inches away from her face. Everyone in the corridor stopped to see what was going on, and in that moment, the screams of a human were then replaced by the wailings of a vampire. She began rolling around the stone flooring, crying in intense pain covering her face with her hands.

The vampire's comrades tried to help her, but they were blocked off by their opponents, who were eager to finish their fights.

Kat looked to see what had happened. A bottle of water was cupped around her tightened right hand with its top unscrewed. A quarter of the bottle was empty.

"Well, I'll be damned," she thought as she realised what had happened.

David raced across the corridor to get to his opponent. He grabbed her by the neck, grasped his hand on her back shoulder, and with his free hand he pulled her by her scalp as tightly as he could with his arm grasped firmly. The vampire woman was in too much pain to do anything and continued squirming for dear life.

Kat quickly got up from the floor and unsheathed her sword. David continued to grasp tightly onto the woman, trying to pull her head off from her torso. He could hear the skin ripping from her neck.

The tip of Kat's sword pierced through the centre of the vampire's breastbone where the heart would be. She pushed it with all her human force and made sure it was pushed far enough to pierce through her back, but not too deep as to hit David.

The pain of the blade going through the vampire caused a blood curdling scream that distracted the remaining vampires to slow down and lose their concentration, giving Tabitha and Laura the upper hand.

Henry kicked his opponent across the room, which allowed Aaron to use his nunchucks for extra damage to knock them to the ground.

David asked Laura to pass him her stake, which she agreed to do, and in an instant he was right next to Aaron. With the strike of his stake, it went through the vampire's chest and punctured his dead heart, ending the vampire's miserable existence.

Tabitha and Laura tag-teamed their way through the lead vampire that started it all. She was ferociously fast and clearly more skilled than her comrades as they kept failing to get a hit on her. It was like they were fighting a ballerina. She, on the other hand, got a couple of punches and kicks at Tabitha. Laura parried around her but still found her to be untouchable.

David, Henry, and Aaron tapped into the fight making it five against one now that the other vampires were dead. Kat ran into the fight with her sword at the ready with the determination to fight despite her vulnerabilities. She had more of an advantage with five vampires fighting by her side, hopefully soon to be six.

The vampires joined in with Tabitha and Laura made it easier for them to get a hit on her. All five vampires launched themselves at her. She leapt up high to avoid the group attack and backflipped far down the corridor, landing like a cat.

Henry quickly aimed his crossbow and immediately pulled the trigger to release the bolt. The vampire caught the bolt with her hand before Kat could even blink.

"You fools think you could defeat me?" she laughed maniacally. "I've been around for centuries and have fought many battles. You all fight like weakling humans!" Her hand crushed the bolt, snapping it in half. "That vampire in the interrogation room is mine. Claudette offered me a new lover and mate!"

Everyone looked at her dazed and confused.

"Why Oliver?" David asked, seeming offended by her choice, which made Laura roll her eyes.

"He has charisma. He seems very obedient as well, dominant when he needs to be - which I find very pleasing. Now," the vampire sauntered towards the group with a look of malice and omnipotence. "I'm going to give you two choices; either you leave me be with my new mate, or I will kill all of you, starting with the human. I could do with a drink." She slowly licked her lips, envisioning the taste of human blood on her tongue making her even more thirsty.

Kat didn't flinch or feel threatened by the vampire's words. She grasped her sword tightly on its grip.

"Go ahead," she told her with a tone of loss.

"Kat!" Laura cried.

"It's okay," Kat whispered. She turned to face the gang as she stood in front, passing a wink over to show confidence that she knew what she was doing.

"Free food?" the vampire seemed happy knowing Kat was prepared to sacrifice herself. "It's not as tastier when it's intentional! But I will take what I am given!"

Kat marched forward at a reasonable pace, not slowing down, nor stopping with hesitance. The gang watched in horror. Each of them were highly tempted to snatch Kat away from the vampire and kill the vampire themselves.

"Will wouldn't allow this to happen," David whispered to Henry. "We need to do something."

"I know," Henry whispered back. "I hope she knows what she's doing."

Kat was now inches away from the vampire who looked down at her like a snake. Her blood red eyes gleamed

351

down at her sea-blue eyes, and she could see the bravery within her soul.

"You truly do have a death wish, don't you?" she indicated.

"I've had a death wish since the day I met these guys," Kat responded. "But it's been worth it."

Kat then raised her left wrist with her palm clenched tightly.

"Take a bite from my wrist," she implied. "There's more blood in that region and I don't think you want to bite me in the neck."

The vampire gazed at her, confused with why she was suggesting this.

"It doesn't matter where I bite you. Blood is blood, no matter where on the body it comes from." She leaned down to roll up Kat's sleeves and expose her skin. She could hear Kat's pulse beating, which made her mouth drench with venomous saliva. The vampire turned to the side to get a better amount of Kat's wrist in her mouth. Her fangs extracted and sharpened as she was ready to take a bite.

Laura almost made a run to her, but Aaron pressed his arm out to prevent her from moving.

Kat then unclenched her palm, exposing the crucifix, then bent her hand upwards like a catapult and pressed the palm of her hand against the vampire's face. This caused the vampire to lean upwards away from her wrist and scream in terror at the sudden unexpected touching of a holy symbol.

"Holy shit!" Aaron screamed enthusiastically and jumped up and down. Everybody gasped, which then grew into smiles.

Kat quickly gripped both hands onto her sword and instantly penetrated the blade right through her chest and out her back, causing black blood and smoke to escape the wound. The blade made the vampire disintegrate even faster than the previous vampires. She pushed the sword upwards with the blade still within the vampire, slicing through her and splitting her upper body into two. The black blood evaporated as soon as it hit the carpet like chemical burns.

Aaron bounced around ecstatically, laughing, and gawking at the intense scenery he had witnessed.

Once the screaming ceased and the body turned to ash, Kat turned to see her vampire friends looking astonished and outright amazed with what they had just witnessed. She placed her sword back into its scabbard.

"Kathryn Rhodes, you fucking daredevil!" David laughed.

"That was ABSOLUTELY EPIC!" Aaron screamed.

Tabitha and Laura raced over to immediately embrace Kat with intense relief.

"Don't ever pull a stunt like that again or else Will is going to kill us!" Laura laughed. Kat giggled and hugged her friends, with her fist clenched to prevent the crucifixes from touching them.

"How did you know that was going to work?" Henry laughed as he approached the girls.

"This sword," Kat began explaining, "was soaked with holy water. I've poured some into the scabbard to keep it soaked. "

Tabitha and Laura both leaned away from her, both stunned with what she had told them.

"You soaked that sword with holy water?" Tabitha asked with astonishment.

"It was Laura who inspired me!" Kat pointed at her. "She told me to improvise and combine my inventory!"

"You're welcome," Laura raised her eyebrows.

"I was kind of gambling my chances there. She was much more gullible than I thought. I should have enough to soak up this blade with more holy water to cause burning damage to whatever vampire I am able to slice."

"That's pretty fucking dope," Aaron chuckled. "Like combining inventory in a video game".

"Shall we go and grab Oliver now?" David suggested to his friends.

"Lets!" Kat nodded.

Everyone raced into the interrogation room. Oliver was seen sitting a chair with his head dropped forward to face the floor.

Laura and David were the first to walk through the door.

"Oliver!" They both cried out simultaneously. Oliver slowly turned his head to look at them and his eyes gave off the impression that he was thirsty. Dark circles had developed under his eye which made him look like he hadn't slept in days. He didn't look nearly as bad as Laura and David did when they were thirsty, but he still looked blood deprived.

"Woah, Oliver!" said David. "You look rough!"

"Thanks," Oliver muttered with a smile. "I'm just thirsty."

Kat and the others came in. She was already prepared with a bag of blood that she knew he would be craving.

"Here," David beckoned his hand at Kat to pass him the bag. He then ripped open the top of the bag with his teeth and immediately jerked Oliver's head as far back as it would go and shoved the bag of blood into his opened mouth. David squeezed the bag slowly for the blood to splash down his throat and sooth his thirst.

When the bag was completely empty, David threw it across the room and stood back. Oliver breathed slowly to allow the blood to quench his thirst.

"Mind if I unhook him?" Tabitha asked David.

"Do it," he told her. Tabitha placed Kat's winter gloves back on and proceeded to break the silver chains. She could see the burn marks on his wrists and ankles from the touching of the silver.

It took Oliver a moment to get back on his feet. He slowly got up and sighed with relief.

"Thank you," he turned to smile at his friends.

Laura quickly walked up to him and embraced him. "I'm so happy you're alright," she whispered.

Oliver embraced her back and the pair hugged tightly for their little reunion.

"You want a hug, David?" Oliver teased.

"Of course!" David gave Oliver the hug, which Oliver did not expect from him. David held him tightly like he had never done so since they had known each other.

"Erm...are you alright?" Oliver queried, unsure whether or not it was actually David he was talking to.

"Now that we've reunited, yes," David whispered.

"Now we need to go and rescue Will," Kat informed the team. Everyone left the interrogation room and made their way out of the dungeons.

Up the elevator the gang went, ascending back into the castle where the endgame was nearby. Kat hoped for there to be no more vampires standing in their way as she was sure they were on a time limit to Will's possible execution, or before he starved to death. Which begged the question:

"Do vampires starve to death?" she asked everyone in the elevator.

Oliver was the one to respond to her nihilistic question. "No. But they slowly turn into very ugly, very skinny, and very dangerous vampires. If there is no blood in their system then their powers decrease immensely, however their urges increase which makes them susceptible to viciously killing a human to the point where their body becomes unidentifiable. It's quite a brutal image, and I think that's what Claudette had in mind when she was trying to put us in an intense hunger state."

Kat remained silent. She stared intensely ahead with the image of Will tearing her apart with his sharp claws and teeth. She was very surprised that he hadn't done so on the day that they met, but thankfully he and the band had found ways to maintain their urge for human blood.

Will had told her that it was difficult for him when he first spoke to her outside the pub, and that he had to go to the van immediately afterwards to drink more blood which thankfully calmed him. Despite having the intention of sucking her blood, her scent was pure to him, one he had never desired before.

The elevator reached the top and opened to the haunted house aesthetic corridor.

"Would you like me to carry you up the stairs again?" Henry politely offered Kat.

"Yes, I'll need these legs for the final battle." Kat was surprised she wasn't completely shattered or hungry from the night she had going on. She assumed the intensity of tonight's events and pure adrenaline were keeping her energy levels maintained, aside from the anxieties of her kidnapped vampire lover.

Henry slouched down to allow Kat to ride on his back. Her arms wrapped around his neck and her legs were held by his arms.

"I would suggest we run to where we need to go, but I don't want to risk getting Kat nauseous or have her in a worse state," said Henry.

"We'll just have to jog our way there," David shrugged.

They all made their way down the corridor and back up to the second floor, with Laura leading them to their destination.

"We need to go to the ballroom," she informed them all.

"You should have seen the fight we had in there!" said Aaron, seeming proud of it.

When they got to the ballroom, Laura and the band saw the aftermath damage from the fight Aaron had spoken about. Shattered glass all over the floor, damage done to the tiling, and damage to the pillars and walls.

"Fucking hell," said David, seeming surprised at the state of the ballroom. "That must have been some fight!"

They left the ballroom and approached the piano room which triggered a thought in Aaron.

By the time they had reached the lobby, Kat's heart was racing at its fastest, causing major discomfort within her. This was it.

Down the stairs they went and approached the large door at the end of the corridor. Behind the doors Kat knew she wasn't going to be leaving that room the same as she did before she entered, which made her think about her parents; her small group of friends back in Bristol; Sally and Luca at the Golden Barrel pub; the life she may never see again, or at the very least will go back to them as a changed person.

Henry slouched down to let Kat off and mentally prepare herself for the final fight. Laura and Tabitha both looked at her whilst the boys stared on ahead at the doors.

"Are you ready?" Tabitha asked her, seeming concerned for her wellbeing.

"Before we go in, each of you should take one of my stakes," Kat suggested to them as she revealed her chest belt containing her wooden stakes.

"Are you sure you want us to take them?" Oliver asked.

"I'll be alright with just the one. I have a feeling she's not the only vampire that's behind those doors. Even if you can kill some vampires with your own two hands, I would rather you had the extra weaponry at your disposal."

Each of the vampires approached Kat and took one of her stakes from the belt, leaving her with only one left.

Kat grasped tightly onto the grip of her sword and took a deep breath in, and then out, and then in, and out.

She confidently nodded her head, then said, "I'm ready.

Chapter 30:

♥

Claudette

Laura had insisted that she and David were the ones to open the door in case of any sudden ambushes. Kat settled with this, and the vampire crew circled around to make sure Kat was centred to give her a full three-sixty protection circle.

Kat felt the intensity of anticipation once the doors swung open. The revealing of the courtroom sent chills down her spine. Her eyes scanned the room in the hopes of finding Will, unfortunately, he was nowhere to be found.

The courtroom was the largest room in the entire castle. A long silky red carpet draped on the ground making its way to the end of the room. At the end of the carpet were a set of stairs which led to where the golden throne of the Head Vampire stood. At the end of the courtroom where the throne stood, they could see the woman of the hour, the queen of all vampires in the United Kingdom, the head of the Matriarchy vampire, *Mistress Claudette Hemming*. Her large blonde curls were tied up in a hive hairstyle, with black and red veil that wreathed the hive. Her long black and red laced dress had made it impossible to see her legs and feet. Claudette's shiny lips were painted the darkest of reds, making it seem like she had painted human blood on her lips, which, along with her intense beauty, was very intimidating. She remained seated on her golden throne watching them approach her for the trial of the century.

Kat's eyes gleamed at Claudette from afar; her eyes filled with dread and resentment. She despised her for kidnapping, torturing, harming, and wishing death on her vampire friends and her love.

Many large chandeliers hung from the ceiling to illuminate the large courtroom; giant red flags dropped from the ceiling, that had a golden symbol in the middle of the letter C, with a rose pattern painted around it with the images of blood dripping from the rose.

Each side of the room contained seated rows which elevated diagonally like the benches of a football stadium. The seats were filled with vampires, all rumbling aloud against the vampires that walked down the path of transgression. It was a scary sight for Kat to behold, to be the only one in the room that wasn't a vampire. A mere mortal that had killed several vampires with the help of other vampires.

Claudette waved her hand to calm the audience down, which succeeded as the room turned silent.

"Fellow vampires of the country!" She began, the tone of her voice sounding primitive and royal, which echoed through the large courtroom. "I welcome you all today for the trial of these despicable vampires and their. . . human pet," she spat in disgust at the word *human,* "that have shown transgression against the vampire laws, which are as follows." At the snap of her fingers, a vampire came racing towards her, passing her a piece of paper. He bowed to her before leaving.

Claudette slowly walked down the stairs whilst reading from the piece of paper.

"The killings of many members of the Head Vampire's coven - may Sven rest in peace, we will miss him." Laura faced the ground when she mentioned his name, remembering the fight at Tottenham Stadium, which made her feel further resentment at the mention of his name. "Marissa, Jack, Mark, Olivia, Felicity, Vikki, Rachel, Clive, Donavan, Molly, Jade, Joshua; we will miss them all."

Kat and the vampires didn't react to the names being spoken aloud by Claudette; the names of those they had killed and had no regrets killing. Those who had names were nobodies, they were nothing, just parasitic monsters.

"Exposing our kind to a human and refusing to either kill the human, hypnotise them, or turning them into a vampire; killing a human in the middle of a populated city; and refusing to cooperate with members of the Head Vampire's coven!"

The entire room roared in anger at the gang after Claudette finished listing their crimes. She allowed this to go on for a full minute before telling them to stop.

"William Crowell, David Barrett, Laura Bates, Oliver Stokes, Henry Halstead, Aaron Goulbourne, and Tabitha Davis, you are all charge for the crimes I have read aloud and there is no excuse, nor can you deny to these transgressions."

Tabitha leaned over to whisper at Henry "How does she know who we are?" Henry couldn't respond.

David stepped forward to object to this.

"Why call out Will's name when he isn't even here?"

Claudette chuckled viciously. Which made Kat shiver and feel heavy beneath her feet.

"Oh, he is here."

Kat felt her chest pounding again.

"Where is he then?" Kat called out from the centre of the circle. She almost ran out to confront her, but Laura prevented her from moving.

"Ahhhhh," she smiled, her eyes looking down at her so menacingly. "Kathryn Rhodes: the vampire killer." Her face scanned the room to look at everyone in the crowd, which made them scream maliciously. "I have been looking forward to meeting you. I have heard so much about you!"

She remained halfway up the stairs staring down at them.

"Come forward, puny human," she laughed, waving her hand to beckon her to approach.

Kat took a deep breath in before moving out of the circle. Laura became very hesitant and tried to stop her, but a group of vampires holding onto spears surrounded the gang, prevented them from protecting Kat. She strode forward and stopped halfway between her friends and her enemy. Claudette examined Kat. She struggled to understand that a human overcame vampires and had vampires side with her in her attempt to kill the Head Vampire.

"I see you stole one of my swords from the weapons room, you termite!" Claudette hissed venomously.

"I borrowed it, actually," Kat responded mockingly. "It looks better on me than you."

Claudette's eyes squinted; her eyebrows arched angrily. "Tell me," Claudette continued. "Why did you decide to come all this way to kill me?" Kat felt the silence around the room. The eyes of all the hungry vampires darted at her as they waited for her response. Kat knew she was going to be telling her the truth. There was no way she could lie her way out of this. Her heartbeats would give her away.

She sighed and then begun. "I was told that by killing you it would reverse vampirism and have vampires that are below one hundred years old transmute back to human."

The audience roared with laughter at her answer. The laugher of a hundred vampires boomed through the giant room.

"SILENCE!" Claudette screamed, which shut the audience down. "And you believe this hypothesis? This rumour that an imbecilic thought of many years ago?"

The latter part of the question had Kat confused.

"Wait? So, it was just a theory that someone thought about?"

"I will be asking the questions here, human!" she growled. Her high-volume tone made Kat even more anxious, like a mouse being looked down on by a lion instead of a cat. "And who told you this hypothesis?"

The images of her and Will's first night back at her flat came into her mind. She relived the moment where Will was suggesting to her that there was a possible way for him and the band to become human again, but that it was a suicide mission that may or may not even work.

His beautiful face made her feel further anxieties due to his absence.

"TELL ME WHO TOLD YOU!" Claudette's voice had gotten louder with each shout. "If you don't tell me, I will kill you and your stupid friends, and we can all go about our day! Tell me the name of the person who told you about the stupid theory! I will not ask you again!"

Kat really didn't want to tell her. It made her feel like telling her would betray Will. She had devoted her human life to him after he had saved her that night in Southampton. Her life was now part of a bigger picture that no human knew about. She had stumbled into a mythological world that was now her norm, and the life she had before seemed more alien to her. Stumbling into the vampire world was something she did not take for granted as it added more than just excitement, it gave her hope.

Her eyes continued to stare at Claudette's grey and enraged look, showing no mercy at her intimidations.

"I told her." A voice came from the group behind her. Everyone in the room murmured when they had spoken. Kat turned to see who it was that exposed themselves and lied to Claudette.

"David," she whispered. She saw the horror of Oliver and Laura's face when David stepped forward. Laura tried to reach for him but failed.

"I was the one that told her about the theory of killing the Head Vampire and turning us back to human," David lied. Kat was immensely confused as to why David, of all people, was doing this as he was against the idea of becoming human and wanted to remain the monster Will described himself to be. Plus, she was sure that he thought very little of her.

"Quite funny coming from you rather than the human," Claudette chuckled. "Is this true, Kathryn?" Kat could feel the pain in her chest getting stronger and stronger. It was becoming too much for her that she had to do something to stop the pain.

Maybe David had a plan? Maybe he wanted Kat to go along with the lie to build up the plan? She couldn't figure out what he had planned.

"Yes, it's true." She gave in and went along with the lie, not being so sure as to why he wanted her to admit it was him.

"Tell me, Mr Barrett," Claudette continued. "Why did you tell her this nonsense?"

David stared at her with a look of intimidation. He wasn't afraid of her; he had never been afraid of anyone.

"Because I didn't have a reason to become human until the night we met Kat," he confessed. "Before, I was a lonely, spiteful, cynical, rage-filled person with big enough daddy issues to kill my own father and show no remorse for it. I had nothing. I had lost my girlfriend because of my depressive state of mind; my sister had moved away, leaving me to stay with my drunken, miserable, abusive father who wanted nothing to do with me. I wanted to kill myself the night I turned because I was no one and had nothing."

Kat looked at David, finally understanding his way of thinking. His humour was a coping mechanism for his trauma. It now made sense to her why he didn't want to go back to being human. David had a very hard life back in his human years and becoming a vampire had given him the strength to carry on and do something good with himself.

"I then met these guys and they had finally given me a reason to exist! They are the reason I am still here! They are the family I never had! I want our band to succeed and become something more than what it is now. Of course, we cannot do that as vampires because, you know, the sun and shit. So, I suggested that if we wanted the band to become successful, we needed to turn back to our old human selves to make that happen. And yes, we needed help from a human to do this, hence Kat being our makeshift vampire killer."

Laura and Oliver couldn't believe their ears at what they were hearing. David, who was always snarky and sarcastic, was potentially sacrificing himself to save Will.

David was never the sort of person to put other people first, so this came as a shock for both Laura and Oliver.

"Let me get this straight," Claudette placed both her hands together and touch the tips of her index fingers against her blood red lips. "You persuaded a human to attempt an assassination on the Head Vampire, killing many vampires along the way, so that you could become human, and kickstart your band?"

"Am I not being more obvious?" David asked with a hint of sarcasm, shrugging his shoulders.

Claudette couldn't help but laugh at the absurdity of the situation. Kat turned to face David, still confused with what he was doing. He shrugged his again shoulders in response.

"I have never heard such a pathetic reason," she laughed. "Did you hypnotise her into doing this?"

"We were originally supposed to, after the incident in Southampton, where Will killed a human for sexually violating Kat, but we, I mean, *I* had the idea of convincing her to do this for us as a 'thank you' for saving her life." David's initial lies were getting more and more clever. He blurted it all out like he had written it as a script in his mind. Was David's special vampire ability to be a convincing liar? Did he have a high skill level of persuasion?

"So, that makes you the culprit of this whole operation?" Claudette asked him.

David shrugged, "Yes?"

Kat's heart was still racing swiftly, which gave off a negative vibe to Claudette. She turned to look at Kat with a sinister smirk.

"Bring in the vampire boyfriend!" Claudette commanded, her voice increasing in decibels "I think we could do with hearing what he has to say."

Kat's eye widened. The anxiety built up within her again but was much worse than it was before. Two vampires approached the bottom of the throne's stairway carrying a limp, lifeless body that Kat was awfully familiar with. His body was dragged by his arms with his legs falling behind.

364

His head dropped to avoid the horrendous, weakened look he had developed from the lack of nourishment.

The two vampire guards dropped him off, with his back turned at Kat and the others. He knelt on the red carpet with his head still dropped. He could barely move a muscle.

Kat's breathing began accelerating as the urge to embrace him swelled up with herself. She needed David to hold her upper arm to stop her from doing so, or else she would start something dangerous.

"William Phillip Crowell," Claudette announced. "You've been a vampire for almost ninety years now! Surely, you would want to return to your old human self before you reached that milestone, correct?" Will remained silent, which made one of the two guards that carried him in nudge him with his foot, then proceeded to kick the centre of his back. Will groaned trying to lift his head up to face Claudette.

"I…" it was painful for him to talk. It felt like he was swallowing razor blades every time that he spoke. "I want…to live."

"Don't we all?" Claudette chuckled mockingly. "I suppose you didn't want that until you met Miss Rhodes?"

Kat held her breath, waiting to hear what Will had to say to that.

"Yes," he confessed with a raspy voice.

"And were you the one who told her about the supposed idea that killing me would revert you and your clan back to human?"

David knew he was screwed. Will wasn't a very good liar; he was too sincere and honest to be a liar. Everyone in the room glanced at him, waiting to hear the word they dreaded.

"Objection!" Laura called out. "He's not in a fit state of mind to be doing this!"

"Overruled!" Claudette yelled, flashing a wicked smile at her. "He will answer to my queries in whatever state he is in. Whether he is dying or in Behemoth form, he will answer what I ask him, and he will tell me the truth!"

David was running out of ways to get out of the situation. Kat eagerly tried to think of a way to get Will out of this mess.

"May I please feed him some blood to get his energy going?" Kat begged. "If he has enough energy, he can tell you everything. Let me feed him and I will hold myself responsible for this and face the consequences."

"Kat, don't!" Laura screamed.

"Kat," Will wheezed. "No."

"You truly are a pathetic human," Claudette sniggered. "Will is in a state where the very sight of blood would cause him to go on a frenzy. We would be getting quite a show if this were to happen."

"Exactly, Kat!" Laura marched away from the group and stood next to her. "If you try to feed him blood, he will rip you to shreds."

"Silence! I have had enough of your stalling! I want answers from William Crowell, and I want them now! Any more interruptions and you will go into the dungeons! Even though SOME of you should already be in there!"

Kat had run out of options. She accepted her defeat and waited for Will to tell Claudette everything.

"I will ask you this once, and only once: were you the one who told her about the hypothesis that killing me would revert all vampires within the age of a hundred years old to go back to their old human selves?"

Will gasped as he opened his mouth to respond to her question. A couple of breaths later and he finally spoke.

"No," he finally spoke. This took the band and Henry's coven by surprise, especially David, and most certainly did it surprise Kat. Did Will know what was going on? Did he hear David's lie from wherever they had kept him before bringing him in? The latter seemed more logical.

"Who was it that told her?" Claudette continued.

Will gasped and closed his eyes from the pain he was suffering.

"David," he whispered faintly.

David raised his hands to the side when he shrugged his shoulders. "You see? I did it! Now, can we please give

Will some blood so that we can have him back to his normal vampiric self?"

"Not so fast!" Claudette objected. "I'm not done with Mr. Crowell just yet!"

David rolled his eyes and turned around in frustration. "The guy is in a bad state, woman! Show some dignity and have this be a fair trial! I'm going to keep moaning until my friend is given the appropriate treatment!"

"SHUT UP!" Claudette's scream was so loud that it caused the chandeliers above to rock sideways.

"I'd do as she says," Laura whispered to David.

"Enough of these distractions! Guards, take this one away! I will deal with you later, Mr Barrett!" The two guards that took Will to the front grabbed hold of David by his arms and began dragging him away from the group. He began fighting for them to release him.

David saw Kat and the others watch him being dragged away, not being able to do anything about it. Kat wasn't going to allow this to happen. She stepped forward away from Laura and approached the guards holding both her palms out making sure they both saw what she was doing.

"Hold it right there!" she cried out at them. They both turned and were horrified to see two crosses that were on her laced gloves. The guards and David closed their eyes and hissed in horror trying to avoid seeing the cursed symbol that were in view.

Laura raced over to David and grab him away from the guards who were still busy trying to avoid eye contact with the holy symbols of God. David remained blind, flinching as Laura embraced him. He breathed slowly as her scent wafted into his nostrils. The scent of her apple spice perfume relaxed him.

Kat then pulled out one of her water pistols and took aim at the guards.

Claudette loudly laughed at her. "Don't you look adorable with your little toy gun?" Kat ignored her and continued holding her aim at the guards and the palm of her hand out. She then turned the gun onto Claudette without hesitation, leaving her palm out and aimed at the guards.

"Don't fucking test me," Kat muttered angrily. Every vampire in the courtroom started to murmur at the sight of their overlord being held at gunpoint, like they were witnessing a theatre show rather than a court seating.

"Did you not think that by killing me would cause the vampire society to collapse?" Claudette asked her. "Why do you think there are Head Vampires around the world besides me? Simple: our job is to keep our kind a secret and kill those that threaten to expose us or are transgressing the laws that were laid down for them. If I die, then vampires will roam the streets and it will be catastrophic for humanity. Which is why we are hidden in plain sight, camouflaging ourselves to fit in with the society of humans without exposing ourselves. What baffles me most is that you are willing to kill me and put our kind at a great risk of exposure, all for this sad, pathetic excuse of a vampire. What a cliché that is, I must say. Pretty darn pathetic!"

Kat didn't move a muscle. She allowed Claudette to let out her thoughts on the situation. She hated to admit that she was correct about certain levels of the situation. Yes, she is the Head Vampire and it is her job to keep the vampire community hidden and for it to be maintained, but it meant keeping those who had turned into vampires hidden away from their friends and family without consulting on the idea that maybe they could compromise on something to remain in their lives. She thought about Tabitha and Aaron in particular: young and ambitious people who had their lives stolen away without achieving their goals or saying goodbye to their loved ones.

"She's doing it for us," Tabitha interrupted. Everyone except for Kat turned to look at Tabitha to see what she had to say. "It's not just for Will. It's for everyone who has ever had the displeasure of being a vampire. Hiding away, being unable to enjoy everyday activities, wanting to do whatever their hearts once desired only for it to be restricted due to their condition. Kat doesn't want to kill you because she was told to or because she wants to be with Will. She wants to kill you to end the corruption." Kat smiled slightly at Tabitha's objections.

"Besides!" Oliver added. "Couldn't someone take over your role if you were to be killed by a human? Can't someone be elected rather than having to fight to the death to receive your role as Head Vampire? Surely, there could be other ways to do so without breaking the Head Vampire line. Have a different vampire be elected as the Head Vampire?"

Claudette stared at them, stunned with what they were saying to her. Nobody in the courtroom said a word. All that could be heard was the creaking sound of the swinging chandeliers above them.

Laughter suddenly roared from Claudette, louder than she had ever laughed before. Her laughter was sinister and bitter, and contagious as the whole courtroom joined in.

"You lot are the biggest bunch of imbeciles I've ever had to put on trial!" she told them. "I'm getting tired with your excuses and reasons for your crimes. I think it's time that we end this trial once and for all."

At the snap of her fingers, every vampire that sat in the trial stood up. The band looked around the room, knowing what was about to happen. Each of them stood in a battle stance with their weapons at the ready.

"Let the feast begin," said Claudette with a menacing smile.

Chapter 31:

♥

Endgame

The gang gathered around Kat to form their protection circle again as they all watched the vampires crawl down from the balconies. Blackened eyes were staring at the vampire coven in the most bloodthirsty, venomous, and intimidating way.

Kat had her eyes locked on Claudette and kept the gun pointing at her. Her finger rested on the trigger, the temptation to press it increased per second. The sight of Will on his knees looking weak and deficient from blood had her feeling even more tempted to pull the trigger. His starvation was getting the best of him as he was listening carefully to the sound of Kat's heartbeat increasing its rate; the only heartbeat that could be heard in the room. The pain of withholding the urge to suck her blood dry, like a child drinking on a juice box. It was the strongest pain he had felt in almost ninety years.

"We need to get the blood from Kat's bag and feed it to Will," Henry suggested to the others.

"Or at least get him away from this place," said Laura. "David, get Kat away from this madness and let us kill off the hoard. I'll get Will away from here. The rest of you, fight them off."

"No. We need to stick together," Oliver rejected the idea. "Tabitha, stay with Kat and make sure nobody gets to her."

Tabitha nodded and quickly approached Kat, standing right next to her.

"What about Will?" Henry asked them.

"Don't worry about him. Let's sort out the hoard first," Laura assured him.

Kat and Tabitha watched Claudette raise her right hand in the air. This caused all the vampires in the room to stand motionless. The sight of a hundred vampires standing completely still was a haunting sight. The band waited for the charge, knowing it was going to be absolute chaos. A pit filled with bloodthirsty vampires.

It was so silent that all that could be heard was the rapid sound of Kat's heartbeat, and that she could feel the pain of adrenaline as she waited for Claudette to drop her arm to signal the attack.

The arm dropped, and the chaos began.

Vampires hissed and launched themselves towards the band, who charged themselves towards the vicious hoard. Within a blink of the eye, the band were immediately caught up in a crowded battle around the courtroom.

Kat immediately pulled the trigger of her holy water gun and the water landed on Claudette's exposed chest. She cried out in pain, and smoke came from the surface of her skin due to the burning. The two guards in a flash, immediately grabbed Kat's hand holding the gun. The grip of the vampire's hand was tight, causing Kat to drop the gun. Kat was expecting bruises to show later.

Tabitha, thankfully, pulled the sword out of its scabbard around Kat's belt and quickly slashed the guard's hand that had grabbed her. The holy water-soaked blade sliced the hand clean off without any effort. Black blood and smoke came gushing out from the wound and bubbled up like toxic liquid when it landed on the floor.

The vampire guard screamed as he looked at his missing hand. When he looked back up at Tabitha, the edge of the sword was the last thing he saw before his head was sliced off from his neck, killing him instantly. Tabitha ran towards the second guard and used the sword to slice off his head.

The black blood from the decapitation sprayed onto Tabitha's white shirt, causing holes to develop into the fabric, which made her sigh with disbelief before running back to Kat, who ran towards Claudette with her palm out and water gun at the ready. Claudette launched herself high above the courtroom floor, laughing manically as large, black bat wings ripped out from her clothes and expanded from her back. Her hands mutated to claws with large red nails and sharp pointed ends.

Aaron used his nunchucks and martial arts skills to fight off whatever vampires approached him. Using his strength, he knocked them heavily against the ground before staking them through the chest, killing them instantly. One by one vampires launched themselves across the room towards him, and one by one was Aaron able to knock them down.

David and Laura teamed up together with their backs against each other, manoeuvring their attacks so that they were able to kill off whatever vampire was ahead of them. Pirouetting around their radius punching, and kicking whatever vampires were gliding their way.

Henry used his crossbow to hit the ones that were above ground as some were in their Behemoth form. His fast vampire speed helped him to reload bolts and race over to retrieve the ones he had launched. Each vampire he critically hit through the chest would crash to the ground and disintegrate into smoke and ash. He would use his stake against any vampires that were trying to grab hold of him or get in his way.

Oliver had managed to leap his way around the vampires and swiftly stake several of the vampires along his path. At one point he joined Henry with attacking the airborne vampires by leaping into the air and tackling them onto the ground.

Screams from the vampires could be heard as they crumbled into nothingness.

As the others were fighting the courtroom attendees, Tabitha helped Kat with fighting Claudette.

"Pass me one of your water guns," she suggested to her. Kat didn't hesitate and passed her the one that was in her holster; its capacity filled to the brim with holy water. Tabitha handed back her sword in exchange.

"I'll distract her for a bit while you help Will," Tabitha told her. "Do keep your distance, though!"

"Be careful," said Kat. "And try not to kill her. Just stall her while I get Will sorted."

"Pinkie promise!" Tabitha winked, raising her pinkie finger and bending it. Tabitha slouched to the ground and allowed her wings to expand out from her back and immediately launched herself at Claudette's level. She began shooting holy water at her, but she parried around her to try and slash her wings. Tabitha controlled her wings and had them deflect her attacks.

Kat ran to Will with her backpack unzipped. She hastily searched for the bag of blood desperately wanting to help Will. Her instinct was to look at Will's face to see him but was worried that the very sight of her would have his bloodlust kick in and immediately tear her apart. She kept her distance as she knelt to the ground to take out the blood bag. She pulled out her pocket knife from her jacket pocket to open the bag. When it opened, she gently tossed it to him. The blood started oozing out from the bag and onto the carpeted floor right in front of Will. He wasn't responding to the free food. He stared at the ground motionless and unresponsive, which made Kat panic.

A small group of vampires suddenly came charging towards Will as the metallic smell of the blood caused them to seek out the source of the scent. Their deadly blackened eyes aimed at Will thinking he was the source of the blood.

"Will!" Kat cried out to grab his attention. He still was not responding to her cries. The vampires were getting closer. Kat quickly lifted her hands up to reveal her palms to scare away the vampires with her crucifixes. This thankfully worked as she warded away the group of vampires that wanted a piece of the blood bag that was leaking on the floor in front of Will. They hissed in horror at the sight of the crucifixes on her palms.

"Will! Please drink the blood! We need your help! Please!" Kat screamed at him, trying to encourage a response out of him. He remained unresponsive to her calls.

Kat could see her friends fighting around the courtroom. The brutal killings of vampires, the horrific screams as they withered away after being staked through the heart; the grunts and shouts from her friends as they parried, dodged and attacked each vampire that attempted an attack on them. Every few seconds a vampire would be killed by one of her friends. Ash would rain down from above from the ones that were killed.

An idea then struck Kat.

"I need someone to help me with something!" she cried out to her friends. Immediately, David was at the ready for her commands. "We need to get these vampires wiped out quickly. Do you think you could help me lure these vampires away and we blast them with a molotov?"

David stared at Kat for a brief second to take in what she had just requested before saying to her "Fuck it, let's do this."

"Grab the vodka bottle and rag from my bag while I cause a diversion," David nodded and did exactly that. Kat moved herself towards the edge of the room away from Will. Her pocketknife was taken out of her jacket pocket again and she pulled her sleeve up to reveal her skin.

"I've self-harmed quite a bit today for the sake of vampires!"

Kat could hear the fight between Tabitha and Claudette from above. She wanted to look up and see how she was doing but couldn't afford any distractions as it sounded as though she was trying really hard not to get herself or Claudette killed.

And for the second time tonight, Kat pressed the knife hard and broke the skin deep enough for blood to escape. She flinched from the pain of her self-inflictions and a thick line had developed, and dark red liquid began soaking down her forearm.

For a split-second, silence filled the courtroom. The sounds of bloodthirsty vampires taking a big whiff of the air as the scent of blood filled their nostrils and encouraged their bloodlust to overcome their instincts. All vampires in the courtroom ignored the coven and made their way towards Kat. Since the coven were resistant from Kat's scent due to their times together, and the blood they had consumed recently, they watched what they assumed was about twenty to twenty-five vampires all scurrying across the courtroom towards the source of the blood. It only took one millisecond for them to be inches away from Kat before David grabbed her with his arms wrapped around her stomach. He ascended and carried her away from the vampires. A few of them tried to leap up and grab hold of her, but Henry was able to fire a shot at the ones that attempted to with his crossbow.

David had the bottle in his hand ready for Kat to light. She quickly pulled the lighter from her coat pocket and flickered it before placing the open flame onto the vodka-soaked rag. Once ignited, David immediately dropped the Molotov onto the crowded vampires down below. The sound of broken glass was heard, followed by the birth of flames that built up with the vodka that had spilt onto the red rug.

Many of the vampires became engulfed in flames, most of the damage took place at the front of the crowd.

David flew her to the back where the others stood watching the vampires disintegrating right before their very eyes. The smell of smoke replaced the aroma of the courtroom.

"Will won't nudge," Kat informed them once David had landed onto the ground, releasing her from his grasp. "I can't get him to do anything. It's like he can't hear us."

"I'll try and get through to him," said Henry, who took off immediately to help his father. Laura went through Kat's backpack to get some bandages for Kat's forearm. They watched Tabitha above who had gotten a few hits on Claudette with the holy water, but she was almost running empty. With a swipe of her claw, a critical hit smacked Tabitha across her face causing her to fall towards the flames below.

Kat gasped and watched in horror as her friend was approaching the large fire filled with dying vampires, and she was about to become one herself. Thankfully, Henry was close enough to leap up and catch her tightly before the flames even touched her. He landed on the balcony above and checked to see if she was hurt.

"Tabs? Are you hurt?"

"No. But I managed to do what I promised Kat," Tabitha smiled. "I should be fine. Let's finish this." Henry and Tabitha got up and leaned over to see the fire dying down with the vampires crumbing onto the grave of the flames. They could see the others standing around one another watching the fire burn in the centre of the courtroom.

Claudette hovered above the gang looking down at them, enraged by their actions. "I have had enough of this!" she screamed loud enough to shake the chandeliers again. Much like the other vampires they had fought previously, her skin turned dark grey. Her dress ripped apart as the muscles on her upper body violently expanded. She grew taller, more vicious looking. Her mouth and teeth grew five times the regular human size, making her look like something from a nightmare. The room shook violently, and black smoke began circling around Claudette's monstrous body.

"Looks like it's final boss time!" Aaron called out, swinging his nunchucks at the ready. The others prepared their weapons, ready for the ultimate showdown. Kat could still see Will on his knees near the throne's stairs. Henry and Tabitha leaped down and raced over to Will. They pulled him away from the storm that occurred above them, with Tabitha grabbing onto the bag of blood that was now half full and Henry dragging his father back. Will remained nonresponsive.

The smoke cleared away and Claudette's metamorphosis ceased, revealing her terrifying Behemoth form. Kat thought that Claudette had turned into Sven's Behemoth form, but twice as large and twice as terrifying.

"That is pretty fucking terrifying," David murmured. "How is Kat going to kill this monster all by herself?"

"Simple," said Laura. "With the help of us, of course!"

"We need a strategy," Oliver added. "A way to get Kat close enough to sustain damage onto her."

"I have an idea," Laura told them. She then allowed her wings to rip out from her back and expand. The others backed away to give her room as she explained the plan. "I'll fly Kat around and try and get her close enough to attack her with her weapons. You guys will need to fly around as a distraction and get her confused."

Aaron could see Henry and Tabitha trying to help Will. Tabitha tried desperately to get Will to drink the blood from the half empty bag.

"If you don't drink this right now, Old Man, then Kat is going to die, and we fail the mission! It will all have been for nothing!" she yelled. "So, stop brooding like an emo boy and drink the fucking blood!" She pressed the bag close to his mouth, which caused his lips to tremble, a positive response.

"I think we're going to have to force feed him the blood," said Henry. "I'm just worried it isn't going to be enough as he is almost drained dry."

"Henry," Will whispered. Tabitha's eyes widened and immediately took aim at Henry. "Son."

"I'm here, father," he assured Will. "You need to drink. Please. For me. For Kat. For us." Will slowly lifted his head up to look at Tabitha who held the bag of blood in front of him. He inhaled; the scent of the blood entered his nostrils. His vampire instincts kicked in. In a blink of an eye, the bag was snatched from Tabitha. She didn't immediately register what had happened but was surprised to see Will reacting at last. He shoved the opening of bag into his mouth, with the opening resting on his lips. The blood partially soaked his bone-dry throat, and he could feel his energy slowly regenerating in his system and his strength returning.

Henry and Tabitha both smiled with relief; he was beginning to respond and recover.

Kat couldn't see what was going on as she was preparing herself for the final battle. Laura wrapped her arms around Kat's stomach as they prepared for their attack above ground. Oliver and David allowed their wings to also expand from their backs to help with the distraction.

Henry, Tabitha, and Aaron stayed on the ground for any sudden attacks that may rise. They had suspicions that Claudette may summon more vampires from left, right and centre.

The band left them to it and took flight. Kat was determined to finish this. One hand had her sword while the other had her holy water pistol at the ready. Oliver and David immediately flew over to Claudette and began circling her. She paid no attention to them as her eyes were aimed towards Kat, her primary target. The boys tried to attack the head vampire with their stakes, but she was too fast for them as she immediately flew above and dove back down onto them. Oliver and David were hit and began falling back onto the ground at a fast rate.

Laura quickly flew Kat towards Claudette, trying to get a good distance for her to do a range attack before a close-range attack. Kat pulled the trigger to her water pistol and the holy water flew past as she dodged the attack. Kat rapidly pulled the trigger to squirt out holy water, but Claudette was much too fast to take any hits. Claudette zigzagged her way over to Laura and came very close to hitting Kat, but before her vicious claws were able to grab her, a figure stood in between them to prevent her attack. A tall male with black hair shielded himself to protect the girls.

Laura flew back to see what was going on. Both her and Kat gazed at the monster that they knew, despite never having seen them in that form before.

"Will!" Kat cried in shock. His wings had grown out of his extended muscles. His hair seemed more ragged, no longer slick and smooth. His black shirt had torn from the grown muscles. His hands were now sharp claws, his legs had extended, ripping through his skinny jeans. He had become something Kat had never thought she would see Will become: a bloodthirsty monster.

"William Crowell!" Claudette growled. "You finally snapped out of your brooding and decided to join us! Now, you can properly cooperate with me!"

"Told you feeding him would do that!" David cried from below.

"I am…" Will muttered at her. "I am never going to cooperate with the likes of you!" He kicked her hard enough for her to crash against the stone wall above the throne. Debris crumbled onto the throne, causing it to bend and break.

"Fucking hell, Will!" David laughed. "I've never seen him act so vicious before!"

"What happened to him?" Oliver asked Henry, Aaron, and Tabitha who approached the boys.

"We fed him half a bag of blood, but I don't think it was enough for him to sustain his thirst and he's still in a bloodlust state," Henry informed them. "We need to keep him away from Kat."

David rolled his eyes. "So, we've solved only HALF the problem, then?"

"Or have created a new problem!" Tabitha gasped.

David and Oliver got up from the floor and launched themselves back into the air. They flew next to Laura and hovered side by side. They watched as Will launched himself over to where Claudette had crashed, hoping to finish the job. Being in a bloodlust state made him unaware with what was going on, losing his sense of reason and understanding, which was why they needed to make sure he wasn't close to Kat, or else his bloodlust would kick in and possibly cause him to shred her to pieces. He may even kill his bandmates in the process.

David and Oliver charged after him and attempted to grab him by the arms to drag him away, but Will wasn't having any of it. He flung his strengthened arms left, then right, causing his bandmates to fly across the other ends of the courtroom.

Laura and Kat both watched in horror as they saw Will becoming a big issue now.

"Giving him the blood was a huge mistake," Kat whispered.

"You're telling me," Laura commented. "If he kills Claudette, then we've failed. David! Oliver! We need you to continue getting Will away from Claudette!"

"It's easier said than done, Laura!" David cried. "He is much too strong!"

"Let us help you," Aaron offered. "I have an idea. But we will need Kat's help."

Laura saw Aaron signalling for her to come down. She agreed and did exactly that. Once her feet were on the ground, they raced towards them and grouped up. Kat could see Will and Claudette clashing their claws viciously at each other. Their bodies were flashing in every direction, making impossible for Kat to see what was going on.

"We'll need to get Will back on the ground and pin him down," Aaron began explaining his plan. "David, Oliver, Henry, you guys, and I will have him pinned down and have him away from the fight. Laura, Tabitha, take Kat and try to get some damage done to Claudette in the meantime."

"Wouldn't it be easier if half of us grab hold of Will, and the other half fly above to get Claudette?" Tabitha suggested. "Three down here and three up there?"

"Fine. You, Laura, and I go above ground while the rest stay here. I figure Henry will be the best at trying to reason with Will."

"Right. Let's go!" said Tabitha. They all flew back up into the air with Laura grasping onto Kat. Henry's team approached Will who grabbed Claudette's neck and came very close to finishing her off. Thankfully, they were able to remove him by having Kat flown behind Claudette with her palms revealed in front of him. He began screaming and loosened his grip which gave them the opportunity to get Will onto the ground. They used their combined strength to get him away from her. Kat then saw the opportunity to try and stab Claudette with her sword. Unfortunately, Claudette saw this coming and immediately twisted herself to the side to dodge the attack.

"Nice try, puny human!" she smirked, facing the opposite direction from her.

Aaron was then able to grab Claudette by the neck with his arms wrapped around her from behind, with Tabitha grasping onto her arms, preventing her from trying to escape.

Laura quickly flew to get Kat in front of Claudette. Kat quickly pulled out her sword and was ready for the finishing blow. However, Claudette's gargantuan wings defended her body from Laura's approach and pushed her out of the way. Kat's quick reflexes caused her to swing her sword and unintentionally sliced Claudette's wing. The blade soaked in holy water caused intense burning on Claudette, making her shrill out in pain. She began rotating around in the air and had gotten enough momentum to get Aaron and Tabitha to loosen their grip. She twirled her body at an intense rate, crashing onto a nearby chandelier. The fire from the candles hit Aaron and Tabitha, causing the pair to let go of Claudette and fall onto the floor with the chandelier, which crashed loudly onto the ground.

"Oh shit!" Henry cried as he watched his closest friends slowly catching fire. Tabitha immediately started rolling around on the floor to get the flames to stop building up. She succeeded and immediately went over to save Aaron, who was having more flames building up within him.

"Roll around!" she told him. "It'll stop the flames!" And Aaron did exactly that. The flames died off shortly after and his clothes had been badly burnt. Thankfully, neither of them had sustained any damage to their skin.

Henry sighed with relief.

Claudette remained hovering above them. Her eyes became an immense shade of black. Laura and Kat both looked at her, feeling lost with what they could do. She was too powerful for them no matter how many of them there were to fight her. If Will wasn't in his bloodlust state, they would be able to get her pinned down onto the ground by combining all their strength to even theirs with hers.

Kat then had an idea.

"Get me back to the ground," she whispered to Laura. "I have an idea." Before Laura could answer, a monstrous Claudette spotted her and had no one around to tackle her.

"Get ready," Laura replied. "David!" Before Kat could respond, she found herself descending at a fast rate. David immediately leapt up to catch her halfway. Claudette growled at her and tried to glide her way over to grab hold of Kat. Before she could touch Kat, Laura caught up and grab her. Tabitha and Aaron were back on their feet and quickly flew up to prevent Claudette from getting her hands on Kat. David was successful with his catch. He raced Kat to the other end of the room. Kat failed to register that she was far away from them until three seconds later. Her stomach felt a little queasy from the sudden high speed.

"Fuck," she muttered.

"I'm sorry, I needed to get you the hell away from there!" he told her.

"No, it's okay. You did the right thing anyway. I need to be here." Kat winked.

"Oh?" David seemed surprised. Kat then pulled out her pocketknife from her jacket.

"Just like in the dungeon. Only, we have no molotovs. But I've got this." David stared at Kat, thinking about how when he first met her, he resented her immensely for disrupting the band's lifestyle, and resented her even more for trying to remove the only pride in his existence: immortality and super strength. Now though, he looked at her and felt the resentment become a distant memory. He understood why she was doing this, and how the journey had given him a different perspective of life. He had found his purpose, his reason to becoming human, he couldn't help but smile.

"Be careful," he nodded.

"Go and help Laura," Kat commanded. Within a blink, David flew off to help Laura, Aaron, and Tabitha. Aaron tried using his nunchucks to get a hit on her, but her reflexes were five times faster than a young vampire such as himself. Tabitha parried around Claudette, trying to get a good aim for her to take a stab at her wings as she believed that they were what gave her the extra agilities.

Laura and David attempted to grab hold of her whenever she was hit, but they weren't having any luck.

Meanwhile, Henry and Oliver tried to get Will to snap out of his bloodlust state, but they were also not having any luck.

"Father!" Henry called out as he pushed Will, whilst Oliver held him from behind. "It's me, Henry! You need to snap out of it!"

"It's no use," said Oliver loudly. "He's in too deep! He needs more blood!" Will growled trying to violently shove Oliver off. He then caught a hit on Henry with his claw, making him fly backwards across the courtroom and crash onto the wall of the upper balcony.

Will then stopped. His face rose, taking in a long whiff of the air. His eyes suddenly turned black as he turned to see where the elegant scent was coming from. His red coloured vision saw a young woman at the far end of the room near the doors to the courtroom. The sound of her heartbeat entered his ears as it was going at an accelerated rate the longer he stared at her. The red vision turned Kat into a pink silhouette where her outline would echo outwards with each heartbeat like a ripple in water.

Both of Kat's palm had been cut. Blood dripped out from her wounds and trailed to her fingertips, dripping through her fingerless gloves and onto the ground. This was the first time Will had ever smelt her blood, and it was an excruciatingly delicious smell. Will became go frantic and immediately chase after the samples of blood that was being offered to him. The scent grew stronger with each step towards her.

She looked at him with determination rather than fear. Her vampire boyfriend was coming after her with the intention of harming the love of his afterlife without acknowledging his actions. Will ran at a speed she had never seen him go at. It terrified her.

Henry and Oliver watched in horror, unable to stop him. Neither of them would be fast enough to prevent the kill.

Within a second, she lifted one of her bloody hands and revealed a necklace. A silver necklace with a cross pendant covered in blood reflected onto Will's sight causing him to completely stop. He then closed his eyes, viciously shook his head, and growled vastly. Kat slowly approached Will with the necklace at hand. He started frantically walking backwards at the sight of her necklace, creating fear within the monster.

"You gave this to me!" she screamed. "Remember? It was your Christmas present to me! You wanted me to use this to deflect vampires, well, I'm using it to deflect a vampire. A vampire I happen to love from the moment he saved my life!" Will breathed heavily. The pain of the thirst that dwelled within him caused him to kneel to the ground as he fought the urge of bloodlust.

"Remember everything we've done in the last three months! The night you took me flying across Southampton; our trip to London; the tour around Cardiff and the museum; the night we got intimate; all those moments you made me feel special because, despite being a weak human, you still loved me, right? You saved my life that night because you felt something towards me!" Kat pushed her arm further to try and get the silver cross he gave her close enough to him to stop. "I made you feel human! That was why you chose not to kill me that night at the pub! Talking to me made you feel human for the first time in ninety years!"

Her fingers then loosened, the cross quickly fell onto the floor.

"And if you still love me, you wouldn't allow the bloodlust to take over and have me killed. You want to be human again so that you can have back the life that was stolen from you. A wife, a child, a home, all of that was taken from you. But your son is still here, and I can be the missing piece that you've desired for so long, Will! I love you."

Kat took in a deep breath of air before speaking again.

"*These rivers once flowed red. Tho' winter conquered my world. The roots of beauty are now dead. And my heart and soul cry and yearned. For the life that was once*

384

mine. Tho' now shackled by a curse. These frozen lands stand lost in time. Unknown to when the frost will reverse."

Will stopped screaming and opened his eyes to see Kat standing dangerously close to him. She took another step forward and allowed herself to be as dangerously close to Will as possible. He didn't react to her despite her hands being a food source for him to take.

She then embraced him tightly with her mouth by his ear. The sensation of holding her lover caused her pulse to accelerate like a chaffinch bird's call. Will surprisingly did not respond to this.

"For eternity these lands remain pale. Until further notice, or never at all. My home becomes a wasteland and stale. But some day, the warmth of you may come. To thaw.

"I love you," she whispered to him. "It's okay."

The intense pain of the thirst and the urge to fight the pain made it difficult for Will to control himself. His throat felt hot, like he had drunken lava rather than blood. Her pulse was close to his ear, causing the thirst to increase.

Kat's repeated words continued through his ear.

"I love you, Will. I love you. Will. Please. Remember us. Remember the band."

Her voice was so beautiful, a choir to his ears. The voice made him remember who she was. The memories of their time together in the last few months flashed through him, as his body retracted its Behemoth form, and became the Will that Kat and the band once knew.

Chapter 32:
♥
Sacrifice

Oliver and Henry both looked at will with amazement. They were surprised that Will hadn't taken a chunk of Kat's neck off and create a bloodbath.

Laura, Tabitha, David, and Aaron were still high above the ground fighting off Claudette, stalling for time whilst the others tried to get Will to snap out of his bloodlust state. Claudette would try to push past them to get to Kat but wasn't having any luck as one of the three would prevent her from leaving the fight.

Kat's head rested on Will's chest. She could feel his muscles relax and heard his claws morphing back to his regular vampire hands that once touched her smooth human face. His wings drew down into his skin.

Will's hands slowly made their way to cup her face. His height decreased to his usual six foot two, which meant he rested his forehead onto the top of her head. She dropped her head onto his chest, still whispering 'I love you' to him.

"I love you too," Will whispered. Kat lifted her head and was given what she had hoped for; a beautiful smile from the handsome vampire she knew and loved.

"Hi," he breathed.

Kat then embraced him tighter, still in disbelief that her plan had worked.

"That…actually worked!" Henry laughed. Oliver pressed his hand against his head and sighed with relief. He quickly turned and flew up to help the others to fight Claudette as she begun to lose her ability to parry their attacks. Aaron took some hits with his nunchucks, Tabitha threw a few punches at her, and Laura kicked her many times, but it was barely effective.

Henry raced over to the lovebirds. "Father!"

"Oh, Henry!" Will quickly embraced him. "I can't believe you're here!" He was so pleased to see both his human lover and son.

Will then let the embrace end and looked at him, feeling proud of his son for helping Kat get to their destination.

"Could you maybe save the love reunion for later and help us?" David called out from above. Will turned and saw his bandmates and his son's friends fighting off Claudette above ground.

"I'm off to help," Henry informed his father.

"Be careful, son," Will told him. Henry passed him a smile as he turned to fly up towards the fight.

"Right," Kat said to Will. "Are you ready?"

"Yes," Will gave her a determined smile. "Let's finish this."

Will and Kat remained on the ground, watching their vampire comrades attempt to bring Claudette to their level and deliver their final blow. All Kat could see were flashes of bodies zigzagging around the monster Claudette, kicking and slashing at her but barely sustaining much damage with each hit. Claudette deflected any attempted attacks that could potentially have her descend onto the ground. Will remained elevated, trying to wait for the opportunity for the final kill, but it looked like it was going to be challenging for them.

Claudette's wings shielded her for a few seconds before expanding outwards and knocking off the vampire crew and pushing them far enough to come crashing onto the balconies, dealing further damage to the stone walls and the velvet seating. Laura leapt off instantly and landed next to Will and Kat to provide extra support.

Claudette let out a loud screech that was ear piercing for Kat but had no effect for the vampires.

"It's her summoning call," Laura muttered. "She's bringing in reinforcements! Brace yourselves!" David, Oliver and Aaron were back above ground with Henry and Tabitha down below. Henry had his crossbow at the ready, knowing what was to be expected.

The sounds of scattering vampires could be heard behind the closed doors getting louder and louder with every second that ticked by. The band looked at the doors waiting for the vampires to barge through and begin the next wave.

"Will and Kat," Laura approached the lovers. "I need you both to remain on the ground. Oliver, David, Aaron and I will try and get Claudette to fall to you both."

Laura raced over to Henry and Tabitha to give them their task. "Henry and Tabitha, both of you need to help Will and Kat with the vampires. There won't be as many as there were last time, but we're going to need to eradicate them before killing Claudette."

"We're on it," Henry nodded, reloading his crossbow. Laura vanished to approach Oliver, David, and Aaron.

Will, Kat, Henry, and Tabitha all stood steadily, ready for the incoming attack. The others flew up into the air to fight off Claudette and weaken her enough to get her on the ground.

The heavy wooden doors came crashing down as a spawn of vampires came racing in after hearing Claudette's command call. Laura was right: there weren't as many as before, but there were still a large number of vampires they had to kill. Their red eyes glowed greatly like little laser lights.

Kat immediately raised both her hands to reveal the crucifixes, causing the nearest vampires to retaliate and withdraw their attack. This in turn helped Tabitha and Henry use their weapons and fighting skills to barge in for an attack. Tabitha leapt onto one of them and tore their head off from their torso. Black blood started oozing all over the red carpet, burning it in the process.

Will growled aggressively as he launched himself onto the vampires nearest to Kat, and in an instant tore off the limbs of the vampires in a fast swift movement that Kat failed to see. She had pulled out her water pistol and began taking fire at the vampires that were racing over to feast on her blood. Her determination and bravery conquered her anxieties. She smiled at the damage she was doing to the vampires as the holy water caused the monsters to screech from the burning, their skin melting from the religious blessings of the water. With the vampires distracted and in pain, she had the opportunity to use her holy water-soaked sword and penetrate the pained vampires through the heart, killing them instantly.

More vampires were in sight heading towards the vampire slayer. She swiftly revealed the crucifix to prevent them from further approaching her.

As they backed away from her, Will and Henry were able to grasp onto them into a headlock and pull their heads clean off their torso. Tabitha managed to pull Kat away from the scene to prevent black blood from getting onto her clothes and burning her skin. She was pulled further away from the vampire attacks while the boys were killing more of them. One by one with enough strength to instantly kill them.

"I had to pull you away," Tabitha apologised. "Sorry for not warning you."

"It's fine," Kat assured her. "How are you all able to kill these vampires so effortlessly?" Kat wondered aloud.

"Don't ask me!" Tabitha shrugged. She grasped tightly on the handle of the dagger as she searched around for signs of approaching vampires.

Above them, the battle between Claudette and the rest of Midnight Devotion was getting intense. It was difficult for Kat to see what was going on as it was all happening in flashes. David, Aaron, Laura, and Oliver each found it difficult to grab hold of Claudette whilst she was in her Behemoth form, but even if they couldn't get her to the ground, it was a good enough distraction for them to keep Kat safe with the others down below.

Claudette twirled a hundred and eighty degrees to her right with her wings shielding her body before going at full force and swung her body back to its default position, creating a strong gust of wind with her wing. The bandmates spun rapidly away from her and came crashing onto the balcony chairs.

Claudette suddenly realised that Kat was alone with the youngest vampire in the room. This made her eager to grab hold of the human whilst the others were busy fighting off the vampire hoard. She dove downwards at a rapid speed.

Will looked up to see Claudette flashing downwards towards Kat. The distraction was enough for Will to let his guard down for a split second for the vampire that was in his clutches to push him away and escape. The escaped vampire launched themselves towards Kat at a high speed. Tabitha, after realising that Kat was facing away from the approaching vampire, as well as Claudette coming at her, instinctively, she pushed Kat to get in front of her. Kat stumbled backwards, shocked at the unexpected push from her vampire friend. The force was so strong that Kat had to process what had happened for a brief moment before realising that Will had grabbed hold of her.

"Are you alright?" he asked her.

"I think so," Kat responded.

Tabitha instantly stabbed the vampire in the chest with her dagger, causing it to deteriorate in an instant. Once it had turned to ash, she was immediately ambushed by Claudette who had the intention of grabbing Kat. She hissed angrily when she had realised what she had caught, but then grinned maniacally when the opportunity to eliminate one of the coven members had been presented to her. Her monstrous claws grasped tightly around Tabitha's arms, preventing her from escaping or attempting to attack with her dagger.

Henry had just killed another vampire when he realised what was happening to Tabitha. Aaron, Laura, Oliver, and David had been pushed hard enough to penetrate through the ground and Henry was worried that there wouldn't be enough time left to save her. Will had to protect Kat in case any of the vampires would notice that she was alone. Even if Kat killed the vampires herself, it would still put her at risk of Claudette getting her hands on her since she could easily drop hold of Tabitha and immediately go in for the final kill.

The image of Henry's two friends from his human years came back into his mind as though he was reliving their demise. The images flashed back and forth, from his past to the present. He was one second back in Germany where he and his comrades in the army were standing in preparation for the sudden German ambush, then the next second he was back in the courtroom.

"Run, Henry!"

"Get back to base! Warn the others!"

The sounds of their agonizing screams as the German vampires tore them to shreds haunted him. "Not this time," Henry angrily gritted his teeth. He took aim of the crossbow and without hesitation, he pulled the trigger. The bolt flew across the room at high speed, but was immediately deflected by Claudette's monstrous bat wing which shoved it away without inflicting pain.

Henry instinctively dropped the crossbow and raced over to Tabitha at the speed of a bullet. He swiftly placed himself in front of her, making him the primary target of the attack instead of her. Claudette's claw was caught in Henry's grasp with his hands pushing against the giant red nails as hard as he could physically handle. Her claw shook from the pressures of Henry's grasp, whilst he was pushing it away from himself and Tabitha. This encouraged Claudette to act immediately by throwing Tabitha across the far end of the room.

Before Tabitha could register what had just happened, and why she was no longer facing Claudette, she heard grunting coming from behind, a sound that was so close to her that it was one that was bound to scar her for life. The sound of a close friend being penetrated by the sharp claws of a vampire.

The realisation hit her when she had figured out what had just happened. All Tabitha could see was Will's face when he caught her in mid-air and immediately landed on the floor.

"HENRY!" Will's voice screamed loudly. The cries of his father made it clear on what had just happened. He saw his own son impaled the same way Will had impaled Kat's attacker Declan Shaw back in October on the night they first met; his claw penetrating through his chest and held up in the air, but instead of red human blood, it was black vampire blood that was pouring from his body. His arms collapsed onto his sides as he lost his strength. Black blood escaped from his mouth and dripped onto the ground.

The image that was presented to Will was bound to haunt him for the rest of his eternity.

"No," Tabitha exhaled as Will released her and had her stand next to Kat, who gazed in horror at the scene.

Aaron raced over to Tabitha who stood frozen in place as if she were held by chains attached to heavy boulders.

The extraction from Claudette's claw caused Henry's body to collapse heavily to the ground. The loud thud came later than expected as time slowed down for everyone as they watched in horror. Claudette ascended above them to watch her prey morn the fall of their loved one, creating a sense of achievement and to viciously smile.

Will was immediately at his son's side within a second, cradling his broken body. Claudette had penetrated a large gaping hole through Henry's chest, meaning his heart was in the hands of Claudette.

"Father," Henry whispered chokingly.

"I'm here, son. I'm so sorry."

Will looked up to see that she had indeed taken Henry's black stone heart, which was then crushed in an instant as Claudette closed her palm as tightly as she could. She handed Will a villainous grin while the ashes of his heart rained down onto the ground.

Henry's lifeless body began deteriorating into ash. Will watched as the essence of his son, the only figment of his deceased wife that remained on this earth, was taken away from him again. The thought of having his son in the band was stripped away in a second. The future he had desired since finding him was deteriorating along with his corpse. All that remained of his son were the ash that crumbled in the palm of his frozen dead hands.

"Henry," Will whispered full of grief. He grasped tightly onto the ashy remains of his son and held them tightly against his chest.

Aaron embraced Tabitha tightly as soon as Henry was gone. He could feel the pain within himself building up, the urge to kill Claudette crept up on him. Tabitha couldn't respond to his embrace. She remained frozen in place.

Oliver, Laura, and David remained still at the far end of the room. They had just crawled out from the hole in the ground when they heard Will's scream for Henry. None of them could say a word at what they had just witnessed the moment they had emerged from the pit.

Kat desperately wanted to race over and hold onto Will and help him with his grief, but she knew it would be too dangerous for her to be close to a grieving vampire that was still deficient from blood. Laura raced over to protect Kat from any sudden attacks from Claudette, even if she was too busy being triumphant over Henry's death.

Will loosened his hands, letting the ashes of his son rain down onto the ground, his skin now a lighter shade of grey. Will clutched his hands as tightly as possible before letting out an agonisingly loud scream, a scream so loud that Kat had to cover her ears and close her eyes from its intensity. The room vibrated violently from the high decibel of Will's monstrous scream. Laura held Kat close to her chest and pressed her elbow onto her hand to further silence the noise.

Kat tightly pressed herself against her chest to protect her human hearing from being damaged.

Will's screaming ceased after a full thirty seconds before he launched himself up from the ground. Before Kat could even blink, he was immediately at Claudette's side to get his revenge. His Behemoth form had returned before he came into contact with Claudette. Their claws clashed violently, creating the sounds of sword fighting with their nails. Will's teeth gleamed, revealing his long grotesque fangs that were thirsty for blood and vengeance.

Will violently lashed out towards Claudette, but her agility was greater than Will's.

"Oh, fuck," David muttered. "Will's lost it completely."

"If he kills Claudette, the whole mission will be ruined," Oliver stated the obvious. "We need to stop him. Me and David will go and grab him and pull him away from Claudette. Laura and Tabitha will go and help Kat kill Claudette. Get Aaron to join us when he's done with Tabitha."

"Right," Laura nodded as she pulled Kat away from her chest, revealing Kat's tear-soaked face. Her eyes reddened from the sadness and grief, her cheeks pink and puffed up. "Listen to me. You need to focus. David and Oliver are going to sort out Will and you and I are going to kill that vampire bitch."

Kat slowly nodded. Her eyebrows bent downwards as her hand tightened around the pommel of her sword.

"For Henry," Kat whispered.

"For Henry," Laura repeated.

Tabitha stood frozen from the shock of hearing her closest friend perish. Aaron tried desperately to get through to her, but his voice was just white noise to her as all she could think about was Henry's sacrifice to save her.

"He. . . saved me," Tabitha exhaled. "He shouldn't have done that."

"Tabs!" Aaron called to her, grasping onto her shoulders tightly. "Listen to me! We can grieve for Henry later, but for now, we have to focus on the mission!"

Tabitha's rage-filled eyes shifted onto his, making Aaron retaliate by stepping back.

"I'm going to fucking kill her!" Tabitha screamed as she aggressively pushed Aaron out of the way so she could morph into her Behemoth form again. Her large bat wings extended from her back as she leaped upwards to join in on the fight with Will, and her dagger at the ready.

"Fuck!" Aaron shouted. "Guys!"

Laura and Kat turned to face Aaron and saw him pointing upwards to where Tabitha was. They could see her fighting alongside Will, whose wings had extended out and his arms became monstrous claws.

Before Laura could command the boys to help, they were already in the air trying to get Will and Tabitha away from Claudette. David tried to grab hold of Tabitha, but she shoved him away. Oliver was doing the same to Will and was thankfully successfully holding his arms around Will's biceps and dragging him back to the ground.

Aaron leaped back up to help David with getting Tabitha away from Claudette. Tabitha was screaming as loud as she could whilst trying to grab hold of Claudette's neck, with the intention of snapping it off from her torso.

"You fucking monster!" she screamed as the replay of Henry's death looped on repeat in her mind. "I'll fucking kill you!" David and Aaron managed to pull her away from Claudette, which then gave her the opportunity to pull back her elbow, and with all of her force, she slapped Tabitha and the boys. All three came crashing down onto the ground, creating a small pit on the ground from the impact.

Will tried to fight off Oliver's restraint. He screamed loudly, his teeth exposed as he screamed, his eyes turning black all around. His thirst for revenge was greater than ever.

"Give it up, William," Claudette intimidated him as she came floating down. "You should be blaming yourself for the death of you son. You could have just carried on living your vampire life without any interference and maybe, just maybe, you could have started your new vampire life with your son. However, you decided to drag him into your suicide mission and now look what's happened. You've practically back to square one!" Claudette's laughter encouraged Will's anger to conquer his senses. Oliver kept hold of him as he squirmed furiously to escape their clutches.

"I am now going to give you all a choice," Claudette continued. "Either you all leave, and I never see your faces again. And if I do, I will eliminate each and every one of you. You must also convert this human into a vampire, hypnotise her into forgetting all about you, or kill her; it makes no difference to me what you do with her, though the latter part is more satisfactory. Or, you can continue fighting me, and die here tonight, and I can continue my role as the Head Vampire of the United Kingdom. The choice is yours."

Everyone stared at Claudette in defeat as she descended to the ground. They all knew what they had decided without having to second guess. It was pointless for them to just walk away now when they had come this far to obtain the very thing they had desired for so long: humanity.

Claudette glanced over at Kat who stood at the other end of the room. She had her holy water gun at the ready if Claudette were to make any sudden movements that were aimed towards her. The leering of Claudette's eyes sent shivers down Kat's spine, but she didn't let it get the best of her. She put on a brave face and stared back at her.

"The more you continue brooding, the faster I am losing my patience," Claudette announced. "I will kill the human before any of you can even move if you don't decide soon. I know you're not at your strongest since you were deprived from drinking blood. Not one of you is evenly matched with me."

Everyone's vampiric eyes scrutinized Kat. They were surprised to see her reacting calmy about the threat, and how she just stared back at Claudette with a look that could kill.

"Fuck you," Kat whimpered, tears building up in her eyes. The tightening of her hand around the handle of the sword caused it to redden and feel minor discomfort. "I came here to kill you to turn my friends back to humans. But now, I will kill you to avenge one of my closest friends, and for torturing my partner and our friends."

Claudette laughed hysterically at Kat at the absurdity of her motives. "I'd like to see you try, puny human!" Immediately, she was right next to Kat, which triggered Will into snapping out of his grief for a moment to save the last part of his broken heart. The rest of the band followed behind him for extra support.

Kat raised her left hand out to stop Claudette's attempted attack. The crucifix became visible for Claudette to see, but it wasn't visible for her long enough to react. Kat quickly jerked away despite knowing that she wouldn't be able to outrun a Head Vampire. Claudette was inches away from Kat but suddenly stopped. Her dark red eye gazed at Kat in horror; Kat exchanged a similar look at Claudette. She saw that something sharp had penetrated through her right eye as black blood squirted through the wound and smoke came out. A silver tipped bolt had been forced through the back of her head from a projectile weapon.

Kat held her breath for a moment before she was pulled away by Oliver, and immediately exhaled when she returned to the others. She saw that Will had Henry's crossbow in his hands, meaning he had been the one to take the shot.

Claudette wailed in agony trying to pull the bolt out from her wound. This gave the vampires the opportunity to race over to her and have her put in her place. Kat struggled to keep up with everything that was going on around her as it all happened so fast for her to see.

Tabitha seized the opportunity to deal damage to Claudette by leaping onto her shoulders and penetrated her with the dagger through her other eye, completely blinding her. She pushed the dagger as deep as she could manage until it was not possible to go further. Tabitha gritted her teeth tightly, avenging her fallen friend.

Oliver and Aaron held her by the torso, with Laura and David ripping out her wings from her back to prevent an aerial escape attempt. Will held her in a headlock as if he were to twist it and pull her head clean off, but her refrained from the temptation and waited for Kat to perform the final blow.

Kat looked up and stared at her vampire friends, taking one last look before they were potentially human again. The pale skin and red eyes may soon become natural and in various natural shades. After glancing at them, she took her stake - grasping hard enough for her to obtain splinters in her skin - and drove it straight through Claudette's exposed chest where her dead heart rested. The penetration of the sharp wood pierced through her rough skin and caused a great deal of pain as Claudette screeched loudly.

All the vampires stood away from Claudette, watching her shake violently, screeching loudly, watching her slow and painful demise. Black smoke came from every inch of her body, her skin burnt into ash. It was a violent and traumatic view for Kat to watch that closely. However, she remained still and continued watching with no remorse or emotion.

The black smoke that was coming from Claudette's body aimed its way towards the triumphant vampire killer. Kat backed away slowly to avoid the smoke from entering her airways, but the smoke rapidly circled around her, shielding her from view.

"Kat!" Will screamed, desperately running over to pull her out from the smoke. No matter which way he went, the smoke would push him away from her at full force, rejecting his rescue attempt.

"What's happening to her?" Oliver queried.

"Claudette's powers are entering Kat since she was the one who killed her," Laura informed him and the others. "When a vampire kills a Head Vampire, their powers are drawn into the victor for them to become the new Head Vampire."

"How does that work with a human?" David wondered.

"Nobody knows. Kat's the first to kill a Head Vampire."

"We have to get her out of there!" Will cried out to the others. "She could get killed if the powers are too strong for her fragile body!"

"We don't know that for sure, Will!" Laura cried back at him.

Kat's screams suddenly caused the vampires to turn and see the black smoke forming a sphere around Kat's body. Her screamed made Will feel very uneasy and powerless to help her, thinking that this was how she was going to die. Losing both his son and his lover in one night gave him a sense of dread.

The smoke entered Kat's nostrils, throat, and ears, causing a great internal burning sensation strong enough to paralyse her. She found it difficult to breathe, making it much more difficult to scream for help. Her vision darkened, making it difficult for her to see her surroundings and find her vampire friends.

The burning grew stronger with each second that went by. All Kat could think about was how this would end and how Will would react if he saw her dead. Even if she could try to use all of her strength to pull through, the burning was just too painful for her to bear. She felt as though the smoke was running through her veins and into her heart, which she wouldn't be surprised if that was happening, especially since she couldn't move any part of her body. She was both paralysed and blind.

The smoke begun to disappear. Kat could see a small ball of light expanding through the smoke. A familiar voice called out her name from a distance. She couldn't make out the following voices afterwards as they sounded too distant for her to make out. The pain died down as the smoke began to disappear, giving her a sense of relief that she wasn't dying, not just yet. All she could think about was Will holding onto her and securing her through the pain.

Will's face showed through the light but was still blurry for Kat to see. She could see her friends in one colourful blur in the far distance behind the blacked blur in front of her that she knew was Will.

"Will," she gasped lightly.

"Can you grab hold of her?" she heard a female voice ask behind Will.

"I don't think it's a good idea," another female voice responded. "We could cause more harm to her than what's already been done."

Kat tried desperately to speak louder for Will to hear so she could tell him that she was fine and that she was going to survive. It was too painful for her to release any words from her vocal cords due to the strong pain in her throat, which made her wonder if this was what being thirsty for blood felt like.

"Am I becoming a vampire?" Kat thought to herself. *"Please don't let that be happening to me. It would destroy Will and the others."*

"Kat?" Will's elegant voice became clearer for her to hear, creating a sense of comfort. She longed to be safely in his arms to comfort him for the trauma that they had both endured in the last few days. "Can you hear me?"

Kat struggled to move her head to respond to his question. She was still paralysed and unable to communicate to any of them properly without being in severe pain. She was, however, thankful to see that she had been given her vision back to see her friends.

"I don't think she can hear you, Will," Kat heard David's voice. "The non-responsiveness makes it obvious."

"Maybe she's in a trance and cannot respond to us in any way?" said Aaron.

"No. It's not a trance. It's a transformation," Laura told them. "Her senses will be frozen for a period during the transformation as the Head Vampire's powers begin to conquer her body."

"You seem to know a lot about this sort of stuff, huh?" David said to Laura, amused with her extensive knowledge on the vampire lore.

"How long does the transformation last?" Will asked her.

"It should have ended by now," Laura responded. "I'm not sure why it is taking this long."

"Maybe her body is rejecting the power," Will thought aloud. "Since she has human blood within her instead of vampire venom, the powers that are entering her could be struggling to find the source of vampire activity within her, causing it to fight against her blood cells."

Kat wondered if that was why her body was burning internally and frozen externally. It was dying off now, but she wasn't so sure what the outcome was going to be. She could feel her chest tightening and a strong beating sensation within, so she figured that she wasn't a vampire, unless her heart was slowly giving in, and that she was indeed turning into a vampire. But she had hoped that the latter wasn't going to be the case of this outcome.

Chapter 33:
♥
Reborn

The black smoke completely disappeared, releasing Kat from her temporary prison, causing her body to collapse into Will's arms. He grasped onto her tightly and then placed her gently onto the floor. The other vampires surrounded the lovers as they examined the damage done to their friend.

"Kat?" Will moved her head so that she was facing upwards. She looked peacefully asleep, but Will was determined to check to see if she was still alive.

"Check her pulse?" Oliver suggested to him. Will immediately listened to Oliver and placed his index and middle finger onto her neck to try and find a pulse. He struggled to feel anything pumping through her veins.

"I can't find one," Will panicked. "Please don't do this to me! Please, Kat!"

Tabitha grasped tightly onto Aaron's hand for support without looking at each other. They had already lost their friend today, losing another would be twice as painful for them, but not as painful as what Will would be going through if Kat had died.

"I don't think she made it, Will," Laura said, defeatedly.

"No," Will rejected her statement. "I don't believe

that."

"Denial is the first stage of grief, Will," David told him. Oliver heavily slapped the back of his head, hard enough to push him forward.

Will stared heavily at Kat's lifeless body. She looked so peaceful with her eyes closed and her body so still. The enormous room remained silent, with no sound to be heard.

THUMP

THUMP THUMP

Will quickly looked at Kat's motionless body as he heard the sounds of life coming from her.

THUMP THUMP

"She's alive," Will whispered as he smiled greatly.

"What?" Laura gasped. "It cannot be!"

"Kat! Can you hear me?" Will caressed the side of her face with his cold hands to try and wake her up, hoping his cold sensation would encourage her to awaken.

She instantly opened her eyes, and the first thing she saw was the vampire she had fallen in love with. Will's smile grew greater, with the others smiling at one other in relief.

Will saw that Kat's eyes were still blue, but the shade was a lot more vibrant than it was before; shinier and more abstract.

"Hey," Kat sighed, smiling back at Will. "We won." Will didn't respond to her immediately; his smile withdrew back to sadness when he suddenly realised what the outcome of killing Claudette had become.

"Not exactly," Will stated with disappointment in his tone. Kat noticed that his eyes were still red, his skin was still white as snow; he was still a vampire. She pulled off her laced gloves before slowly placing the palm of her right hand against his skin. She lightly gasped when she realised that his skin was not as cold as she was used to feeling. She figured that maybe her body had become used to the coldness of his skin, but after spending some time away from each other, she would have guessed that her body would have forgotten what his skin felt like. Added to the fact that she had been dealing with the intensity of the cold weather on top of the largest mountain in Scotland.

Her heart dropped when she saw that what they had set up to do did not occur.

"You're still…"

Will closed his eyes in response. "Yes."

Kat felt the strong sense of disappointment when he spoke.

"How are you feeling?" Oliver asked her, trying to change the subject. "Do you feel different in any way?"

Kat thought about it before answering. She did notice that her hearing senses were much greater, and her vision was much more vibrant, clearer. The colour of everyone's clothes were brighter, the room itself was lighter and easier to distinguish the shades of each colour.

"I feel…stronger," she informed them. "Everything around me is brighter. I hear things so clearly. I physically feel like I can fight off against anyone."

"You don't feel thirsty for blood, do you?" Laura queried.

Kat slanted her mouth to the side whilst she thought about it. "No?"

"So, she's not a vampire?" David turned to Laura, expecting her to answer right away.

"It doesn't look that way," Aaron answered instead. "Maybe she's half vampire?"

Will turned to face Aaron, shocked at the idea that Kat could very well be half of what he was: a parasitic monster that feasted on human blood. A killer.

"You mean a *dhampir?*" Kat pointed out, trying to sit up so that she could see all of her friends. "Half human, half vampire?"

Everyone looked at Kat with confusion.

"I know they don't exist in this world, because you guys cannot procreate with humans or yourselves, so maybe I am the very first dhampir?" The idea of being a unique breed of vampire made her feel somewhat special, but also quite frightened. If she was indeed a half vampire breed, what were the chances that the Head Vampires from around the world were going to find out about her?

"How could that be possible?" Oliver wondered. "Wouldn't the strength of a Head Vampire either kill her or turn her into a complete vampire? I don't quite understand how this works."

"Laura?" David turned to her. Laura looked at him with visible confusion.

"I don't know!" Laura shouted. "When a vampire kills the Head Vampire they go through the same transition as what we had just witnessed, then they are awaken with the Head Vampire's powers and become one of the strongest vampires in the world! With this, it seems we have a lot to discover!" Kat started to feel further anxiety building up the more they spoke about the possibility of Kat potentially being a strong half vampire breed that could easily kill any vampire that attempted to fight her, or even humans that attempted to fight her!

"Try running around the room?" David suggested to her.

"David," Will growled.

"No, it's okay," Kat stood up, refusing help from Will when he offered it to her. "I want to see for myself."

"Are you sure?"

"Yes." Kat turned to face away from the others and saw the broken wooden doors at the end of the room.

She began to run across the hall as fast as she could. To her disappointment, she found herself running at much slower pace than she thought she would be. She had hoped that she would be running just as fast as her friends could. This caused her to stop halfway down the hall and immediately turn to face her friends. Disappointment turned to confusion when her friends came into view. She shrugged her shoulders in defeat.

"I guess I can't run as fast as you guys can!" Kat called out; her voice echoed through the hall. She ran back to her friends and immediately approached Will with a question. "Do I still smell mouthwatering-ly tasty still?"

Will raised his eyebrows. He hadn't thought about how she had smelt since he was so fixated with grief and determination to kill the vampire that murdered his son. He took a great big whiff to answer her question, his eyes closed, and his head raised back slightly. Once the scent had entered his nostrils, he sighed.

"You smell less human than before," Will smiled. "But still smell exquisite, nonetheless."

"What exactly do I smell like?" Kat asked.

"Lavendar and coconut," Will continue to smile. Kat smiled back at Will, with the anticipation to kiss him, but figured that he had too much going on in his mind to respond to a romantic gesture, even if it was coming from her.

Will's smile withdrew the longer he looked at her. Even though Kat was still alive and well, she wasn't exactly the same person she was yesterday, or the days before yesterday. Then, his attention drew to the other person in his life that he had lost. His face turned to look at the piles of ashes that scattered around the courtroom, knowing exactly where the remains of his son laid. He slowly approached it, passing by the group without looking at any of them; his eyes focused solely on what was taken from him.

Kat and the others watched him walk grievously to the ashes, kneeling to examine what was left of Henry Halstead.

"I need a bag," Will requested. "Anything to pick up the ashes."

Kat was the first to respond. She unhooked her bag from her shoulders and unzipped it in search of something for Will to use. She hastily pulled out all her items, examining each of them to see if they could work. The first aid kit came into view and Kat unzipped the bag to see what was available for him to use. There was a plastic lock bag containing latex gloves that she knew would be of use. After taking out the gloves, she quickly approached Will, feeling anxious with his possible response to the situation. Thankfully, Will took the bag and thanked her kindly. After unlocking the bag, Will scooped up the remains of his son and placed the ashes gently into the see-through bag. The further into the ashes he dug up, the more he could see something metallic at the bottom of the pile, each scoop was painful for him.

Will could see the letter *y* and *d* engraved in the small circular plate. He had a vague idea of what it was buried in the ashes.

After collecting all of Henry's ashes and placing them into the bag, he saw that he was correct. Under the ashes were two circular tags - the size of a two pound coin - that soldiers would wear in the army, specifically during World War Two. Engraved on them were Henry's details.

Will picked up the tags. In a state of deep grief, he grasped the tags tightly and kept it close to his chest.

"Will?" said Kat, leaning down slightly to see what was happening. "What is it?"

He doesn't respond to her question. All he could think about was the image that repeated in his head over and over again and again. The last image that he saw of his offspring: penetrated by the claw of the Head Vampire while trying to save his companion. The shock on his face when he realised what had happened to him. Despite knowing that he was dying, Henry seemed at peace knowing that he had just saved a friend.

Will quickly got up and walked away from Kat. The others watched him walk away, confused with what was going on through his mind.

"Do you think Will is at the grieving stage of brooding?" David whispered to Oliver.

"No. He's just grieving, full stop," Oliver whispered back.

"Will?" Laura called out. "Where are you going?"

Will stopped halfway down the red carpet. Silence filled the room as everyone waited for his response.

"We need to go back to Southampton," Will finally responded, with no remorse to his tone. "Let's get out of here." Will continued to march heavily down the red carpet with the anticipation of leaving a place that he now sees as a cursed location.

The rest of the team remained silent, looking at one another with different reactions of awkwardness and uneasiness. It was going to be a difficult trip back home.

Chapter 34:
♥
Changes

Laura navigated the team all the way back down to the lower floor where there was an exit at the end of a stony corridor. The walls were made from mountain boulders that were drenched from the cold atmosphere of winter. Will followed behind Laura closely, not paying any attention to the others who were walking behind them feeling rather uneasy.

Kat couldn't help but feel guilty about the entire situation despite knowing that none of this was her fault. The pain that Will was dealing with, along with grief, disappointment, and loss of hope, was something that Kat was not sure she was experienced enough in to be able to support Will. Vampire counselling was something that she was still very new to.

Tabitha held onto Kat's hand after noticing how anxious she was due to her fast heart rate and the smell of her sweat. Kat tightened her hand and began to calm herself. She felt incredibly thankful to have Tabitha there for comfort. She knew Laura, Aaron and Oliver were going to offer the same level of support. David, she wasn't entirely sure about.

"The exit is at the far end of the corridor," Laura filled the silence to break up the awkwardness. Will didn't respond to her. He wanted to be snarky and state the obvious, but he knew that would be something that David would say to her.

"I have a strong feeling that we're going to be having the most awkward nine-hour van journey of our lives," David whispered to Aaron and Oliver.

"No shit," Aaron whispered back. "I'd much rather run back."

Will growled under his breath and scowled. Kat squeezed Tabitha's hand when she heard him growl so vividly. The world around her was not what she remembered. Despite it being colourful, louder, faster, and more alien to her, she had never felt stronger in the twenty-four years she had been alive. Unfortunately, it was not how she had intended to start her new life. She could have ended up as a vampire instead and nobody would have to have died.

Laura had led the team to the end of the corridor where there was a rocky dead end. However, she immediately started hovering her hand over the edges of one large boulder like she was looking for something.

"There should be a lever somewhere to open the exit," she informed them all.

"Jeez! How advanced is this castle?" Aaron queried loudly; his voice reverberated through the rocky corridor.

"Claudette installed many contraptions and upgrades here," Laura responded. "She wanted to have 'the best lair' possible."

"I wouldn't necessarily call this place 'the best'," Tabitha muttered.

Laura pushed down on a piece of boulder that stuck out and successfully activated a contraption that would pull up the large boulder standing in front of the group to reveal the outside world. The external cold air breezed its way inside the mountain, making everyone's clothes and hair sway with the wind.

Will immediately marched passed Laura with a quick thank you nod and didn't stop. Everyone followed behind Laura despite Will leading the pack.

"Do you even know where you are going, Will?" Laura called out.

"The car park, right?" Will called back with a hint of sarcasm. Laura turned to get a response from Tabitha and Aaron. Aaron responded with a nod to confirm Will's comment.

"It's literally down the hill," Aaron responded.

Will was gone in an instant once Aaron confirmed the location. Laura sighed with frustration. The others had to race after him - with Tabitha holding tightly onto Kat. Because Kat had potentially been given partial vampire powers, being carried at a high speed no longer phased her or caused any nausea. Instead, it felt like a blink teleportation, because once she blinked, she immediately found herself by the purple van.

"Open the door, please," Will had requested with little emotion in his tone. Aaron dug through his pocket and took out the van key. After pressing the unlock button on the fob, yellow indicator lights flickered, and the sound of unlocking echoed through the car park.

Will opened the passenger door and got himself inside, waiting for the others to get in after him. Kat did not feel like sitting next to her grieving boyfriend, especially if they weren't going to be interacting for nine whole hours.

"We'll go to a hotel if there's possible signs of sun," Oliver informed the gang.

"No," Will growled as he opened the door. "You drive, and do not stop unless it's to fuel the van."

"Since when were you in charge?" David questioned Will's authority. "Do you want us to fry to death when the sun hits?"

"Winter sun isn't as strong. We should be fine."

"Bullshit," David huffed. "You're just making up excuses so that you can get back to Southampton as quickly as possible to brood in your room because you were proven wrong." David was truly pouring fuel into fire as Will was suddenly out of the van and grasping onto his neck and held him up high. David stared down at Will and was horrified to see his eyes turning into a colour that could be described as an infinite void. Absolute darkness. Pitch black. Evilness.

"Do you want me to rip that tongue of yours out? Or are you going to shut the fuck up and get in the fucking van?!"

"Will! WILL, STOP IT!" Kat screamed in protest. "Please don't hurt him!" She ran as fast as she possibly could away from the others, trying desperately to get Will to listen to her. She knew that he was not in the right mindset, and she needed to talk sense into what he was doing to his friend. Her hands grasped tightly onto Will's forearm. With every strength that she had, she tried to pull him away from the situation, even though she knew it wasn't going to make much of a difference since he was a thousand times stronger than she was, it was worth it to try and get him to stop.

"Will, let go of him, please!" Kat continued to beg. "You're not thinking straight! If you don't let go of him, I will make you stop!" Her telling him this made him turn slowly to face her. His darkened eyes caused her to step back a couple of inches with terror on her face. Immediately, Tabitha was standing right next to her, ready to shield her if Will had planned to act back. Will's eyes suddenly reformed back to dark red before he dropped David from his grasped. Without even apologising, Will headed back to the van and waited for the others to follow. Laura approached David and rested her hand on his shoulder.

"I'm fine," David assured her, not looking at her. "It was my fault."

"No, it wasn't," Laura muttered, which took David by surprise since everything that happened after he said something was always his fault. This seemed to be the first.

Kat remain frozen next to Tabitha. Tears began to dwell up in her eyes, causing a strong emotional sensation that was begging to escape her hold.

"You should sit in the back with me," Tabitha recommended. "You'll feel much safer."

"I'm not afraid of him," said Kat. "Though, I think he may be afraid of me."

For four long hours, Kat slept through the van journey, despite feeling very uneasy about the entire situation. She slept soundly on Tabitha's legs, with a coat being used as a pillow. Tabitha would have spent the majority of the journey looking through her phone and distracting herself for hours on end with endless videos and photos people she followed had posted. However, she felt a strong sense of guilt wither within her. She wasn't sure if it was survivor's guilt, or if this was grief, or a combination of both. Henry's death replayed in her mind on repeat, and she knew that Will and Aaron were repaying that moment on repeat, but their guilt was different to each other's.

Laura sat in the front with Will, with David and Aaron sitting at the back with the equipment. David saw Aaron looking down in disbelief, his face plastered in sadness. David knew that the best way to help him was to remain silent and let him be since he wasn't good with handling other people's grief.

Nobody said a word to each other. Silence had birthed the moment the engine started, and the gang left Ben Nevis with disappointment. It grew into a long period of silence until Oliver stopped to fuel up the van at full capacity to try and get them to Southampton without stopping. Not once did Will turn to look at Kat to make sure that she was okay. He felt as though he had ruined her. His curiosity and strong sense of hope had costed him so much and had ruined him, creating a possible fracture in the band's relationship.

By eight o'clock, the snow began to pick up again, and there was no sign of sunlight as they drove down the motorway. For the remainder of the journey, Kat had managed to get her six hours of sleep before she was fully awake. She checked her phone and saw that her mother had sent her a text message asking when she was expecting a visit from her daughter. The realisation that she had her parents to think about now that she was half vampire.

"Oh, fuck!" Kat called out, breaking the silence.

"What?" Tabitha snapped out of her deep thinking and looked at Kat.

"My mom and dad! What am I going to do about them? What if I begin to crave blood and want to rip out their arteries? Will I have to quarantine myself from society until we know for certain what is wrong with me?"

Laura turned to face the back of the van. "I doubt it. If you're half vampire, you might just be a little stronger physically, and can still eat normal human foods. We'll just have to look into it and learn from experience. Okay? It's going to be alright."

Will gritted his teeth. This was not how he had wanted things to go. If this was how it was going to be, he may as well have turned her into a vampire the first night they met, even if he was against it. If he hadn't lost Henry, he would have given Kat further attention and support, but his mind was so fixated on the fact that his hypothesis was incorrect and that it had cost him the lives of two important people. One dead and one that had been genetically altered, with no knowing on how she may act around humans.

By midday, they were back in Southampton. The snowing had now ceased, but the ground was blanketed by thick white powder. The sky remained grey, hiding any hint of sunrays, making it safe for the vampires to be outside. Oliver pulled up to the front of the building of their flat and cut off the engine, the only sound that had been running in the last nine hours. The torture had now ended, and Will was the first to leave the van. He immediately marched through the front doors of the building, aggressively pushing through them, and angrily made his way up the stairs.

"Someone's desperate to get to the flat," David muttered. "He looks like a teenager being told to go to his room for swearing or was caught smoking."

Aaron and Tabitha both gazed at the building in awe. The pair of them were not sure what was going to happen to them now that they were away from Birmingham and had lost their creator and closest friend.

"I suppose this is our new home then?" Aaron asked Laura as she left the van after Will. "Considering we have nowhere else to go, and that we've grown fond of you all. Maybe, we can join your coven?"

Laura handed him a smile before closing the door. "Of course. We'll talk more about that later. Let's just get our things into the flat first and settle down."

Oliver and Laura pulled out the suitcases from the back, handing Kat hers in the process. The weapons they had obtained from the hideout were noticed next to the amplifiers. Laura quickly pulled out the amplifiers, passing them to Oliver, before grabbing the tarpaulin and covering the weapons before closing the door.

When they all got to the flat with their equipment and instruments, Aaron and Tabitha's jaws dropped to the floor.

They had never seen a flat so huge and so spacious for four people to live in.

"It's like something from an American sitcom!" Tabitha gasped. "How do you afford this place?"

"We bought it," Oliver answered, smiling with pride. "All that money we made over the years from not eating and not paying for human necessities can get you sweet cribs such as this one!"

"Wow," Aaron mouthed as his eyes examined every inch of the living room.

Kat noticed that Will was nowhere to be found. She saw that his bedroom door was closed, giving her the indication that he had caved himself in his room away from the others. She wasn't so sure whether to comfort Will, or to allow him to live in temporary isolation.

"Right! I'll be in my room if anybody wants me for anything!" David announced all of a sudden. He vanished before anyone could respond to his announcement.

Kat continued to stare at Will's bedroom door, wondering what he could be doing in there.

"He'll be fine," Laura assured her, wrapping her arm around her shoulder. "Why don't I grab you something to eat?" Kat responded with a nod. "It's still overcast outside so let me finish unpacking everything from the van and I will be on my way to get you some food."

"I am pretty hungry," Kat admitted softly. "I want human food, thankfully."

"Give me half an hour and I'll have your lunch ready in no time."

"Pizza and chips?" Kat requested.

"Of course," Laura nodded before leaving the flat.

Aaron and Tabitha both sat on the L shaped sofa. Aaron placed his nunchucks onto the coffee table before they both began to think about how their coven of nomads had now become two and joining a coven of four and a half.

Aaron stared at the ground as memories resurfaced of the times he had with Henry before his death. The times they spent doing martial arts training in desolated locations that no human could find them; sneaking into cinemas to watch the latest movies. The memory of Henry saving Aaron from bleeding to death by transforming him into a vampire and giving him a second chance of living, but with limitations involved. Aaron believed it to be a gift rather than a curse.

Tabitha, too, thought heavily about her time with Henry and Aaron and how they saved her from the brutal beating of two evil men that drugged her and assaulted her. The gruesome deaths of them were still imprinted in her memory like a frequent rewinding of a movie. It was the moment she rebirthed into an elegant creature that managed to tackle anyone that threatened her or an innocent person. She felt proud to have prevented multiple assaults and possible murders, and she owed it to Henry and Aaron.

The survivor's guilt, however, trembled within her.

"Hey," Aaron nudged Tabitha, causing her to slowly face him. "It's not your fault." Tabitha knew that if she could cry, she would be shedding every tear her body could release. All she could do was nod her head in agreement.

"What are we going to do about Henry's ashes?" Tabitha wondered aloud. "Do we keep them? Or do we scatter them somewhere?"

"I'm not sure," Aaron responded. "We'd need to speak to Will about it. We have a say in this since we've known Henry longer than he has. Will didn't even know he existed until last week!" Aaron released Tabitha for them to glance at each other for a brief moment before Tabitha leaned her head against his shoulder looking gloomy, with Aaron wrapping his arm around her shoulder and pulling her closer to him. Oliver sat next to the new members of the coven to comfort them, leaving Kat on her own.

Kat sat at the dining table with her elbow resting on the glass and her cheek on her hand. The end of the tour had ended in tragedy and the changes made to the lives of those within the coven were never going to be the same. They had all witnessed gruesome images, horrific murders, life changing experiences, and had hopes and dreams crushed.

Three months ago, Kat was living a mundane human life and wanted something exciting to happen. This was on a whole other level that she could have ever imagined. She wanted something like a better job opportunity, a potential partner to date, something positive that most humans could experience at least once in their life. However, she was led down the path that was dangerous but exciting, life-threatening but rewarding, for she was now a powerful human being with potential vampire gifts that she was yet to discover.

Despite knowing that she could fight alongside her vampire lover, the thought of Will grieving made her feel hopeless. She desperately wanted to enter his room to offer him closure; but at the same time, she wanted to give him the space to grieve until he was ready. Everyone in the coven was grieving in their own way – aside from David, she reckoned, who got what he wanted: to remain a vampire. She felt a strong sense of guilt when she realised that even though they had succeeded in the mission, it didn't come with the reward they had hoped for. Nobody got what they wanted. It wasn't even a bittersweet conclusion to the mission; it was absolutely grievous.

Laura returned with a takeaway pizza meal for Kat.

"I suppose you wanting human food means you're definitely not a vampire," said Laura as she placed the boxes onto the table. Kat shifted herself up, her mouth watered up with the excitement of her meal.

"Do we know for definite that she's part vampire?" Oliver queried, sitting on the opposite side of Kat. "This could be something we're going to have to be cautious about."

"I agree," said Laura. "You may need to stay here for a bit so that we can monitor your behaviours and how you function as a dhampir."

Kat stopped chewing and looked at her vampire comrades. She swallowed before responding to Laura's idea. "So, you're saying I need to be put under quarantine?"

"I wouldn't necessarily call it quarantine," Laura answered. "You can leave the flat, but you will need one of us to stay with you in case your vampire side suddenly lashes out and causes mayhem." Kat's heart skipped a beat at the idea of biting the necks of random civilians with no control to her actions. She shook her head to remove the images from her mind and continued her fixation on the food.

"Could I at least get some of my things from the flat first?" asked Kat. "Or, better yet, couldn't Will stay with me to keep an eye on me?"

"I'd rather we're all keeping an eye on you," Laura objected. "Plus, if we're all with you, and someone from the Vamperium or one of their associates comes and finds us, we need to be there for you in case it goes down."

"I would roundhouse my through those vampires to keep Kat safe!" Aaron called out from the sofa. He sat on top of the sofa and dangled his legs. "We can take on the Vamperium if we work together."

Laura crossed her arms and turned to Aaron and said, "You do know the Vamperium are a large group of powerful vampire rulers and there is one in every country and continent. I would love to see you try and kill more than one of them."

"You dare question my moves," Aaron jokingly pointed at her, feeling offended by her judgement.

"Let's worry about them later," said Oliver. "We have someone more important to worry about." Oliver smiled at Kat, which made her smile in return.

"Will I be okay seeing my parents, or my friends?" Kat queried. The idea of not being able to see her parents again made the pit of her stomach heavy. She waited patiently for Laura to inform her of the idea.

"So long as you are with one of us, I think you'll be alright. Besides, so far you're showing no signs of vampirism in you," said Laura.

"What are we going to do about the eyes?" Oliver pointed out. "They're so shiny and vibrant that no human would be able to not acknowledge it."

Kat had forgotten about her eyes. They were still beautifully blue but shone as bright as sapphires. "Contact lenses? Maybe?"

"We'll have to bulk up on them if you're going to be visiting people," said Laura. "I'll go and order some now."

After finishing her meal, satisfying her human hunger, Kat sat next to Aaron and Tabitha on the sofa. Just like Will, they were both grieving for their loss of their creator, their friend. Kat knew there wasn't much she could do to make them feel any better, but by being there for her friends, it was enough for them.

"Hey," Kat said quietly.

"Hey," Tabitha and Aaron said simultaneously, still offering small smiles despite the circumstances.

"How are you feeling?" Tabitha queried.

Kat tilted her head to the side and said, "I feel better after eating something."

"Good," Tabitha said gleefully. "If you begin to crave any blood, just let us know and we'll find something that can quench your thirst."

Kat clenched her teeth in fear at the idea of wanting to drink human blood.

"Is drinking human blood technically cannibalism?" Kat suddenly thought aloud.

"Not if you are a vampire. Even half vampires, I am sure!" Tabitha shrugged.

"I think I'll be alright anyway. But if anything were to change, I'll let you all know immediately. But what about you two? This is much harder on you than it is for the rest of us, aside from Will."

The two remained silent for a moment. Aaron grasped Tabitha's hand.

"We're doing okay, surprisingly," said Aaron. "I think it'll come to us when we decide what to do with his ashes, you know?"

Kat nodded lightly. "Whatever you decide, we'll be here for you."

The vampires and dhampir suddenly turned to see their friend's father walk through the threshold and into the living room, looking absolutely miserable.

"May I suggest something?" Will inquired, his voice sounding fatigued. Laura closed her laptop to pay attention to Will, whilst Oliver turned himself round from the dining table chair. Kat stared at Will with worry, as well as surprise; she hadn't expected him to be out of his room this quickly. "I actually have two suggestions. One, we take some of his ashes and turn them into memorial gems, place them on a gold ring or necklace, no silver. It will take up to six weeks to have done, but the sooner the better."

"I like that idea," Tabitha agreed. "We can have a piece of Henry with us at all times." Tabitha's face would glow if she had blood in her veins rather than vampire venom.

"I agree," said Aaron. "What's the other suggestion?"

Will stared at the two for a moment, and then glanced at Kat who looked at him with concern. It was going to be a difficult thing for him to suggest, but, to him, it felt right.

"I wanted to ask you two first since you've been with him for so many years, and I only knew him for a week. This may sound ridiculous to you all, but to me it will give me some form of closure." Will paused and took another glance at his coven, his family. "I would like to spread Henry's ashes onto his mother's grave in Birmingham. And since his birthday is coming up, I would like to do it on that day."

Nobody responded right away; they all sat in silence thinking about the idea. Aaron quickly glanced at Tabitha to see her response.

"Are you sure you don't want to keep them?" Laura asked.

Will grasped onto the name tags that rested on his chest, supported by string. "I'm sure. It would just be too painful for me to have them."

"What about Aaron and Tabitha? They should make the decision on whether they want to keep them."

"We'll have parts of him with us when we get the memorial jewellery," said Tabitha. "It's not like we'll have nothing of him. Right, Aaron?"

"Right. I am in favour of these decisions. But I have a condition," Aaron pointed out.

"What's your condition?" Will asked.

"That me and Tabitha get to spread some of his ashes as we say our goodbyes," said Aaron. "We both want a third of his ashes as well."

"That's fair," Will nodded. "One third of his ashes each. We have a few weeks until his birthday. So, this should give us time to grieve and think about what we would want to say."

"Do you want us all to come with you?" Oliver stood up from his chair. Aaron, Tabitha and Kat turned to look at Oliver. "I can drive us all to the cemetery."

Will gave Oliver a look of appreciation. "That would be very kind of you, Oliver," said Will. "I think Henry would have loved for all of us to be there."

"Including David?" Aaron raised his eyebrows.

"We'll drag his arse with us," Laura responded. "Whether he likes it or not, he's part of this coven, and so was Henry." Will gave Laura a nod, indicating his gratitude.

"I'll take Kat back to her flat and have her bring more clothes," Will announced. "We shouldn't be too long."

"Just make sure you bring her back, even if she feels sleepy. I'd rather we all look after to her, not just you." Laura told him.

"Whatever," Will whispered bitterly. "You ready, Kat?"

"What, now?" Kat seemed surprised how sudden her departure back to the flat was. "I have my suitcase here filled with clothes?"

"I figured you may want different fresh clothes to wear," Will informed her. "Let's get going. We'll be back before you know it."

Kat sighed in defeat. "Okay. I'll see you guys shortly." Tabitha and Aaron both returned a smile.

Chapter 35:

Hope

The cold night of Southampton was bitter. Despite being a dhampir, Kat still felt uncomfortable with the coldness of winter. She crossed her arms as tightly as she could to warm herself, even if it didn't make much difference. Her human instincts were still present for her to be cold rather than walk around like she felt nothing,

Kat's hearing had become clearer. The world that she once knew seemed louder, colourful, and very distracting. She could now hear distant sounds of people talking, vehicles driving through the city, but she decided to talk to Will to distract herself from the sounds.

"Déjà vu, huh?" Kat asked awkwardly. "Remember when you were walking me back to the flat after saving me and your intentions were to hypnotise me into forgetting you and the others?"

Will walked in silence, paying no attention to Kat. Guilt withered within her, making her feel as though she shouldn't have said anything. Much like their first night, it was an awkward walk to the flat.

Will and Kat entered the flat when they arrived. Since the heating hadn't been on for some time, it remained very cold, which encouraged Kat to keep her coat on. She turned to the wall on her left where the meter was and turned on the heating, making sure it was on a high, comfortable temperature.

Kat caught a glimpse of herself in the mirror on the wall. Rather than a pale woman with heavy makeup and dyed hair, she saw a glowing woman with shiny gem-like eyes and brightly dyed hair. She then turned towards the hallway leading into the living room. Her new eyes saw brighter shades on everything she glanced at. Her horror movie posters – which were often visually darker – seemed colourful, which was somewhat off-putting with how out of character the theme was.

"Do your eyes see vibrant colours?" Kat asked Will.

"At first, yes, but overtime the vibrancy begins to dim when we aren't drinking blood as regularly," Will responded casually.

"So then, why are my eyes seeing vibrancy when I've never drank blood? Is it the partial vampire venom that's within me?"

Will shivered at the idea of poison running through his lover's veins, even if it's partial, or the ratio of vampire venom is much lower than human blood.

"I don't know," Will said defeatedly as they both sat on the sofa. "We have a lot to learn about you now. You're one of a kind."

Kat pursed her lips; feelings of anxiety swam inside her at the thought of being abnormal. But then she thought about the night she met Will and how she had requested that he turned her into a vampire. If that had actually happened, would she still feel this way, or worse? This seemed like the better deal than the vampire route she could have taken; she's still somewhat human but with some vampire powers that are yet present themselves.

"If I'm part vampire, how come my powers aren't present yet?" Kat began to wonder. "Do I need to drink blood in order for my powers to appear?"

Will cringed. "I don't know. And I don't want you to drink blood, nor do I want you to have vampire powers. I'm not trying to control you and tell you how you should be living your life now, but I'm just speaking from experience."

"You're right," said Kat, "you cannot tell me how to live my life. But I've already decided how I want to live it. I want to live it with you, with the others. I finally feel like I've found my place."

"Even if it's highly dangerous and you could potentially get killed?" Will asked worryingly. "If the Vamperium find out about you, they may not hesitate to kill you, especially since you're a new kind of vampire."

Kat remained still. She never would have thought she would become the primary target of a group of superior vampires that would potentially see her as a threat to their kind, whether it's due to strength or exposure.

"I've faced death so much this last week, but I have defeated it with the help of you and the others. We may have failed the mission, but I'm going to be completely honest, and you won't like what you hear." Will heard Kat's heart beat higher as she prepared herself for her confession. He had a vague idea on what she was going to say given how he had gotten used to her the last four months.

"I'm sure I won't be offended," Will gave her an assuring smile.

Kat released a breath of relief and said, "I feel like I had gotten an award from this mission. I've been given something special and have never felt so strong in my life. I feel fucking awful for feeling that way given how you guys didn't get anything out of it and had lost so much."

"That's where you're wrong," Will interrupted instantly. Kat gazed in confusion. "I got more out of this tour than I would ever have imagined. And, yes, you're right, we didn't get what we set out to achieve, but we did get new fans, new friends, closure, and I still get to be with you. While you're not purely human anymore, I don't have to worry so much about harming you physically by accident or feel the need to feed off of you." Will continued to smile, making Kat feel reassured that he wasn't disappointed in her views on the situation. "If anything, it's made me love you even more. You gave me hope. You gave all of us hope. And, in the end, our hopes weren't achieved, but our lives are still spared and we're still here." A strong sensation dwelled up in the pit of Kat's stomach. The sensation encouraged tears to build up within her, tears of relief, happiness and sadness mixed together.

"I love you," Kat sniffed. "It makes me feel better knowing you still love me."

Will gently held Kat's hands and pulled them onto his lap. The coldness of his skin still sent shocks though her but were less abrupt. "We're going to get through this. I'm not going anywhere. We are all going to help you adapt to this."

Both of their eyes connected; the windows to their souls peeking through.

"I'll go and pack more clothes to bring with me," Kat leaned forward and gave Will a peck on the lips, which then grew into a passionate kiss. It was their first kiss after Kat became a dhampir, and it felt normal to Will, like she was still Kathryn. Her scent was still the same as it was before, making her seem more human.

Will ceased the passionate kiss and said, "Who knows? Maybe someday we will find something that will make us both human."

Kat looked at Will, confused with his statement. He pulled her closer until she was resting her head against his chest and wrapped his arms around her.

"But what if this is the best we're going to get?"

Will didn't respond. In response, he kissed the top of her head and continued to hold on to her.

"Are you still going to pay me like you promised?" Kat jokingly said. She expected him to remain silent but hearing him chuckle instead gave Kat the sense of relief.

"We'll work something out."

Epilogue:

Goodbye

2nd February 2010

It was past midnight when Will and the others arrived in Birmingham. The sky was clear but filled with thousands upon thousands of stars.

They pulled up outside of a cemetery which was fenced off and locked up for the public to visit. This never stopped the vampires from trespassing.

After leaping over the gated fence – with Laura holding on to Kat – Will directed his coven over to the grave he had never intended in visit since the day of their death. The last time he was there he was hidden in the distance watching the funeral from afar on a stormy day. The heavy rain added to the grimness of the funeral, the usual cliché of funerals seen in movies. After Elizabeth's funeral, Will left Birmingham with the intention of never returning, until Laura decided it was time for him to return for a gig. This decision had transpired into a turn of events Will never would had thought would be possible. He not only found the son he never thought he would see, but with the added bonus of two new members of his coven, who were able to guide Kat to the hideout of Mistress Claudette and save him and his band.

Aaron and Tabitha walked closely behind Will, with Oliver, Laura, David and Kat trailing behind. Laura held on to Kat's hand as she knew Kat was going to need the support.

Will was carrying the small medical bag filled with Henry's ashy remains.

Aaron and Tabitha stood side by side next to Will. They read the tombstone of Henry's mother:

Elizabeth Henrietta Crowell
June 6th, 1896 – February 2nd 1921
Loving Wife, Daughter, Sister, and Friend

Will read and reread the carvings of the grave repeatedly with the image of his deceased wife appearing through his mind. Her elegant smile, beautiful blue eyes, and long luxurious auburn hair that blew along with the breeze, all came crawling back to him as he relived the happiest moments of his human life before it was taken from him too soon. He had wondered what life would have been like for the pair if their fates never took place. The pair of them with their handsome son, playing on the beach with another child that was due soon. The father and son bonding they could have had together, the grandchildren they could have had; all of it a distant fantasy, locked in the back of Will's mind.

Will stared blankly at his wife's tombstone, grasping tightly to the urn containing the ashes of their deceased son.

"I'm sorry, my love," Will sighed with grief. "I failed to protect our son. I wasn't so sure if I was ever going to see him again, let alone meet him in person within our circumstances. But you would have been so proud with what he had grown up to become. A soldier. A brave warrior. A loving individual with a heart of gold; just like you.

"Happy birthday, Henry."

Kat felt the tears dwelling up as she heard Will's sadness. She grasped tightly onto Laura's jacket to withhold the tears and get herself a grip. She watched as Will tipped some of Henry's ashes onto the grave. The dust amalgamated with the dirt and grass. Without looking at him, Will passed the remains onto Aaron, allowing him to say goodbye. He stood up and allowed Aaron the space to say his goodbyes.

Aaron knelt down with the bag of Henry's ashes and began his eulogy. "My dear friend. You saved me and gave me a second life. It's one that wasn't what I wanted, but I accepted. You gave me strength, courage, and guided me through this new life. And for that, I thank you. May you find your way through the afterlife, and hopefully, someday, we may meet again." Aaron tips the bag over for some of his ashes to continue soaking down with the dirt before standing up and passing on to Tabitha.

"If only witchcraft was a thing so that we could resurrect you," Tabitha sighed. She knelt to the ground and stared at the bag in her hand. The image of Henry appeared before her. All of her memories of him flashed in her mind of their times together. From the day he and Aaron saved her, to their times 'shopping' at the shopping centres, to their times at music events and gigs; his laughter and smiles, it would make her cry waterfalls if she were able to shed tears.

"Thank you for saving me. I wouldn't have met such an amazing group of friends if it hadn't been for you. But, Henry, you didn't need to sacrifice yourself to save me. How am I going to return the favour? I wasn't worth saving, you know."

"Hey," Will knelt down and placed his hand on top of her shoulder. Tabitha dropped her head as soon as she felt it. "Don't think like that. You were worth saving. I just wish it hadn't had turned out this way and that both of you were here. And don't think for a second that I resent you for this. You're one of Kat's friends, and one of us now, so that means something to me." Tabitha looked up and turned to see Will smiling at her. It was a genuine smile that she knew was honest, and that he meant what he had said.

Tabitha nodded, looking back at the grave and holding onto the gemstone that was made from Henry's ashes.

"Goodbye, Henry."

Tabitha continued holding onto the gem of her necklace as she tipped the final remains of Henry onto the ground.

Will got up and walked past his coven and quickly approached Laura and Kat. Laura stepped aside to allow Will and Kat their connection as he embraced her. His face dug into her shoulder. She returned the embrace by holding on tightly to his torso.

"It's okay," Kat whispered. Will didn't respond. She knew how difficult this was for him, having spread his son's ashes on the day he was born onto the grave of his wife who died the very same day. The second day of February was always a cursed day for him.

Will released Kat from his embrace and gently pressed his forehead onto hers. She cradled the side of his face, which was still cold to her but manageable.

"So, what now?" David disrupted the moment.

"We go home," said Oliver.

"Continue our lives like they were before, but with some additional bonuses," said Laura. "We killed Claudette, but the outcome wasn't what we had hoped. However, at least we're still together, and we can focus on getting ourselves ready for the next tour."

"May I suggest that we then start thinking about recording a new album? I think we've managed to grab some fans throughout the tour that may want more from us." David suggested impatiently. "I am itching to get new content out there!"

Tabitha and Aaron approached the others.

"You will need a social media account then," said Tabitha. "May I request to be recruited as the band's social media PR?"

Oliver shrugged. "Sure thing! You know more about it than any of us do." Tabitha smiled at Oliver with thanks.

"Will?" Kat asked him. Will withdrew his close connection to her and looked down at her. "We're going to be okay, aren't we?"

The sparkling blue eyes of his dhampir lover showed concern. He still loved her despite the changes. She was no longer completely human, but she was still Kathryn Rhodes, the human who he had fallen in love with and had given him a sense of hope for the first time in decades. No vampire connection was going to separate his feelings for her.

"We're okay," Will assured her with a smile. "I'm going to be by your side for as long as we're together." Kat felt safer knowing that Will didn't love her any less.

"Let's get back to Southampton before the sun rises," Oliver informed the others.

"We have plenty of time! It only takes a few hours to get back!" said Tabitha.

"Do either of you have anything here that you would like to take with you whilst we're here?" Will asked Aaron and Tabitha, remembering that they had their hideout in Digbeth where they first met.

"Not really," Aaron shrugged. "We have our clothes back at the flat, but I don't think we need anything else. I could do with new reading content though. Some manga or something."

"I'll order you some books of your choosing tomorrow," Laura smiled. Aaron smiled and nodded back in gratitude.

Will wrapped his arm around Kat's shoulder and drew her closer. She held onto him tightly as they all walked away from Elizabeth's – and now Henry's – grave.

The band left the cemetery together, ready for their next plan of action. Their original plan had shifted into a completely different direction, but they weren't going to completely lose hope.

*

In the far distance of the cemetery, standing next to a Hawthorne tree, dark golden eyes gleamed in the darkness, gazing at the vampires and dhampir from afar. They waited until they left the cemetery to finally let out a soft vicious growl.

A small audio recorder was held by this stranger closely to their mouth as they pressed down on the record button and said into the little device, "February second, two thousand and ten, ten minutes past midnight; I am standing in

429

the Birmingham Cemetery and I may have found the culprits to Claudette's murder. Seven vampires and a human. I will report back to the Vamperium before taking action."

To Be Continued...

Playlist

Music that inspired the writing of 'Midnight Devotion'

Only Thing - *No Devotion*
Poisoned Heart - *Creeper*
Vampires - *Godsmack*
Silence - *Esoterica*
Miss Murder - *AFI*
Ghost - *Blue Foundation*
Join Me - *HIM*
The Ghost of You - *My Chemical Romance*
Solway Firth - *Slipknot*
Destroy Me - *Salem*
October and April - *The Rasmus feat.Annette Olzon*
One of Us - *Creeper*
Sleeping With Ghosts - *Placebo*
Franklin - *Paramore*
Love Has Led Us Astray - *Thursday*
Fall Out of Love - *Salem*
Elements - *Orestea*
It Rains - *Esoterica*
Afterlife -*Avenged Sevenfold*
Black Mass - *Creeper*
Vampires Will Never Hurt You - *My Chemical Romance*
Stand Inside Your Love - *The Smashing Pumpkins*
Help I'm Alive - *Metric*
The Story - *Thirty Seconds to Mars*

Acknowledgements

This book would not have been possible without the tremendous support I have received, from both friends and family, and the writing communities I have corresponded.

A massive thank you to my first reader of the draft and my first editor, Philip, who has been by my side since the start of my new life. Our sharing of music has created a bond so strong and indestructible. He is also this book's biggest fan as he has read it more times than any one!

My volunteer editors Jeff Stevens and Lisa Conn who I met at my new workplace that are part of the book club they have. Your eyes have helped make this book concise and better!

To my grammar editor Edward Jones who helped make this book shorter and easier to read!

To Kim Nash, who has helped me achieve my dreams of becoming an author and being able to partake in author events and do signings.

My partner, Matthew, who's tremendous support and encouragement has helped me overcome so much and changed my life for the better. Your love for me has helped me love myself, and I cannot wait to see what's next for us. (Also, you introducing me to the wrestling world has ruined me emotionally but has given me the confidence to stand up for myself! Golden Lovers 4 Eva!).

To my partner's family, who are the most loving and welcoming family in the entire world and even before dating him, I was welcomed into the family already!

My parents, Louise and Richard, who, despite our trials and tribulations growing up due to my difficulties, made me who I am today. My step parents Alyson and Dave for helping my parents find themselves and become better people. My siblings: brothers Greg and Curtis; sisters Holly (who did the logo for the band!) and Summer, along with her partner Dan and his family, including the pets!

Speaking of pets: my two bunnies Bucky and Kit who are my heart. They fill me with joy and happiness and their mischievous 'bunter' will always be amusing and worth every destroyed phone charger and internet cable!

My partner's guinea pigs, Dorian and Emmett, the noisy ones!

Both grandparents, Aunt Jules and Uncle Kevin. Aunt Teri, cousins Shaney and Lucas, Jade and Iggy.

My friends: Nick, Zach, and everyone at the Derby *Fools and Heroes* LARP group. Andy, James, and the people who run our local games club every Thursday! Raven and her wonderful family! James Sedge and his family! Corrie, who I don't see as often, but she will always have a place in my heart. Amanda - my missing third sister - and her husband Adam. The *Rycaida* D&D group: Ryan, Brandon and Andrew. Captain Jack, the almighty shipmate! Andrew and Stuart. Rob. Aaron, who I don't see as much as I want to due to distance, but you're encouragement and support has been gratefully appreciated. Ash and Amber, who my partner and I cannot wait to share couples activities together in future!

To all the musicians and bands whose music inspired me both creatively and emotionally. The list is very long, but I would like to acknowledge a small independent band whose music has comforted me in many ways and had given me the most amazing experience seeing them live: *Esoterica*. I have followed them since 2009 and I look forward to seeing more music from them!

To my guitar teacher, Jack Edwards, who taught me not only how to play many songs on guitar, but for also answering my many questions on how bands create albums, book gigs, and how to run a band.

To the *Asylum* venue in Birmingham where their owner, Jack, allowing me to insert the venue into the story as my way of saying thank you for running the weekly Uprawr events as well as being the birthplace of this story!

To all the English teachers that had taught me how to read, write, spell, and grammar correctly! I've had many over the years, but if they ever read this, know that your teachings strived me into writing, and I also apologise for my cringy behaviours as a child, I wasn't aware with what I was back then.

And before we conclude, I want to speak up for the Autistic community. As a fellow autistic person, I have struggled throughout my life with mental health issues, self-depreciation, trying to mask myself to 'fit in' which would result in burnout and severe depression, and if there is one thing I would like to say to anyone out there with autism who is struggling:

Embrace your flaws
See it as a blessing, not a curse
Be yourself

And last but not least, I want to thank YOU, the reader, for taking the time to read this. It isn't a masterpiece by any means, but I'm thankful that you read through it and may even have some comments! If you do, please feel free to write them on Amazon, or if you have a YouTube or BookTok account, rant and rave about it, positively or negatively! I encourage honesty! It's what helps us grow!

The coven will return in

TARNISHED HEARTS

Coming 2024

Printed in Great Britain
by Amazon